David's
STORY

WOMEN WRITING AFRICA
A Project of The Feminist Press at The City University of New York
Funded by the Ford Foundation and The Rockefeller Foundation

Women Writing Africa is a project of cultural reconstruction that aims to restore African women's voices to the public sphere. Through the collection of written and oral narratives to be published in six regional anthologies, the project will document the history of self-conscious literary expression by African women throughout the continent. In bringing together women's voices, Women Writing Africa will illuminate for a broad public the neglected history and culture of African women, who have shaped and been shaped by their families, societies, and nations.

The Women Writing Africa Series, which supports the publication of individual books, is part of the Women Writing Africa project.

The Women Writing Africa Series

ACROSS BOUNDARIES
The Journey of a South African
Woman Leader
A Memoir by Mamphela Ramphele

AND THEY DIDN'T DIE
A Novel by Lauretta Ngcobo

CHANGES
A Love Story
A Novel by Ama Ata Aidoo

COMING TO BIRTH
A Novel by Marjorie Oludhe
Macgoye

HAREM YEARS
The Memoirs of an Egyptian
Feminist, 1879–1924
by Huda Shaarawi
Translated and introduced by
Margot Badran

NO SWEETNESS HERE
And Other Stories
by Ama Ata Aidoo

THE PRESENT MOMENT
A Novel by Marjorie Oludhe
Macgoye

TEACHING AFRICAN
LITERATURES IN
A LITERARY ECONOMY
Women's Studies Quarterly 25, nos. 3
& 4 (fall/winter 1998)
Edited by Tuzyline Jita Allan

YOU CAN'T GET LOST
IN CAPE TOWN
A Novel by Zoë Wicomb

ZULU WOMAN
The Life Story of Christina Sibiya
by Rebecca Hourwich Reyher

David's
STORY

Zoë Wicomb

Afterword by Dorothy Driver

The Women Writing Africa Series

THE FEMINIST PRESS
at The City University of New York

Published in 2001 by
The Feminist Press at The City University of New York
The Graduate Center, 365 Fifth Avenue, New York, NY 10016
feministpress.org

First edition.

Library of Congress Cataloging-in-Publication Data
Wicomb, Zoë.
    David's story / Zoë Wicomb; afterword by Dorothy Driver.
    p   cm. (Women Writing Africa Series)
    ISBN 1-55861-251-3 (cloth: alk. paper)
    1. Coloured people (South Africa)—Fiction. 2. Racially mixed people—Fiction. 3. Political activists—Fiction. 4. South Africa—Fiction.
    I Title. II. Series.
    PR9369.3.W53 D38 2001
    823   00-052829

This publication is made possible, in part, by grants from The Ford Foundation and The Rockefeller Foundation in support of The Feminist Press's Women Writing Africa Series.

Publication of this book is also supported by public funds from the National Endowment for the Arts.

The Feminist Press would also like to thank Mariam K. Chamberlain, Johnnetta B. Cole, Florence Howe, Joanne Markell, and Genevieve Vaughan for their generosity in supporting this book.

Printed on acid-free paper by Transcontinental Printing.
Printed in Canada.

08 07 06 05 04 03 02 01   5 4 3 2 1

45284694

My final prayer:
O my body, make of me always a man who questions!

Frantz Fanon, *Black Skin, White Masks*

Adam Kok I (d. 1875)

Cornelius Kok I (d. 1822)

Adam Kok II (d. 1835)

Adam Kok III—Margaret   Adam Eta Kok
(d. 1835)   (d. 1889)

Eduard la Fleur

X————X

Adam Muis Kok   Abraham le Fleur
(d.1878)

Rachael Susanna Kok ⊤ Andrew (Andries)
                     Abraham Stockenstrom
                     le Fleur
                     (1867–1941)

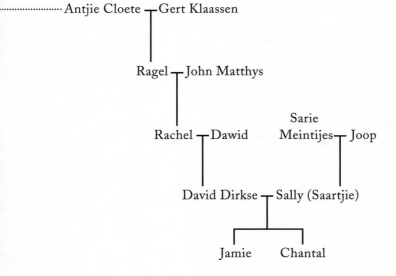

PREFACE

This is and is not David's story. He would have liked to write it himself. He has indeed written some fragments—a few introductory paragraphs to sections, some of surprising irony, all of which I have managed to include in one way or another—but he was unwilling or unable to flesh out the narrative. I am not sure what I mean by *unable;* I have simply adopted his word, one which he would not explain. He wanted me to write it, not because he thought that his story could be written by someone else, but rather because it would no longer belong to him. In other words, he both wanted and did not want it to be written. His fragments betray the desire to distance himself from his own story; the many beginnings, invariably flights into history, although he is no historian, show uncertainty about whether to begin at all. He has made some basic errors with dates, miscalculating more than a hundred years, which no doubt is due to the confusing system of naming centuries; but then, as I delighted in the anachronism, he was happy to keep it.

David's story started at the Cape with Eva/Krotoa, the first Khoi woman in the Dutch castle, the only section I have left out. He eventually agreed to that but was adamant about including a piece on Saartje Baartman, the Hottentot Venus placed on display in Europe. One cannot write nowadays, he said, without a little monograph on Baartman; it would be like excluding history itself. And perhaps he is right, although I do believe it a pity always to be gazing into a dim and hallowed past as they do in the Old World— that curious name for Europe—refreshing themselves on the mustiness of things. There is also the question of literary research.

I doubt whether he had read the numerous poems and stories about Baartman; otherwise a shrewd person like David who believed in shortcuts would surely have quoted the existing texts. And in his eagerness to historicise, to link things—his own life with the lives of Baartman and the Griqua chief—he made a mess of the dates and lost a century. This bungling, however, gives quite the wrong impression of David, who was conscientious and methodical; it was simply that he did not take the project of writing as seriously as perhaps he should have done.

In our discussions about events in his life, he did not encourage questions, or rather, he left many direct questions unanswered. Which is not hurtful if one considers oneself purely as amanuensis. We have never been close friends—possibly his very reason for choosing me as collaborator—although we have since developed a curious, artificial intimacy. I would hate a reader to think that my failure to provide facts, to bridge the gaps in the narrative, has something to do with the nature of our relationship. Or with my gender. David was simply unable/unwilling to disclose all. He believed it possible to negotiate a path between the necessary secrecy and a need to tell, a tension that caused agitation which in turn had to be concealed, but it drove him to view the story of his life as a continuous loop that never intersected itself. I confessed to being unequal to the task, to not understanding such a notion of telling or for that matter of truth, to having a weakness for patterns, for repetitions and intersections; but he insisted that my views did not matter. If there is such a thing as truth, he said, it has to be left to its own devices, find its own way, and my role was simply to write down things as he told them. All he needed was someone literate and broadly sympathetic to the liberation movement; my prattling, as he called it, about meaning in the margin, or absence as an aspect of writing, had nothing to do with his project, and as for understanding, he had no expectations of me. David believed it possible to father his text from such a distance.

I am, in a sense, grateful for the gaps, the ready-made absences, so that I do not have to invent them, but I take no responsibility for the fragmentary nature of this story. I am, as David outlined my task, simply recording. Aesthetics, he said, should be left to the so-called artists, to the writers and readers of fiction. There is no need to fret about writing, about our choice of words in the New South Africa; rather, we will have to make do with mixtures of meaning, will have to rely on typographic devices like the slash for many more years, he predicted. Some may call him a philistine, but it is a label that he would willingly accept. For my part it is comforting to know that my occasional flights of fancy, my attempts at artistry, would not be detected by him: proponents of plain writing are notoriously vague in their definitions of that category.

It is a matter of some concern to me that David has not read all of the manuscript, although he was happy with what he saw and made only minor amendments in the interest of accuracy. It was much later, during the final draft and with an anxious publisher breathing down my neck, fearing that historical events would overtake us, that I took liberties with the text and revised considerably some sections that he had already approved. I can only hope that I have not disappointed him in any way.

David wanted the following to be the last words of the text, but I have, for reasons which may/may not become clear in the course of the narrative, transferred them to this position, where I hope they will serve another function.

Nkosi sikilele iAfrika—God Bless Africa
Viva the Struggle, Viva!

Ouma Sarie has hobbled down the hill bold as you please, smiling to herself at her own boldness, but the world had changed, it was mos the New South Africa, and she'd just ask, just say plainly, Listen, I hear you people put in a new foyer, jazzed up the whole place, as the children used to say, and I've come to have a look. This is also my place: for fifty years I worked here in this grand Logan Hotel, and the old Farquhars will tell you there was no better worker in all those years, not a single day off and all the girls under me just so sharp-sharp. And scraping together her palms in a dry rustle by way of showing the sharpness of her girls, that's just what she said to the woman with the cropped blonde hair. Which is now something, 'cause how often do you think you're going to say one thing and it comes out the other side as something quite different, something quite wrong. But no, she just said it straight, and the young woman smiled with Oubaas Farquhar's skew smile, which really spoiled her looks. Ouma would have known her as one of the straw-haired girlies who'd get under a busy person's feet with nuisance questions of Sarie this and Sarie that, although she could not be sure, what with hair these days coming out of bottles. The woman said politely, You go ahead Mrs. Meintjies, and we shall be most interested to hear your verdict on the blah blah big-words. Still, very nice she was, and left Ouma Sarie in the hallway to inspect at her leisure the renovations, the brand new plush chairs, the rag-painted walls, and the newly stuck-on cornice with its fancy this-tle pattern.

My word, she sighed, her hands on her hips as she craned her neck to look at the ceiling, a picture of heaven with gilt-edged clouds and angels swarming like bees. What a funny idea of fixing up the place; this was no modernisation, the foyer now was ancient as the Bible, and the pictures on the parchment-coloured walls looked as if they'd been rescued from a fire, though she could have sworn that some were the same portraits of the old gentlemen with their horses. She folded her hands in the deep small of her back to admire, like any guest, the gleaming hallway of the Logan. The floor made her smile with pleasure: the same old tiles of blue and white and terra-cotta, all laid out in the geometrical pattern that repeated itself, over and over. How she used to linger over them in the olden days with her rag of Cobra polish and lose herself in the triangles and squares and rectangles, and forget her troubles. Not that there has ever been such a thing as forgetting your troubles; the very moment of thinking that you've forgotten them, the demons would rush in, and you'd regret not savouring for longer the moment before remembering, impossible as that might have been—but then thinking is a business that drives you mad. And in those bad old days there was no such thing as thinking things through; there was only thinking yourself into knots and endless sums of rands and cents.

Checking for dust, Ouma Sarie ran an expert eye along the window ledge, along the pretty blue leaded glass, but glad as she was about everything being nice and clean, about the things that had been left, she was disappointed. She had imagined the place airy and modern, brightly painted, and as for the cornice, well, what a business it would be keeping that clean. No, altogether it would be too much work, and just thinking of it made her tired, so tired that she sank into an antiquish velvet armchair—ag, the sort of thing even she wouldn't have in her old-fashioned house. She used to always make a turn in the hallway, look up at the ceiling of wooden squares and triangles that dear God had clicked so neatly into each other, before slipping off into the disorder of her world. Then she would hurry through the green gardens, averting her eyes from the fountain decorated of all things with naked figures in stone, and through the brush until the garden petered out into the karroo that would not acknowledge its presence, that loudly and abruptly announced itself as the stony karroo, where the grey scrub of the veld would have nothing to do with the greenness.

The walk down the hill had taken it out of Ouma Sarie; she found herself drifting off in the chair, and so, not remembering to say something to the nice young woman, she hurried out as of old, through the garden, into the veld, and towards the clump of houses behind the ridge, out of sight of the hotel. Towards the newly whitewashed, wobbly-lined rectangles of a child's drawing, their flat roofs sloping backwards to a wall considerably lower than the front: the steek-my-weg location of unmistakably coloured country houses, the houses of farm labourers. These houses have blind backs with no windows. The door, more or less centred at the front, is divided horizontally, so that in the evenings a person could rest her folded arms on the latched lower half and watch the daylight slipping into dark. On either side of the door the unglazed windows with wooden shutters, sometimes just one, like a postage stamp, but she had insisted on another. And above, on the right, an apologetic chimney from which smoke curls all year long.

In the smart black dress with white apron and cap—the Logan Hotel always looked well after its staff—she would halloo up to the house where young girls sat with legs spread around their game of ten-stones-in-the-hole. They were coloured girls; they wore the cut-off ends of stockings—or rather those modern panty hose—on their heads to flatten their hair, swirled smoothly around the skull after a punishing night in rollers. They pored over stones raked nimbly with fingers out of a hole in the earth, returned some with the heel of the hand, raked and returned, made split-second judgments on which to leave behind, so that there was no pause between raking and returning. Their tilted, stockinged heads were those of guerrillas deliberating over an operation. The karroo wind whipped up little whirls of dust from which their hair was well protected. They leapt up from their clandestine game as Ant Sarie, the enemy-general of games, approached, shouting commands, so that, pulling the stockings rebelliously over their faces, the girls scattered to the tasks of sweeping, collecting eggs, and emptying forgotten pisspots.

Ouma Sarie rubs her eyes as she sinks into a chair. If only she had known at the time to thank God for her good fortune, but who could have imagined trouble overtaking her like that, one day the children playing ten-stones in the yard and before you blink they're out there in the terrible world of fighting, as if she hadn't done her best to bring them up as Christians. And as if that wasn't bad enough, to have her child called a guerrilla, a word sounding so like baboon that it took her back, right back to the day she and Joop arrived in the district. When they put down their bundles under the eucalyptus trees in front of Baas Hennie's shop and the little Saartjie, her first, oulik as anything, scrambled off her back and practiced her crawling right up to the stoep where she giggled and babbled into the face of the oubaas, who said, Better take away the little baboon, otherwise it'll get trampled underfoot. Kindly, she supposed, but she should have known then that it was an omen, that the girl should have been kept on a short leash. Ag, she wouldn't dwell so on the past if it weren't for Joop being dead and gone. It would be so nice for him to know that everything turned out alright in the end: that the girl, the apple of his eye, is alive, that she, Sarie, is now an ouma, and that everything is busily settling down. That the Boers have all these years kept Mandela clean and fresh on the island so that when everything had gone stinking rotten, there was someone clean and ready to take things in hand. Yes, everything is going to be just so nice-nice, rubbing her palms together—and it is the very scraping sound that makes her bolt out of her chair. This is no his time for brooding; she would go to Cape Town, go and see the children, because it's pure longing for her little ones that's given her such a turn, and before that she'll go back to see the nice young woman, say the right things about the foyer looking grand and make some excuse about rushing off like a mad old thing. And she casts an appreciative eye over her own modernisation, the glazed windows and the lovely patterned lino that looks just like a photo of the Logan foyer. No, she smiles, the bad old days of dung floors are over.

This is no place to start. But let us not claim a beginning for this mixed-up tale. Beginnings are too redolent of origins, of the sweaty and negligible act of physical union which will not be tolerated on these pages and which we all know comes to nought but for an alien, unwilling little thing propelled damp and screaming into this world to be bound in madam's old, yet still good, terry cloths.

Saartjie arrived like any other baby born in the airless rhomboid of a coloured house. The same muffled cursing and mewling and heaving behind the unglazed shutters, the same rush of amniotic fluid and Ant Sarie's final heroic push that propelled her into a recoiling world. And a clutch of anties held her by the ankles to dislodge the last of the foetal phlegm, ascertained that she was a girl, and got ready the nylon stocking to pull over her head, for there was much woolly hair that had to be smoothed and flattened over the pulsating crown. This was the decade of brave baby girls with tightly bound guerrilla heads, which goes some way towards explaining the little-known fact that the Movement managed to recruit so many coloured women.

Who does not know that resourcefulness and frugality are virtues next to godliness and cleanliness? In the stunning heat it was not surprising that bare-legged young women found a new use for the charity bags of old stockings—We cut them up for pillows, Madam—but they came to serve the sinister function of fighting the curl in the hair of women who found that it took no more than a swift tug to drag the nylon across the face and radically transform their sleek-haired selves into guerillas. Thus killing two birds with one stone, they saw in the Movement a liberation from laying their weary heads on the discarded panty hose of the rich. That Africanisation would at the same time discourage the fight against frizzy hair was an irony which they could not foresee.

Saartjie, the ten-stones-in-a-hole wizard, turned Sarah at high school, and thereafter, boldly, since recruitment by the ANC, the more distinctly English-sounding Sally, clocked into her first clerical job at Garlicks with the required English accent and sleek hair flicked up at precisely chin level. Thus no one would have recognised her, wearing in broad daylight a stocking on her head like any rough, roesbolling girl, on the afternoon she first met David. It was a minor assignment, in the early days of her training. On a suburban train bound for Simonstown, between Wittebome and Retreat stations, with collar drawn up and a cap turned back to front, he slouched through the third-class carriage and joined her on the wooden seat she had in a sense been reserving for him.

He said, tugging at the red scarf draped around her neck, Miss Rooi Scarf, hey! seeming to note neither the telltale stocking on her head nor the redundancy of his observation, as she correctly replied, Rooi soes 'n rose—red as a rose—so that he slipped a package deftly into her shopping bag, so deftly that she could not be sure. Then he moved on, teased another young goosie but returned to glance at her, and she looked deeply into his green eyes before he leapt, nimble as any skollie, from the already moving train at Retreat Station. There was no knowing if she would ever see him again. Indeed, she knew nothing of him, could make no enquiries in Cape Town where everyone knew each other because she did not know his real name. But believing in destiny and touching wood whenever an opportunity arose, Sally waited. In the meantime she summoned his face in her mind's eye as often as possible, not realising that the features blurred and blunted and the lines shifted with the passage of time, so that when she finally met him almost two years later, in the community centre where she was now nominally employed, he only faintly resembled the mental picture she had been carrying around. But the eyes were the same, the very bewitching shade of green.

As for David, he had no memory of her, retained no image of the woman, although he recalled the event with clarity. When he gave her an awkward long-stemmed red rose and tried to pin it to the red chiffon scarf she had taken to wearing, she spoke of their meeting on the train. Had she been content with the repetition as coincidence or remembered that red roses are routinely given by young men, Sally would never have learnt from his own mouth how he had not recognised her as the girl on the train—a woman now, with all that weight of carrying around an image with which to fall in love. How could he have told, he pleaded, without the stocking on her head, for having not yet been to bed with her, he had not seen her wearing it at night. Then he castigated her for being indiscreet, for speaking, although her words could not have been more carefully chosen, more cryptic. How could she be so sure, what if he were not the man, could he not after all say the same of her? Forgetting the disintegration of features, the shifts in bone structure, the shrinking of his form, she shook her head emphatically and with her hand over his eyes declared that this was not at all possible, that they were who they were.

Months later, during rush hour, when the old Ford Capri broke down in Long Street, she leapt out of the passenger seat to help him push the car into a side road. Shamed and perplexed at first by such odd behaviour, he thought of her training in the Movement as explanation, and tossing in bed that night decided that a woman who did not sit respectably in the car with head tilted and legs crossed at the ankles while he pushed was perhaps not such a disadvantage; indeed, there was a curious lightness in his heart as he thought of marriage to such a woman, a cadre, a comrade to whom he need not always lie about his activities.

David Dirkse, alias Dadzo, or rather Comrade Dadzo: Has no illusions about war and so accepts both the acts of glory and the acts of horror, neither of which will be or need be disclosed by anyone.

Age: 35

Race: 'Of no consequence'

Training: Angola, USSR, Botswana, Cuba, and, of course, sessions within the country, under their very noses, where nothing untoward had happened.

Only once, recently, in the hills of Natal where the ground gives spongily and the whispered words of the dying lie in scattered syllables on the surface, has he felt his own weight on the earth, on time, on the very murmur of decomposition, until the muffled silencers of the gunshots amplified into thunder in his ears. The doctor called it tinnitus and prescribed a week's rest, but a day of doing nothing did the trick. Others have lost limbs, but nothing untoward has happened to Comrade Dadzo. Only there were deep scars on the soles of both his feet, and the dislocation of the bone on the ball of the left foot gave him a slight emphasis on the right when walking, a mannerism which both men and women with an eye for detail found attractive.

As one would expect, Sally asked questions, to which he replied jokingly about initiation rites. David's discipline and loyalty were legendary among his comrades. No stoic could have imbibed army codes more thoroughly, so that his replies were curt. She knew not to badger him, knew that there were limits to probing.

To Sally it may have seemed like an adventurous life; he would not have used such a word. Not that he had any replacement. He would never have attempted to find a descriptive word, like the arbitrary names on a Dulux colour chart—personality blue, stratos, sailboard, sea rhythm, or soft rain—names that gave one no idea of the actual shade of blue. No, it was simply his life. To put a name to it would have invited disappointment, would have left him unprepared for the unexpected. So now, with the unbanning of the Movement, he does not lament the lack of adventure, although there is much to do here at home that demands even greater vigilance, greater secrecy. But nowadays there is also more time to think, and turning an eye inward he finds a gash, a festering wound that surprises him, precisely because it is the turning inward that reveals a problem on the surface, something that had stared him in the eye all his life: his very own eyes are a green of sorts—hazel, slate-quarry, parkside, foliage, soft fern, whatever the colour chart may choose to call it, but greenish for God's sake—and that, to his surprise, he finds distasteful, if not horrible.

It is, he supposes, unlike the rest of his life, personal, a matter entirely unconnected with the Movement or with the way he relates to his comrades.

They saw little of each other during their courtship. Only once, at the beginning, they were on a mission together in Gaborone, but the pleasures of combining work and play were limited and laced with guilt. After that, their activities overlapped only here and there, in spite of attempts on Sally's part to influence locations. Moments stolen from the Movement in unexpected places were like feasting on the sweetest watermelon, but whole, pips, rind, and all, for the next morning as they slipped apart there should be no trace of the fruit. Naturally they never went away together, and naturally months would go by without them knowing of each other's whereabouts, without knowing whether the other was alive. When they found themselves in Cape Town, David said that they should not be seen together too often, that this made them easy targets, but they met up at night at various safe houses, with their ordinary red stoeps and neat lawns. You must have a wife and two-point-four children hidden somewhere in town, she teased. Sometimes on sultry evenings they sat in cafés to drink coffee without chicory or even a beer, and then in public his hand would linger deliciously on hers. But stranger than the eating places of Harare or Gaborone were the drinks in Stuttafords or on the seafront, under the Apostles—places that still held the taste of the forbidden as black people entered defiantly. Sally felt the chill of discomfort at those tables of trimmed carnations and muted conversations.

Were they being watched? she whispered. When she looked surreptitiously about the room to identify that Boer, the lone, dark-skinned white man with blunt features, David laughed. The young, flashily dressed black couple behind them were no less suspicious; there was no telling in these days of treachery and flux and things being all mixed up, no telling who was who and where danger might lurk. If it were not for the pleasure of being together in public, the seductive whiff of the illicit, Sally would not have bothered learning to sit around in cafés, spending money, inventing personas that spoke quietly about subjects such as gardening or holiday resorts or even a baby called Tracy, and behaving, except for the customary hushed tones and the eavesdropping, as if there were no one else about. She could not tell whether there were looks and whispers when they entered, or whether she imagined it; she hated the less discreet raising of eyebrows, although such things were of no consequence. David stretched and yawned comfortably, had no difficulty remembering at all times not to raise his voice, and if he knew about the devices she sometimes carried in her handbag to record a muted conversation at a nearby table, he said nothing.

Sooner or later he would suggest marriage. Sally laughed, It's all that talk about Tracy and blue kitchen cupboards. But no, he was serious. The struggle had made unprecedented progress; despite the government's bravado, it would not be long before the country would be free, before democracy would reign; it was only sensible that they should think of the future, of leading normal family lives; they were no longer spring chickens. Sally had not realised the extent of his influence: she was released from her underground work after protracted debriefing and that was that. The so-called part time job in the community centre became real, full-time, and community issues were to be her domain. Which was an important aspect of the struggle, David assured her, but there was an emptiness, a hollowness inside as if she had aborted, no, miscarried, and a rush of unfamiliar hormones left her listless for weeks. It was not surprising, then, that she fell pregnant soon after, vomited for three months after every meal and forgot at night to swirl her hair in a nylon stocking. When the baby came, a healthy boy whom they could not very well call Tracy, Sally was an emaciated scarecrow of a woman with uneven, vegetal tufts of hair and liverish spots on her brown skin.

A child of the struggle, she sighed, as she turned on the radio to drown the sound of his wailing. President Botha was at that very moment making his tough Rubicon speech. The newsreader called him an invincible crocodile, which made her snort with rage, and pulling herself together, she once again pulled a nylon stocking over her head at night in imitation of her old self. Which signalled that it was a happy marriage and that the struggle was going well.

David was partial to the sight and smell of the red plastic bucket into which she dropped the nappies. Homely, he thought, and cooed with pride at the boy's natural functions. The baby was obliging in this respect and on evenings when Sally went to UDF meetings soiled his nappies repeatedly, challenging the most robust plastic pants. David could not pick him up on such occasions for fear of leakage, and his cries after an hour or so tried even that most patient and adoring of fathers. Sally's return was a relief to both her men, who were unstinting in their appreciation of her skills. The baby gurgled and David ran a meek hand over her groomed hair.

Later, exhausted after the washing of nappies, she reported back on the meeting. He asked questions about impossible details, such as the tone of voice in which people delivered their speeches or who faltered when, and advised on what she should say and do. Ag, she didn't mind. Ventriloquising for him helped her to distance herself from the more unpleasant decisions. Not being at the centre of things, she did not always appreciate the possibility of treachery, the selling of information for a slice of bread, the need to be tolerant of the ways in which the poor would turn a penny.

In this amalgamation of family life and the struggle she found a pattern, so that when the little girl came there was no hesitation, no search for a new routine. Chores took somewhat longer; she got to bed a good hour later at night but she knew things would become easier. The girl would give up nappies earlier, would learn to speak sooner than the boy, and hardly had the little mite uttered her first word than her hair was pulled tight in preparation for the stocking. It was only as she drew the nylon over the head of the squealing child that Sally thought otherwise. They had been speaking of nothing other than liberation. It would be, they were sure, only months before the overthrow of apartheid, so that the little girl would be no guerrilla, oh no, she would be a doctor, a lawyer, or even a scientist; only months before children would sit in neat rows on their school benches, reciting their multiplication tables rather than running wild and being mown down in the streets; only months before rows of girls would whip the stockings from their heads.

She remembered her first day as a sleek-haired filing clerk at Garlicks department store. How proud her mother was to have a daughter who worked in an office, and in Adderley Street too. So that she never spoke of the sneering voice of Mrs. Upton, who flung across the desk the customers' dockets, the MacKeowns, McKeowns, and McKeoghnies: Do you not know your alphabet? I demand strict alphabetical order. Which made her stutter in up-country English before all the Town girls in the office, Yes, please, Mrs. Upton, it won't happen again. She'd since taught herself to type, had been running the community centre for some time, but no, her little Chantal would never work in an office. Neither, for that matter, would she ever marry and have children.

The house on the sandy Cape Flats was comfortable. Sally did not understand the lowered eyes of white comrades who tutted and shook their heads in sympathy. Perhaps not lovely, as she would have liked it to be, but that was no doubt her own fault, her own lack of resourcefulness. She had once found a beautifully carved wooden crow in the gutter, had taken it home and painted it black, which David called a waste of time and Mrs. January swore would bring bad luck. Why one bird should be better than another she did not know, but nowadays it was the guinea fowl with its white and black speckles that was in fashion. A garden would have been nice, but she soon gave up on that strip of coarse sand where marigold seedlings would wobble for a day or two like undernourished toddlers before keeling over for good. Instead, there were her curtains which she had sewn by hand, had saved up and waited for Zhauns's buy-one-get-one-free offer—and what a picture it was, that deep green foliage, the posies of rich red roses and baskets of velvet-cheeked fruit tumbling into the green and transporting her into a fairy-tale world of certainty and abundance. She could have done with a television—she liked to hear others discuss the goings on in the American and Australian soap stories, and the children would be still in front of a screen—but she did not mind. She could always go next door if she really wanted to, Mrs. January loved people coming to watch, but there just was no time. They were really quite fortunate; so many had lost their lives or had watched their children scatter and fall before the Casspirs, yet so far, touch wood, they were all still alive, her entire little family. Yes, she had much to be thankful for.

Steatopygous Sally, turning to the tune of the collapsed springs of the mattress, presses a buttock into David's thin hip, and offering warmth and well-being that brings a sleep-smile to his lips, does not as yet know of the epithet or its meaning. Neither does she know of the queens of steatopygia, the Griqua Lady Kok and Saartje Baartman, the Hottentot Venus displayed in Europe whose private scientist, Georges Cuvier, gave to the world those spectacular parts. Which makes her a comfortable wife to whom all will no doubt be unfolded in due time, but more importantly, an appealing character: innocent, naive, a woman who responds artlessly and whose feet, exquisite in spite of their childhood buffeting in the stony karroo, are kept firmly on the ground; a character who will arouse sympathy across oceans and landmasses as she lies tossing and turning in her Soweto bed on the Cape Flats.

It is, however, not to her credit that she lies awake in the clutches of an unprepossessing insomnia, finding the ceiling oppressively low, when not so many years ago she, Saartjie, had stepped out of a crooked raw-brick coloured house in the veld where the bandy-legged walls threatened to cave in and the roof brushed against the thatch of her hair. Resilience: that is surely what such walls had taught her, would have taught any human subject, but they had not prepared her for the convulsive horror of jealousy. Poison fountains from the pit of her stomach as she thinks of Dulcie, but if she is not all sweetness and light so much the better, for one soon tires of a good woman. Besides, David would like his wife to be something of a character; steatopygia, being a given, is not enough.

David falters over the word that has fired his imagination, that has set the story on its course so to speak, for he is anxious, having found the fancy name, that it will not be understood simply as natural fat padding of the buttocks but rather might be read in white people's pathological terms. A pity, for he loves new words, loves flicking through a thesaurus and finding one that captures precisely a meaning, which cuts down on explanations, on ambiguity and argument, on the struggle through forests of words and the attendant meandering of the mind. It is due to this precision that David has done so well in MK, the Movement's military wing— has risen so fast, as they say also in the corporate business world. In any case, no good starting with a woman's two eyes, nose, and mouth, although these features, even in her sleep, are distorted with jealousy. He knows that she is suspicious about the trip he is planning to Kokstad, but he does not yet know that Dulcie is the source of her anguish. Silly girl, and he smiles affectionately, for her tossing and turning has woken him up.

~

DULCIE washes the sticky red from her hands, watches until the water runs clear and then shakes them vigorously; she does not like wiping them on a towel. When they are dry she rubs olive oil from the little Clicks bottle into her hands, but it won't be enough; it will never be enough as the skin, washed over and over, laps greedily at the oil. Like Lady Macbeth, some would say, but that would be a poor comparison and there is no point in trying to explain, David says. You would get it wrong, quite wrong; besides, power has never held any lure for her. Or so he believes.

Her hands are beautiful; the fingers, in spite of her large frame, are long and slender. She lifts her left arm gracefully, as they do in the movies, holds it above her head before dropping it slowly onto the table while curving her torso towards it. Her teeth are clenched, her neck stretched; she holds up a face smiling through clenched teeth. She had once, as a child with fantasies of being a ballerina, admired a photograph of a woman in that pose. No one has ever called her beautiful but at times like this—and there are more and more times like this—she tries to think of her body, to recall the grace of an earlier time, and feel the muscles under the loose shirt ripple into beauty. As in the days before she took up slouching and hunching her shoulders and standing with her legs apart like a man.

One day, she muses, someone will take these hands washed clean under running water and kiss each fingertip, a nice man of whom no questions will be asked and who will ask no questions about her left thumb with its neat crisscross-patterned tattoo. She stares at the thumb as if she has not seen it before. The corner of each diamond is marked by a darker point where lines cross and where the fine instrument lingered, burning into the flesh. These points make her long for the lick of a fierce Capricorn sun, long to leave the city, to go north to a peaceful village where the earth is red and tea grows in bright green rows and where sculptors recruit suggestive shapes of wood, turn them into human figures with knives, carve life into them, chisel out the eyes in their shallow sockets, produce the new through gouging and stabbing at wood. Not flesh.

There, on a training mission in the Venda, in a cave, she had watched the sharp black shadows of young women as they entered, crossing from lurid light into darkness. They came in traditional dress, gaudy green shifts under pink crossover pinafores draped over straw bolsters for buttressing the hips and buttocks into exotic insect shapes. When they left days later with piles of wood balanced on their heads, they filed past her searching gaze, their bodies a mere hint of movement within the sculpted shapes, the AK-47s perfectly concealed. Her own body, always in trousers and shirt, lives in the curious past tense of the Venda dress, taking its aspect from the gaze of a viewer who cannot undress it, who cannot imagine the criss-cross cuts on each of her naturally bolstered buttocks.

Her back is strong, broad, almost a square depending on where one considers the back to end. This square is marked with four cent-sized circles forming the corners of a smaller inner square, meticulously staked out with blue ballpoint pen before the insertion of a red-hot poker between the bones. The smell of that singed flesh and bone still, on occasion, invades, and then she cannot summon it away. Each circle is a liverish red crinkled surface of flesh, healed in the darkness under garments that would not let go of the blood. One day a nice man of her own age will idly circle the dark cents with his own thumb and sigh, and with her bear it in silence, in the deepened colour of his eyes. Perhaps a man called David, who will say nothing and who will frown when she speaks of a woman in *Beloved* whose back is scarred and who nevertheless is able to turn it into a tree.

A huge trunk of a tree, and she dries her hands on a towel after all, rubs in more oil, and leaving hurriedly, barely pats her hip and then her right inner trouser leg to check that she has everything.

A windbroek, that's what you are, what you've always been, that's why you mess around with kaffirs, his father shouted, taken in by kaffir talk.

He had had enough of the fellow's stubbornness, his madness really. God had seen fit to bless him with one son only, a son who has since turned out to be no blessing at all. A moffie and a windbroek.

David patted his trousers foolishly as if to beat down pockets of air that turned him into a windbroek. Yes, he was slim-hipped and his legs were perhaps already beginning to grow thin, but he had naturally not thought of himself as a windbroek. Perhaps he was called that by his colleagues at school, where he would not be promoted, would never achieve his father's ambition of having a school principal for a son. As for the implications of moral turpitude or cowardice, well that was just plain absurd. He was one of the bravest comrades, whose skill and stamina had soon earned him an honourable position—but that his father would not hear of, would find infuriating. That Oliver Tambo himself had held his hand in both his own and called him my son ought to be enough for anyone. Why did he go on caring what his father thought of him? If it were not for the Movement, which occasionally brought him to this Namaqua dorp, he would, perhaps, not come to see old Dawid at all. How was it possible that a reactionary old man could make him quiver with an unnameable feeling, turn him into the stuttering child in short khaki trousers, anxiously waiting for approval? Perhaps his father was right; perhaps his son was a windbroek after all.

They sat in the sitting room crowded with shiny dark furniture. In the corner, his mother's display of treasures, her altar to finery. A bench across the corner housed her brass knickknacks: a pair of scales with brass weights, a brass vase with wax-red carnations now faded and askew, and a little bell with which to imagine the summoning of guests to a grand dinner table. These were arranged on a linen cloth embroidered with irises and poppies strung gaily on a green chain of leaves. On a second tier were her china ornaments of shepherdesses, ladies in crinolines, his favourite jug with the pattern of crowded yellow and orange nasturtiums. A ragged fern draped itself over Ouma Ragel's painted plate, bearing the maxim, De môrgenstond heeft goud in den mond—the dawn holds gold in its mouth—so much nicer a message, his mother said, than the English version of an early bird with a mouthful of fresh worms. Leaning against the lower bench was a framed magazine print of a Swiss landscape of tall, snow-clad peaks and fir trees, which cooled her down in the Namaqua heat.

The old man has added to this collection her tin of buttons, on which Queen Elizabeth's youthful face had grown leprous with rust. She would never have left it there, the functional tin, and David itched to take it away. Never mind being poor, you can still keep the place nice. In that room it was impossible not to hear her, not to be again the boy to whom she took the strap in fear of spoiling him—God will punish the parent who does not chastise the child—but whose hand she held tightly and called Mamma-se-boklam—Mamma's darling—and to whom he swore obedience. The old man sat in her chair, surrounded by the aura of his dead wife, by the order of her treasures, willing her voice to whisper sense into the ears of her son. That is where he has taken to receiving David, in that room where he read his Bible at night and listened to the news on the radio. A good boy he had always been, no trouble at all, obedient and anxious to please. The old man shook his head at the memory of her death last year, when David couldn't be found, had disappeared clean off the face of the earth; it was then, on his return from God knows where, that he confessed to working for the Movement. But the father would not listen to that rubbish, would not be replaced by new loyalties.

It's people like you who give coloureds a bad name. What do you think I worked so hard for, getting us out of the gutter, wiping out all that Griqua nonsense, just so a windbroek like you can tumble the family right back into the morass? No one could have set you a better example, a life of decency and sacrifice so you could have an education. And what are you throwing it away on—politics! Going against the law, getting up to all sorts of terrible things and associating with people who are not our kind. What has been the fruit of my labour but shame? Yes, it's like a tree in the front garden just laden for all to see with the shiny apples of my shame. Your Uncle Hennie, whose children never went to college, now sits through the sunny afternoons in an armchair with his grandchildren playing all around him. Oh yes, those motor mechanics and factory workers have time for their fathers; they're not too busy with politics, they don't lecture old people on keeping their independence, on the privacy of their lives, no, they've opened their doors to their fathers while I have to make excuses for you, about what a busy and important person you are when you're wandering about God knows where, disappearing like a vagrant, a drunk. You, you, he stuttered in rage, you—a bladdy communist who hasn't been to church for years and who went missing when your mother died. Do you know what your principal said? The man had to look out the window to say, Mr. Dirkse, I'm sorry to say your son is one of those who needs a lot of time off; we've been covering up for him for years, keeping his, shall we say, keeping it from the officials. . . .

His father summons the scene every time David visits, summons the school principal turning to the window, stroking his thin goatee, but has from the start excised the word *condition,* the unspeakable stab of the man's fading voice: Keeping his *condition* from the officials. It is a thing Dawid has fought against all his life: the coloured condition—drunk, lawless, uncivilised.

I hang my head in shame and when Hennie says, Dawid, this education brings nothing, just loneliness and godlessness, what can I say? Must I just shut my ears and my eyes for the disgrace? No, I say, I want to keep my independence. Siss man, siss, what is this pigshit of independence, 'cause I'm telling you that nothing will take me away from this place now, that this independence shit is now mine whether I want it or not, it's crept right into my marrow and you can stand on your bloody head but I will look after myself till my dying day. You look after your communist kaffirs.

People in the liberation movement don't need looking after. We look forward to toppling this government, to a better country where everyone will have a share of the good life. Just a matter of months now, he correctly predicted.

Bladdy communist speeches, is that all you can manage? So you admit you still go around with those kind of people. I don't know why I even allow you in my house. Just shows that I've more decency under my fingernail than you'll ever have. I'll tell you something about the kaffirs and the Hotnos, they just don't want to work. Look what it's taken your mother and me, sweat and blood, to shake off the Griquaness, the shame and the filth and the idleness, and what do you do? Go rolling right back into the gutter, crawling into all kinds of dirty hovels to speak with old folks about old Griqua rubbish, encouraging the backwardness. Don't think I don't hear about these things. Ja-nee, he sighed, his face drawn in self pity, all our sacrifice for nothing. Once a Griqua, always a Griqua. Then, in a fit of irrational rage, And all because of the kaffirs. Your mother must be turning in her grave.

His mother was a gentle soul, who said, It's best not to ask any questions. Just do as your father says. How he adored that father, a man who could do no wrong, who knew everything there was to know in the world and who would pull a length of string or a twist of wire from his pocket and fix anything at all. You just name it, he boasted, and turning around with bits of bicycle still in his hand, frowned at the black man in a blanket who seemed to come out of nowhere, asking for directions, and if the mister could spare it, also a slice of bread or some pap.

Don't smile or laugh with them, Dawid instructed the little boy.

Why not, David asked. He looks like Oom Frans, just blacker.

You must do your Christian duty but don't ever let a kaffir see your teeth. See how your mother keeps her head down.

I watched her hunt for an old tin mug and pour rooibos tea for the man, who kept his own head down and whispered his thanks, and feeling an inexplicable rush of shame for both of them, I dropped my head too.

Later, I came upon him by surprise. The man whom I imagined trudging through the veld in search of the gypsum mines sat propped up behind the kraal wall, sleeping through the afternoon heat. I stepped slowly, putting one foot before the other, gingerly, watching him and not knowing what I wanted, except that the man would tell his story and show that there is no need to keep one's teeth covered. But when he opened his eyes he looked at me with such an emptiness, his story sealed deep down inside, that I fumbled hurriedly in my pockets and offered him a stone. Only the day before I had found the milky white crystal on the river bank, a precious stone that sure as eggs would bring good luck. The man smiled without showing his teeth. The black pupils softened and he took the gift, gazed at it, nodding, before slipping it into either a pocket or a bag hidden under the blanket. Searching under his blanket, he drew from it a shell with a shiny oyster-pink lining and handed it to me. I took it without a word and dropped it into my own pocket. Then, not knowing what to do as the man once more shut his eyes, I crept away with my secret, which turned out not to be a secret at all.

You liked kaffirs even when you were small, going against my wishes and talking to people I'd told you to leave alone. I should have put my foot down from the very start; I should not have listened to your mother, and you wouldn't have got into this dangerous business. No respect for your elders, that's your problem, think your education gives you the right to put aside everything your elders have taught you.

Old people, Father, do not have a right to the respect of the young; they have to earn it like anyone else. Just as those in power do not have a right to that power; the people over whom they rule must not only agree—

The old man interrupted in the thunderous voice of his youth: Don't you dare preach your politics at me, you who can't even accept yourself as a coloured person. That's what we are— decent, respectable coloured people, so to hell with you and your rubbish politics. A bladdy windbroek Griqua, that's what you've become. And, heaving himself out of his chair, he stumbled off, flushed with rage.

David believes that it was his father's irrational rage that fired his interest in Le Fleur, the Griqua chief who succeeded Adam Kok and founded the settlement in Namaqualand.

❧

Brown people take the cigarette between thumb and index. They prefer wearing glasses and look you quietly and steadfastly in the eye (but not at one another). They are stiff until unexpectedly shaken loose by a spasm of laughter. Nobody blows out smoke through the nostrils anymore.

Breyten Breytenbach, *Return to Paradise*

CAPE TOWN 1991

Sally has splashed out on a new pair of glasses. She sits reading, or rather pretending to read, *The Argus,* with her legs folded awkwardly under her, pens-en-pootjies as her mother disapprovingly says. The glasses are large with a fashionable transparent pinkish frame that was not designed for cheekbones of such prominence. They are not reading glasses, so that it is something of a strain flicking through the paper. Which adds to her irritation as she waits for David to say what he thinks, or rather to say how nice they are.

David has always wondered about the way women seem to take refuge in reading. He would say to Sally when the troubled look settles on her face, Have you been to the library? Why don't you get a book, read a story? It is an indulgence not worthy of a cadre, he privately thinks, but better than knitting, which infuriates him with the click-clack of the needles and, quite out of sync, the waggling of her slippered foot. Her foot has waggled uncontrollably of late, as if it has a life of its own. But now that she is reading he sinks into his favourite chair and shuts his eyes. She allows him five minutes, then rises with a deep sigh and says that the food is ready, that he should set the table.

Like any couple their dramas are played out at the dinner table. They are silent, bent over their plates, over their bredies with potatoes and rice, or on Sundays a roasted chicken. With sweet potato, browned and ginger-sweet. Sometimes curry. Shall we have a lekker chicken curry for a change, she would announce by asking the children, smiling with pleasure. And pudding on Sundays: baked sago with coconut, or this time, because she is listless, just Ouma Sarie's canned peaches with evaporated milk, and green jelly for the children.

Nice coloured food. Not the stiff pap with meat eaten by blacks. Nor the meagre pasta and pesto favoured in the homes of white comrades, where what seemed to count was the napkins printed with their favoured icon of liberation, the black-and-white stippled guinea fowl.

The children fidget; they don't want to eat. Do you know how many people have nothing but pap? David asks. We had pokkenkô in Namaqualand, he says, straying from the rebuke, my father called it Hotnos food, but mealie meal's much nicer in that crumbly form, especially with the crispy fat of kaiings, nicer than sloppy pap.

Sally is disgusted by the nostalgia in his voice. Do you remember how it's made? she asks.

No, what a pity, he says, unaware of her sarcasm.

Today they are having chicken curry. Sally has fretted and fumed along with the sizzling spices and has tapped too recklessly at a red chili, dropping all its fiery seeds straight into the pot. Which makes the children cry out loud and David gasp with the heat. The dinner table may be the appropriate place for family dramas, but he would rather Sally did not let loose her feelings in this manner. Her mouth is set with resentment; she chews prissily while her knife and fork stab angrily at the meat, at the rose-patterned china, long after he has lain his own down and the affronted children have sailed out of the room, unnoticed, on their bellies. He thinks as one ought to, of the waste, of the hungry and homeless, as she pushes aside the plate of mashed food.

Today Sally is clairvoyant; she beats the haft of her knife on the table and shouts, Let's think about ourselves for a change. Then, noting his bemused look, revises it to, Let's feel sorry for me, the one who doesn't know what's going on in her own house.

He has no idea of what she means. He has not noted her reserve of the past few days, so that the outburst takes him by surprise. He has no stomach for this kind of talk.

Shu-ut, he soothes, don't shout.

Why, have we turned white or something that we no longer can speak loudly? I will shout and shout until you come clean about your trip. You've been lying to me. Why won't you say what it's all about, where you're going, and why—she lowers her voice—and with whom?

Really, he does not understand such an uncharacteristic outburst. Sally knows that questions are out of order, that she should
not know anything about his missions; having been a cadre herself,
she has never had any problem with secrecy. But this time, and he
shakes his head, this time with the trip being primarily a private
matter, he has in fact not concealed anything. Whatever could the
matter be with her? Women, he silently exclaims, throwing his eyes
heavenward according to custom.

I have told you everything there is to tell. That it's been suggested that I take a break. Things have been hectic; there are new
tensions building up in the cell that I can't quite put my finger on—
everyone's wound up, I suppose—and I haven't been feeling myself
of late, especially after the last crisis. As for this trip, everything's
aboveboard—well, almost everything. I said that I'd take the long
weekend, leave on Wednesday—Dr. Abdurahman will give me a
certificate—and be back the following Tuesday morning. In time
for school. That I'll be staying in the Crown Hotel in Kokstad. Why
Kokstad? Because I've been thinking about the Griquas. All the old
stories that Ouma Ragel told, about Chief Le Fleur, and my
Great-ouma Antjie trekking down from Namaqualand. I'd just like
to find out more about that history, about the weird Griqua chief.
Dunno why, it's just interesting, part of my history I suppose, and
I might even write something; it will take my mind off things. As
the doctor said, I need some diversion, a hobby or something. And
that's all there is to it.

With whom? Sally persists.

With no one. I've just said it isn't Congress business, although
I do have to drop into a meeting at Umtata on the way back.

Everything he says enrages her. Don't try to fob me off with
nonsense about roots and ancestors, she shouts. Rubbish, it's all
fashionable rubbish. Next thing you'll be off overseas to check out
your roots in the rubbish dumps of Europe, but no, I forget, it's the
African roots that count. What do you expect to find? Ours are all
mixed up and tangled; no chance of us being uprooted, because they're
all in a neglected knot, stuck. And that I'd have thought is the beauty of being coloured, that we need not worry about roots at all, that

it's altogether a good thing to start afresh. We've got our brand new AMC pots of stainless steel and Ford Cortinas, she mocks, so why burden ourselves with the dreary stuff of roots and tradition? But no, people like you must also have your fake toorgoed dangling from the rearview mirror. What's happened? You've always been the first to say it's rubbish.

But that doesn't mean you just dismiss history—

She interrupts, her eyes fixed on his as if there were a secret to extract. She cannot believe that he has fallen for that kind of nonsense, and putting on a faintly familiar deep voice (Dulcie's voice?) she mocks, So you need to go away to reclaim your culture—surely Kokstad isn't quite the place. Too well-known in Namaqualand, hey, is that it? Is that not where your roots are? It's rubbish David. There's nothing to reclaim. We are what we are, a mixture of this and that, and a good thing too, so we don't have to behave like Boers, eating braaivleis and potjiekos and re-enacting the Great Trek by waiting half the day for the fockin' thing to cook outside when we've got perfectly good microwave ovens at home. It's precisely having a microwave that makes people crave potjiekos. Like picnics—only when you're sure of a good roof over your head would you even think of eating out of doors, of making a song and dance about eating under a tree. Same thing, dressing up in leopard skin and feathers and baring your tits for the nation. And now I suppose we'll be getting ourselves up in Khoisan karossies, strum our ramkies, and stomp around being traditional hunters and gatherers. Nice and phoney, hey, which is why the leaders who preach this nonsense sit buttoned up in their four-piece suits. Might as well do something brand new like . . . like—and she flings her eyes around the room—like wear a telephone on your head. We can do as we please. It's ridiculous going around looking for Griqua history and traditions when you know that they're just ordinary coloured people like everyone else, just ordinary gullible people who fell for the nonsense of that madman Le Fleur. Ugh, Sally snorts, the things that pass for freedom these days. Then, irrationally, she adds, So leave people like myself to straighten my hair if I want. Why should I not be able to cover my forehead with a fringe or have hair curling here, there, and she tugs brutally at the wisps in question. And it's not about aping white people; they don't straighten their hair. Straightened hair looks nothing like European hair; it looks only like straightened hair; it's different. I'm sick of people with their so-called ethnic bushy heads. If freedom is about looking awful then I leave it to your revolutionaries like Comrade Dulcie. I'll have none of it and I'll have none of your lies. Liberate yourself and face up to being a Tupperware boy, light, multipurpose, adaptable. We're brand new Tupperware people and should thank God for that.

David is bewildered by this outburst. He had no idea that she bothered herself with things like that, held so many views on trivial matters, and such extreme ones at that. He supposes that they haven't talked much of late. Things have been difficult with all the tensions about Mandela's release, about a new dispensation, which only goes to show how badly he needs to go away. So he answers methodically, careful not to upset her further, though why she should want to discuss her hair is beyond him.

Number one, I have told you nothing but the truth and can think of no reason to tell you any lies.

He uses his spread fingers as usual to tick off the points.

Secondly, it's not like that, not really about roots and tradition; it's about myself, my private needs. I can't explain because it's not clear to me either; everything's so confused. I suppose it's all bound up with our changing roles, the tensions around our new offices in the Movement. Let me get sorted out and then when I get back we can talk things through. Like we used to, hey! All I ask is that you bear with me. You know that I can't afford to be troubled in this way. But, and he hesitates, you're wrong about just being ourselves, about being simply what we are. We don't know what we are; the point is that in a place where everything gets distorted, no one knows who he is. And he gives her cheek a consoling tap.

And number three, I have nothing against your hair. I have always found you lovely, loved your hair just as it is; in fact, if you were not to sleep with a stocking on your head would I not choke in the night with all that hair in my mouth?

Only then does he notice her new glasses, which he says are all the more successful for not being so noticeable. She allows herself to be held, her hair to be stroked, and David makes a pot of strong tea before putting the children to bed. Nothing like a cup of tea, he thinks, to soothe the troubled mind and wash down half-baked ideas. They have long ago given up smoking but on such occasions they both savour the memory of a cigarette, of blowing smoke through the nostrils, by way of calming the nerves.

Only the following day as he speeds along De Waal Drive does he think of her reference to Comrade Dulcie. Why on earth should she mention Dulcie? he wonders. Dulcie, and he indulges in the pleasure of thinking her name once more.

Not everyone has a good electric iron, but then, not everyone knows how to use it. Properly, that is. First you sprinkle each item, like baptising it with a flick-flick of your fingertips. Then roll each tightly and pack them like sausages, snug in a plastic basin, where they lose their identity as shirts or sheets and become ironing, taking on the name of the activity. Just as they have earlier become washing, smelly limp things to be passed through soap and water, then dried into warped shapes in the sun. It is the act of ironing that brings them back to life, that resurrects the damp sausage into the lovely fresh sheet, the lovely fresh shirt, the smell of sunlight sealed in with heat. To call so many stages of transformation by the single name of laundering is to take the difference out of washing and ironing—and how else do you get through your days, your life, without dwelling on such differences, without probing their meanings. No one has taught her to do these tasks, just as no one would teach her own children, but as sure as she is Saartjie, or Sally, that is what everyone does when she first looks at the ironing—she dips her fingers into water and sprinkles each item thoroughly.

Except for David, who is too busy to tell that things need washing or ironing; he thinks in terms of laundry although he does not, of course, use the word. Ag, today she is grateful for having work on which to concentrate. You test for heat by spitting onto the hot surface—yes, even on the electric iron, which does not have a dial for controlling the heat—and when the hissing spittle rolls off, you use a cloth, taking care not to burn while you clean the iron once more, making sure that the edges will not smudge the garment. Shirts are the most demanding but the key lies in the collar. It is a mistake to move in a straight line from right to left; you'll only end up with unsightliness. Instead, start at each edge in turn, burrow the hot arrowhead of the iron into each collar tip, resisting the temptation to carry on. Only after each tip is smoothed do you iron the central strip, lifting and switching sides, easing the fabric—for there is always somehow an excess—and there you are, a perfect collar without a crease. She hangs the shirt on the back of a chair.

In her mother's house there was the magic of lighting the Primus stove, of staring into the heart of that fire flower, of holding the plump brass belly while you pumped life into the flame, until the heart glowed red and the flames were blue and orange petals hissing evenly around it. And every household somehow had an old blanket, an old scorched sheet, a ring on which to rest the hot iron, and a set of irons, for while you used one, the other would be heating on the Primus. Not that one bought such things in a shop. Her own had come from their neighbour, Ouma Sanna, whose house at the bottom of the hill hummed with death just as she, Sally, was preparing for her marriage. She came home in time to greet the ouma, and in that airless room, close with the breath of singing women and camphor to cover the smell of death, the ouma sucked at her gums searching for words until those ancient lips parted and in the voice of a ghost whispered, looking into the distance as if she were not there, Die strykgoed, vat vir Saartjie-goed—that she should have the ironing things.

It is a trick she has learnt some time ago, part of her training: to block out all else while she concentrates on physical tasks, on the minutiae of things that have to be done. So, she thinks, and not without bitterness, it has not all been wasted, even for a wife that training has its uses. She folds his shirts into neat rectangular bibs, the buttons dead centre, the arms folded under. Perfect; she could wrap each in cellophane, and even after weeks in a suitcase they would need no further ironing. She packs his bag and oh, if only she could pack her broken heart, pressed and flattened for

David to find bleeding in the folds of his best shirt. But she says carelessly, I've packed your good shirt for going out.

Going out? I won't be needing best wear in Kokstad. Just clothes for messing about in. I'm going to check out the Griquas, remember?

For a special outing, a dance, she says, as if she hasn't heard him. She knows in her bones that the trip has something to do with the woman, that she will be with him at the hotel, although she, Sally, will say nothing, not a word. A woman whose name she knows but will not utter, not ever again.

Does such a woman iron shirts?

Certainly such a woman, with muscular arms and an eye that misses nothing, can aim with deadly precision, knock out a strong man with a fleet-footed move.

And are there women in the world who do both?

She thinks not.

~

Midway between the extremities Nature had been extremely prodigal, so as to make walking neither easy nor graceful. This lady might have sat for a model to a Parisian dressmaker, without any artificial aids in order to set forth the grotesque feminine disfigurement which the freaks of fashion made popular in the middle eighties. Had "Lady Kok" once walked along the Champs Elysees in Paris or Rotten Row in London, the steel mills which were then running day and night to assist in producing this horrible artificial excrescence might have all gone into liquidation at once.

The Reverend Dower, *Early Annals of Kokstad*

THE GRIQUAS OF KOKSTAD IN ONE SHORT CHAPTER— AND OUR ARRIVAL AT THEIR HISTORY

How strange that in his hotel room in Kokstad there should have been right next to the Bible a copy of Buckland's *Curiosities of Natural History*. But no, David insisted, not strange at all;

there were several old bound books of the kind that no one reads, the kind that people buy in boxfuls from auctions. Six books of even size selected to match and flank the faded maroon spine of the Bible. He had nevertheless chosen that one, had opened it at the very reference to Cuvier, and if there is, as David says, no meaning to be found in coincidence, there are certainly effects, for it was that page that persuaded him to cut out from the story the lengthy piece on the scientist whose very name so enraged him. But I say none of this; the question of coincidence seems to be a touchy one.

Although he called the piece on Georges Cuvier and Saartje Baartman his first attempt at writing his own story, it had really been an exercise in avoidance. Besides, he found his interest deflected from outrage on Baartman's behalf to fascination with Cuvier's mind, with the intellectual life he imagined for the anatomist. David saw Cuvier pacing furiously the length of a long book-lined room, a corridor really, as the struggle took place entirely in his head; saw the new system of natural classification thrashed into being, the deadly combat of ideas as military fronts where function finally triumphed over form. That Cuvier, rejecting the obviousness of form, should have invented a system based on features hidden from view appealed to the guerrilla, but he did not like to think of the learned man's anatomical studies of Baartman's genitalia that revealed those hidden private parts. For it was not only the spectacular steatopygia that she strutted in her cage for all of England and France to giggle at—no, the entire world, thanks to Cuvier, could peer in private at those parts of which no decent person would speak, let alone make drawings. On display, the Hottentot Venus may well on a good sunny day have snarled or giggled at her plane-backed viewers. It was the shame in print, in perpetuity, the thought of a reader turning to that page, that refreshed David's outrage.

And so, since outrage must be fuelled, he flicked through Buckland's *Curiosities* to see if Saartje was included. But there was only a description of the fountain erected in honour of Georges Cuvier, outside the gates of the Jardin des Plantes in Paris, and it was this that struck at David's pledge to keep to the facts. Having memorised the passage from Buckland, he recited it to me in high dramatic fashion, lingering over the scientific words:

> Here is represented, first, an anatomical impossibility, *viz,* a crocodile turning his head at right angles to his body; secondly, a zoological absurdity, *viz,* a walrus, a graminivorous rather than a piscivorous animal, holding a fish in his mouth, and that a freshwater fish. Surely Cuvier, if he could see his own fountain, would be much pleased to observe the good use that had been made of his investigations into the secrets of nature by the artist.

This jeering at the artist's ignorant representation of the natural world made David smart at the transparency of his own writing on Cuvier, which he then rightly came to see as a simplistic act of revenge, the product, to use his phrase, of a mind not fully de-colonised. For his portrait of a scientist discoursing on the private parts of Baartman was an ill-researched one of a portly, concupiscent gentleman with a deficient posterior. In short, a windbroek, not only an absence of flesh but a weakness of spirit, which after all could not be true of Cuvier, the father of biology. Besides, the passage was largely irrelevant, no more than a warming-up exercise, a digression from the real subject of his narrative.

And what, I ask, taking advantage of the opportunity, is the real subject of your story?

David finds it hard to say that it is about himself; he mumbles about problems with this year's Youth Day celebrations, about things being so mixed up since the ANC is being established within the country; one has to expect all kinds of sabotage from unexpected quarters. I remind him of his previous answers about the trip to Kokstad, about the Griquas, the maverick chief, Le Fleur, and also his own ancestors, who were among Le Fleur's converts in Namaqualand. Yes, yes, he says, hiding behind impatience. He will not/cannot say how these are connected, so that we skirt about a subject that slithers out of reach, and I am reminded of the new screen saver on my computer that tosses the text hither and thither, prettily rearranging and replacing, until the letters, transformed, slip into fluid, abstract shapes of mesmerising colour.

With Cuvier now removed from his story, David flew off into another fiction, into the European origins of the Griqua chief. But the anatomist would not be deleted without a trace, so that the historical figure of Madame la Fleur was transformed into Cuvier's housekeeper, the good woman being lifted out of her period and grafted onto the wrong century. Charmed by the way in which one collapsing story would clutch at another in thin air, I suggest that, in spite of the error, we keep her after all. David giggles boyishly at the image of Madame la Fleur flitting between centuries, a Protestant angel dithering in time. It is nice to see him lighthearted.

But what, he asks, if a reader should try to find meaning in the historical disjuncture?

Nonsense, I say, it's clearly an error. I begin to tell him of the misrecorded *Come in* uttered by James Joyce in answer to a knock on the door, and included in the text by his scribe, the young Beckett; and then, uncharacteristically, I shriek as I remember. Youth Day—Soweto Day, the sixteenth of June—that's also Joyce's Bloomsday, I gabble excitedly, Day of the Revolution of the Word. Imagine, black children revolting against Afrikaans, the language of oppressors, on the very anniversary of the day that Leopold Bloom started with a hearty breakfast, eating with relish the inner organs of—

David grimaces, shakes his head, interrupts: Don't, that's horrible. What on earth are you talking about, eating a man's organs?

Not a man's; the inner organs of an animal. Oh, forget it, I say, just another coincidence. But wasn't that also the day you met Dulcie, in the Soweto Day celebrations?

Yes, yes of course, he says, but what's that got to do with your Mr. Blooms? You must understand, be clear about this, that Sally is jealous of nothing at all. It is by no means that kind of thing, what your kind call an affair, my relationship with Dulcie.

We banter about my kind, skirting about Dulcie, a protean subject that slithers hither and thither, out of reach, repeating, replacing, transforming itself. . . .

•

The stout widow, Madame la Fleur, of sallow skin and emerald eyes, was a Huguenot of stout spirit who had kept her religious beliefs a secret. Even from her master, the good doctor Cuvier, who had taken responsibility for her son's education and who indeed seemed prepared to do anything to ensure a bright future for the boy. For all her Protestant principles, she knew of no better education than the Jesuits could provide and, distinguishing between mind and soul, trusted in her own ability to undermine their influence on the latter.

That Madame la Fleur left on a false alarm of a new wave of persecution is a possibility that she never allowed herself to contemplate. For her plain-speaking, no-nonsense God, she braved a wicked night of howling storms to collect her darling boy, and tossed on a choppy English Channel until days later they reached the cliffs of Dover where Protestant fathers, wet crows in their sodden, sombre garb, welcomed the Parisians and drove them in the driving rain to Spitalfields. Here, much addicted to a rickety Queen Anne chair, she sat wrapped in a cashmere shawl, a bashful gift from the celebrated Cuvier, and trembled for the treachery that he would undoubtedly have read in her actions. Walking through the dreary London markets of food fit only for dogs, she choked back her tears. Who could be trusted to provide the master with a perfectly baked brioche for breakfast? And how would the eminent doctor, occupied with learned thoughts, know how to describe to a new and ignorant housekeeper precisely how to prepare his tourtière de poulet?

She chose not to remember those months in London. She had never spoken to an English person before; she had only heard from a rakish relative incredible tales of his adventures as manservant accompanying one such personage on a sentimental journey through France and Italy, a distinguished gentleman of letters much discussed by Cuvier, who could not abide his style of beating about the bush. And now, from her own experience, it was not difficult to attribute the man's legendary strangeness to the national character. How indeed they beat about the bush even in discoursing about their weather; besides, the language was impossible, slippery and barbaric, and she had to rely on her reluctant son for translation and instruction.

The expensive education and refinements of the young Eduard

la Fleur allowed the boy to resist adaptation to his new impover-
ished circumstances. His habit of rocking to-and-fro as he memorised the religious texts to which they owed their condition made
his mother fear for his sanity. Besides, she detected a disturbing tone
in his voice, as if the syllables were infused with venom; but then,
perhaps his voice was breaking once again under the strain.

In Spitalfields her strong hands rummaged helplessly through
heaps of yarn. Only faith kept her from despairing of the puckered
fabric that issued from her loom. She wove because no one believed
that she could do anything else. If she was a Huguenot she would
have to be a weaver, for that was what Huguenots did so well and
in no-nonsense England that was that. Until divine intervention came
in the form of a ship bound for the Cape Colony, where the last of
the surplus Huguenots were being sent. Hostile and cold and
themselves clamouring for employment, the English were best left
behind. Certainly Madame la Fleur did not relish the thought of
real barbarians, but without the skills needed to be a real Huguenot
in London and with a son who languished in a creaking chair
with theological texts, the idea of the veld seemed preferable. In any
case, here was an opportunity for austere worship of God, who could
try her faith anew with droughts and locusts and an absence of boule-
vards and boulangeries. Little did she know that after the standoffish
English there would be enforced assimilation at the Cape, where they
would have to merge with the Dutch, speak their language, and
worship with the brutes so hopelessly deprived of the civilising
influence of European women. Or that her weaving skills would have
to be replaced by winemaking, for that was another thing Huguenots
did so well. That's life, she sighed resignedly, an endless shuttling
back and forth between opposing worlds. Besides, who was she to
set herself against the making of history and tradition.

On the ship, the green-eyed Eduard vomited copiously or
stared across the vast blue reciting his psalms, roused not at the thought
of brave colonial adventures but by the souls of the poor barbarians, clumps of disfigured steatopygous people whom he imagined
as stonefaced congregations chattering in a wild tongue throughout the service. As they neared the equator, where flying fish

broke through the tepid water, curving into the tepid air, Eduard contemplated the mirror smoothness of the ocean and thought of Cuvier, the benefactor who beckoned him into his room to see the grotesque drawings of a woman's vast buttocks and other parts that he knew were sinful to look at. There were also sketches of a delicate face with high cheekbones, shell-like ears and slanted eyes, but these were severed from the bodies. It was the buttocks that made the boy sigh deeply, as the silver fish fountained out of the sea, those mountains of insensible flesh that would have to be infused with a love for God.

The rest of Eduard's story can be found in Mrs. Sarah Gertrude Millin's narrative about miscegenation, although the reader should note that she has taken several liberties with the tale, including casting the boy as an Englishman and adding some years to his age—in other words, that her narrative is as unreliable as David's.

Adam Kok I begat Cornelius Kok the Careless (who even after his death lost the diamond fields of Griqualand West) who begat Adam Kok II who begat Adam Kok III who more or less begat Adam Muis Kok. All without the interference of women. Which was just as well, or the Paramount Chief's Staff of Office, bequeathed by the Dutch colonial government and responsibly passed on from generation to generation, would undoubtedly have been sold by a faithless wife. (There is the indisputable example of the first native woman of no parentage, Eva/Krotoa, who in spite of being taken into the cleanliness of the Dutch castle, in spite of marriage to a white man and fluency in his language, reverted to type and sold her own brown children's clothes for liquor.)

But women—and complication—will intrude, and thus Adam Muis Kok begat a daughter, Rachael Susanna, who, sitting on the knee of her esteemed relative Captain Adam Kok III, listened to marvellous and greatly exaggerated stories about M'Ntatisi, the giant Batlokwa warrior-chieftainess, and Victoria, the small, fat, and cross British Queen.

Bewitched by the child, the captain said, Why not—if she were good and quiet and obedient—why not a female successor? Her father,

Adam Muis, whose name in any case did not bode well, could keep an eye on things until she was ready to rule. To which the captain's chair-bound lady of steatopygous fame nodded vigorously, congratulating him on his good sense, for she, too, having thrilled at the tales of female rule, came to think of the child as her very own. When Adam Muis Kok, whilst leading the Griqua rebellion in 1878 against British annexation, was shot by a dashing high commissioner in a scarlet coat, old Lady Kok leapt more nimbly than her figure would allow out of her chair to assume the heavy staff of office which, despite the shaking of beards and grizzled heads, she held with a steadfast hand over her feckless people.

Rachael Susanna Kok, growing up in the shadow of her aunt, tried not to think of the threat of ladyhood and indeed forgot all about the destiny pronounced by the captain until she married none other than Andries le Fleur, the grandson of a queasy young Huguenot, Eduard la Fleur, whose limp, linen-clad figure we have left in an earlier century, insensible to the silver flash of flying fish at the equator as he stood vomiting on the poopdeck.

On the autumn equinox of 1867, when Andries Abraham Stockenstrom le Fleur shot headfirst into the world, the cry of the departing stork was quite drowned by the scream of Ouma Truida, the midwife. The good woman had once before delivered a cauled baby years ago in Griqualand West, and that one's legendary powers of vision had not stood him in good stead.

But such a caul!—a veritable lisle stocking pulled tightly over the little one's head, as if he could not risk entering the world without a guerrilla's disguise. Ouma Truida's skilful scissors trembled as she removed the membrane, but like Baby Jesus the infant uttered not a single cry. Po-faced like his implacable grandfather—she might as well have left him imprisoned in his caul for all he seemed to care about the world. Not that he was not alert. The mixture of Malayan-Madagascan slave, French missionary, and Khoisan hunter blood had produced a perfect blend of high cheekbones, bronze skin, and bright green almond eyes that stared with such knowledge that his mother, whose name no one remembers, wept and turned away.

The nameless woman trusted no one, not after the lies and the loss of land, the interminable trekking, and the bad manners of the British who were supposed to be their saviours. As for expectation, well, she had learnt her lesson in Griqualand West that it was only sensible to stand such a thing on its head and await the opposite. No matter how old the legend of the caul, the world was becoming horribly modern and she would not believe that it would bring her son good luck.

Against death by water, the midwife insisted. Sailors would give you anything for such a caul.

Now that's just the sort of good luck you need when you live miles inland, the mother retorted. Did I not see with my own eyes how you had to cut this blue-in-the-face baby out of captivity? And now look at him.

The baby's old-man eyes narrowed into points of green light, hard as diamonds.

Bury the thing and not a word to a sailor or anyone else, said the mother.

Ouma Truida had to agree. Klaasie Fortuin, her first cauled child in Hopetown, could see right through the earth to where the diamonds lay glittering in the deep. And what fortune or hope did that bring him, led as he was by the collar like a sniffer dog to show white people where to dig. And his potbellied children running about barebummed with nothing to eat. If anyone should ask about Andries's caul, they would simply deny it.

Andries, unlike other children, did not like playing with water. Some say that it stemmed from the day of his christening, when old Dominee Joshua's trembling finger missed the font. Insensible to moisture, the horny digit traced a perfectly dry cross on the baby's brow. On reaching home, his mother, reading an omen in the accidental lack of water, gave him a sprinkling that even the indomitable infant could not withstand.

His stylus eyes filled with a liquid that dispersed the light; his toothless mouth gaped once, twice, resisting, before he gave in to a hearty wail. It was then, through snot and tears, that he heard the first voice: *Fear neither water nor the absence of water. Listen to the waves lapping at Robben Island, and look to the radical moisture of the desert where your Grigriqua ancestors tended their stock.*

The voice that at first sounded incomprehensible was in fact in Xiri, the old Griqua tongue, which was then still spoken by the older generation.

That he was able to access the language came as no surprise. The mixing of blood may have been old hat in the melting pot of the Cape; what the infant Le Fleur, guerrilla-in-arms, understood was that above the new roar of eugenics, the Khoi, oldest blood of all, spoke at once most clearly and in code. And that the imperative, its preferred mood, made for its clicking clarity.

From the diary of Andries Abraham Stockenstrom le Fleur, Paramount Chief of the Griquas

Kokstad, 16 June 1885. Standing on the crest of Mount Currie like Moses of old, I cast my eyes across the valleys of Nieuw Griqualand, across the rich, brown paps of earth, across God's green grass beckoning in the breeze, along the veins of water coursing loudly under the surface of the land. A rising sun spread her golden rays evenly over the earth, over the tattered pondoks and the prosperous homesteads alike; flocks of steaming livestock stamped their feet, bellowing their morning prayers. And there on the mountain, the others having eagerly gone ahead, I stayed and watched the sun travel across the blue dome until it reached the zenith. Then all grew dark for seconds as she withdrew her light. When the blood red circle of sun appeared once more, her rays surveyed the earth, marked out the rectangle of Griqua land, from the Umzimkulu across to Umtata, and the voice of God called from a bush burning with the fire of the sun, Andries Abraham Stockenstrom le Fleur, and I said, Lord, I am your servant, and the voice said, These are your people who have lost their land, who have become tenants on their own Griqua farms. It is you who must restore to them their dignity.

And when I went down into the valley I saw a people of running sores, of filth and idleness and degradation. What had become of the warriors of the Great Trek of '62? Where were those who, driven from the diamond country of the West, scaled the mighty

Drakensberg and, fired with freedom, built the roads and tamed and tilled this fertile land? Reduced by annexation to a people without a patch of earth to call their own, a people without pride, a yawning people, following the sun around the crumbling walls of their pondoks, a dispossessed people who had given up and who had lost their God. And according to my word I will stir them from their slumbers, imbue them with the courage to fight the white man, recover our land, and with the help of God breathe fresh vigour into their slack veins. Annexation! There can be no such thing; we will not acknowledge their cheating bits of paper.

Captain Eta Kok gave us a warm welcome and boasted of the handsomeness of the town, but what was there to boast of except a church with the arrogant Reverend Dower in the pulpit and a Scottish magistrate's office right next to the Kok palace. My heart bled as Captain Kok saluted and bowed to the enemy, to the chief constable, so that I had to relieve my distress by going for a walk, past the plots now owned by thieving settlers. I took the rich brown earth in my hands, watched it trickle sluggishly through my fingers, and knew that there lay a hard task ahead.

Griqualand for the Griquas and the Natives. This is our land. We will wipe out the stain of colouredness and gather together under the Griqua flag those who have been given a dishonourable name.

When I returned to the palace, Father was giving thanks to the Lord for our safe arrival. Through the humble Griqua voices woven in descant, the spirit leapt into our hymn, Juig aarden juig—Rejoice, earth, rejoice—and gathered us together in a flash of fire that streaked across the firmament.

When Abraham le Fleur, pioneer of the Great Trek across the Drakensberg into Griqualand East, erstwhile secretary to Adam Kok III and later adviser to Lady Kok of steatopygic fame, sent his son, Andries, in search of a pair of mules whose hind legs he had failed to tie together, he could not have imagined the consequences.

Mules, he mumbled, more trouble than they're worth, obstinate like these wretched Griquas. Why God should allow such breeding, I do not know. I'd trade twenty of these wretches for a good horse.

Which both grieved and frightened the pious son, for not only does the Creator know best, but before his eye flashed a vision of his father's downfall brought about by a vengeful horse. (Reverend Dower's readers will note how, within a short appendix, that author uses the young man's vision to transform the father from Griqua-agitator-for-compensation to Abraham-the-horse-thief.) Mistaking the young man's glazed look for one of contempt, Abraham sternly warned him not to return without the animals.

On the first day the youth roamed the veld, eagerly sniffing the forest pines, praising the blue sky, and, if the truth be told, not thinking too much about the errant mules. Such delight brought inevitable guilt, but Andries, thoroughly questioning his heart, decided that to rejoice in the earth was as much a holy duty. Day two, however, found our hero somewhat disheartened. He had slept badly in a recess, hardly a cave, where the stars in spite of sealed eyes burned on his retinas. The entire night sky crowded into the canvas of his mind: the three kings of the Orient danced with brilliance, a meteor with ominous tail of fiery stars travelled steadily across, and sleep came fitfully only with Venus's morning light. Still there was no sign of the mules.

He had brought only one day's supply of bread and lard but found a small bag of kaiings that his mother had slipped into his sack. To punish himself and the indulgent woman he resolved not to eat the kaiings but on the second evening succumbed, only to find the cold twists of fried tail-fat unpalatable without bread. On the third day the hungry Andries cursed the mules, the stubborn, sterile offspring of male donkeys and female horses. Stupidity and laziness, that's what made them wander off; they deserved no better than to be used as beasts of burden. But given to self rebuke, he thought of his Khoi ancestors who wandered at will to and from the castle because they would not be enslaved, which according to the Dutch showed that they were lazy, irresponsible, and without ambition. Could it be the mixing with European blood—for he would not allow the knowledge of slaves from the East—that later enslaved his people? The

young man shut his eyes and gritted his teeth. He roared his rage
into the veld and felt the blood galloping through each vein, separately and distinctly, with a force that made it perfectly possible,
he thought, to turn up the earth with his bare hands.

On that third evening, sitting on a promontory with his face
buried in his knees and resolving to let the mules be, to leave them
to their freedom, he heard a voice calling, Andries, Andries, lift up
your eyes and see the glory of God. Before him lay a valley of breathtaking beauty and on the horizon a burst sun edged the clouds with
its signature of gold. The voice continued: Servant of God, heed
your task. Gather the scattered bones of Adam Kok and lead your
people out of the wilderness.

The youth trembled. For looking again at the valley he saw that
the pebbles were not pebbles and the hills were not hills. Scattered
in the valley were acres of bones, bleached bones picked clean by
sun and rain. He fell to his knees calling, My Lord, I am your humble servant, but the voice, not without a hint of impatience, said,
Rise Andries, rise, and be a man so that you may lead the Griquas
out of slavery. Return to Kokstad and announce to your people the
death of Lady Kok at sunset tomorrow.

He sprinted for half a mile before the voice returned to
admonish him for not taking the mules who, on his return to the
promontory, were waiting, clearly wearied by freedom—of which
he thought nothing until decades later when he lay propped in bed
dictating his broken thoughts to a fool of an amanuensis for
whom weariness could never mean anything other than lack of sleep.

Lady Kok's death at the appointed time established in the
eyes of the people the young man's powers, his special relationship
with God. Andries set about pondering the enigma of God's words.
Some elders thought that the bones in the vision meant that he should
consult the medicine men of Sigcau, the Pondo chief, but the
pious Le Fleur forbade any mention of such savage practices.
Patience, he said, and slow, careful thought would reveal its meaning in the fullness of time, and in the meantime they were to turn
their thoughts to the building of a Griqua nation. The bones of Adam
Kok were scattered far afield, and the nation was one that did not

recognise itself as such. It was to him that the task of upliftment and unity fell, and to that purpose he received the gift of tongues, so that his voice dropped an octave to resemble that of God as he discoursed in the many languages that found their way into his preaching.

One of the unexpected benefits of hearing the voice was the sharpening of his vision so that in the weeks of still, deep thought he found solace in the patterns of miniscule seedpods, or in the infinitesimal wing of an insect, a wisp of gossamer crisscrossed with veins. The world was transformed: a casual glance fell nothing short of penetrating the molecular arrangement of things; a pimple, no longer a blemish, became a honeycomb of cells; a path of dust was like the Milky Way stuffed with stars. In his intense absorption with the microscopic world he failed to notice Rachael Susanna Kok. He did not see her slow sad smile, for that lady, in her starched bonnet of mourning with frills as rigid as etched waves, allowed her eyes and mouth to droop sadly after all those deaths. Whilst her hands and feet were indeed of miniature proportions, they were not to be compared with stomata of leaves or spores of dust. But it was while tracing the flight of a concupiscent pollen sac, a fluffy little thing normally quite invisible to the naked eye, as it settled on the virgin crisp bonnet of Miss Kok that he chanced, some weeks after the voice, to alight upon those sad black eyes. And peering into her heart he saw the first stage to the fulfilment of the prophecy and understood his role, for that heart was a well of kindness, docility, and above all obedience which would ensure that history unfolded without a hitch and according to the vision.

Andries had never before found reason to speak to a woman. How was he to secure this wife? He cast his eyes about the troop of willing disciples gathered about him for an emissary, but then remembered the Word. He was to be a man, a leader of men, and therefore had to accomplish the terrible task himself. Which was just as well, since an emissary might well have missed the lady's assent. Miss Kok had been expecting a proposal ever since he had peered so boldly into her heart and thus by way of reply inclined her head, a barely perceptible nod that was recognised by Andries as a cipher. He took the miniature hand in his own, thanked her courteously, and explained how her nod had triggered off a series of unstoppable events: that he would eventually have to take her away from her beloved Kokstad; that the Griqua bones scattered across the barren wastes of the Free State, the Eastern Cape, and even far-flung Namaqualand had to be gathered. In short, her nod had signalled a life of trekking. But before further discussion he would have to have the Staff of Office which Rachael Susanna had secreted in her voluminous skirts ever since the death of the captain, which is to say the death of old Lady Kok. As she rose and loosened a tie in the deeply carved small of her back, he felt in the swell of her full-grown steatopygia a spirit moving him to husbandhood. She handed over without a word, and without betraying an iota of the fear he inspired in her, the symbols of authority passed on by Adam Kok I.

It was around this time that Andries anglicised his name, a process which in spite of his growing Scoto-Anglophobia occurred without a hitch. (The implications were wider than he could have imagined. Not only did it show that Griquas were in this respect indistinguishable from coloureds, but the practice gained momentum until the next century, when parents realised that children could from the outset be christened with English versions of their forebears' names or even with brand new American ones. Such defiance of tradition in turn discouraged nationhood, so that Andrew came to regret setting a trend that so undermined his own project.)

Marriage to the freshly named Andrew did little by way of cheering up Rachael Susannah Kok. All his fine talk about the alchemy of marriage stabilising the humours, making things clear for a person, well, it was all stuff and nonsense, more like a conspiracy that she simply did not understand, even though conspiracy was the very thing on which she had been raised. Her new husband's energetic to-ing and fro-ing exhausted the good lady. Having become Paramount Chief by dint of marrying Adam Kok's heir, he was given to practising on her patient ear long sermons on the role of duty, industry, thrift, sobriety, and chastity in the upliftment of the people. As for the long lost diamonds in Griqualand West, the farms stolen by missionaries, or British annexation of Griqualand East, these topics made him storm about the place in fresh rage, beating the syllables of *re-tro-cess-ion* or *com-pen-sa-tion* on the table with such force that his knuckles surely bruised. She dutifully praised his speeches although she wished for the sake of her unborn child that he would not get so carried away. Her slow sad smile grew slower as his obsession with work left little time or inclination for cheer. (There is some dispute about the distinctive smile. Some say it came after her marriage; others, that it stems from the misreading of a photograph in which a woman with just such a smile sits demurely to the right of the lively Rachael, a lady I identified as Annie Kok, of purer Griqua stock. However, since we have come to know her by this distinguishing feature, to wipe away the smile or to replace it with another characteristic would only add to the confusion of this story.)

Rachael shook her head in the privacy of the room where her husband forbade an afternoon nap. Sleep was the downfall of the Griqua people, he said. As First Lady she had to set an example so that they would no longer laze about in the sun, dither wantonly before time's tricks, and be caught out once again by history. Only vigorous shaking of the head would stop her eyes from drifting to the pillow. Andrew had fortunately a number of collars to be turned, socks to be darned, coats to be mended, worn sheets to be cut in half and stitched side to side and the monogram of *AAS* embroidered once again on the worn edge since the seam, having swallowed an initial, left a sorry *AS* in the centre.

The many letters that Andrew composed every day, demanding justice from governors, all kinds of deputies, secretaries, and even the queen, he dictated to her, or would give to her to check his writing for words missed in haste and passion. When she said at first that no, she was sorry, but she was not so good at reading and writing, that it was not her kind of thing, he looked at her sternly and said, Never again do I want to hear such nonsense. You have a duty to me, to God, and to your people; your kind of thing is that duty and nothing else.

She noted the order—that he placed himself before God—but said nothing. Husbands and schoolroom talk, she'd had enough for one day. She developed the habit of holding out her bonnet strings like taut reins while he talked, and as he stopped, of tying them into a bow with firm clipped movements which, functioning like an amen, prevented him from starting up again. He took the gesture as a sign of her resolve to obey. She thrilled at the possibility of his wondering how they came to be untied whenever he spoke, but not once did he ask.

It was not that Rachael was unfamiliar with the business of politics. She had after all been a girl when her father, Adam Muis, organised the rebellion of 1878, but that was an exciting cloak-and-dagger affair of midnight gatherings and the gallop of horses carrying brave warriors into danger. And she too had galloped across the hills with her uncle, the Chief, who said yes, of course, she need not wear a bonnet in the veld. Bareheaded on the barebacked Prince, she knew every inch of the valley, roamed freely across the hills around Kokstad, travelled far in the mind to distant countries, to the cross queen's green England of babbling brooks, where swashbuckling men on horseback—fine men quite unlike the silly captain who had killed her father—annexed picturesque villages, all while her own horse charged through the dry tamboekie grass. She had sat for hours watching a dying sun paint the sky in streaky, miserly gold, watched the night advance with bolder purples and dreamt of wrapping herself in just such an up-to-date colour, for modernity itself was peeking over the fading hilltops. That such a wrap was inspired by the elaborate dress of the Hlangweni chief, whose furtive visits were growing more frequent, she would be the first to admit. But she had also seen ladies fresh from Europe being lifted out of carriages, so that it was difficult to separate out the influences, for there in the twilight, with time in her hands, things grew wonderfully strange as the colours of the sky leaked into one another.

Her new husband—and the newness stayed until the first imprisonment, when she got to know him better in his absence—said that galloping about the countryside was not dignified, and as the grandson of a missionary, she supposed he knew all about dignity and decorum. Dignity, it seemed, meant a bundle of dreary things for a woman: she had to keep her head covered at all times, was not to throw it back and roar with laughter even in private, and above all, was not to venture outdoors after sunset without an escort. A horse was to be ridden for a purpose, to get somewhere that you had to be; cantering idly across the hills was out of the question. A pity, she thought, and just as well that marriage had brought so much to do; otherwise she would not have managed the business of being a dignified wife.

Now her evenings were spent reading the *Kokstad Advertiser* in lamplight, for more often than not there was something about the Griquas: the vulgar writings of the Reverend Dower, who chose to believe that they could not read; the devious arguments against retrocession; or the vicious misrepresentation of Andrew's words and actions. These were her task to collect and relay to her good man. But how her eyes strayed to Mitchell & Co.'s notices of the new consignment of fabrics—voiles, shantungs, white piques, poplins, and silks—frocks and dresses promised in the prevailing styles of Europe, finished according to the correct idea of the moment. There was surely no need for a busy and sensible person to look a fright. Oh, she was not going to give up being a modern woman in the matter of dress. Being a deft seamstress, she would peer into those windows and then re-create the imported styles, and he, it seemed, did not mind. Or did not notice, as long as the newspaper was properly scanned and the cuttings carefully filed. For he would take his place in the evenings, in the upright chair with wooden armrests, and ask her to read an article once more. Then she would remember, without having marked the phrases, to leave out again all malicious references to his person while keeping the flow of the sentence. No mean task in the flickering lamplight, but that, she supposed, was what marriage was all about—keeping a woman on her toes.

But the Chief, David's Ouma Ragel said, came to understand women in the end. All the troubles turned him into a better, a more loving husband. You see, there is nothing like a prison sentence to soften the most masterful of men, also to keep a man out of trouble and intrigue, she whispered, and most important of all, to keep the politician's hands clean. And so, you see, he came to call his wife Dorie. His voice was always stern as he said *my Dorie,* which was, of course, not her name, but it was so nice to hear him sometimes say *my dearest Dorie.*

Why Dorie? David asked. Was that Rachael's other name?

No, Ouma said, it wasn't, clipping his ear for the disrespectful use of Rachael's first name, it was just the Chief's pet name for our volksmoeder. Who knows, she said, perhaps it's short for dorinkie—little thorn. A marriage is never what it seems to others, perhaps that sweet and mild woman was a thorn in his side. Or perhaps not. Your own Oupa Gert, bless his departed soul. . . .

But it was the fantastic stories about the Chief that David wanted to hear. Thus as a boy he learnt the skill of steering a conversation that later came to stand him in such good stead in the Movement, and in a manner so mild and a voice so girlishly soft that he would be the last one to be accused of manipulation.

And Oupa (whom he never knew) was the Chief's Man in Namaqualand, who brought together hundreds of Griquas from miles around, he recited. I think the Chief said to him, Gert, her name is Dorie because, because she didn't believe in the miracles. . . .

Ag no, never; she was the best, the wisest woman in the world, and the Chief came to rely on her more and more. A thorn isn't always a bad thing, and what's more my boy, love has a funny habit of speaking in many tongues.

She stopped to cut the daintiest piece of konfyt for their tea. Just the two of them, washing down the sweetness in the still afternoon heat.

Ja, he didn't speak to women as a rule, but he became, in a way, a special friend of your great-grandmother Antjie. In her presence he was quiet and respectful, spent many hours at our house just quietly drinking coffee.

Come on, get these sticky konfyt hands clean. Ouma held a mug of water over the chipped basin, but before David washed his hands, he would rub a finger—ouch—into the sores on the enamel.

When you grow up to be a politician, you'll remember that Ouma kept your hands clean, she laughed, And wipe, just here on my apron, she said as she drew him close. So that with his nose pressed against her he gabbled, More, Ouma, more. Please tell another story, another miracle. But the day was getting long in the tooth; she had a million things to do.

No miracles today. Just the plain old Chief being quiet for a change. Yes, he spent many an hour in our house and never did he call your Ouma Antjie anything but Mrs. Klaassen. In that strong voice that somehow made people remember their failings. But he loved children. He was like a father to me.

This world, my good wife, Andrew explained, drawing up his newly patched breeches without a word of admiration for the fine stitching, but with his back modestly turned, This world is not the place we thought it was. Who could have imagined that the Commission of Enquiry for which I have fought tooth and nail could be turned into such a travesty of justice by Stanford. Chief magistrate, my foot! No, we shall have to petition the colonial secretary in London. God has given each one of us the knowledge of right and wrong, yet everywhere we see the taint of Satan, and it is sadly the case that missionary zeal turns out to be nothing other than enthusiasm for the Prince of Darkness. Note the zeal with which our imperial missionary friends, our men of God, have been stealing our land. It was in good faith that Adam Kok put Clydesdale in the hands of the missionaries to be used for the good of the Griquas, where our people would have owners' rights and titles in their own names. And what do my enquiries bring to light? That in 1883 the bishop registered Clydesdale in his own name, as his personal property. Let me assure you, there is no confusion over title deeds, there is only the swindling by missionaries. Imagine, that arrogant Reverend Dower on the Forty Years' Money, and Andrew affected an absurd voice of rollicking *r*s with which to mimic the little man: Och, I have pursued this matter for your people but there is nay solution. I rather fear that all church registers of marriages, births, and baptisms up to 1861 were uplifted for official purposes, eh, and now have clean, eh, disappeared, so that even if we were able to sort out this very, eh, complicated matter, a just, eh, distribution of the land would be impossible. Och aye, I would strenuously advise you to forget this, eh, business of the past, when so many mistakes were made on both sides. Far too complicated to follow so let's look, eh, to the future.

Andrew hunched his shoulders and drew in his neck to imitate Dower's nodding and wagging, but as Rachael's giggle reminded him of the seriousness of the matter, he leapt up to proclaim, They will not get away with it! As you all know—forgetting that he had an audience of only one wife—I have been blessed with vision that tells me of the great changes to come about in this land, changes that will leave the greedy capitalist gangs squealing in their ponds of avarice. Yes, he repeated, pleased as punch with the image, squealing like piglets in their filthy ponds.

But Andrew, she soothed, you shouldn't speak like that of missionaries, remember your own grandpapa from across the waters. Then she saw his green eyes blaze with rage, his body grow rigid, while his voice softened—things being always the wrong way round with him—as he finally spoke: Rachael Susanna le Fleur, there is only one thing with which we need concern ourselves, and that is justice. That is our duty. We are Griquas and it turns out that we must fight foreigners for rights in our own land.

She would have liked to hear about that missionary forebear. About the stories from faraway places told to the child in a foreign tongue. But not a word did Andrew say about him, not a syllable of French could be prised from his tongue, just as if, she thought, there had never been a laughing child dandled on the knee of old Eduard. A pity, for that would surely have stopped him from ranting about foreigners. She knew, of course, nothing of the anachronism, of the century lost between Eduard's arrival and Andrew's birth. (Nor could she have known that the celebrated writer Mrs. Sarah Gertrude Millin, then still stumbling about in bulky nappies, would one day turn Eduard into a lily-livered Englishman lost in filth and apathy, and stunned into silence by his own motley brood—in other words, an ancestor that Andrew would later completely disown.)

Not only will the land be restored to us, but the charlatans and hypocrites will be exposed, he shouted, as if she had not spoken. Take the Clydesdale farm or the claim of poor old Johannes Kok. Who would have thought that a magistrate would stoop to such low tricks, swindling a blind man so carelessly, so contemptuously? As if it mattered not in the least that the rest of us can see and know of their dishonesty. If it takes my life, I swear by the God of justice that our poor will once again swing their hoes and lift their heads with pride. And we will have our Forty Years' Money. It was a disgraceful agreement with the Koks, a pittance for driving us out of Griqualand West, and now, predictably, they won't honour it.

She understood little of what Andrew said; she had never before heard anyone speak like a book. Besides, he never gave her any details, and since she was not allowed to ask she learnt little of his clandestine activities.

It is safer that way, he said. These things are too complicated for women. Which sounded to her much like the Reverend Dower's speech, but she knew better than to say that. So he did not explain about the discovery of the deed of sale which was supposedly signed a good couple of years after the owner's death. How would they get themselves out of that fraud? No, there was no other way, he frowned, tapping the leather pouch he had taken to carrying with him at all times, if demanding justice is about agitation then yes, I am the Great Griqua Agitator. And yes, I am working with the chiefs of the Bhaca and the Hlangweni; we will fight together to restore the land to the Griquas and the natives. Our land will be purged of these white thieves and the rinderpest they have brought to kill off our livestock.

Thus he resigned his partnership in the wagon-making business and preached anew the virtues of frugality, for he knew instinctively of the extravagance of women, of their frivolity. Andrew would even have had her do her own housework, both for her own good and as an example to the people, but the very people would not see their lady stoop to a scrubbing brush. It was they who sent Siena, collected a wage for her, so that a humbled Andrew in turn insisted on employing her himself. Rachael supposed that the people paid their meagre dues as always, but certainly house-keeping became a business of juggling with copper coins.

Rachael's moment of high adventure started as a rude distur-bance in her sleep. Andrew had been in conference for most of the night with his right-hand men, Lodewyk Kok and George Abrahams, and when finally, in the early hours of the morning, he came to bed, he sighed and fidgeted so horribly that she woke up. Resentfully, she stroked his fevered brow while he grunted and ground his teeth, until at last he sat up and, being in touch with anoth-er world, spoke in a strange monotone, punctuated with long silences that caught her nodding with sleep: There is a hand slid-ing across a sheet of paper. It is the chief magistrate with a war-rant for my arrest.

He drew away peevishly, ungratefully, she thought, from her own soothing hand. Now Andrew don't fret, she said firmly. The Griqua chief couldn't possibly go to prison. They wouldn't dare—

It can't be helped, he interrupted. Such things will happen in the quest for justice. Shu-ut, Rachael, shu-ut, I am troubled—blessed or burdened with vision. I see three dark figures . . . they move about furtively . . . thieves in the night . . . I can't tell. Then, bolting out of bed, he whispered, I do not know the third, but there, unmistakably, are Lodewyk and Abrahams, their plotting heads bent with shame. Don't think that Judas is not ashamed from the start; from well before that money is mentioned, before he has even agreed to the act of betray-al, he suffers the shame of knowing his own weakness.

With no man in the room whom he could trust, he turned to her and how thrilling it was to open the bedroom window inch by inch, to slip out together into the night and in the light of the ris-ing moon to dig up right by the gatepost, for heaven's sake, the leather pouch of documents that he had, with the help of the abominable Judases, those snakes in the grass, Abrahams and Lodewyk of all peo-ple, buried for safekeeping. In the moonlight the bag shone eerily.

Take it, Rachael, I cannot bear to touch it, for already it jingles with the shekels of treachery.

She dusted it down fastidiously while he replaced the soil and smoothed the earth. And only then did she suggest that they take out the documents and rebury the bag. Again they dug into the earth, making for a second time a hole where a hole had already twice been. Taking the spade out of his hand she carefully lifted out the earth, sensing from the density the site of the original walls of the hole, for a hole being a thing of absence, she focused on the presence of its walls. She would have liked to replace the plug of earth precisely as it had been, each clod packed into the very same ill-shaped cylinder that the men had dug earlier; in other words, she wanted the hole to remain theirs.

Meekly, he turned to her: And so, Rachael, where do we bury the papers now?

No, she said, and felt for the first time the chill of the night so that he put his arm about her. No, leave them with me.

They climbed back through the window. He looked distastefully at his soiled hands but again, and not without relish, she said, No, no, it's only God's earth; we can't risk fiddling with water buckets now.

So they wiped their unwashed hands and slipped into bed. But not before she had tied the papers into the centre of a strip of sheet which in turn, under the voluminous nightdress, she tied around her body, the package settling in the curve of her back, in the generous space shaped by steatopygia, where it would never be found. He slept like a child with his head on her breast while she lay awake awaiting the day.

At eight o'clock the following morning, as he predicted, Chief Constable Demmer arrived to arrest Andrew, who by now had had a good wash and had returned to his manner of curt instructions, telling her only what he thought necessary. It was safer, he said, as he hastily shook her hand, that she knew nothing, and he turned his attention once more to the constable, demanding to know what the poor man, who after all had not issued the writ, understood by the word *sedition*.

Some hours later, Rachael watched impassively the arrival of the magistrate and his boy—who was, of course, a grown man. The man/boy tethered their horses to the gatepost. She carried on kneading dough as she waited for him to yoo-hoo at her window. Then she went out to where the magistrate paced her yard. For as long as she could manage, she rubbed her hands, watching the little worms of dough shower to the ground, before looking up at him.

Good morning, he cried jovially, and in an admonishing tone rushed headlong into fast English, which she claimed not to understand, but following her uncle Captain Kok's advice about speaking to white people, replied, By the grace of God, my husband and I are well. And how goes it with your good self?

He looked alarmed for a second, then launched into another passionate speech that she assumed to be about his horse, to which he pointed several times.

Ag ja, she said, oh shame, yes, nodding sympathetically; she knew how strongly these people felt about animals and so concentrated on cleaning her hands of the flaking dough. When his sluggish man/boy appeared with a spade, he informed her that they were unfortunately obliged to dig for information by her gatepost. By which he meant that the other would do so, for the red-faced magistrate kept his hands folded behind his back throughout. Emboldened by the knowledge that red faces come from drinking tumblerfuls of whisky, she begged him to be careful; she was particularly anxious that the earth should not be too greatly disturbed. If the precise plug of earth could be lifted—for if there had indeed been a burial of information, there would necessarily be such a plug—and replaced, so much the better. Her husband did not like things disturbed in his absence. And by way of buttering him up she said what a fine horse he had.

His eyes gleamed as if they had found diamonds when the boy held out the bag. As he bid her a grave good-day, she tied her slackening apron strings in the small of her back while the slow sad smile developed like a photograph on her face. She could not stifle the feeling of well-being that made her anticipate the smell of baking bread and think of the sunny days ahead as something of a holiday.

•

Prison made no impression at all on Andrew Abraham Stockenstrom le Fleur. She supposed that nothing would. He had been born with the caul, which was to say, she now knew, with a complete, already printed history book in his head, so that his behaviour amounted simply to a matter of reading aloud, intoning like a preacher and in the strange language of books. Something like the reading of a recipe, acting upon instructions and awaiting the expected dish. Take this, sift that. Which is a strange way to treat a recipe, she ventured, for a person should be prepared to throw in an inspired pinch of nutmeg, to do without a second egg, to mix the wrong way round and hope for the best.

So he stepped after all those months of waiting for his trial into a kitchen filled with the warm breath of her perfectly risen loaves, shook her hand, then crossed the room to shut the extravagant fender of the stove. He looked exactly the same, had lost not an ounce of weight and declined a slice of bread.

Surely, she said, you could do with a nice slice of this. Look, I've put raisins in the loaf. The people brought raisins for your return, also cabbages. We'll have a nice cabbage bredie tonight.

He had predicted the precise hour of his release, and the faithful carrying gifts had shamed her into believing, into the festive baking. She had looked forward to celebrating and above all wanted to see him enjoy the warm, fragrant bread. But, offended by the exuberance of the fire, and as if they ate nothing but fresh raisin bread in prison, he drank his bitter black coffee, then said kindly, Perhaps tomorrow, my Dorie. It will keep until tomorrow when Lodewyk and Abrahams and Kleinhans come over.

Lodewyk and Abrahams, she shrieked, not noting the new name he had given her. Not those vipers. What would they be wanting here? They'll not eat or drink in my house; this is no place for traitors.

They are our people Dorie, and we have things to talk about, to plan our next move against the settlers.

They are treacherous vipers who sold you to the enemy for a few shillings; they are no longer my people.

It's your womanly heart, Dorie. You don't understand that this is war and that one has to put up with people behaving strangely during war. It is not their fault. In topsy-turvy conditions people can't always tell right from wrong; they get confused and fall by the wayside. The same God who showed me the day, the very hour of my release, the very drops of rain as I would step out of the prison door, that God has also shown me that people will, like stubborn oxen, turn to the devil; that we must be patient, swallow our pride, and think of our land occupied by the thieving settlers. There is too much to do to hold petty grudges.

Well, she could not believe her ears at the nonsense he was talking. So he had changed after all; he who had never been tolerant of wrongdoing. She could not believe that he had been born with that speech in his head. Plain madness, if you asked her, that she who had slaved over a raisin bread was to serve it to the vipers themselves. She would never understand the ways of men and their politicking, of how they passed off their inconsistencies as good sense. Which made her speak boldly, waving the bread knife she still held incredulously in her hand: The bread I always make with my own hands I would rather feed to the dogs. Siena can make something for them. I, for one, will need some time to think of Lodewyk and Abrahams as my people. As far as I can—

Rachael, he interrupted, they will be here tomorrow at three which gives you, the mother of the volk, twenty-four hours in which to remember that they are your people. What would happen to us if we do not forgive? How will we learn humility? No, traitors cannot be banished; they must be taken into the bosom of the volk. Forgiveness can only strengthen us. Otherwise, how will we ever become a nation independent of the lying missionaries?

He patted her hand on his way out to inspect the garden and Bleskop's new foal. She thought of having a slice after all; she thought that this new lenience might allow her to canter bareheaded on her horse. But as she held the knife to cut, the raisins turned into sores, so that she sprinkled the loaves instead, wrapped them to steam off in the bleached flour bags, and knew, not least from the mad glint in his eyes, that the all-change would never be to her advantage.

•

From the photograph captioned *A. A. S. le Fleur and following, Kokstad gaol, 1898,* there is neither indication that he has lost his marbles, nor that he has had any brush with humility, although a person can nowadays take comfort from the new knowledge that the camera often lies.

The gaol is a low-roofed building designed not for maximum security in the usual sense of the word but rather to reassure Griqua inmates, who prefer the familiarity of an oppressive ceiling. On the western side of this gaol there are two windows. The lower half of each is boarded up with six vertical wooden slats, with an extra crossbar dividing it from the six panes of the upper half. Light bounces off the glass of the window on the right; the panes on the left have been painted a cheery white, for the glare of the afternoon sun can at times be unbearable. Brightness in any case is not desirable in a prison cell where easily incited Griqua passions can flare uncontrollably. The windows are open at the maximum angle of twenty degrees.

Le Fleur has centred himself between the two windows with sixty men or more arranged around him. The ones in the front kneel on their right knees, their left hands resting on bent left knees so that their chests are bravely pushed out, and erect postures are maintained even by the bowlegged. An old man holds on to his knobkierie; another appears to be injured, for his jacket is buttoned peculiarly as if across a bandaged arm, and he wears a doek under his hat. All the men look at the camera directly, in stunned defiance, as if that instrument is the very source of their outrage.

Andrew Abraham Stockenstrom le Fleur, standing at the front of the group surrounded by seated men, cuts a tall, dashing figure, the only one who is fully visible. His right arm is crooked, allowing his fingers to be tucked between the buttons of his jacket, which gives him both an air of solemnity, as if he had just made a pledge, and one of supreme indifference. He is the only one who has turned his head away from the camera, who looks to the left. Standing at ease with his left foot slightly forward and the brim of his hat elegantly curved, he carries an air of exquisite disdain.

The men are all in hats, wide-brimmed hats, not all of which are worn soberly. There are brims turned wholly back in a girlish fashion, there are rakish angles that leave not only an ear but a good inch or two above the ear exposed, and there is one excessively floppy hat, the front of which seems to be pinned to the crown. The wearer holds something peculiar in his left hand, a pair of shears perhaps—but no, the second blade is in fact the shadow of the object, thrown onto his jacket. His brooding face betrays the act of defiance: he has just before the click of the camera whipped out the pointed weapon.

The rebel has tucked back his hat to ensure that even a casual glance at the photograph will draw the viewer's attention to him. He is the sceptic who scoffed at Le Fleur's messages from the Archangel Michael, who warned against bloodshed and who promised that no bullets would enter their bodies. It was he who persuaded the Chief that they should at least carry rifles, even if they did not plan to use them, that an unarmed brigade was a sorry affair that the godless settlers could not take seriously. Then came the miracle that he for one could have done without: the rifles that many of them found necessary, after all, to try and fire at the imperial force refused point-blank. Which was surely no way to go about a rebellion, but what could he say in the face of a perverse God and his prophet, the Chief. So whipping out his own reliable dagger was indeed, as the picture shows, a two-pronged act of defiance for which he would later pay with a sound beating.

The Reverend Dower, poring once again over his own well-thumbed book, flicking between the photographs of himself surrounded by his deacons and those of Le Fleur with his rebellious riffraff, noted three things: that Le Fleur was the very demon of pride; that standing whilst others were on their knees made for a more impressive portrait than being pressed in too large a chair by native deacons who stood around in what he now feared was mock humility; and that a new edition should therefore be printed without the photographs.

•

Rachael sat hunched over the report in the *Eastern Province Herald.*

> A widespread hostile agitation was undoubtedly got up by the Griqua agitator, Le Fleur, but has been nipped in the bud by the prompt action of the Chief Magistrate and the patrol of the East Griqualand Mounted Rifles.

Was she becoming like Andrew, dependent on the yeast of their writings to feed her rage? She had on first reading crumpled the page in her fist but, remembering her duty, had released the paper, smoothed and patted and pacified the creases as if they were her very own babies. It was then that the task of collecting and filing struck her as an odd thing to do. But there she was, with the light quite gone, reading in the dark, for she knew by now every word. No mention of Sigcau, the Mpondo chief, who had betrayed the Griquas. Oh, no, it was all the work of their own intelligence, and she snorted at the peculiar word that in politics had unhooked itself from wisdom or cleverness in order to bow and scrape at heroic lies. How, Rachael wondered—and the thought unscrolled word for word, in line, like print—how would those who tend and nurse the bits of paper escape their tainted messages? Ag, she said aloud, impatiently, she was becoming like Andrew with his visions, and she rolled the thought back into a tight scroll; she had no business getting mixed up with ideas, even if these days auras and revelations were two a penny.

As the nineteenth century leaned on tiptoe, poised to somersault into the new, the air was indeed sulphurous with the clashing of centennial hopes. For Le Fleur there could be no doubt about the fruits of his efforts. After the travels across the country, the secret meetings and the spit-flying speeches, the planning with men not fit to lick his boots, it was only right that the land would be restored to those who had been swindled, that the documents would be signed as the bells tolled in a new era of Griqua men and women ready to till their own land. Instead, sentenced to fourteen years of hard labour, he found himself at the Cape, flanked by colonial guards as they set out on the choppy sea for Robben Island. Maintaining an erect if greenish cast, he was prevented by belief from leaning over to vomit into the ocean like his feckless French ancestor. God's ways were mysterious; the miracle was simply being postponed from his vision of a public land base to doing private time. Thus no one was less surprised than the Paramount Chief when an amnesty released him after only five years of quarrying stones.

Andrew held her hand tenderly as he told of the triumph: See, Dorie—and he did not stop as she flinched at the name still new to her—I said to the man, just as he turned the key, Only five short years before you unlock to let me out for good; you may as well mark the date in your calendar. In fact—and I asked him for the time—it will be precisely at two in the afternoon.

I'll eat my hat, the warden laughed scornfully.

At the sound of his laugh the mist rolled back and the vision flashed clear as a summer's day before me.

Actually, I said—hesitating as humbly as I could—before you eat your hat, you shall have to pay your respects by lifting it to salute me.

Being a rather coarse man, he laughed uproariously, and on many an occasion taunted me with my own words. Well, my dear, and he rubbed Rachael's hand vigorously, when the time came it was impossible not to gloat.

On the sunny afternoon of the third of April 1903 at the precise hour of two, post meridian, I was escorted by the governor, who had brought a personal pardon from the new King Edward. Which only goes to show that our petitions have not been in vain, that the world is not entirely devoid of justice. But the poor warden . . .

Then she started as Andrew actually laughed aloud, with a queer, neighing, adolescent sound jerking from his throat.

Yes, the warden turned puce with disbelief; the poor man had no choice but to salute me smartly, just as I said he would. I shook hands with the governor and turned back to make sure that he would carry out his promise. There he was, a man of honour, from whom the governor could have learnt a thing or two, gagging on the first mouthful of greasy felt, so that, my dear Dorie,

I drew the hat out of his mouth and gave it to a beggar at the gate.

She supposed then that God had a sense of humour after all, but Rachael's mouth drooped sadly at the paucity of the miracle. The century had, to the sound of fanfares and trumpets—noisy gongs and clanging cymbals, the enraged Chief shouted—crossed over, and still the people crept about their huts, whilst Andrew brooded afresh over land and volk. And what an unhealthy and accommodating business the idea of nation was, she thought—just as well that her husband had given her the new name of Dorie with which to face this idea.

It was at this stage that some came to speak of her slow sad smile of subterfuge.

～

In other parts of South Africa, among the Zulus, the Pondos, the Swazis, the Damaras, and other such tribes, the people were big, and black and vigorous—they had their joys and chances; but here, round about Griqualand West, they were nothing but an untidiness on God's earth—a mixture of degenerate brown peoples, rotten with sickness, an affront against Nature.

Sarah Gertrude Millin, God's Stepchildren

KOKSTAD 1991

It is a clear bright winter's morning. Light streams in through the plate glass, and the reversed gilt letters of The Crown Hotel seem pure gold, even from the inside. From his table David has an unimpeded view of the square, its trees and grass and benches, where a public life even at this early hour begins to murmur. Opposite the hotel, on the other side of the square, are the grand buildings of the courthouse. The blue white and orange of its flag fall into the tranquil folds of a lovely day. There is no evidence of the mental snort, the not-for-much-longer look, on David's face. On the western side of the square, beyond a screen of oak trees, a bus screeches to a halt and lets off a steady stream of people from the townships and outlying villages who have come to work in town. It is this bustle, this winding up of the Kokstad day, that stirs his reverie.

A shaven-headed man in the extravagant red-and-black livery of the hotel has for some time thought of waving his hands to get David's attention. He may not have wanted to interrupt the thoughts of the earnest young man with close-cropped woolly hair and green eyes set in a matte mahogany face. David is alone in the dining room, the first; not many of his kind come to the Crown. The man starts towards David in a curious gait, almost a dancing shuffle. David, suspecting him of buffoonery, stares at him cold-ly so that the man is driven to further parodic servility: he doffs an invisible cap, braces his shoulders and coaxes a croaky voice to con-certina his Yes Sir No Sirs into a televisual Deep South drawl. So that David resolves to get through his meal quickly, just cereal and toast even though he had planned on a full cooked breakfast. Not only because it is paid for, but just in case, he knows not of what, and now, regretfully, he simply has to get away from this odious man who makes him feel uneasy, reminding him of someone whose image he cannot quite summon.

He has not managed things as well as he might have done. How good it was after the clandestine trips out of the country to be trav-elling somewhere of which he could speak freely, but perhaps the request to his unit had been too brief, a symptom of the new slackening of discipline, as someone at the meeting suggested. Was the comrade not perhaps taking for granted the right to go away? He explained that he wanted to go to Kokstad for something of a holiday which he needed badly. Yes, he would stick to Kokstad and its environs, mainly a walking holiday he thought, climb Mount Currie and so on, and yes, he would go to a meeting at Umtata on his way back, suppressing the unreasonable feeling that he would have pre-ferred to keep the trip entirely free of Congress business.

Why Kokstad?

He shrugged, just part of the country he's always planned to get to know.

He took care not to show his surprise at the next question: Some turmoil in his private life? A woman?

He hadn't thought of the stress in such specific terms, but perhaps, yes, things were tense at home, though it was not quite like that, and in his anxiety to reassure them that whatever it was did not have a destabilising influence, he succeeded, he thought, in doing the opposite.

There was surely mockery in the laughter in that bare room of Comrade Y's where they huddled over decoy liquor bottles arranged on the table, real enough brandy poured into glasses from which no one was drinking, but which left the aroma of the spirits lingering as they sipped at their Appletisers. Just men drinking and gossiping and telling tall tales. In their cell there was to be no let up of the teetotalism imposed at meetings.

Well, David carried on, tapping at his glass with embarrassment, he would do some research on the history of Griqualand East, find out about Chief Le Fleur and the Griquas.

Ethnic identity, someone laughed, a problem for the comrade? And why did he think they moved uneasily, suppressed their sniggers, or something he could not quite put a finger on.

Winks and nudges. Was there perhaps someone else he might like to talk about, anyone in Cape Town on whom an eye should be kept while he was away?

Nope, he said, not on my account, as Comrade Dulcie's name hovered in the air. But the trip was approved and the business in Umtata, fortuitously, could only be entrusted to someone of his rank.

The day is surprisingly warm. It had been a cold night, just as the girl at reception had said, although one is of course supposed to say woman these days. Why an attractive young thing would want to be called something frumpish like *woman* is beyond him. But she said in her offhand way, as if addressing the ochre tints of evening, Sunlight's deceptive, the nights are bitterly cold here.

Thank you, he replied inappropriately. He could have added that it was hardly warm then; that he expected nothing, certainly not clemency from the weather, which in all his life seemed to offer nothing other than fierce heat or dry, cutting cold. But he smiled and rushed off to eat a sandwich in his room. David spent a comfortless night under heavy covers tossing on a rough sea that flung him repeatedly from the rigid shores into the hollow centre of the bed and back again. So that he groped at the wall, searching for cracks to heave himself out of the tumult. No less bitter than the camps of Angola.

Nevertheless, today he looks fresh and handsome, a slight puffiness around the eyes giving him the distant look that the young find distinguished in a man. He worried about hanging his clothes in the narrow wardrobe but there are no unsightly creases. David does not know of the pressing service offered by the hotel. To tell the truth, for all his travels this is his first time in a real hotel—that is, not counting the trip to Britain, where his accommodation was called by the discursive name of bed and breakfast, which allowed it to be of dwarfish proportions and where conveniences meant nothing more than a washbasin and somewhere to empty his bowels, and smutty comedy on television in a room with shiny furniture and stony-faced patrons who pretended that he was not there.

The woman at reception is delighted for him. Her hair is pinned up, allowing her long brown neck to swivel freely. Ooh, she smiles, you've got such a nice day. Doing business in town?

No, he replies, just visiting, and barely glancing at her neck, hurries off.

She watches the man through the plate glass. A tall, dark, handsome stranger in town, in spite of his frizzy hair, should be seen as a stroke of luck. Class, that's what he clearly has, not like these cheap white chaps sidling up now that the Immorality Act's gone, but what a disappointment this one's turning out to be. Broomstick-up-the-arse sort of chap. She is not fooled by that easy smile. Must be from Cape Town, doesn't have a Jo'burg accent anyway and certainly doesn't know how to be friendly, although not for want of trying. Like educated people; that's what they must learn at universities, how to keep formal. A chap who'd back off from the least bit of fun. What would he know, she thought bitterly, about the loneliness of a dusty town like Kokstad, of how a girl could sit through an entire weekend staring into the blue of Mount Currie. No point in telling him about the dance, and she kicks the rickety swivel chair contemptuously towards a shelf buckling under last year's box files. Dust flies as she lifts out the September file, so that she falters and jumps down from the unreliable chair. Damn these blinking files, damn the twenty-second and twenty-third, for those are the days that Mr. Ebrahim asked her to find. Barking his orders—find this, do that, and don't forget the Mister—but she, oh yes, she is to be called just plainly by her first name.

What for? she asked, but all he said was, Never you mind, and switched his look from the lecherous to the inscrutable while she debated whether to say, If you want to accuse me of cheating you'd better say it out loud. For why should she invite vertigo, snap her own ankles on that crazy chair in order to help along her own death, but it was then that Mr. I'm-So-Serious came through the door and old Ebrahim turned so quickly, as if he didn't want to be seen by the stranger, that it was best to drop the whole thing. One day, though, she would like just once to make him call her Miss Bezuidenhout. Mister Ebrahim indeed!

And why in bloody God's name would the twenty-second and twenty-third, of all the days, be missing? A trick, a trap, or has the silly old fool forgotten that he has removed them himself? She lifts her head, the better to think through what happened yesterday, when a car speeds by and from its mirror flashes a beam of light which, refracted through the plate glass, dazzles her into momentary blindness. A punishment for her blasphemy—the apocalyptic beam, like the Sunday school pictures of a bearded Old Testament God frowning in the forked light. A punishment of complicated calculations since light, she remembers, is refracted through glass. School, she snorts, stuffed with useless information and foolish tasks—calculate the angle of incidence, a skill required by God alone—and she laughs at the silly selectivity of memory. Who would have thought that she'd remember all that nonsense about refraction and incidence? There is, as far as she can see, going to be no bloody incidents at all and she certainly would not be angling for any.

Men—siss!—always ready to think the worst, to get the wrong idea as if there's anything wrong in wanting to talk to a stranger in a boring town. No, she would not even mention the dance. And as she settles down in her chair she sees David across the road, turning away from the courthouse. He has no camera and she wonders why, if he is a tourist, he does not photograph the building as tourists do, but then, she supposed, coloured people have only recently become serious tourists. Come to think of it, why does he stay in a hotel; coloured people stay with family or friends of family. If it were not for his stiffness she would invite him to her parents' home, but then why should she put herself out. Really, she should let the strange young man be.

David, gazing up towards the metallic purple of Mount Currie, its slopes green with trees, starts at a voice by his side, a tap on his elbow.

That's Mount Currie, the toothless man who greeted him earlier on the square announces. He smiles a slow generous smile, the pink gums parted to suggest that teeth may be nothing but a barrier to genuine smiling, that as targets of toothpaste advertisements we have foolishly come to associate smiling with a display of teeth. Offering an unimpeded view of the interior, the toothless version insists at once on the boldness and the vulnerability of deep smiling, its origins in the solar plexus, its projection up through the alimentary canal, inviting another to the warmth of what is known as communication. Ice cold by comparison is the enigmatic, thin-lipped smile of the Mona Lisa. Or that of a seal that lifts its sleek body out of the water to flash an idiotic and patently insincere smile at its viewers. But this open-mouthed smile of brotherhood reaches out to make human contact with a stranger in town, David, singled out by one of its residents, even though he be unemployed, toothless, and nosey.

Gradually swallowing the smile, but with its influence still visible around the eyes and the lines of the mouth, he launches into conversation: Are you visiting, my bra? This place is now made for visitors and tourists, full of history man, jeez-like, chockablock full of history. Now take the Cape. Mister is mos from the Cape, hey? He pauses for David to nod. You can tell; all the classy people come from the Cape. Now everybody thinks the Cape is where it all happened but I'm telling you, for action, for real bladdy action, you should've been at this place. Right here in Kokstad.

The man sucks his gums then, spreading his palms on his thighs, sinks to his haunches. His right hand gestures an invitation to sit, but David hesitates. It is not that he cannot bring himself to squat on the grass where barefooted women rest with their bundles, it's just that he thinks it, well, unwise to encourage the man, or rather, to draw attention to himself in such a public place. He pats the briefcase under his arm by way of announcing that he has to go, but the man laughs it off.

The battles man, he continues, ignoring the discomfort of the man whose embarrassed eyes swoop and dart about the speaker's raised face.

David asks politely, Which battles d'you mean, although he has not given up all hope of getting away.

For the land, of course. This is a helluva piece of land with rivers and mountains all round and good grass for grazing, not like those dry parts of the West. Everybody wanted it but, of course, it belonged to us Griquas. Yirrer, there were some battles here ou pal; too hot for Captain Kok to handle so he just had to up and die. And then all hell broke loose. Between the English, the Griquas, the Boers, and the kaffirs.

Africans, David says.

What? No it wasn't just that lot.

No, Africans, not kaffirs, that's what decent people say, and in the heat of the moment, without realising, he sinks to his haunches in order to deliver the word directly to the man's face. Delighted with the gesture, the man flashes him a conciliatory smile.

Okay then, Africans, but, he warns, you should be careful of those people, man. You defend them, you treat them good, and they shit on your head.

David explains. (He believes that you should not leave things because they are incidental, that every instance of ugly speech should be challenged. He takes the opportunity to lecture me on the matter.) The man listens, nodding impatiently, then he takes David by the elbow and points to Mount Currie.

Look, that's where our Griqua history starts, man. Through that tooth-gap in the mountain the oxen stumbled—imagine, drenched with sweat and tossing their horns—and Captain Adam Kok, sitting bolt upright on the first wagon, cracked his whip, and the valley, rumbling with the echo, replied, Welcome Home. 'Strue man, take it from me, Thomas. They all heard it: old Mr. Le Fleur, the big Chief's father, who checked out the land beforehand, all the big men. You ask any old people here and they'll tell you how their forefathers told them. This valley spoke to those Griquas tired of trekking all the way from Griqualand West, 'strue's God. God's sigh of relief that they made that helluva journey came through the echo of his whip, Welcome Home. The captain saw it all, the new world, lying before him.

Waving his hand proprietorially across the town, he waits for David to take in the panorama. This green and fertile land, the tamboekie grass—it's yellow now 'cause it's mos winter—but then the grass was bright green, calling out, waving at them, and what could the captain say with such glory staring him in the face?

Thomas pauses, but David, insensible to that which stares him in the face, has no reply, so that his disappointed informer supplies the obvious: Glory, glory, hallelujah! That's what the captain said. Pointing vaguely towards the mountain, he continues, That's where they stopped with the wagons still at a dangerous angle and fell to their knees to pray. The captain didn't have much learning, you know, but he could pray like a professor. Then they built a monument; you can see the four tall fir trees from here that the captain planted that day. And they were mos tired, so they made their houses right there as they came down the mountain. Now it's the Nature Reserve and Reservoir, 'cause you see we moved further away from the mountain into the valley and that, if you ask me, was our first mistake.

Moved by the suggestive gap in the mountain, Toothless Thomas rubs his upper gum tenderly in remembrance of the first extracted tooth and its absence, the soft pink gap in a white edifice. A beautiful tooth it was; no sign of decay but it ached like an ox, kicking free the cloves stuck in on either side. What a struggle it was to get her out. David's tongue moves nervously across the denture at the front of his own teeth where he gratuitously and in accordance with coloured fashion had the two front teeth extracted in his youth, but with the passion-gap now decently plated with plastic, he leaps to his feet. Around him people have stretched out in the morning sun and he really ought to be off. Thomas, fired by the memory of the patriotic gap, places a firm hand on David's arm.

No, man, I've left out the voorloper, the chap who leads the oxen. The captain wouldn't have been the first to come through the poort; it must've been the voorloper 'cause why, look, the oxen would not have wanted to do that terrible climb and even with God's help they need a strong young man to lead them.

He smiles demurely, lowering his voice, That was my own great-grandfather, my very own Oupa Grootjie, strong as anything and a man who could do what he liked with an ox. Those beasts were just putty in his hands. A born voorloper he was, and the faithful, trusted right hand of Captain Kok.

Rewarding himself for this freshly discovered family history, he draws two oranges from his pocket. David declines and is about to leave, but the restraining hand falls once again on his arm. In his right hand Thomas pummels an orange pugnaciously. With hardened gums he digs out from the top a plug of skin and flesh which he spits out and putting his mouth to the hole, sucks contentedly at the fruit, pummelling it all the while like a babe at the breast. He aims the deflated, disembowelled globe—no longer a fruit but still bright and orange in colour—at a wastebasket.

Well done, says David, biding his time.

Do you then keep yours in your pocket ou pal? You spoil your smart suit that way my bra, he laughs. Come, let's go. I'll show you this town. We Griquas, man, we're civilised; we don't leave a visitor stranded on his own. Sir, your trusty guide, Thomas Stewart, at your service.

He removes his hand to salute. Upon which David grabs his right hand and shakes it firmly. He has some business to attend to; he is indeed grateful, lucky to be in such a friendly town, such reliable hands; he would be very pleased to avail himself of Thomas's services at another time, and turns away briskly. But Thomas deep-smiles and begs to detain him for just another second. From his breast pocket he draws a paper, remarkably clean and freshly folded, a picture of the Kokstad coat of arms.

See the crown, here, these diamonds the Free State Boers stole from the Griquas. They drove Adam Kok off his own Griqualand West without a diamond in his pocket, that's mos why we're here in the East. Thomas folds the paper carefully and returns it to his pocket, patting it as if to check for precious stones.

Hey Mister, he calls after David, swaggers up to him, and, after an intimate display of gums, whispers, Diamonds are forever, hey.

Another clear, bright winter's morning. Toothless Thomas slides out of a doorway and lurches with a peculiar thrust of the shoulder at David who, in shock, lashes out with his left hand while his right plunges into his breast pocket. Touching the metal, he collects himself and smiles, patting his chest in disappointment at such uncharacteristic jumpiness.

The old heart's not on its best behaviour these days. What a fright you gave me, he laughs.

Steady on, my bra. What's the matter man, are they not treating you right at the Crown? There's that smart goosie at the desk; just keep in there and you'll be alright, he winks.

He looks David straight in the eye, pausing and nodding by way of encouraging a reply, then, without a hint of reproach, says, No man, we mos didn't finish our chat about the history 'cause you were too busy, but I tell you what, we go get a lekker cup of coffee at the café and we sit right there in the square where you can see a thing or two about life. Sit in a motorcar like the larnies and the world passes you by. Nay, don't worry ou pal, we'll make up for lost time hey. Nothing like a Kokstad cup of coffee. Kô ons waai Meraai— Let's fly, Maria. See, I know the Cape lingo also. Adaptable, that's me. And he takes David's arm to cross the road.

It is chilly in spite of the bright light and clear blue sky. Thomas is wearing two very similar brown tweed jackets of the same size, the outer being rather too small over the buttoned up inner, giving him a stuffed look. Catching David's eye, he laughs, You like my coat, hey? Kokstad winter fashion, you know, so that David, ashamed of looking, allows himself to be steered to the café, where he orders two cups of coffee to take away. Once settled on a bench on the square, Thomas excuses himself. His breakfast is not to be compared with that at the Crown; if he could trouble David for a couple of rand he'll just nip across the road for a hot dog. I'll be back just now, he says.

David had planned to spend the morning at the offices of the *Kokstad Advertiser* and after waiting for some time considers leaving to do just that, but as he gets up Thomas comes rushing out of the café, waving from across the road with a fresh set of coffees.

Sorry ou pal, you getting tired of waiting, hey? Had to make a phone call to put off my appointment with this guy I'm doing a bit of business with, but he's now a slippery customer I can tell you. Thinks I'm some kind of coloured baboon. Nay, my bra, you can't mess with Thomas, make no mistake, hey.

And the hot dog? David asks.

No sir, there's no messing with Thomas, make no mistake, he says pensively.

In quiet companionship they sip the sugary Ricoffee with globules of powdered milk floating on the surface.

Nothing like a Kokstad coffee. Nothing like Kokstad, really, says Thomas. You see the big mistake the old guys made was with the diamonds. Now a diamond is a funny thing, you know. Have you ever seen one? And he pats his breast pocket as if to check for one with which to demonstrate. It looks like nothing special, just a little dull grey stone, but my motto is, always look a second time; on the face of it you got something worthless, but take nothing for granted, look again, otherwise you come to grief like the old guys. Now even a rough diamond: you look again and again and 'strue's God you see like through a pinhole the light come shining through and that thing glitter man, I tell you, it just glitter, blinding you for a second or so. Then you know aha, something's up with this grey little stone.

But the Griquas weren't blinded by the glitter then, David reminds him.

No-o, you see it's mos always like this with our people: they're blinded by wanting to ape the white man. Say after me: this is not a diamond, and then that's what the eyes also tell you 'cause, why, the eyes follow the heart. So Adam Kok just sold it all, even when his own people said, Look here Chief, there's more to this than meets the eye. But what did that Hotnot care, just as long as there was good hunting and grazing and then, then when Griqualand West got swallowed up by the Free State Boers—even though England swore to them, Don't worry, that won't happen—he just got the trekgedagte in his head and so he said to the people, Come on you lot, no more lazing about and resting on your laurels, we've got to get over the mighty Drakensberg, and see, then our Great Trek started. See—

David, fearing that he would tell the same story again, leaps to his feet. He crushes the paper cups in his hand and, looking round for a rubbish bin, avoids Thomas's eyes, as he explains hurriedly, Got to go. I didn't realise the time but I've got an appointment with a chap at the *Advertiser*, and now I'm late.

Thomas leaps to his feet. No, that's okay, pal, I can see you're a man of your word. Not like these bladdy Griquas who keep kaffir time. Wait, I'll walk down with you, he says, limping somewhat as he struggles to button each jacket in turn against the cold.

You might like to think, Mister Kaffir, of your own time-keeping over there in the café, David reprimands.

Okay, okay, black time, he laughs. Look here, never mind that now, you see, he says, attempting to take David's arm, but the restriction of his too-tight jacket allows David a neat side step. You see, you see, and he pants, trying to keep up while puffing at his hand-rolled cigarette, this trekgedagte was in the Griqua blood. Once they got themselves nicely settled down in Kokstad, fires burning, kettle singing on the stove and the goatmeat stewed nice and soft, then they want to get going again. Now me again, I'm a modern man; I like to keep steady. Stay in the same place, get to know the lie of the land, keep track of what's coming and going, keep my feet on the ground and listen to the bones of my ancestors 'cause why, when you walk around with your troubles—and mister, I can mos see you got mighty troubles—just keep your ears pointed man and listen and you'll hear the ancestors whisper their advice. Look at old Chief le Fleur, mad with the trekgedagte, but then you could say that trekking was the fashion then. See how the Boers just trekked around, then there was the kaffirs, I mean blacks, doing their own serious trekking. Just the British in their offices, staying put on their flat backsides, but cracking their whips and just herding others along. Like we were all flocks of sheep sweating our way over the mountains, carving out roads, then they come, ice cool in their smart red uniforms, just shouting in English, telling everyone where to go next. No good you don't understand English in those days, you jus' had to learn quick-quick 'cause otherwise you wouldn't know which way you wanna go. Anyway, it's mos Le Fleur's treks you want to know about. Man, he had now a lust for trekking, 'cause you see he started out as a wagon-maker, so naturally he would say to himself: Look here, I take all this trouble to make a beautiful wagon so now it must travel somewhere. What use is a wagon that stands still in a garage. Three treks he organised, but it's mos the trek down from Namaqualand, there from Leliesfontein, you want to check out. No, man, that won't be in the *Advertiser*. Look, I got a better idea. We could take a walk out of town, perhaps up to the mountain and see if we can hear the spirits of the ancestors 'cause it's not something like a wireless you just switch on, no, my bra, you have to learn how to tune in, learn how to get in touch with your roots.

David feels a chill rising from his feet to his head. He has mentioned neither Le Fleur nor his interest in the trek from Namaqualand. They are a few yards from the building. He stops, takes Thomas's hand, and smiles, declining the offer. Another time perhaps, but he had better keep his apppointment. Thomas shakes his hand vigorously, promises to be around and at his service.

At the top of the steps he looks back to see Thomas's generous toothless smile still beaming, and before he turns the handle of the door, the man winks, waves, and singsongs a merry see-you-later-alligator.

•

David finds the day in Kokstad exhausting. Far worse than a day's training in the mountains. He spends an hour in the little museum, making polite conversation with an attendant who behaves as if no one has been there all year and who will burst if he does not there and then relieve himself of the details about starching of bonnets and greasing of wagon axles. Then the municipal library, where he reads Halford's *Griquas* and is charmed by women of old Kokstad-Scots pedigree who are anxious to display their lack of prejudice. How fascinating, they say, as he speaks of Le Fleur, the maverick chief. No, they have not heard of the man, but they give him a cup of tea, which is nice, sitting like that in a library of all places as if it were their parlour, drinking tea from a tray covered with an embroidered cloth, chatting with the ladies. Who wear uniform: two-piece suits in baby blue polyester, as do the bank clerks on the Main Road, only theirs are a darker blue. Soon the entire country will be in uniform; that seems to be what freedom has boiled down to, free of the burden of choosing something to wear, from the tyranny of colour coordination. For most people the leap is from rags to uniform. People want to look smart even as they leave their smoky hovels, and who can blame them. Pride and discipline, that is what uniform brings to people, that is how an armed force keeps itself in order. David has long since overcome his adolescent distaste of uniform and now has no patience with arguments about individuality.

From one of the many carryouts he buys fish and chips, which he plans to eat on a bench in the square but loses heart when he sees the number of people converging at lunch time. The workers pouring out of the surrounding shops in their deep blue suits of cotton drill carrying parcels of food, the hailing and chattering in many tongues, the screeching of buses and taxis, and the beggars after a morning's slumber perking up with the rustle of food wrappings— all these make him uneasy, so that he takes the Matatiele road out of town and, after dithering about suitable places, sits down to eat and falls asleep under a tree. A drugged sleep from which he half emerges only to be dragged down again, so that feeling himself pulled hither and thither by sleep and wakefulness, he rises quite unrefreshed.

David spends the afternoon at the offices of the *Kokstad Advertiser,* going through old newspapers for entries on the Chief.

It would be gross negligence on the part of Her Majesty's government not to keep a close eye on the impudent Le Fleur. In the crowded village hall with no regard for the representatives of Church and State, he ranted afresh about retrocession and the Forty Years' Money. Affecting not to acknowledge annexation, he accused Her Majesty's government of dishonesty and in his vulgar tongue advised the naive Griqua people to move to the Cape where he has established a Griqua church independent of the influence of missionaries. If ever there were need for guardianship of these poor people it is now that the gullible Griquas cannot see through Le Fleur's scheme of lining his own pockets in the improbable guise of Robin Hood.

'We will pool our resources and distribute them equally on farms and farming equipment. There through hard work, sobriety and independence from corrupt European influence we will prosper. It is in agriculture that the future of the Griquas lies,' he raved.

With characteristic arrogance he refused to answer the practical questions put by Mr. Fraser, the town clerk, claiming that he had not addressed himself to colonisers and owed the town no explanation.

That the charlatan, Le Fleur, should have the gall to appear in Kokstad testifies to the fellow's lack of shame.

David smarts at this branding as if he were himself accused of being a thief and a charlatan. He would go the next day to the coloured township, speak to some old people who would surely have stories to tell. He has no interest in the details of the earlier treks, of Le Fleur luring so many Griquas to the unsuitable plains of Touwsrivier where they lost everything to drought, disease, and what the *Advertiser* calls incompetence. These he reads cursorily, and withholds judgment. It is the later, Namaqualand trek that interests him, the agitation for a Griqua homeland in the Western Cape, which culminated in a strip of godforsaken desert that the Chief nevertheless believed would flourish with their labour. How had Le Fleur come to be converted to separate homelands before the Nationalists had even dreamt up that idea?

So what's the explanation? I ask.

Lost his marbles, David says without hesitation. You should see the ridiculous sycophantic letters he wrote to the prime ministers, Botha and Hertzog. And pride, he adds. When it transpired that the Boers were not prepared to put any money into a homeland for a handful of Griquas, not a penny towards irrigation schemes, he persuaded himself that he and God would see the project through without water.

∿

DULCIE is surrounded by a mystique that I am determined to crush with facts: age, occupation, marital status, what she wears, where she was born and raised—necessary details from which to patch together a character who can be inserted at suitable points into the story. But David cannot or will not answer such questions, except that she is single and works as a researcher for a nongovernmental organisation, which accounts for the flexibility of her time. Her story is of no relevance to his own, he says weakly, but he has already betrayed the belief that some trace of hers is needed for his to make sense; he has already betrayed the desire to lose her story within his own. So I persist.

David will answer no questions about her life as a guerrilla, perhaps because he does not know; he has never operated in the same cell as Dulcie. I ask about the conditions of female guerrillas.

Irrelevant, he barks. In the Movement those kinds of differences are wiped out by our common goal. Dulcie certainly would make no distinction between the men and women with whom she works. So I gather that, like him, she is high-ranking in the military wing, probably a commander. David appears to be surprised by this inference. It is impossible to know whether he has deliberately given the clue to the power she wields, whether he is genuinely naive about language, or whether he is keeping up a pretence about giving nothing away, pretending either to himself or to me.

I try to imagine a woman who takes that kind of thing seriously—protocol and hierarchy, the saluting and standing to attention, the barking of orders, the uniform. Someone who sees no contradiction between military values and the goal of political freedom. Such a woman does presumably not rifle in her handbag for a lipstick, does not pause briefly before a passing mirror to tug at her skirt or pat her hair into shape. Or perhaps she does just that, taking pleasure in her double life as she dabs perfume on her pulse points before target practice. Just as others might pray to a God for safekeeping.

David refuses to acknowledge my need to know more. He mutters about personal and professional lives running along quite separately, then, as if realising that that might not be the right thing to say, he waves his hand as if to delete. It would seem that there is in any case no point in discussing her clandestine career: things are in a state of transition; the army is in the process of redefining itself.

So in the New South Africa militarised men and women will enter civic positions without declaring themselves as the military? I ask.

What else can we do, he shrugs. Such lives that have always, necessarily, been wrapped in secrecy can't be unwrapped at this stage. Besides, what's wrong with military values? See how far it's brought us all, including the likes of you, who believe in keeping your hands clean at all costs, who reach for lace handkerchiefs at the thought of bloodshed, and choose not to notice that that fine thing, freedom, is rudely shoved through by rough guys in khaki.

I do not defend this presentation of myself, or of freedom.

A fine word, hey, he smirks, *li-be-ra-tion,* beating out the syllables with his fist on the table. And fine people just prefer to believe such nonsense as the *Cry Freedom* vision of schoolkids bursting into spontaneous rebellion over the Afrikaans language. Get real, old girl, without a military movement orchestrating the whole thing there would not and could not have been a Soweto '76. Brilliant, isn't it, how your arty lot just love these lies about irrepressible human nature and the spirit of freedom bubbling in the veins of the youth.

Yes, I say—I am miffed at being called old girl; is there no such thing as a young woman over thirty?—but that's no reason for keeping up the lies. That surely is the point: you start with secrets and lies as you have to, you do things that aren't nice, as I suppose you have to, and then before you know it's just second nature—military values that go against the very notion of freedom for which you originally set out to fight. Does Dulcie approve of these kind of lies?

David shakes his head in disbelief. Look, forget it; it's not nice, he mimicks. Let's remember that you'd be the last person I'd come to for a political discussion. All you need to know is that there is nothing irregular between myself and Dulcie. She is not pretty, you know, not feminine, not like a woman at all.

As with the preservation of all prejudices, he will no doubt go on clocking exceptions rather than question the stereotype and its rules. How many exceptions does an intelligent person have to come across before he sees that it is the definition of the category itself that is wanting? But I won't discuss womanhood with him, won't be lured into another subject. Since there is little to go by other than disconnected images, snippets of Dulcie, I must put things together as best I can, invent, and hope that David's response will reveal something.

Dulcie recognises the stinging sensation in the bridge of her nose as one that signals the desire to cry. One that converts the recognition of danger into a curious amalgam of fearlessness and terror, triggering another signal that ensures that she will not cry. She associates it with the dust of the playground where boys in school uniform dance mockingly around her, tug at her gymslip of which only the patches are in the right shade of blue, and chant Dulcie-pulcie-kroeskop-poeskop. It was then, as they rhymed her blackness with her cunt, that she bit back the tears and discovered the strength in her thin arms and legs that sent the little shits flying one by one into the dust, even if her gymslip got torn to shreds. Those limbs, since built into solid trunks of muscle, are still activated by a stinging in the nose.

The men in balaclavas come like privileged guests into her bedroom, in the early hours, always entering the house by different routes, ridiculing her reinforced bolts and locks, the secret code of her Securilarm system. She wakes up and with every sense aquiver, mentally follows them over the fence, along the garden path, through the chosen window. Bessie, her old dog who barked feebly on their very first visit, was summarily shot. Now they come without a sound, but the stinging in the bridge of her nose precedes conscious knowledge of their arrival. So that her sleeping body bolts upright as she waits the long seconds for fear to metamorphose. Then she arranges herself on her back with her eyes open, her hands folded behind her head, looking straight ahead at the door—she has moved her bed for this purpose—where a polite knock will be followed by the gentle turning of the handle, as if they do not wish to disturb her.

Each time a kindergarten rhyme jingles in her ears, mingles with the smell of dust:

> Miss Polly had a dolly who was sick, sick, sick
> So she called for the doctor to be quick, quick, quick
> The doctor came with his hat and his bag
> And he knocked at the door with a rat-a-tat-tat.

Dulcie has never had a real doll.

For the occasion of the school concert she took along a length of evenly stuffed nylon stocking. The head was shaped by a throttle of tied string; eyes and nose were marked out with blobs of blue ballpoint pen, red pen for the mouth. Standing in line with other girls, Dulcie rocked the length of doll to the rhythm of the Miss Polly song; the boy whose jaw she had later broken was the doctor.

For a while, in her teens, as she pulled a stocking over her hair, she had the grotesque image of herself as Miss Polly with infant's skin stretched like a caul over her head. Which may have led to her losing the desire for straightened hair.

One of them carries a doctor's Gladstone bag filled with peculiar instruments and electrical leads. Occasionally a real doctor is brought along. He is uncomfortable in the balaclava and the black tracksuit, from which his white hands dangle pathetically; his movements are stilted, reluctant, shot through with self-hatred. He keeps his eyes averted, does not speak, but shame leaks from his fingertips into her wounds. Sometimes in the delirium of pain she wishes to say something soothing, comforting, for she knows that he does not understand the ways of the world, the ugly secrets of war, that he has stumbled upon them without warning, without training. But she cannot trust the words to come out unmangled. Out of delicacy she does not speak, remains dry-eyed. One day she will weep like a gargoyle. Tears will fountain from every orifice, including the man made ones, washing away the grimy contact, washing her retinas clean, so that she can see clearly how things stand in the world. The new world, that is.

David stares at me impassively, shaking his head, refusing to speak. I have forgotten about his training.

Alright, he says at last, I've remembered something Dulcie once told me. Can't remember exactly when or why she did but perhaps you'll find it significant. He places equal stress on all four syllables of significant. I have no idea why. Is he making fun of me, of my Miss Polly piece? I am grateful all the same for the story.

Dulcie told him of an incident in the desert of Botswana, as a young recruit, when rations were low and everyone was sick of bread and sheep's fat. She suggested taking honey from a bees' nest. David can't remember why the others pooh-poohed the idea, mocked her, wondered if she were man enough to do it by herself. She took off her socks, twisted and knotted them, held a match until they smouldered and intrepidly stormed the nest wearing only a balaclava as protection. Her hands, eyes, mouth were stung; bees covered her face, bored through the fabric of the balaclava, but she carried on, had to, since it was a matter of honour, and managed to fill a basket with dripping honeycombs.

She swelled up into a roly-poly, hands like loaves of risen dough, eyes buried beneath layers of swellings, mouth a drunken pout, face an undulating hillock of yellow-brown flesh. For several days she writhed in agony, unable to take anything except water. When she recovered sufficiently to try a honeycomb, she found that the others had eaten every scrap of it, had left her nothing.

Dulcie leaned forward to show him the trace of her ordeal, a slight puckering of the eyelids, an excess of stretched skin, she claimed, although, even as he stiffly bent closer to look, he could see no evidence of that savage attack.

But otherwise, she said, see how the body recovers and renews itself.

~

KOKSTAD 1917

Rachael, squinting severely after the years of grass widowhood and reading newsprint by lamplight, could see nothing wrong with the report in the *Advertiser*. They had, after all, printed most of her good man's statement on the trek he had organised to Touwsrivier, but he seemed to have forgotten that he had written it himself; indeed, he had handed it over too hastily, had changed his mind since on a few points perhaps, and had forgotten that the paper had not been revised accordingly. It worried her that he was becoming forgetful—but who wouldn't after sitting with seals and dassies on Robben Island, just a little rock surrounded by water, so that he no longer found it easy to distinguish between various versions. And that was the trouble, she thought, that was life, just bristling with different versions of things.

But he hissed and steamed, claiming that they always distorted, that it was after all their function, and when she said in surprise, But Andrew, that nice Mr. Renfrew from the *Advertiser*, he asked you for a statement, he wouldn't deliberately tell lies, Andrew calmed down and took her hand.

My dearest Dorie, you are a sweet, innocent, trusting little thing—had he not noticed that she had grown large, twice her original size as her stomach, swollen by a diet of mealies and so many children, came to match her steatopygia?— *but you know nothing of the world. Where in this country of colonists will one find a white man who is not a liar and a cheat? Why do you think they cannot give me back the original if it is in fact an accurate copy? No, they've conveniently lost it, just as the missionaries then had lost the deeds to the Clydesdale farm.*

But, she persisted, then they would know that you know that they are lying and that would be so embarrassing.

Really Dorie, he exploded, *that may apply to their own people but not to us. Such is their contempt; they don't care what Griquas think. Have they not lied under oath and sent me to hard labour in the full knowledge that it was not just? The Griqua Chief must be discredited at all costs. What do they care about truth or embarrassment when there is money or land at stake? No, there is no such thing as shame, and that is why I will go on fighting, why their prisons are nothing to me.*

Rachael said nothing. The years on Robben Island had changed him, though she could not quite say how—except, how like his own description of the enemy he was beginning to sound. She supposed that hearing the water day and night, watching the tide come and go had made him restless, for he would think of nothing but trekking and establishing a new settlement. But really she wished he would not brood so much, flare up so easily. She read through the statement once more. It was a fine piece of writing. She had grown to love the no-longer-new husband for the fine words that just tumbled out of his mouth, leaked out of his pen, tinted with the fire of his spirit so that the very ink glowed red on the page. But really he ought to stick to words. He had no common sense, no idea of money, failed to do his sums properly. Once she had ventured, as nicely as you please, to say something about his calculations, but now knew better. She would have done things quite differently; she who in his absence had performed miracles of housekeeping with a miserly guinea, she would not have laid herself open to charges of embezzlement. Oh, she could have told him then that the whole scheme would flop, that the horses would not take to the dry conditions, that the fields could not possibly yield the projected quantity of grain, that Touwsrivier of all places was the most unlikely Promised Land. Instead she smiled her slow sad smile and hoped for the best. Which did not always come: the Spanish influenza took sixty souls in spite of her tireless nursing.

When the first rains fell she felt ashamed at her lack of faith. In the new village hall they had built in Touwsrivier she sang in her full contralto, with the tenors weaving in their own praise to God, and the Good Lord gave his message through the deep voice of the Chief. Then she sank to her knees as Andrew the artist painted God's message in words. And for a people with nothing of their own, smothered in the greyness of the veld, they were pictures of hope, promising the colours of the world: terracottas and the butter yellow of a gentle sun, oranges lanterned in their dark green foliage, and the ivory pumpkin that holds like the earth herself a jewelled secret in its belly, the gold and diamonds and rubies for those who believe in His Word. His words were a symphony of colour, and who was she, O woman of little faith, to question the man who made people rise from their ash heaps and flick aside their fleas so that their voices rose in one song of praise—Juig aarden juig—to a humming earth that would in time bare her bosom to her chosen people.

Seventeen different tunes they had by then composed for that one hymn, their voices woven in harmony as they waited for the earth to jubilate in justice. It was best to keep to the same words: same God, same story as of old, of being led out of bondage; the yearning for the new would find outlet in wordless sound. And so she went about humming, clinging to the words of the hymn, but trying out new tunes—blocking memory's chosen moments—with which to wipe out Andrew's brand new words on the trek, or migration, as he called it in the *Advertiser* of seven December. He had not dictated that statement to her. The thing already in print, he read out hastily only from the trials of Touwsrivier, his acknowledgement of her help, only the paragraph with her name:

It is quite natural that we have had great responsibilities thrown upon myself and Mrs. Le Fleur in first aid and sickness, in seeing to the spiritual needs of the people, their bodily needs, and in teaching them how to use economically their small sources of income.

As for the rest, which she had read for herself in disbelief, the stuff about outcasts and things, well—and she shut her eyes for a moment, shook her head which had grown heavy with disbelief—well, that hymn to God would have to preserve her, for if she could only get the correct emphasis, the correct rising note for the last line, Eer Hom met 'n lofgedig—honour Him with a song of praise—or even, and yes, there she had it: a repetition of *lofgedig* followed by the entire line once more, that would do the trick, restore the harmony. And thus came into being the eighteenth tune for Juig aarden juig, which, people still say, is the most powerful of all, and not surprising too, since its birth had given the Mother of the Nation, overnight, a head as uniformly grey as that of an ostrich.

Andrew said not a word about the disappearance of the cutting. He kept silent too about the chronological muddle in the file where Rachael had replaced the piece with the fifteen-year-old, yellow-edged cutting of the letter to the *Advertiser*, previously kept in her Bible. This she read daily, nodding to the familiar words that now slipped into the melody of her famous eighteenth tune. The letter sang:

> Sir, will you allow us space to refer to a certain book written by the Reverend William Dower, called 'Early Annals of Kokstad and East Griqualand.'

She held the rough paper with both hands, reverently, as if it were the tissue-fine page of its old home in Ecclesiastes.

> Why does Mr. Dower not tell the readers of his book that he and his sons were treated like burghers by the Griqua government when farms and plots were granted to them by

Captain Kok and his Council? And yet he mocks them today re their custom of parliamentary sittings. . . . Why does Mr. Dower not tell the readers of his book that in 1881 or 1882, he got a bond passed on the church properties, in his favour, for the sum of £300. . . . We are now coming to what Mr. Dower says about the wife of our Paramount Chief.

She hums through the quoted description:

'olive complexion, short, woolly, peppercorn hair, sleepy eyes, high cheekbones, small hands; her type of beauty was not exactly queenly; in truth she was but a wrinkled piece of womanhood.'

She shuts her eyes at the closing line:

. . . a want of refinement in a minister of the gospel which is simply astounding to us. We are, etc., Griqua Committee.

Rachael finds the *etcetera* especially fine. Delicate, commodious, all-embracing, and repeatable—like *lofgedig*—so that she sings once more, We are, etcetera, . . .

And what do we know of our ancestors, the little people who, loping along the strand at the Cape of Storms/Good Hope, watched a smudge on the horizon feed on the indeterminate space between sea and April sky, and before whose amazed eyes grew steadily, with the help of a conniving wind, the full white sails of a Dutch ship? Only that which is passed down by word of mouth, for there was no one to record those momentous times.

Surely there was someone who could have written it down for them, Le Fleur asked himself.

But that history is one that has failed to imagine the world from another's point of view, even if the other were, strictly speaking, the hosts. Did the little people like beads and bits of shiny things, or did they, having exchanged their treasures out of politeness and hospitality, toss those worthless trinkets at their children? What we do know is that they were impossible, ungovernable, that Van Riebeeck found them too lazy to be enslaved, for they both worked and wandered off whenever they pleased, with no regard for the needs of their new master-benefactors, no grasp of the principles at play, and no notion of obedience, so that real slaves had to be imported.

But of those, the ships from Madagascar or Malaya, Le Fleur did not wish to think, and in any case, the high cheekbones, the oriental eyes were as likely to come from the native Khoisan. Of his own European ancestry, well, that blood was by now so thin, so negligible, there really was no need to take it into account.

Only there remained a distant memory of the defeated French missionary taking a dry cure of warm ashes packed around his scaly white feet, discoursing on his ill health, for that, he claimed, blinking in the harsh light, was what kept him in darkest Africa. Eduard, whose psalms had over the years been replaced by secular texts culled from an interrupted education, had muttered an immortal passage about health that rumbled through the years to haunt the imagination and resonate in the soul of Andrew Abraham Stockenstrom le Fleur, who had been waiting since childhood for its meaning to be revealed. The old man, staring into the ashes, talked wildly about an Irish writer, Sterne, to whom the words once belonged, and told a mixed-up tale about an uncle who had been manservant to that mad writer of tall stories, foolish pranks, and prevarications as he journeyed through Europe. Twice daily he recited:

> O blessed health! thou art above all gold and treasure; 'tis thou who enlargest the soul—and openest all its powers to receive instruction and to relish virtue. The whole secret of health depending upon the due contention for mastery betwixt the radical heat and the radical moisture.

The word, *radical,* rushed like wine through the boy's mind: root burrowing into the earth, root as conduit, root as source, God as the root of his being, or plucking that which is undesirable by the root. Still he could not get to the root of what he believed to be a sacred text. Body and soul; radical heat and radical moisture; open and secret. Tormented by the tug of opposites and haunted by these words that he believed would someday reveal his destiny, the young Andries disappeared from time to time, roamed the hills in search of ancestral history, and waited for a sign on how to conduct the struggle for justice, how to fan the dying embers of self-respect of a people driven and crushed and robbed of their land, which is to say of their selves. Until, years later, on a soggy winter's morning, finding his chest constricted, he rolled up his sleeves, for to interpret is no less than to act.

Another trek, he declared, and this time to the border of Namaqualand, where our Grigriqua forefathers tended their herds in the radical heat and payed not the slightest attention to the secondhand stories of the ghostly foreigners and their sails billowing in Table Bay.

Ag, no shame, Andrew man, Rachael sighed, fortified by a fresh reading of the letter, there is nothing left. Neither people nor livestock, nothing with which to trek. We've lost everything in the last one, and the poor people who escaped the Spanish flu so far away from home, still left on those plains of Touwsrivier with blighted crops and dead horses. All our plans have come to nothing and now we must be off again, and to such a terrible dry land. How can you be so sure that that's what God wants?

She was careful to use the plural, to take responsibility for the failed trek, to make no mention of the charge brought against him by their own greedy and ungrateful people, who did not want to share their resources with the poor. Not that she had not foreseen it all, even though seeing into the future was a business with which she would rather have nothing to do.

Then she had said meekly, Chief—using his title by way of buttering him up—it will not do to spread the money across, for the equality plan is only popular amongst the poor and really what the poor think has never been of any interest to the world. Were there not rich and poor even in the times of Jesus?

Andrew drew himself to his full height and, drilling his eyes into her own, said that people had to be forced into decent behaviour and that making a fine pumpkin fritter did not mean that she could comment on weighty matters.

And now she had once again overstepped the mark, but who could blame her. Not even the great man himself, who knew that a trek to the Western Cape seemed like madness, but what else could be done. They had been sorely tried, and now there was no looking back: if they were to be a decent God-loving people, natives in their own land, tilling their own soil, they would have to trek, just this last time, for there was no salvation other than in a land base. He would bring the scattered volk together, search them out, those who had in bygone times strayed like mules away from Griqualand West into Namaqualand. That too was the vision of his youth, the bleached bones in the valley. Gather together the bones of Adam Kok, that was what the voice had said. So instead of chastising Rachael, he explained patiently that they had gone in the wrong direction, that a whirlwind conjured up by Satan had distorted earlier messages, and that like the Israelites of old they had to be patient. Now God was finally leading them to their rightful place, the cradle of the volk. Kokstad, Kimberley, Leliesfontein, these were places they had been driven to by Europeans, where they lost sight of themselves and followed the foolish doctrines of missionaries. Naturally those early treks had come to nothing, were plagued by droughts and locusts, but this time they would return to the ancestral land of the Grigriquas, the land of radical heat.

I am done with politics, Andrew declared. At which she looked up in alarm. Yes, Dorie, he said firmly, we must apply ourselves to the tilling of the earth. It is in agriculture that our salvation lies and that is just what I have written to the new prime minister, General Botha. That is now a man of good sense. He has shown great enthusiasm for our idea of a Griqua volk living in a separate territory, and I have no doubt that the Afrikaner Landbank will give us the help we need.

He did not manage to disguise the pleading tone. Rachael Susanna sighed. She was his wife, and foolish as she knew it to be, she would obey, fling herself into the new plans, outstare those who were hostile, who thought him a cheat and did not understand or could not imagine his zeal. Oh, she understood only too well how irksome he found living amongst the shameless settlers, so that there was no need to remind him that the Landbank would once again refuse to help natives. As for General Botha, well, she would rather not know what they had to say to each other; would rather not have Andrew air his strange new views in her presence.

~

Namaqualand, Home of Strange Tales: Coloured people seldom manage to hang on to their money.

Lawrence G. Green, *Karoo*

BEESWATER 1922

On the crest of the last hill, the new Griqua trekkers saw before them the promised land of Beeswater rolling down from low hills in the west, hemmed in by the Soutrivier in the east, and in the distant south the gleam of Varsrivier's white rocks. Here were the radical opposites: these rivers, salt and fresh, dragged their meandering beds of stones for fourteen miles apiece before joining the Olifantsrivier that bounded full tilt just within the boundaries of the white village. Already a red hot sun hovering above the horizon sent quills of heat as they descended into the plain where the Grigriquas of old once roamed.

A godforsaken place, Rachael murmured under her breath. Was this what his new trust in the Boers had brought? Her eyes, searching for shelter, found only a scattering of ragged grey tamarisk trees along the river, but the Chief, oblivious to the heat, spread his arms at the wonder of the hills, encrusted in white pebbles that shone in the light.

Look, he cried, common stones glittering like diamonds. What a sign of the marvellous treasures, of colour, to be found in the depths of the earth. Rubies and garnet, beryl and jade.

Why not diamonds themselves, she ventured, fighting the bitterness in her voice.

He said soberly, They would have speculated, Dorie; they would not allow diamonds to pass to us, and for that we must be grateful. Let us not get involved in their squabbles over riches; we are here to till the land and to watch our food grow through our own efforts. God will provide; He'll enrich our lives with the colour of precious stones. And this, he exclaimed, picking up a fragment of shiny layered rock, testing its mirror smoothness against his cheek, if this is not a sign of prosperity, I'll eat my hat.

Namaqualanders call it baboon's mirror, Gert Klaassen, his righthand man, explained. He prised off several layers to show how a number of mirror surfaces were embedded in the rock.

So, the Chief laughed, even the baboons have not been neglected. But let this rock be a warning against personal vanity. God has provided mirrors for baboons in order to remind us that we are human. The lower species may be given to peering at themselves; we have to rise above such vanity through toil.

The evening was cool, and in the hum of the earth releasing its balm of wild thyme and buchu, the people lay to rest their implements. The young men from the north, watching the thornbush crackle and fire its stars into the sky, and rejoicing in the smell of roasting meat and the curled smoke of mutton fat, unpacked their ramkies fashioned out of paraffin tins, wood, wire, and sheep's intestines. Their bodies curved around the instruments as they touched the strings; sound trickled like fresh water through their fingers, and around them tired feet tapped in anticipation of the feast, of dancing the kabarra under the stars.

Bounding down the hill where he had been exploring, the enraged Chief waved his arms and thundered: No, it cannot be, there will be no heathenish music, no dancing like savages. The instruments of the devil have to be laid down, here—he stabbed his finger into the air—right here by the fire.

One by one they laid them down. Hungry fingers lingered over the pattern of zigzags and waves burnt into the wood. Like invalids, the tin guitars with cut out bellies coughed and spluttered their feeble notes of protest.

They must burn, he said, rubbing his hands over his ears, up and down, as if he could not believe those organs, as if to wipe away all sound, the very memory of music, the mocking echoes from he knew not where. God has given us the human voice, and that is enough for singing his praises.

Then Rachael, trusting in the hymn, put in a trembling Juig aarden juig that would stop all action. There was no choice but to take up the singing, the sullenness of the young people drowned in descant, so that by that last line—Eer Hom met 'n lofgedig— all was well, the meat cooked, and Rachael risking all, stooped to gather the instruments.

We'll put them out of harm's way, store them with the ropes and harnesses in the wagon kists, she said briskly.

That night she ate too much meat. That was what brought the dreams, the frightening cacophony, and the picture of a bearded God stretching a single goatskin taut across the sky, across the moon and stars, stretching all into a drum of darkness.

The faithful from the Eastern Cape wilted as soon as the sun rose. The Namaqualanders whom the Chief had persuaded to trek southward may have been used to the heat, but they were unused to his regime of physical work. Having secured contracts from the Boers in the dorp, he sent them out to dig a canal, set the vine on the banks of the river, and build large houses with cool verandahs and lawns until the dorp gleamed like an oasis, white and lurid green in the parched valley. At the end of each week as they returned to Beeswater he collected their meagre wages and distributed the money among all the families. For some stayed at the settlement to till the fields, dig at the quarries, and build small raw-brick houses, wobbly-lined Griqua houses with postage stamp windows.

There was no end to the work, Ouma Ragel remembered her mother, Antjie, complaining. From first light to sunset it was work, work, work. Through sickness and health, women tied their babies to their backs and hacked at the hills for red and yellow ochre with which to paint the buildings. Of course, not on the outside. The Chief did not approve of decoration. No place for frivolity, he said, but after all that hacking and carrying in the sleepy afternoons and watching the piles of ochre grow, he gave in: Alright, no harm in colouring the inside walls, but no patterns. Even the dung-smeared floors had to be smoothed down without the old decorations, not even the plain old swirl pattern of fingers swivelled around the thumb. No, that was what savage natives did and we are no cousins to Xhosas; we are a pure Griqua people with our own traditions of cleanliness and plainness and hard work. Which is why they didn't complain, even those who hacked at the quarries. For the semiprecious stones, the Chief said, but the men knew that it was for no reason other than to keep them busy.

Ag, but it was hard to get used to drinking Jantjie Bêrend. No more coffee, Chief Andrew said as the depression fell on them and the Boers paid even less for building the village with water running in and out of their houses and through their orchards and vineyards. So for those who worked on the settlement there was no coffee. It was harder for the men, who had already given up drinking at weekends: no ready-bought wine, no corn beer or mtombo brewed at home, and not even a drink of magou, in case the mealie-meal fermented too long and went to the head. No, they had to pick bitter Jantjie Bêrend pods in the veld and brew what the Chief said was God's own healthy drink that would strengthen them in body and mind, yes, even in church they took it for holy communion. Although there, Ouma Ragel said, a bitter drink is to be expected, but after a morning's hard work in the sun, aai, and she shook her head.

Only when he was away did old Miss Rachael bring a billy can of sweet black coffee to the quarry. Which they drank without saying a word, for they all had to pretend that it was the bitter medicinal herb, but it was as if the sky had gone deliciously grey and cool, and the coffee was brought by an angel from heaven.

And now my boy—even though he was no longer her little boy, was already a revolutionary who had gathered the youth to raid shebeens, preach at the political apathy of adults, and pour their flagons of wine and home-brewed skokiaan down dusty township lanes—they say we're a drunken people, so just you stick to coffee and remember that it was Jantjie Bêrend that built us into a strong, God-fearing nation. See, the Chief would not allow drinking, not after Touwsrivier, where he refused to have prohibition, believing that people should practise self-restraint. And of course that didn't work; they travelled, in the end, the ten miles for drink, especially when things didn't go so well on the farms.

Your Oupa Gert's cousin, Japie Boois, who dared to brew mtombo, was beaten outside the church hall for all to see, seven lashes of the aapstert, the whip which was of course not a monkey's tail at all, and that was exactly what Japie shouted, insolent with brave beer: Why call it an aapstert when the whip's made of cowhide, why not call things by their right names? he wailed. It's cowhide tanned by my own hand; I made that whip myself; it's not right to beat a man with the thing he made himself.

Which made the Chief say, Give him two extra strokes that the lesson might sink in. And he turned away in disgust and disappointment.

Oh, we were a hardheaded people with so much to learn. What a job the great man had to civilise us, to get the message through our peppercorn heads. And now they say we are a drunken people, Ouma Ragel sighed. We Griquas have never been a drunken people, not since we became Griquas. Struggling drunkenly to her feet, for she was now all but blind, and shaking her fist, she shouted, But I ask you, as I ask these little police brutes in their safari suits who come to search out our dagga-smokers and drunkards, Who makes the wine? Who owns vineyards? Yes, it is we who built their canal, we who planted the vines that made them rich and turned our children into drunkards. Only now do we understand the great man's prediction that children will rise against their parents.

Kill your children, he said, kill them now, for the next generation will rise up against you, will turn you into their own bald and grey-headed children.

Ouma Ragel, by then an apologetic carrier of steatopygia, had little more than disconnected anecdotes about the old Griquas, about the Chief or the great-grandmother, Antjie. She would stop halfway through a story, only the slack muscles about her mouth would go on working soundlessly for a while, as if she were swallowing her own words; then she'd stare into the distance and shake her head, unable to remember how things came about. But it was Ragel herself, who was given to mystification and who made much of sharing a name with Rachael Susanna le Fleur, the Griqua First Lady, whose muddled tales seemed to suggest an irregularity of her birth. Which brings us once more to the field of concupiscence, a subject that after all cannot be avoided in the writing of this story. For David and I were left to patch together a family history, and more's the pity that it would seem to support the colonial assumption that concupiscence and steatopygia are necessarily linked.

With his own hands and in secret, Andrew made her a coolbox of coke packed between two layers of chicken wire stretched across a wooden frame, and watched with shiny eyes her regal acceptance of the gift. Over which she poured brackish water that evaporated in the draught of the afternoon wind. Here her mutton packed in salt would keep maggot-free during the day. In the evenings she hung out the meat to dry.

We must be patient, Dorie, he pleaded.

Yes, she replied cheerfully, for in that enervating heat and drought she had also learnt to ventriloquize, all will be well when we find the radical moisture.

At the new Griqua settlement at Beeswater, Antjie of small Khoisan stature bends over a pile of wood. Stomping with her new veldskoen, she crackles and flattens the dry bushes into fans for stacking on the fire. She is alone in the cooking shelter. In the growing darkness her silhouette is that of a mythical creature, which she transforms again and again with movements of her wiry torso, snaking hither and thither as she builds the fire. She is unaware of her sorcery. When she stops, stretches, lifts her arms in adoration of the full saffron curve of a rising moon, her loose shift draws up over the high step of her buttocks, lifting the hem immodestly towards the swell of her calves. Perhaps she stretches her arms to relieve the stiffness or to feel the pleasurable ache of the muscles. Her torso is not lifted in pagan obeisance—she has been baptised into the new Griqua church—but because she has carried the pile of wood for some distance. All along the dry bed of the Eersterivier, Antjie has been making wood, an appropriate expression since it is not simply a matter of gathering the wood. The land is bare; only the practised eye finds the dried stumps of last year's shrubs, rust red as the earth. These she has worried like loose teeth until they lifted out of the sand. The bundle, a tall mast balanced on her head, was surprisingly heavy.

The full moon looks directly at Antjie. Across the high cheekbones the skin is taut, and the forehead is smooth above the severe slant of her eyes. Is she beautiful? Gert Klaassen, the local leader, ordained by Paramount Chief le Fleur himself, has certainly not chosen her for her beauty; it was the serenity, the quiet dignity in so young a woman that drew him to her. That she remains childless does not matter to him; there are enough mouths to feed and besides, God does what God sees fit to do.

There are no traces here of the Old Ones, the Grigriqua ancestors who once roamed these plains and whose spirit the Chief said they would capture here as a new nation. The Old Ones had left the world as they had found it, their waste drawn back into the earth, their footprints buried. In the still evening with the smoke spiralling joyfully to heaven, Antjie hears the pounding of ancient hooves. Her nostrils flare with the smell of goats, the fresh herb of their droppings, and her eyes follow the purple shadow below the ridge. Here she hears again the words of the Chief as they arrived in the Promised Land: Lift the scales from your eyes and look. Where the herds of our forefathers grazed—listen how they stamp the ground—here we will stay where the Lord has given his blessing. And for all the world like a farmer inspecting his invisible flock, he swept his arm across the empty plain, calling, Griquas, take up your shears, roll up your sleeves, and let us work God's bounty.

Then she blinked and shaded her eyes with the visor of a hand, for the sun scorched mercilessly on that spring day, and blinked again until the heat waves quivered with the sound of hooves. And now, under the swelling moon, she hears once more the stamping of a flock. Which goes some way towards showing what a good Griqua she is turning out to be.

•

Naturally David finds his height, his slim hips, pleasing. He imagines it to be an immeasurable advantage to look another man, of any colour, squarely in the eyes, or even tower over him, so that his voice remains steady, so that his words flow in effortless economy. But he is not vain, as Sally thinks. She creeps up behind him as he stands in front of the mirror trimming his moustache and laughs. Admiring those hazel green eyes? Her laughter is affectionate—there is still much affection between them despite her jealousy—but it is she who admires his green eyes. There is no hint of a Griqua slant in those eyes. They are a soft, feminine green flecked with the pale lights of his fury. Sally will never guess how he hates those eyes, fake doll's eyes dropped as if by accident into his brown skin.

It is, rather, the mirror that he loves. In the shape of a ship, a three-masted, lateen-rigged galley, the kind of vessel, he imagines, from which Van Riebeeck stepped on to these shores. The sails are divided at the base but curve towards a single point at the top. The galley base, a separate glass, is attached only at the two endpoints of the sails, and behind this mirror, in four parts, the whitewashed wall paints the absence between base and sails, an illusory sea of unimaginable depth. Shaving, David observes himself in four parts.

Ouma Ragel had it hanging above the deal dresser, a place of honour barely in reach of the grown-ups. It had been her mother's treasure, hung high to discourage vanity, the only object in the house which was not fashioned by their own hands. How had it come to be hers? Ouma Ragel did not know. In her dark front room the mirror sucked at light. Only towards evening did she open the shutters and allow the half-light to rush through the unglazed windows. During the day thin beams burst through the cracks in the shutters; a crowd of dust motes sailed lazily in each silver line.

To keep the place cool, Ouma squealed in her high-pitched voice as she shooed out both light beams and the boy who stole into her parlour to look at her treasures, the ship of mirrors and the glass jars of canned fruits on the dresser shelves. David would help her cut patterns into the edge of newspapers with which to line the shelves. He bit his lip as he steered the scissors, crumpled and tossed the cutout ovals and diamonds into the bin, and admired the absence of paper, which now in the late afternoon light projected its elongated shadow of lace aslant on the wall. In that light the fruit jars, with their heavy metallic lids, turned to jewels: garnets of quince, peaches packed in sickle moons of amber, red plums of ruby, prettily perched on his paper lace edging. When he grew into a man, he would have rows of jewelled fruits shining in the light.

Ouma Ragel dusted her unused parlour every week, the ship and, to the right of the dresser, a photograph of the founding fathers of Beeswater: Paramount Chief le Fleur, Oupas Cloete, Diederiks, Snewe, and her father, Gert Klaassen. And then there is her mother, Antjie, the only woman in the photograph. She looks bashfully at the camera, unprepared for the momentous click that would freeze her forever in the orb of founding fathers. She had been unexpectedly summoned from the kitchen. The broad noose of her apron hangs askew around her neck and above her right ear a short, curved horn of plaited hair escapes from her doek. No doubt awed by the presence of the Chief, she dared not ask for a moment to tuck in her hair or tear off her apron for this, her first and only photograph.

Ouma Ragel claimed that this was the very first photograph taken.

In all the world? little David asked.

In the whole world, she said, her lips puckered with pride.

Great-ouma Antjie stands to the left of the Chief. His face, not quite turned away from her, bears the usual stern expression, the lick of fire in the emerald eyes. The other men look perplexed, disapproving.

The Chief has shouted, just as the photographer ducked under his black shroud, Antjie—wait for Antjie, and the woman, drying her hands on her apron, has dutifully joined them. The Chief offers no explanation, but his eyes flash dangerously. Around them is the vast empty veld, with no landmarks.

Ouma Ragel said that the photograph was taken at the dabikwa tree, on the historic day of the Beeswater settlers' giving thanks to

God. September the tenth. But David now sees that it was taken on the plain, near the houses, some distance from the ceremonial tree; otherwise Antjie would not be wearing her apron. Where had they found a camera and at what cost? Could the stern and pious Chief be guilty of vanity? Whatever the case, the official camera-man arrived by horse cart two days late, the awe of the moment long passed, hence the unusual placement of Antjie as founding father.

David remembers an ancient Antjie squatting in a half-moon cooking hut of reed, mud, and tightly stretched sacking. He remembers the hut blackened with smoke, washed by the winter rain and bleached grey in the sun until it became a dome of inde-terminable material, a swelling of the earth, a hemisphere in miniature. There she spent her last years lying in a quiet curve, frag-ile as a doll. On dark afternoons his head lolled against her volu-minous skirts that wrapped round and round, so that drugged with the smell of smoked old age, he fell with her into ancient sleep. The memory is meshed with a figure in the diorama of the Natural History Museum, where a wrinkled Khoi woman squats by a fire. David does not remember Great-ouma Antjie's death.

He nevertheless imagines the cataracted eyes tracking back time through paths of mote-speckled light that steal through the door, a tucked-back flap of sacking. On the screen of ochred wall, images of the past flicker by. Antjie is a young girl with legs that are too thin to be beautiful. She unwraps a lump of tail-fat and for the first time greases her legs until the ash grey disappears and her skin gleams dark. She settles into her bower of new ghanna bush, protected from the vastness of the world now fully covered with the yearly chorus of Namaqua daisies. Her arms burrow into the red sand, dew-damp and cool. It is still early. She has been out since dawn to move the herd along to better pasture, and now low cloud obscures the sun. She wriggles to accommodate the new pro-tuberance of breast. Above her the glare of the suppressed sun; below the coolness of the earth pressing into her strange new body. Resting on her elbows, Antjie plucks at the twigs of a shrub, sur-prised at its suppleness. She pulls off the grey skin in strips that curl instantly; underneath, the fibre is moist and bright green, so that she puts it on her tongue, tumbles it in the cavern of her mouth until its saltiness slips through her entire body, and the earth, as she buries her face in the red sand, stirs beneath as if to receive her.

She jumps up, crying, Heitse! and spits out the fibres. What if the bush were to be as poisonous as the tongue of a puff adder? She could die a lingering death over two days—like Oom Willem's Booitjie, whom they say turned a mottled yellow—as the poison spread through her fingertips, her new breasts, her shiny brown legs to her toes. And then—and she feverishly works up a saliva with which to wash out her mouth—and then, ice cold dead, she would never have loved. She has to know, and so, peeling strips from another twig, she chants with each: I will, I won't, until the last I will, which brings confusion. She has started too hastily. Does the stripping mean that she will die or that she will love? Or do they mean the same thing? Antjie rises from her bed of sand, shakes the earth from her shift, and chides herself for the sinful fancy of peering into God's holy plan.

Driving her flock, she sees the flash of a springbok on the ridge, its fawn coat blending with the geel-bush that have not yet come to life, so that it seems as if the bushes themselves, bored with rootedness and last year's dress, are taking a rebellious leap towards the hills, quick as the springbok. That is what her man would be like. Quick and lithe as a springbok. His whistle will gather a herd and send the sun scuttling behind the western hills. Antjie pulls her kappie over her head, for the sun has started scorching with all the fury of one too long suppressed.

When Gert, dressed in his Sunday clothes, crumpling his hat in both hands, explained in his slow steady voice that he had been called by the Griqua chief, that he needed a wife to accompany him from Ezelsfontein to the new territory in Klein Namaqualand, her heart thrilled at the adventure, at the earnest man who was to be hers. The hardships of the trek were as nothing; the empty land of Beeswater that lay just beyond the yearly outburst of Namaqua daisy, free of baas or overseer, held all the promise of the new, and if the Chief was frightening, he also knew how to keep them working day and night, so that in no time at all a church was built. During the week the building would be used as schoolroom where Miss Rachael taught the children to read and write.

On that first Sunday of worship in their own church they marched solemnly to the riverbank for Thanksgiving under the great dabikwa tree. Then she saw the true magnificence of the Chief, felt a surge of blood as he stretched out his arms to embrace his ragged congregation. Her lips moved along, silently, as if she could see the prayer bursting from his heart, awakening the words that lay dormant in her own.

To give thanks, Almighty Lord, for giving us direction, for leading us through salt pans and sand dunes to this our Promised Land.

We did not know, Dear Lord, who we were; we did not know to whom we belonged; we did not know why we were languishing on this earth in sorrow and degradation. We were a motley, nameless people, discarded until we were shown the way from the desert wastes of Namaqualand, from the shanties of the Cape Flats, from the Boland, the Free State, and from the lands of Adam Kok to gather here today. Never again will we be slaves.

No longer will we stray nameless across the land of our forefathers. Thou has named us. Thou has brought us together under this tree for which on this glorious spring day we thank Thee.

We, the Griqua people, will commemorate forever this tenth day of September.

We will not forget Thy words: Be a nation for me and I will be a God to you.

Amen.

Her heart filled with pride as the task of holding the sacrificial goat fell to Gert, and Andries Abraham Stockenstrom le Fleur, eyes flashing with holy light, slit its throat with a single movement of drawing the knife and twisting its head, so that the blood bubbled and frothed into the dry earth. Through the growing stain Antjie saw right into the centre of the earth, where a tangle of roots and tubers stirred thirstily to receive the blood seeping down from above.

With the thrill of the quenched earth passing through them, they sang, Juig aarden juig, alom die Heer / Dien God met blydskap—Rejoice earth rejoice, around the Lord / Serve God with gladness—and steatopygous Antjie felt the weight of her body melt away until she was pure spirit flickering in the sunlight. That the Promised Land was barren and the shrubs dwarfed with thirst was only proof of God's mysterious ways.

Ouma Ragel's stories may not have been as reliable as he thinks. In her cooking shelter, with the boy tugging at her patchwork skirt, she bent over the blackened pots of slow-cooking mealies and beans packed on a marrowbone, which indelibly flavoured the story in the child's memory. And so, Ouma, and so? he called impatiently, as she told for the millionth time the tale of the Chief's imprisonment, for sometimes she would remember a new detail. Thus David ought to have seen how truth, far from being ready-made, takes time to be born, slowly takes shape in the very act of repetition, of telling again and again about the miracles performed by the Chief, seasoned and smoked in Ouma's cooking shelter to last forever—stories that made that much more sense than the remaining fragments of the old man's own text. Which, as I pointed out to David, only goes to show that people cannot be relied on to tell their own stories.

Having spent her lungs on reviving the fire, Ouma would sit down for a rest on the packed earth floor, her legs stretched out.

My boy, she panted, it is a faith that he worked hard at, a special Griqua faith of our very own; we cannot even think of doing without it. Pointing to the ridge across the Soutrivier, she said, Look, along there he promised a train would run, right here through the veld, an artery that will carry the riches of the land to the ports of the west coast. And believe you me that day will come, for his predictions have never been wrong. To me, he said—he was always tender with me—Ralie, he said, you will hear the train but you won't see it.

And what about Plettenberg Bay, Ouma?

The beauty of the waves, he said, will be dashed against the rock. They will build a monstrous building, a white tower of Mammon that will scream out its own ugliness and flash its evil glare for miles and miles. And what did the people from the bay tell us at this year's conference?

They had been full of it, the people from Krantzhoek crammed into a lorry on their tenth September visit to commemorate the founding of the Griqua reformation movement and to re-enact the sacrifice of the first goat under the dabikwa tree. They told of the fulfilment of the prophecy, of the new bay hotel on the rock floating like a castle—no, like a ship—on the lagoon. When the tide was in you had to cross the water, and from the other end of the lagoon there was the cutest little humpbacked bridge which was, of course, only for the white people, the guests. Who danced every night in the hotel, even on Sundays, some whispered, the women half-naked and smoking cigarettes from long holders, the men with wallets bulging like their prosperous stomachs, making lewd suggestions to the Griqua girls who dusted and swept and changed their sinful sheets. And the building itself, the gleaming white concrete hotel, just as the Chief had said, except—there was without doubt admiration in their voices as they described the grand structure towering above the water—the evening sun reflected in each window so that the place was ablaze with a million suns. No, with the fires of hell, Ouma interjected, our children, our young men and women, should not work at such a place.

But, said someone, it was better than being idle in these days of scarce work, and did the Chief not drum into them the importance of work. Then someone else started up the hymn: Juig aarden juig / alom die Heer. Little Davie thought of the marvellous sea he had never seen, of water rejoicing around the hotel, and he wondered, if the white people were wicked enough, would God set alight and sink their ship-hotel? And he saw the cheeky Lewiesa, who had boxed his ears and said that hammer-headed children should not be counting the teeth of grown-ups, saw her tilting wildly on a balcony, arms still aloft as she shook crumbs from a tablecloth, the cloth transformed into a flag of peace, but in vain as the building staggered and the first angles of blazing windows sizzled in the sea.

Now that would have been a miracle, especially if Lewiesa, who would have learnt her lesson, were to float back to the beach on a rafter, the linen cloth a taut sail in her stretched-out arms and the lagoon resounding with Juig aarde juig in all twenty tunes sung by the famous Griqua choirs. But he did not care so much for the predictions; anyone could predict hotels if there were rich white people around who did not care to stay at home. It was the real miracles he wanted to hear about, the wonderful things that actually happened like the Chief bursting out of prison gates of iron.

But the railway, I ask, through Beeswater? Did that happen?

Oh yes, it comforted Ouma Ragel in the days before her death. She would listen for the sound; she could hear it long before it appeared—but anyway, by then she was blind as a bat. I had to count the trucks for her. Yes, the Iscor line between Saldanha Bay and Sishen was built alright. But of course all that iron and steel works brought not a penny to the Griquas.

And did you always count the trucks? Or did you make it up for her, I ask.

Of course not, never, he says indignantly. Ouma would in any case have known; she had a sixth sense, a little like the Chief himself.

The way in which Le Fleur with his bare hands burst through the iron doors of prison turns out, from the fragments of manuscript, to have been a metaphor, mistaken by an ill-educated scribe for the truth. Those anxious to preserve the volk's history worried about the newness of the story but the old man, open to grand suggestions, readily adopted it on his deathbed, along with the governorship of Rhodesia, and the scribe, anxious to make a contribution, countered hostile questions by saying that of course he had not been apprehended, that he had not like a common criminal wanted to escape from prison, that he had merely wanted to prove that he was indeed God's right-hand man and had gathered together the wardens to show them his feat, whereafter he retired meekly to his cell. And that was only a taste of what was to come: the pardon and the release that would make a whole row of prison wardens choke on their wide-brimmed felt hats.

As for predicting Lord Rosmead's death, the Chief had seen in the early hours of the morning a vision of that English gentleman sailing home and literally being hauled over the coals by God for leaving him, Le Fleur, in prison, knowing that it was wrong, knowing that justice had not been done. The very morning of the dream, Rosmead, feeling faint, had to be carried on to the deck, where he died within the hour—yes, died within sight of an unusually mist-free coast of England with his fair lady waiting on the pier, waving a sad white handkerchief.

Again, Ouma, tell it again, the child whined. He liked to wince at the story of Rosmead dancing on red-hot coals, crying out for the splash and sizzle of a wayward wave while the ocean swayed calmly all around him.

Okay, said Ouma Ragel, listen carefully and when you're a big boy you can write up these stories. She took off her doek and ran her fingers through the landscape of her head, scratching ferociously along the paths between the network of plaits before tying up the cloth once more into the old-fashioned double knot on top that the child so loved.

You won't believe it, she whispered, looking round as if assassins lurked in the shadows. It was an ugly thing, but twice, you know, twice those grand white people from over the waters hired cheap political skollies to kill the Chief. They just didn't understand that he had vision, that he could see through things and repeat to them their very own words: By hook or by crook Le Fleur must be wiped out. Just imagine such shameful behaviour. Not that his life was really threatened, because bullets just shot past him and the assegais bent against his word.

~

KOKSTAD 1991

The young receptionist, packing her things into a bag of many compartments, much like a filing cabinet—a nuisance to get one's
eyebrow pencil all mixed up with ballpoint pens—is pleasantly surprised by David's friendly greeting as he enters the hotel lobby. So
she cannot resist mentioning the dance that night, which is free for
guests; no harm in it, he doesn't know anyone here, and who
knows—although she just has a feeling that she will not go even
if he were to ask her, but no, he doesn't. She should have known
that this broomstick-up-the-arse guy isn't up to having a good time,
but then, with old-fashioned country formality, he shakes her
hand by way of taking leave, which quite makes up for not being
asked to the dance. But he has not even asked her name, and
there, she supposes, is the proof of his indifference.

David, raised in a squat, flat-roofed house, takes a childish delight
in climbing stairs. Each narrow step of the creaking staircase is
steeped in adventure, a notion collaged from a number of films.
Alone in the room he revels in the luxury of doing as he pleases;
he can even choose not to eat tonight and so save himself a few rand,
which will go some way towards soothing his guilt about this
trip, with Sally and the children never getting away. Tonight he makes
notes—or rather, writes down words in minute writing, hardly notes
—for a meeting, to be held when he returns, on the role of the
army during the transition period. He cannot think without writing things down, a longstanding defiance of rules, but he has developed his own set of rules for the transgression that renders it safe as
houses: he uses the smallest possible slip of paper, which he always
removes from its pad to ensure that there is no imprint; it is never
left unattended; he shoves it into his mouth at the slightest interruption; improvised and inconsistent codes and abbreviations make
it, in any case, difficult to read; and the note exists only as long as
he is busy writing—he destroys it as soon as he arrives at conclu-
sions. And if he should suddenly be seized by a heart attack, well,

he knows that he would instinctively stuff the paper into his mouth and spend his last breath chewing it, ensuring that the letters dissolved in a wash of blue.

His room is above the ballroom, which occupies most of the ground floor, and the thump of the music is distracting. His thoughts flutter about the transgressive act of thinking on paper, so that he loses his thread and finally tears the slip of paper into the lavatory bowl, flushing away his first thoughts on how to maintain an army whilst officially dismantling it. A pity that such deception has to be practised, but civilians simply do not understand, and it is in everyone's interest that energy not be wasted in debating matters about which there can be no debate.

Obladi, oblada, life goes on, yeah, the band blares, and David finds himself trying to summon the original, which amounts to focusing on the deviation, that which jars in its difference, so that the Beatles's rendition just escapes him. The timing, the timbre, the tinny quality of the guitar, these seep in and take root, until he fears that the original is forever lost. David, who prides himself on the ability to concentrate on one thing whilst appearing to be involved with another, is forced to give up. He could look at the chapter he has photocopied at the library, but with all the noise there is no point. Better to go to the dance—or rather, to hang around the dance room, since the very thought of jazzing across a floor, dancing coloured style, as the comrades say, makes him feel foolish. Not that he hasn't, in the old days of watchfulness, hastily grabbed a woman and dived into the centre in order to escape attention. He puts on the shirt that Sally has so expertly ironed and folded for the occasion and slips on his jacket and goes down the stairs he had ascended with such anticipation.

The man at the door rests his eyes on David's well-ironed but unbuttoned collar. He puts out a hand to restrain him, then turns round and, as if he had been given the nod by someone—someone who identifies him as guest?—wishes David a very pleasant evening in a manner that suggests the delay was all about conventions of politeness. The breakfast waiter, with no trace of his earlier obsequious manner, hurries by and nods at David, a professional tower of plates on his arm. There is something familiar about the shaven-headed man, something that lies just underneath the red-and-black waiter's uniform, that he cannot put his finger on, that draws him to the man, whose figure he follows with his eyes across the candlelit room. He loses him and the band plays 'Smoke Gets in Your Eyes.'

The bar is like any other, inviting patrons to lean on it with one elbow, so permitting the body to swing both towards the barman and round to make peremptory conversation with whoever else wishes to linger there. Most patrons return at once to the tables decorated with candles and little glass vases, each hosting a pink carnation. Ebrahim, the manager, attaches himself to David, who leans against the bar. He is a rotund man whose Terylene trousers follow the sagging curve of his belly, and whose trousers would not have deserved a mention were it not for his irritating, intrusive line of conversation. David is adept at chattering companionably without answering too many questions, which drives the man to telling jokes—Hear the one about Van der Merwe and De Klerk, or the one about Gammatjie and the liberation struggle?—desperate stories for loosening the tongue. David laughs good humouredly and wishes he could tell jokes; Ebrahim laughs uproariously and, although he has given up on drawing out his guest, repeats the questions.

So just a little pleasure trip, hey, a bit of business here and there and also to relax? And on your own too; perhaps a nice lady on her way, hey? Listen, you can always change rooms, you know, there's a nice little love nest at the end of the corridor, lovely view. I would've given it to you from the start but it was taken. Business, you know, and he winks.

No, I'm fine, I'm on my own, David says. Just visiting, doing a bit of research in the school break. I'm a teacher, you see, working on a history project. The grandeur of the word *research* appeals to him, helps him to chatter, to fantasise. I'm thinking of enrolling part time for a degree in history, but you have to be sure of what you want to study, it's no good just taking a degree for the sake of the salary like so many teachers do. So I'm finding out about the

Griquas, looking at the museum, the newspapers, and so on. And he surprises himself with the additional, unnecessary lie—My people were from Kokstad. Originally, that is.

Ebrahim fiddles with his keys and explains how all his people have degrees, even from the white universities, that there is nothing like education to uplift yourself, show you the way, and listen, by the way, have you heard the one about Gammatjie and Mandela in the bookshop? But David does not hear the rest. A young woman at one of the tables in the centre of the room waves at him, unmistakably at him, so that he waves back, and Ebrahim is reminded that what the event lacks is a good dose of dry ice to improve the atmosphere.

The woman rises and walks towards him. Her hair is piled high on her head; her neck is long and slender and she teeters on dangerously high heels, holding her head very still to prevent the tower of hair from tumbling down. It is the girl from the reception desk. She holds her hand out by way of inviting him to dance. Better, he supposes, than sitting with old Ebrahim, whom he watches talking to the shaven-headed waiter, who then disappears. With the noise of music and laughter it is difficult to follow the woman's chatter about the band from Umtata, about how her cousins had arrived and persuaded her to come just as she was settling down with a good book. The library in Kokstad is not bad, even though she sometimes finds halfway through a book that she has read it before, but then they do tend to be about the same things, stories, don't they?

On the wall, their moving shadows are distorted by candlelight, and he thinks of the bumpy walls of his childhood, upon which the slightest movement of a little finger could turn an ostrich's head into a fox's. He gets away with uh-huhs, and if she is aware of his distraction she does not appear to mind. Caught up in the romance of sailing through the swirling clouds of smoke with a stranger, it hardly matters to her how he behaves; she has no expectations of this broomstick-up-the-arse sort of chap. He senses this, and his gratitude, spreading into an affection of sorts, makes him draw her somewhat closer.

Typical, she thinks, just like a man, and at the end of the dance she asks if he would like to sit at her table. A quick glance at the arrangement of chairs and the cousins settled with their row of beers shows that he will not get a seat facing the door, that he would not be able to keep an eye on that waiter when he comes back.

No, he says, smiling warmly, we'll carry on dancing.

The receptionist lets herself down. He could've asked rather than assume her willingness; she should say no, but what the hell, she can't be bothered arguing with him, and besides she's seen much worse. At least he's not drunk and you can tell that he can be trusted, no monkey business with him. But that doesn't mean, it doesn't mean—and her body, stiffening with humiliation, keeps its distance. Sensing that he will have to make some effort to keep her longer on the dance floor, from which he can keep his eye on the door, he says belatedly, I should introduce myself. David, David Dirkse, from Cape Town. As if she didn't know. I'm a teacher, just visiting, doing some research on the Griquas, looking around a bit, checking old newspapers and the museum and so on. Got to study further, you know, they're cutting back in education, making teachers redundant; you need a degree nowadays. Keeps you out of trouble, he says, trying to be playful. Failing to raise a smile, he carries on, No, it is interesting, fascinating to find out what went on in the good old days. I also want to speak to some of the old people here. Are you a Griqua?

Course not, what you take me for? There's a Griqua church here, just like any other church, but I'm Dutch Reformed. Griquas are from the olden times; there aren't any left now. We're all coloured here.

He has no time to apologise, for the waiter has appeared in the doorway.

Extraordinary looking man. What an amazing profile, don't you think?

No, I don't. Looks kind of ordinary to me.

He has an efficient air about him. Seems to be quite the man in charge. Is he the head waiter?

Him? He's only been here a couple of days. I don't even know his name, or perhaps he told me but I can't remember it. These people are so forward these days; that's the New South Africa for you.

David decides to let it pass. He steers her back to the table of cousins, who shake hands and invite him to join them, to have a drink, but no, he says, he still has some reading to do that night and, having monopolised their lovely cousin for so long, he had better be off.

The night air was indeed freezing, and when he returned to his room a couple of hours after leaving the dance he was grateful for the kettle and the courtesy-of-the-management coffee, stirring and stirring a whole sachet of sugar into his plastic cup.

Two hours? I ask since *a couple* could mean any number of things, but he waves away the question impatiently. How did he know that someone had been in his room?

Just, is his reply, just knew.

But nothing was disturbed. His notes from the museum lay in the same neat pile; there was in any case nothing to find. His gun, as always, he carried on his person.

The hit list is a cultural variation on sticking pins into a doll or sending a tokolos—a demon—to undermine the intended victim. Except that in such cases the victim would mysteriously sense the evil, be unnerved by moving shadows of something scuttling off, perhaps see what may well be the tail of the tokolos, or in the mind's eye perceive a flash of the fading self as hapless doll, bristling with pins, before all was swallowed into a morass of fear and darkness. The secrecy, the silence of this operation, where all that is required is for the intended to catch an uncertain glimpse, is replaced in the hit list by stark revelation, by making public, for there in black and white is your name in a column with the names of others.

Written down, intended to be read, your name becomes the bearer of menace. And so you are separated from yourself through reading your own name and wishing that you were not the signified, the bearer of that name. You are careful not to utter it, although your lips move in silent articulation, as if to verify the writing. A function of literacy: to read your name on a hit list, but silently, as you do the other names.

In vain he tries to remember when he had learnt to read silently, of how a child is persuaded to give up the loud display; instead he thinks of how Ouma Antjie, in her feeble old voice, had read aloud from the psalms, tracing the words with a trembling finger.

The hit list, a handwritten sheet of paper left under his chair, is an addition rather than a removal of something, so that in searching for an absence, he is disarmed. David recognises the generic features: the cheap lined paper with a name on every other line; the writing in a girlish hand. The letters are drawn painstakingly, with a flourish, as if she were focusing only on the practicalities of cursive writing, of joining one letter elegantly to another, as if there were a master with a stick to rap the knuckles for any mistakes, for flaws in the light upward and bold downward strokes. Always, alongside the anonymity of the producer is this mock regard for the personal, the individual hand. The list may not be typed, but the writing is of such uniformity as to show that the names themselves are simply a column, of no consequence to the writer. And what, David wonders, if the writer found herself scripting the name of her own flesh and blood?

The paper is not pink, but then that is not peculiar. The practice is not without variation, not in every aspect repeatable; there is always the possibility of new forms of terror. He had in the course of his career seen a couple before, dismissed them as despicable enemy tactics, had never thought of the effect on those for whom it is intended. Now he, David, is the intended. Like a girl in that twilight time of waiting to be claimed as wife, a time of gazing at the world through windows that are columns of light; a girl clutching at straws, at the fading light, waiting to be told of the truth. Or, he shakes his head in disbelief, the horror.

The first name on the list is that of a recent victim, Oupa Mtshali. His body was found in a little copse near Khayelitsha—an Unrest Related Death—and the police, after listless questioning, hauled off the black plastic bag with no further ado. David knows a couple of the others as names connected with informers, but it is the one beneath his own that leaps out, as the name of the beloved always does. Just as that name uttered in any crowd leaps out of the murmur, breaking the continuum of sound, and, lifted, is carried on a higher crystal pitch, for all the world as if it were spelled aloud. So that for a moment he would stop in midsentence, as if he had been hailed. Here the name in writing takes on a different hue, lifts out from the rest of the girlish script and starts to tremble in a flush of red, the fancy strokes disintegrating, the letters separating as the colour grows deeper and deeper until they disappear entirely in a pool of blood. Dulcie's blood. He wonders whether she is in the same unit as Oupa Mtshali. Is he, David, responsible for her place on the list? And why, how can he possibly, and he buries his head in his hands with shame or anger or despair, how could he be thinking of her as the beloved!

David does not know what to do with such a thing, a list of names ordered on paper. Like a shopping list, he supposes, in case you forget that you have run out of peanut butter; the biscuits after all a luxury, last on the list; a piece of paper for the housewife's eyes alone. What to do with such a thing, instrument of terror masquerading as aide-mémoire? Should he stuff it into his mouth, flush it away in the lavatory bowl? He stares at the writing on the page, the names that swim towards each other, coupling them in an intimacy that surpasses the charged and awkward moments of their chance meetings, an intimacy of death that displaces all. And if he has never considered such a thing, the possibility of infidelity, it is the schoolgirl writing of her name beneath his own that has driven them into this naked embrace, for which he blushes.

For a moment he wonders, hopes that it might have come from Sally, driven to such bizarre measures by anger and jealousy. But no, he knows that she is not capable of such a thing, that she, his wife, loves him.

And Comrade Dulcie, he decides briskly—he can only guess at her rank—would not be in need of his protection.

⁓

DULCIE after a tortured night sets off speeding through the streets of Woodstock onto the highway, where she sees over the top of the distant mountain her own heart rise over the city, its light in her eyes, and the cracked ribs, the bleeding nipples are nothing, nothing at all, as her swollen heart hovers on the horizon then bursts to bathe the world in soft yellow light, her body lightened of the burden of that sentimental heart now beating out the two dear syllables so that she will no longer accelerate through the iron railing and hurl herself into a death of crushed steel and fire, how could she with that light pushing as tenderly as freedom above the hills, urging her to wait, wait, and see with mundane curiosity whether David, wherever he might be, for she has discovered that he had left town, would see that heart in the eastern sky and feel his own drawn into its embrace of light.

When David, at precisely that hour, slips into a side door of the Crown Hotel, he sees the light glowing on Mount Currie, the world flushed with a promise of pinkness, but he is too preoccupied to stop, to think of its origin. His heart leaps but he will not follow it, he will quell it sternly, put it aside, snuff it out like a candle, for there is no time for dilly-dallying in this way. He will not be seduced by flirtatious light.

Cautiously and wearily he makes his way to the room for the second time. David does not know what to do but is not accustomed to admitting such a thing to himself. He will take time slowly, minute by minute, so he attends to his person, brushes up a lather, shaves meticulously, then packs his shaving things away. Rummaging through his bag he finds a hairbrush that Sally must have packed, and standing in front of the mirror he performs the unfamiliar task of sliding the useless brush across his hair, noting with surprise the grey at his left temple. Then he finds his toothbrush and brushes as his mother has taught him to do, up and down, getting the bristles between the teeth and behind as well—Don't forget behind the teeth, you can never brush too carefully, too hard. He draws blood from those unsuspecting gums, which makes him spit several times, expecting to hear the teeth clatter into the basin, expecting all to disintegrate, but no, they remain in his mouth. He packs the shaving things, the toothbrush and paste, the hairbrush, into his bag. Could it be that he is leaving? And where would he go?

He takes the loathsome thing out of his pocket and looks once again. The list is now marked by four fold-lines, across the girlish writing. He rests it in the veined brown hand, a hand unmarked by manual work that has been waiting in the world these thirty-five years to be on this day transformed into that of the intended, the hand of a girl to be married, a girl in a haze of innocence—and he laughs harshly—waiting in the ambiguous light for the truth that will be withheld from her. Can it be, he asks, can it be true that he does not know the truth? Or worse, that it stares him in the face, the truth which he cannot bear? And is truth not what he has been pursuing all these years of trouble and strife and dalliance with death—the grand struggle for freedom?

And now, can there be no turning back, now that he has allowed the blood to be quickened by her, the beloved? Once he had put his hands on her shoulders intending to deliver a fashionable peck on each of her cheeks, but had been unable to remove those willful hands. Now, having held her, even at a distance, even if that holding was a holding off, is there no going back? Once there is acknowledgement, once their eyes have spoken, is there no going back? And does this betrayal of his family brand him as traitor through and through, someone on whom his comrades have to keep a watchful eye?

No, and mentally he clicks his heels, his honour is unquestionable and the truth lies in black and white, unquestionably, in the struggle for freedom, for the equal distribution of wealth, for education for all, for every man and woman and child's right to dignity. . . .

Inviolable like the tokolos, a hit list cannot be amended in any way. To pluck the pins out of the wax doll is not a possibility, for there is no longer a subject to perform such a task. What David does is therefore something of a miracle, something performed in the trance of his freedom mantra. He can, of course, not touch his own, but he scores her name out with a pen, repeatedly, so that it can no longer be recognised. The terror mounts with each stroke of the blue ballpoint. When the name is completely obliterated, he shudders at what he has done. Has he, the intended, been directed into acting, into becoming the agent for others?

By way of making amends to Dulcie he writes her name on another clean sheet of paper. Below it he writes: It is they who obliterate her name.

Which is surely imprudent. This *they* also occurs in other scribblings, but David does not answer my questions about who *they* are. Thus I can offer no substitute; I must stick with the pronoun. A person must, as David all too often says, each trust to his own judgment. Or hers, as I often correct him.

~

CAPE TOWN 1991

Sally awards herself a quiet hour while the children watch television at the neighbours', but she soon shuts the book in irritation. She has had enough of the bodies of black women: their good thick legs, their friendly high-riding backsides, their great sturdy hams. And if not about unwieldy black behinds, there is always something to read about the tragedy of being coloured and therefore, it would appear, in limbo. If only she were lost, she sighs, so that no one, not even David, would ever find her. She ought to rise from her very own good heavy hams, but remains on the sofa staring at cobwebs under the sideboard. In the afternoon light their gossamer pile winks, but to hell with it all, she will not move.

Sally has no difficulty in keeping still for long periods. Having been brought up in a respectable coloured home, she kept still throughout her youth. For the ambitious Ant Sarie who spent many years observing the behaviour of ladies in the Logan Hotel, the idea of her daughter rushing about like the roesbolling girls of the village was out of the question; in fact, there was no need at all to compare her with vulgar girls who would certainly end up in service. To become a lady, she knew, there was no better practise than simply keeping still; she had watched ladies taking slow, short turns in the landscaped garden of the Logan, stooping now and then to admire a shrub, but returning to their sofas and English magazines, or to their rooms to read improving books.

Thus Sally learned to fill the long, hot karroo hours with reading. There were magazines left in the hotel with the subtle odour of grandeur still trapped between the pages. But even the writing on packages of sugar or mealie-meal brought pleasure, her favourite being the old Bokomo flour cotton bags, washed and bleached for making broekies so that the faded letters trailed off into the seams. Best of all were the occasional novels about nurses or murder mysteries left in the rooms by careless guests. These books Ant Sarie kept for a few days in the broom cupboard, waiting for enquiries, but no one ever asked after them, so that after a week or so she took them home for the child whose hunger for stories could not be stilled. And there was always the Bible, with the best, most educated English in the world, one of the ladies told Ant Sarie as she handed her a little black volume. Reading, lying across a bed casting her eyes over print, was a decent way for a girl to spend her time and could only keep her out of mischief. And so Sally, after a brilliant start in the rough and tumble of five-stone-throw or ten-stones-in-the-hole, settled down, either reading or doing her homework at the kitchen table, while her whirlwind brothers chased after inflated goat bladders or tin cans or other whirlwind children.

Keeping very still did not exempt her from all the tasks a girl had to do, including keeping her hair swirled guerrilla-fashion under a tight stocking, but these tasks were carried out quietly and efficiently, and she was rewarded with a lie down and a chance to read a chapter. Most importantly, Ant Sarie explained, keeping still prevented her from making friends. Friends were the ruin of all God-fearing young people. No one would be led astray were it not for friends. Take her older brother, Danie, a clever boy who had only just managed to scrape through standard seven, ruined by the iniquities of friends. No chance of him becoming a teacher, and if he did, he would be one of those who gave coloured people a bad name—a drunken teacher. For a girl it was doubly important since there was also modesty to maintain; she need only look at groups of girls ambling aimlessly, arm-in-arm, giggling at boys in the alluring crimson light of dusk, to know why a lady did not have friends.

No one had told her that all that keeping still encouraged the growth of an uncommonly large posterior, and by the time Sally thought of taking more exercise, steatopygia had set in for good, lycra had been invented, and she was doomed to long-legged step-ins that turned fresh spring days into a stifling tropical swelter. It was the Movement that offered freedom in the form of loose khaki trousers and a break from reading about the sad coloured condition. And marriage to David, she sighed, that lost her her place in MK—and took her back to the overrated business of reading novels. How could such things possibly be called weapons of the struggle? Perhaps the stuff and nonsense that is said nowadays about culture is meant to placate women like herself, and she rises stiffly onto her own good solid legs to cook sausages for the children, whose voices rollick down the length of the street as they chant: You won't make it to heaven / Without the AK-47.

This night, the second of David's absence, Sally, a light sleeper—her dreams filled with Dulcie—is woken by the sound of footsteps around the house. There is whispering just below her bedroom window and what sounds like an argument at the gate. She leaps out of bed to check the room where the children sleep peacefully and hovers in the doorway with her eyes fixed on the window. There she waits until what sounds like the reconnaisance of her house is completed, the consultations over. Encouraged by their carelessness, their attempts to let her know of their presence, she moves to a window at the front of the house. The arrogance of these people, who even now will not let them be. Through the lace curtain she does not see their faces but notes the last of two men in black pile into a large car and sail off into the black night.

How dare they, and how could she have believed that these were things of the past? Only this time they appear to want nothing: no raid, no search for documents, no questions, just dark figures moving around noisily with something like stockings over their heads of all things, a mimicking perhaps of the comrades? No doubt a new tactic for unnerving her. Are they hoping that she will get in touch with David, betray his whereabouts at the Crown Hotel? Surely they know that revolutionary codes do not allow for that. She ought to consult with someone but decides to let it pass. Should it happen again she'll get in touch with Comrade K.

Sally would like to telephone, to hear whether there is someone in the room with David, for she would know, she would be able to tell. Perhaps these people know of her fears, her jealousy, and she blushes with shame. Is there nothing at all private in one's life? Does everything belong to politics?

Ouma Sarie is in town to visit. It is not often that she comes, but a sudden longing to see her girl, her grandchildren, has overcome her, and there's mos nothing to prevent her from catching a bus, from doing in her old age as she pleases. With her old Joop dead she can do exactly as she pleases and so she got out those rand notes from under the mattress and caught her bus. Thank God there were buses everywhere these days, people moving about like nobody's business, that's what Joop would not be able to understand, that catching a bus to town was nothing these days, that the world being all in a spin with this travelling, no one would even come to greet and sing you off to a safe journey precisely because it was nothing at all, and so she could go to town whenever she longed to see her children. Yes, that's what being a widow was about, don't think of the aches and pains, but of how you can do as you please; no more shirts to iron and collars to turn and socks to darn; and she folded her things into the bag, a nice light bag of plastic straw so you don't have to struggle with the extra weight.

And now she staggers up Kiewietlaan with her zip-up bag, hoping that they'll be there—Saartjie, or rather Sally, and the children—not, of course, that David man who is never anywhere. She should really have telephoned from the village shop. They don't mind at all her using the telephone, yes, even white people have changed, but ag, it's no good, she never thinks of such things in time, will never get used to it, besides, she's just too old to practise a phone voice at her age. But not to worry, there they are; the children see her and come running like puppies, wagging their tails, tugging at her skirts. Ouma's here, Ouma's here, they scream, and dance around her as she unpacks the eggs, real eggs with deep yellow yolks laid by her own hens, and the apricot chutney, and the atjar pickle that Sally loves. She must remember to take some empty jars away with her to make more for Christmas. But Sally is on edge, greets her with an eye that sweeps across the road, and no wonder the child is out of sorts, with all the curtains drawn on such a lovely day, starting every time these show-off Cape Town drivers screech down the road.

Ag, ma, don't worry, she says, it's just these Boers, same old games, I know their tricks but it's just the children that I worry about —a person can't keep them in all day. It will be alright when David gets back, won't be long. No, really, she says, smiling at Ouma's snort of disbelief, he's just gone to Kokstad for a few days. And then she surprises herself with sarcasm: Just a little trip for David to, well, find himself.

Ouma Sarie claps her hands and, lifting a child onto each knee, declares, We'll find ourselves at the seaside tomorrow. Yes, we going to have a nice little Saturday at Seaforth—that's now a good idea, hey, she says, noting Sally's doubtful look.

She packs their picnic, and although Sally objects to the striped plastic bag, she will hear nothing of it: by far the lightest thing, why make yourself tired carrying extra weight? They spread out their blanket on that fine white sand, and how they eat, the little things, their boiled eggs and peanut butter sandwiches, murmuring with pleasure, and she remembers how her own children never got enough to eat, that Saartjie, or rather Sally, was always hungry, ate so much more than the boys. Oh, she tried her best to teach the child the ways of a lady, but no, she turned out rough like a boy, running all over the place, the Lord alone knows, nowhere to be found, a person of no fixed address. Good God, and how she worried, how the girl had let her down, running away from college so that she could only fear the worst: running after men, 'cause for what other reason could a girl want to disappear so mysteriously, and although she did not speak to Joop for days when he said she was whoring around, she knew deep down that he must be right. And how she feared the scandal, the disgrace of Sally returning to the village with child and Joop still an elder in the church. That was what happened to girls who went to town, and to Sally of no fixed address, whom the police had come to look for at the house once, shouting, Ons skiet haar vrek— We'll shoot the bitch—as their tyres churned up her swept yard in a flurry of dust, scattering the stones that she had gathered into a pathway to keep the dust down. And she knew that they would, they would shoot as if the child were a dog, so that she rushed to the res-cue of the flowering red malva that the wheels had caught, nursing it with a jug of water, pinching off the damaged leaves, stroking the bruised stem, coaxing it into recovery, for her bruised heart did not know what to think: if the child was in politics, although they had not made it clear, well, God had to forgive her, but was it not worse than whoring? She could only hope that he had not driven over her malva deliberately, hope that the sergeant with the moustache, brusque as he was, had nipped the plant by accident, that at least would be something. And when Joop came home she said nothing of the malva. He said of Saartjie that it was a relief, her politics, but that one could not be sure of those ANC types, that perhaps being in politics did not stand in the way of whoring.

And now, how everything's turning out alright, De Klerk let-ting Mandela out to help him fix up the country nicely, and her Sally all settled down decently, herself a mother. There Sally is with the little one, holding her as she treads water, Kick your legs, kick. And at her feet Jamie, gathering smooth white stones, muttering to him-self, and the little waves washing at the shore, coming in at an angle, waves on which black-and-white birds bob in the sun, and the honey-combed pattern of light trembling under the water. And in the pleas-ure of it, the pleasure of all that shimmering water in which her children play like fish knowing their way through the waves, she, a woman of the karroo who is not so used to water, listens to the lapping and the sloshing and the lovely cries of children and sees the blue folds of the Buffelstalberg cool in the distance and so her eyelids droop, droop as the water laps and laps.

Sally had not known that she was afraid of water. She loved paddling and took some pleasure in feeling the resistance of water, but required to swim at one of the training camps, she found it impossible to put her face in it. In the thick Mozambican heat the water felt like oil, and the comrade with his hand under her belly barked his instructions, Up, draw up your legs, and out, kick, flap the ankle, hands forward, round, and again. And how poorly she performed, unable to confess her terror.

He said, as they made their way gingerly across the burning sand, A fuck, that's what you need, and she saw his bulging shorts and knew that her time had come, as she had known it would come sooner or later, this unspoken part of a girl's training. And because she would not let him force her, lord it over her, she forced herself and said, Okay, if you want. It did not take long, and she had no trouble pushing him off as soon as he had done, and since she had long forgotten the fantasy of the virginal white veil, it did not matter, she told herself, no point in being fastidious, there were more important things to think of, there was freedom on which to fix her thoughts. Then, cleaning herself in seawater, over and over, she lost her fear, found her body dissolving, changing its solid state in the water through which she then moved effortlessly. Which was, of course, just as the comrade had said.

And now, holding little Chantal, whose plump legs flap without purpose, she panics at the child's playfulness, her gurgling refusal to follow instructions. Then Jamie joins them, and conspiring against the swimming lesson they tumble like seals, laughing and splashing, and oh, what it takes to stay calm, for she is determined that the child should learn to swim today, no later than today. Chantal slips out of her hands, a sea creature tormenting her, so that, exasperated, she smacks the child, and Ouma, surfacing out of the cool blues and greens of sleep, holds out her arms unsteadily to receive the sobbing little girl.

~

DULCIE is a decoy. She does not exist in the real world; David has invented her in order to cover up aspects of his own story. That is what I suspect. For a day or so, while I believe in her fictionality, I feel a sense of relief. But no, he is genuinely surprised that I should think such a thing, so that he sets about telling me about their first meeting in Kliprand, where the Griquas now live. David is unusually expansive; he insists that I would not understand unless the political background is adequately sketched.

It was 1983, a good forty years after the death of the Chief, that the Griquas moved away from Beeswater to Kliprand, the location on the edge of the white town. The new generation were tired of travelling all that way to work and spending their weekends in the bundu; they would rather face the Saturday night collisions with sin in the location than the backward tea-meetings in the church hall. By then the white village had expanded into a prosperous wine-growing town, television had arrived, and the Griquas must have grown pretty tired of being Griquas, especially when the new coloured location was built on the hill, even if it was right by the town dump and the sewerage works. But after the hardships of Beeswater it seemed a grand place, with a new clinic, high school, hostel, and, most seductive of all, water—a tap at the end of each lane. The Boers knew that with unrest in the country people had to be properly wooed; a remote settlement of disgruntled, sin-starved people was just an open invitation to terrorists.

David, however, had not been doing any Congress work in that area, would have been the last one to tackle his own people. They had not forgotten all the teachings of Le Fleur, who from the outset had been hostile towards the ANC. And was the benevolence of the Boers, who were offering safe employment and above all peace, not evidence of the good sense of his separatist teachings? Not even the propaganda machinery could keep news of the troubles away from country people, but the Griquas believed themselves to be nonpolitical and therefore safe from the troubles in the cities.

Only in the cities did rude kaffirs corrupt coloured people into throwing stones at the police. Although where those skollies found so many stones in Cape Town, with its skyscrapers and tarred roads, had many Griquas shaking their heads. That the hills of Kliprand were encrusted with inviting pebbles was, of course, a source of anxiety. A UDF branch would surely mean that lorries full of city people would invade them. Not that Griquas did not know how to be hospitable to strangers—but these strangers would teach the youth to raid the hills, to stone the nice Sersant Van Graan and his constables, the white people who had trusted them, and so would bring shame on a people who have always been God-fearing, respectful of their betters.

Not that there have not been some young strangers around of late, people who've come to work in the expanding white town, and yes, they muttered and mumbled and spoke the politics, but ag, that was young people now, always complaining and thinking they had all the answers. But at least they were respectable, sober young people who sat around at weekends drinking their Pepsis and luring others into their circle of laughter and jokes and yes, sometimes also the old politics nonsense they learned from the television. Many of the old people felt that they should not have left the land that the Chief had led them to, but what could be done, they sighed, what could be done in these modern times when people will no longer put up with the brackish water of Beeswater and are thirsty for the roar of motorcars and the smell of petrol?

David did not think the time right, but the young woman from the Cape Town office who was in charge of the project was confident that enough groundwork had been done. It was thought that David, as homeboy, should be around at the time, but that she would be there as official representative. It was at this time that he would publicly declare his allegiance to the Movement and his father would forever turn his back upon him. As for the woman, he had of course known of her legendary activities for some time, and if anything, disapproved—he did not know of what, except perhaps her boldness, what could only be called her immense cheek.

The atmosphere could have been called electric, although that was not a word that David would have chosen. But he was at a loss; things were no longer the same, as if, like some city slicker, he was viewing the world through sunglasses, its meanings tinted beyond recognition. The old familiar, upright words leaned promiscuously in any old direction, attaching themselves to glossy new contexts. Thus later, sitting with his feet on Ant Mietjie's hearth, he found himself saying precisely that which he had not chosen to say: The atmosphere in the school hall was electric. Her words, of course, but then Ant Mietjie was hardly likely to question him on a matter of style, indeed, hardly likely to know that they were hers, the new woman's—Dulcie's—words. Her words, caught in his cupped hands where his eyes, first, devoured them; he could not remember why his hands were cupped, why he should have been staring at his palms. Now, from his own mouth, wrapping themselves around his own tongue, her words came tumbling into the old-fashioned house to perch on the things he had known all his life, the painted enamel pots and jugs with their sores of chipped old age.

Ant Mietjie poked the fire, fanned with a newspaper at the billowing smoke, and said hoarsely, Talk about 'lectric, I wouldn't have a black and crusty throat like a bladdy chimney if there were some of it in this house. So what brought this 'lectric to the hall?

Well, David said, Oom Paulse did his usual leader of the council talk, explained that we should slow down, be patient,. and allow the government to carry out its reforms at a sensible pace. That, the old man said, was what every Griqua had always known to be a good thing. And then . . .

David hesitated, savouring for a moment the memory of the UDF representative. They'd sent a woman, a young woman, for heaven's sake, in trousers and an oversized jersey and ugly brown shoes like the old-fashioned walkers worn by nurses. Not someone who'd have the respect of the elders. But he said none of that.

David started as Ant Mietjie's questioning hand fell on his shoulders. Yes, electric, he blurted. It was the UDF woman; you should have heard her speak. She said how good it was to be there, how good it was to be among a people who were a real community, principled, reliable—soft-soaping the old man. Then she appealed to reason, to the restlessness of the youth, saying that Oom Paulse should explain why it was a good thing to wait for government reforms, that it was just one point of view and that there were so many points of view that all of them should be considered, so that people could discuss, think about the options, and decide for the good of the Griqua community.

Heitse! Ant Mietjie crowed. That would not please old Paulse; he won't be used to anyone asking questions, let alone a young woman. You know how all our problems are sorted out by the big men.

Exactly. This is it, Ant Mietjie, things are just not the same, David said lamely, for he had not been listening.

He took the cup of coffee sweetened with condensed milk from her worn old hands. She had always spoilt the child with sweet coffee in a little blue-mottled enamel mug that she said was his very own, and warm roosterbrood at weekends. Now that he was a grand city man, she gave him a pink glass cup. The coffee was no longer piping hot. Ant Mietjie sat down with him, sipping at her own mottled enamel mug, and stretched her legs out to cut across the line of light that shot boldly over the lower door into the dark room. Her ankles were grey and puffy like Ouma Ragel's.

Well, he continued, the woman outlined the UDF position very plainly and asked if anyone had any other positions to put forward. Of course no one said a word, even though we know that there are also some kids around who are talking PAC, but no one said a word. She said that people should be allowed to think about the alternatives and come back for another meeting tomorrow. So Ant Mietjie must be there, everybody must come and talk this business through.

People won't like it, you know, won't like a stranger coming to tell them what to do, they won't listen to a woman. Anyway, we've all these years of hardship quite happily been doing things our own way.

That's exactly what he had said to Dulcie after everyone had gone and they stood in the brutal white light, for all the world as if they were on display. Then her eyes scrambled awkwardly, an inept monkey scrambling up the length of the electric pole, to meet the mechanical eyes of the riot lights glaring fiercely across the township.

She said, shielding her eyes, still looking up, And this? Is this what you get when you do things your own way?

He could scarcely contain his irritation. As if they were not on the same side; as if she had no idea what he meant about listening to a woman.

Who is this woman anyway? Where is she from? Does anyone know her people? Ant Mietjie asked.

David had little to tell. She was Dulcie Olifant, lived in Town, also spoke fluent Afrikaans, seemed to know everything about all the trade unions in the Western Cape, about the different industries, the labour situation in Kliprand. A single woman, and not so very young, either. That was all. He said nothing about her clothes, her shoes. Ant Mietjie would not expect him, a man, to notice her shoes, and, of course, he never paid attention to what people wore. He recalled a dimple appearing and disappearing on her chin when she was agitated, but he could not very well say that either. He spoke of her quiet, forceful manner, the way in which even the old people echoed her words and nodded. He spoke with unexpected pleasure, like one picking little threads from her jersey, lightly, so that she knew nothing of his fingers landing and lifting repeatedly.

Perhaps she was related, Ant Mietjie said, to the Malmesbury Olifants, the Mr. Olifant who came to teach in Beeswater, remember, just before we all moved to Kliprand.

David did not know. And then he mentioned her clothes after all. How she was funnily dressed in corduroy trousers that certainly did not suit her heavy legs. The colours she wore, he just realised, were subtle versions of the banned green, yellow, and black, of which he said nothing. He spoke of her bushy hair, her unfeminine stoop, the ugly nurse's shoes. A woman to be resisted, and so he spun around her the invisible threads of his voice, looping them round and round the sagging trousers until she was bound into a glittering mummy of his making.

Ant Mietjie, whose attention had been wandering from this talk about clothes, and who started at the word *shoes,* slipped her cracked feet back into her own unlaced men's brogues, long since outgrown by her own grandson.

My word, I have things to do, and she rose unsteadily in the shoes, their leather cracked like her feet, so that David, transported by the telling, saw a surreal melding of flesh and leather, the solid cap of the shoe separating into five cracked toes.

So, can we count on Ant Mietjie at the meeting tonight? he asked anxiously.

My child, if you see me, you see me. She leaned for a moment against the doorpost. I don't know if I want to hear some grand young thing from Town tell me about the bladdy struggle. I've got my own growing wild in this very pondok and it might as well be signposted Private Struggle—Keep Out, for all the help I get from you professional strugglers.

Not so, he laughed, and gave her his patter about the charter and a future of equal opportunities for all. She would be there alright, vociferous and headstrong but an authority they could not do without. She would see the sense in their arguments; she was one of the few to whom Oom Paulse listened. Ant Mietjie followed David out to attend to the loaves in her outdoor oven.

Keep your head, Davie, she shouted after him.

What could she mean? How could she know how disturbing he found things?

Ant Mietjie's own head disappeared into the depths of the oven with a shovelful of glowing embers from the feeding fire beside it. Only the printed nylon of her housecoat stretched tight across her rear was visible, and he could not very well address himself to that mute flesh to find out how he had given himself away—although he supposed his agitation to be just professional jealousy, irritation that the young woman should have gone against his recommendation that the time was not right to come to Kliprand.

Not long now, Ant Mietjie muttered, withdrawing from the oven and putting one more log on the fire, just in case. And when the embers died down, she would put on the grid for roosterbrood and then she would send for him, like in the old days when she always sent for Davie—her own children scattered across the Cape—and together they would eat the warm, blistered roosterbrood, dripping with grainy sheep's fat.

Oom Paulse was in a fighting mood. He started, as usual, at the beginning, where any Griqua would start. There was no other place from which to speak, he said, than from the beginning, when God spoke to His servant, Chief le Fleur, and showed him the lost mules so that the people could be led out of the wilderness and turned into the proud Griquas they were today. Not a cobbled together, raggle-taggle group of coloureds who do not know where they belong, but a real volk, a nation who had no need to claim kin with either whites or blacks.

Ja, he said—thumping the table proudly, smoothing his hands over the starched cloth embroidered with their emblem, the kanniedood aloe of Namaqualand with its stacked triangular leaves—we are a nation. And the Chief struck bargains for the Griquas with the government of the time. That clever man ruined his wrists signing papers, making treaties, and getting the stubborn Boers to see them as a nation, treaties which he, Oom Paulse, would not dare to renege on, and it behoved any self-respecting Griqua to stand by those bargains, for they were no less than bargains made with God. And if Satan came dangling a rosy-cheeked apple before them, they would cry, Get thee hence Satan, for we are not a hungry, needy people. In the very desert where Chief le Fleur rubbed together two sticks to produce the miracle of fire, he sacrificed a goat, which, like the loaves and fishes of old, fed the entire people. Thorn sticks, Oom Paulse bellowed—and then his sticks got tangled with the thorn tree of Boer mythology—from crushed thorn sticks came the miracle of leaf because thorn trees are like the Griquas themselves. They may have been no more than a bundle of dry sticks, but they could withstand anything, even the crushing wheels of an ox wagon, for with the rain of Le Fleur's prayer the thornbush sprouts leaves and shakes free her sweet yellow mimosa balls, but now once more, and the old man's voice grew vengeful as he beat his fists on the table, now some of us, some of our own sons and daughters want to revert to a scattering of dead thorn sticks.

Lost in his account of cyclical sin and regeneration, he launched a fresh attack on Satan, who came in unlikely guises, at which point Ant Mietjie pounced on his falling intonation and in strong soprano fed into the meeting the opening bars of Juig aarden juig, using the convention of being moved to singing during a church service. And whether it was an interruption or an endorsement of the old man, the hymn had to be taken up by the rest. But the room was thick with tension and uncertainty, so that for several intolerable seconds no one joined her. It was unthinkable. Her lone voice, having reached the second line, began to flutter like a trapped insect, careened around the room, stumbled and lost volume on Dien God met blydskap, before someone—and, shocked, David noted that it was the new young woman—in a clear, strong voice lifted the dying one, Gee Hom eer, so that the room was driven into doing the decent and customary thing.

Voices wove into harmony, and they sang lustily until the end of the third verse, when old Paulse, in the split second of silence before the next, seized the opportunity to boom out as if there had been no interruption: In many guises comes Satan, singing promises of a better life, making seductive offers, but hark at the hiss in that buttery voice. Let us not forget the Breakwater where the unbelievers threw him into prison, or Robben Island, where Chief le Fleur broke his back for us in stone quarries so that we would have a place to call our own. There, in solitude, he prepared the way to lead us out of oppression into Klein Namaqualand, where we have settled as a volk, at peace with our fellow volk the Boers. Do we not have our own church, our own flag, our own emblem, the aloe that lives forever through years of drought? Have we not kept our houses clean, our children God-fearing, and even now that we have left Beeswater, do we not grow some food in the gardens given to us by the Boers? Do we not see every year how the dead vine bursts into green without winter rains? Do we now say, yes, it is good to bite the hand that feeds us? What kind of trouble and plagues are we about to bring upon ourselves?

Here he foolishly allowed his audience a second for the weighty words to sink in, which allowed the young woman time to leap to her feet. At first, in her characteristic stance of hands in trouser pockets, she made David wince at how surely she identified herself as Satan, but then, clasping her hands piously on her chest, she took up Oom Paulse's words, endorsed his reading, appealed to his God, to his Chief who had taught all black people what political sacrifice meant, praised the community values of respect for the elders, and then herself, in that clear and powerful voice introduced the fourth verse of Juig aarden juig to Rachael's famous tune. Thereafter it was plain sailing; she had them eating out of her hand. David admired the thoroughness of her homework.

Had the government not abused and maligned the Chief, called his appeals for justice sedition, thrown him into prisons? And had he not fought back? she declaimed.

Slowly she gathered them into her aura as she spoke of what the Movement could learn from the Griquas' faith and determination to control their own destiny. She praised the elders, appealed to the desires of the youth for change, and then called on David to speak as one of them. When she had brought them to the point of establishing a committee—there was no need, she said, to be calling themselves anything other than Griquas—Oom Paulse himself invited the women and the militant youth to join him, while she listened in humble silence.

Afterwards they went to Ant Mietjie's, where Dulcie took charge of the braaivleis. From the boot of her car she produced a bag of potatoes and several kilos of Namaqua boerewors, which she claimed was the best in the country and which further endeared her to people who knew that the sausage, with its crucial ingredients of coriander and clove, came not from Afrikaners but rather from the Kok ancestors, those slave cooks who would go nowhere without their spices. And so they were steered away from the new municipal building, where they would certainly have been raided.

They drank Ant Mietjie's chicory and coffee brew with sweet condensed milk. David watched people drifting towards Dulcie, bringing her the first potato, watched the young people hanging onto her every word, watched her speak to everyone except him. When the party ended he walked her to her lodgings; they had won the first round, but there was the future of the new branch to discuss.

Again they stood in the wash of the riot lights that swept all night long over the village, that turned the new concrete community centre and its large concrete square, the ugly architecture of surveillance, into an eerie, surreal emptiness. He congratulated her, shaking her hand as if they had just met, a hand that was surprisingly soft. Avoiding each other's eyes, they looked up simultaneously into the crammed night sky and saw a shooting star; she thought it meant something but could not remember what.

That night he resolved not to think of her, the statuesque woman who had not changed her rough corduroy trousers for the meeting but who had drawn a fine black line along her eyelids, turning those eyes—licensed for a second by a shooting star to look boldly into his own—into a dark and preternatural flash.

Those were the days, David sighs, when things were clear and we knew what had to be fought, what had to come down.

And Dulcie, I ask, did you see much of her in Town?

He shakes his head. No, not at all. In our positions it simply wasn't possible, we couldn't afford to be linked in any way. It's only lately, this year, that we've even seen each other again, but it's not like that, not what you think.

I ask again, How can it be possible to know so little about another human being who at some level matters to you?

David responds with the following: Dulcie ran away from home at the age of thirteen, leaving behind a drunken mother who would barely have noted her absence. Coming and going for years between casual jobs and houses of various friends, she was in the perfect situation to disappear for long periods without anyone questioning her whereabouts. At the age of twenty, already a trained cadre, she marked in a crowded open-air gathering the grinning policeman responsible for shooting a comrade standing right beside her. Within an hour she had him pinned in a doorway and in broad daylight shot him with his own Magnum; she pulled his policeman's hat over his face, took out the comb wedged in his sock and flung it away, emptied his wallet and donated the money towards the comrade's funeral expenses.

But she didn't tell you this herself, I venture. He glares at me suspiciously.

It's no use, I say. I give up. This is a task for someone addicted to your cloak-and-dagger struggle stuff.

I suppose, David confesses, that I don't see the need to flesh her out with detail, especially the kind invented by you. You see, she's not like anyone else; one could never, for instance, say that she's young or old or middle-aged. I think of her more as a kind of—and he has the decency to hesitate before such a preposterous idea— a kind of a scream somehow echoing through my story.

A scream, I laugh, a scream? You won't get away now with abstracting her. Besides, Dulcie herself would never scream. Dulcie is the very mistress of endurance and control. Dulcie knows that there is only a point to screaming if you can imagine someone coming to your rescue; that a scream is an appeal to a world of order and justice—and that there is no such order to which she can appeal.

And since when do you know so much about her? he asks.

David knows nothing of the art of inferencing, or perhaps he doesn't realise how much he has told me, even if it is somewhat opaque. Because of his inability to speak of her, he has promised to make notes on Dulcie. Writing things down, I suggested, would clarify what it is you want to say, bring to the surface things that you have not thought important, or simply have not remembered.

You mean, he retorted, make up a story, invent things.

But he promised all the same. What is clear from the sheaf of paper he hands over to me is that having tried and failed, he chose to displace her by working on the historical figure of Saartje Baartman instead. Thus he brought along the meticulously researched monograph, complete with novelistic detail: Saartje's foolish vanity, the treachery of white men, the Boer mistress who would not let her go, whose prophetic words rang in her ears, the seasickness on the ship, the cage in London decked with leopard skins, and, on the catwalk of her cage, the turning of the spectacular buttocks, this way and that, so that Europeans would crack their ribs with laughter. And the bitter cold of a northern winter that lasted all year long.

There are quite enough of these stories, I say impatiently. I believe ours can do very well without. Besides, what on earth has Baartman to do with your history?

But it's not a personal history as such that I'm after, not biography or autobiography. I know we're supposed to write that kind of thing, but I have no desire to cast myself as hero, he sneers. Nothing wrong with including a historical figure.

But she may not even have been a Griqua.

David gives me a withering look. Baartman belongs to all of us.

Ergo, we are all Griquas, I laugh.

A good editor would know what to do with this material, he persists.

There is no point in arguing; it is clear that the Baartman piece will have to stay.

And Dulcie? I ask.

He waves a helpless hand.

The page at the end of the unfinished section on Baartman is a mess, schoolboy scribbles that ought to have been thrown away. The foolscap pages had been torn in one clump from a pad so that they remained glued together at the top. It is possible that he had forgotten about the last page, or chosen to forget—that the following day, in a fit of exasperation, he had ripped out the entire thing and passed it on to me.

Although I have made numerous inferences from that last page, I do not quite know how to represent it. It is a mess of scribbles and scoring out and doodling of peculiar figures that cannot be reproduced here. I know that it is his attempt at writing about Dulcie, because her name is written several times and struck out. Then there are beginnings scattered all over, and at various angles that ignore the rectangularity of the paper, as if by not starting at the top or not following the shape of the page he could fool himself that it is not a beginning.

Truth, I gather, is the word that cannot be written. He has changed it into the palindrome of Cape Flats speech—TRURT, TRURT, TRURT, TRURT—the words speed across the page, driven as a toy car is driven by a child, with lips pouted and spit flying, wheels squealing around the Dulcie obstacles. He has, hauling up a half-remembered Latin lesson, tried to decline it.

trurt, oh trurt, of the trurt, to the trurt, trurt, by, with, from the trurt

But there is no one to ask. You pass by the austere figures sitting erect in their chairs, but their faces dissolve with the first movement of your lips. You hold up a board on which the question is written, but the disembarking figures that file past do not read it; their guarded eyelids drop like shutters. You find the place where questions are asked, a vast sports hall with no windows, flooded in electric light. Your words break down into letters that bounce about the hall, chasing each other until they fall plop through baskets jutting out from the walls, as if they have arrived. But you find a useless heap of play-letters without magnetic backs. There are rumours that if you go at midnight, as the clock strikes twelve, you can slip the words into the silent seconds between the strikes of the gong, but you do not believe this; you cannot see how they will not drown in the din.

There are all the symbols from the top row of the keyboard, from exclamation mark, ampersand, asterisk, through to the plus sign, then all are scored out. There is also a schoolboy's heart scribbled over, but not thoroughly enough to efface its asymmetrical lines.

TRURT . . . TRURT . . . TRURT . . .TRURT . . . the trurt in black and white . . . colouring the truth to say that . . . which cannot be said the thing of no name . . .

towhisperspeakshouthollercolour

Who, dear reader, would have the patience with this kind of thing? My computer has none; it has had enough, is embarrassed, and mysteriously refuses to process the elliptical dot-dot-dots, which I have to insert by hand.

It is with the greatest difficulty that I get David to admit that there is something between them. Then he retracts it immediately, saying that he does not know the meaning of that coy bourgeois description. Yes, they like each other, are attracted to each other, but there has never been any question of anything physical; he has no patience with that kind of messing about. Besides, Comrade Dulcie, herself a disciplined cadre, could not possibly have that kind of interest in him, would, like himself, have nipped it in the bud. It is also for this reason that he refuses to indulge Sally's jealousy, to explain anything to her, for as he says, there is absolutely nothing to explain.

So, I persist, people in your positions are immune to physical relationships, to passions?

He pulls a face. No, of course not, but it is out of the question, can't be tolerated. To indulge in such passion is to betray the cause, and there is far too much of that already. You see, he says condescendingly, it's a different world out there, one you'll never understand.

David instructs me to remove all references to a special relationship between him and Dulcie.

~

KOKSTAD 1991

Kokstad carries no traces of Andrew Abraham Stockenstrom le Fleur. There are no street names, no monuments, and it would seem no memories. In the houses to which the Bezuidenhout woman takes David, he learns nothing. That poor woman has sadly, predictably, let herself down by treating David as her guest, helping him with his enquiries, and now must brave the skinderbekke, gossips young and old, who are already talking about the new suitor. And a married man, too, her mother says bitterly.

This evening they are nevertheless hosting a little get-together for his benefit. People drift in as if for a formal meeting that they have decided beforehand to hijack; they are only too happy to speak about the old days, about what they have heard, but seem unwilling to talk about Le Fleur, and all David's efforts to steer the conversation in that direction are thwarted. There are, after all, not many real Griquas left, says the Bezuidenhout mother, having decided to come to his rescue. Those people of the past have disappeared, passed on, she supposed, with Le Fleur's many treks. That Le Fleur guy certainly messed things up, squandered people's money, puts in a neighbour. But no, seriously, says another, he did what he could, a clever ou; he was like a kind of lawyer, trying to get back the stolen land from those rogues, but there was of course no beating those white skelms. And so on to real politics and the New South Africa, David taking his practised position of saying little while encouraging them to speak.

That they ate dainty meat pies that had fluted edges and were garnished with sprigs of parsley, followed by delicious granadilla cake that must have taken hours to make, is a detail that he does not remember. But Ms. Bezuidenhout surely looks on silently and thinks of the waste as the men speak through mouthfuls of food that might as well be shovels of mealie pap. What, she wonders, is the point of copying in one's best hand recipes from *Cosmopolitan* or *Tribune* into a book with hard marbled covers? She might just as well cut them out and paste them any-old-how into an old ledger, but, she supposes, smoothing a crocheted doily through all that talk, a woman has her pride, has to keep up standards.

Heitse! croaks an ancient toothless woman, a silent, crooked shape who has been sitting all evening in a big chair with a tea towel tied around her neck and a rug around her knees. David, after the many handshakes, has forgotten about her, but now, just as the gathering breaks up, she cries out triumphantly, East Griqualand for the Griquas and the Natives! That's it, she says. That's what's been hiding from me all night. I knew there was a mouthful after the Griquas, and that's just it, For the Griquas and the Natives, that's the slogan the Chief taught us. We would come singing out of the church and form a circle and shake hands, and—she raises with difficulty her own trembling hand to show her height—just such a young girl I was, then the Chief would say, And now the children, and we raise our fists and call out and call out . . .

Her head bobs up and down, but the voice drifts off in the effort of remembering and her trembling fist refuses to lift off her lap.

So Ouma knew Le Fleur? David squats excitedly in front of her, but she shuts her eyes.

It's too late my boy, far too late, she mutters stubbornly, far too late, and her lips begin quivering, so that the Bezuidenhout woman comes to stroke her hand.

Granadilla cake is Ouma Rhodes's favourite and look, Ouma's eaten nothing, she complains.

The slice of cake lies untouched on the plate by her side. In all the excitement with the stranger no one has mashed and fed it to her, and now she shakes her head.

Late, too late, she says over and over, pursing her lips against the spoonful held before her by the young woman and trembling all over.

David tries to speak to her again but Bezuidenhout brushes him aside. No, leave Ouma Rhodes alone now, she needs to get home. So he offers to help carry the old woman next door.

She whimpers and struggles as they lift her into her sagging bed.

It's not the cake, my child, it's the wind in the tamboekie grass, sweeping it up, up sweeping it all. . . . And then, as her eyes fall on David, she says, staring wildly, Goeienaand my Opperhoof—good night my Chief—naand tog my hoof, naand . . . naaaghgh . . . trailing off into a snarled gurgle as her face contorts and her body convulses.

She didn't die, I exclaim.

Well, yes, he says, later that very night that we tucked her into bed. The Bezuidenhout woman said what a relief it was that it couldn't be blamed on the granadilla cake.

And you really don't remember the Bezuidenhout woman's name?

I told you, either Mary or Mandy. Something like that.

•

It is just as well that David is not serious about becoming a student. He is not much of a reader; he looks cursorily at the pages I produce, making no amendments to my attempts at a story. It is a measure of my incompetence that I expect to have several drafts, he says. For him that would be a serious failure, a waste of time; one surely would at least aim to get each section right in one final version. The thing should be kept in proportion: why write and write when it will take no more than one reading?

Even newspapers are of no interest to him. Why read their propaganda or the dreary reports of beauty competitions in dusty dorps? He prefers listening to the news headlines on the radio. Those who, like the comrades in the security department, believe in pondering over messages between the lines clearly have nothing better to do. No point, David says scornfully, in reading about freedom when we should be playing active roles towards attaining it. He just about tolerated the poetry readings at political rallies, and then valued the poems entirely for the passion with which they were delivered and which they whipped up in others; no one, after all, can hear much of the words on such occasions. A weapon of the struggle indeed, he laughs. Imagine the cadres spending time debating such nonsense. It's simply a question of having to humour the mad poets and painters in bandannas bandying about their stuff on the suburban battlefields of Observatory.

Why, then, does David want his story written—which is to say, have it read? Yes, he does feel ambivalent about this project, which invites a reader to perform a task he does not value. But he cannot explain: he is in a sense ashamed of appearing to be vain, of thinking of himself as special. It is not that he wants to be remembered; rather, it is about putting things down on paper so that you can see what there is, shuffle the pages around, if necessary, until they make sense. When I suggest a pseudonym, he looks scornful and says no, not that he wishes to be naive about the truth, but he does want his own story told, wants to acknowledge and maintain control over his progeny even if it is fathered from a distance. And how does truth relate to the gaps in the story? David shakes his head;

the corners of his mouth drop in disappointment or disbelief. It would seem that truth is too large a thing even for those who take on vast projects like changing the world, that it can only be handled in tit-bits: something like a sheet of steel has since fallen between the truth about things in the world and the truth about himself.

Today he does want something added to the text. Instead of deleting and rewriting a misremembered event from his childhood, he insists on the reader going through the tedious details of his own revision.

That David should have been thinking such trifling and inap-propriate thoughts in that hotel room bristling with terror is beyond me. He appears to be so disturbed by the falsehood of a memory that he asks me to rewrite the offending section, which is on one level a ruse; he perhaps regrets telling me about the hit list, or wishes to bring the Kokstad weekend to a close. But I can tell by his agitation, the way in which his jaw is set, that he is gen-uinely concerned about getting things straight, as he so disingen-uously puts it, and perhaps, rusted and ill fitting as it seems, it may be a key of some kind to the story. Clutching at straws and having agreed at the beginning not to overstep the role of amanuensis, I must put up with his digressions.

So it was not the truth, the episode embedded in his memo-ry for so many years that he does not know how it came to be there in its distorted form. But now, in his state of confusion—or what-ever it is called when one's eyes, tired of flitting between the butt of a gun and a list on a sheet of lined paper, settle on the improb-able Bakelite of a doorknob in the hope of being transported, of finding an explanation elsewhere—something else indeed takes over from the present. Sounds and images reel chaotically through time until a picture growing out of the morass, out of the cacoph-ony, slowly flickers into shape like the marks on a developing photograph, unintelligible at first until the black-and-white image, whole and in sharp focus, settles, and there it is—the truth, which he recognises after years of false memory.

David had come upon him by surprise. The man who had asked his father for directions and for food—old Dawid pointing with a bicycle part at the track to Rooiberg—and who he imagined trudging through the veld in search of the gypsum mines sat propped up behind the kraal wall, sleeping through the afternoon heat. His mouth hung open, the lips loose, and a fly made its way across his face, to-and-fro, hovering around the open mouth. Sinking to his haunches, clutching his knees, the child sat staring at the sleeping man, at the black and pink of his mouth, perhaps willing him to wake up, perhaps wanting to hear him speak, tell his story—but there is, in fact, only their mute figures. To read desire into that image is to fabricate once more, and David braces himself for the bald truth, the silence and the lack: just a child and a fly hovering about an insensible figure. There is no stone, no milky white crystal found on a riverbank, no whorled shell carrying the roaring message of the sea, of the world. There is a buchu essence bottle, from which those who travel alone get their comfort, and as if to explain its emptiness, the man gurgles drunkenly.

The child left on tiptoe, but his hands, he remembers, were plunged boldly in his pockets. And yes, he felt, as he stopped to check if the man was still asleep, a reassuring stone in his pocket; he felt no urge to part with it. Under his bed he had a collection of more precious stones, but the one between his fingers was not a thing to pass to another. Only the fly was there, tiptoeing tenderly about the mouth, and he remembers feeling relieved by that presence.

So it is possible, he says, to correct a false memory, in the end to arrive at the truth and find out what really happened.

Yes.

What more does he want? I can tell by the way he drums on his briefcase that this is not enough, that he is disappointed in my response. But have the terms of our collaboration changed? Am I no longer to consider myself as purely listener and scribe? Am I now expected to offer interpretations?

So? I venture.

Don't you see that if I once believed the first version to be true, who knows whether this one is not another invention? Is there any way of telling, when I was once so clear about what happened, the sequence of events, and I am now equally sure about the new version? Why believe anything at all?

So is this what it is all about—searching for a way out, for reasons not to believe his own eyes and ears? In which case the hotel could later become a classroom, the hit list a child's exercise book with the names of his classmates written with a flourish, and Dulcie a page torn out of a novel—a story re-remembered as belonging to another.

It occurs to me that David is, in spite of himself, becoming dependent on speaking to me. I say nothing, but I fear for him. For the telling that will surely take over.

~

CAPE TOWN 1991

It was mid-May, after a glorious spell of still sunshine, winter came suddenly, before dinner, wind pouncing viciously as if it had until then been kept banned behind the mountain. In the northern suburbs lights sputtered for minutes, electricity lost its nerve, and nearly cooked boboties and chicken pie crusts sighed and sagged in their ovens. Only Tygerberg stood eerily illuminated in the dark.

David arrived with fragments of Le Fleur's writings, a faded copy of *Griqua and Coloured People's Opinion* as well as photocopies of several dense, poorly typed or handwritten pages. He stood leaning against the door; his hand traversed the gap between door and frame, checking the cold wind that whistled into the room.

Cape Town houses were not made for winter, he said. The settlers must have persuaded themselves that this was a paradise of eternal summer in spite of the terrible wind and rain in the peninsula. And now we carry on the pretence.

I offered to turn on the single-bar electric heater, but he waved it away, turning to leave. As if he hadn't come of his own volition, I had to persuade him to stay. He seemed not to know whether he wanted to show me the manuscripts. We sat for a while at the kitchen table, listening to the frenzied rain on the tin roof—not huddled, but an aura of sorts spun by the sound of the elements drew us together even as I toyed with the boerewors on my plate. When he broke the silence he spoke loudly, as if to prevent me from picking up on another level of speech, on words uttered on another wavelength that threatened to become audible.

David needed help reading the typescript; he could not understand why it was indecipherable, why it appeared to be written by an illiterate madman when indeed he knew that the self-taught Griqua chief was nothing of the kind. He had seen several copies of the journal that Le Fleur produced, as well as letters to officials with various defences of his position. He looked troubled, made as if to hand over the papers, then withdrew them. This gesture, at the very beginning of our collaboration, came to characterise his relationship with me. David did not at that stage intend it to continue beyond reading the fragments, did not at that stage think about anything other than piecing together the Le Fleur story. He had become obsessed with childhood memories about the Chief, by a sense of mystery surrounding the stories of his own family's relation to the Chief.

What, for instance, he said, do you make of this letter to his son, Adam:

> Wees versigtig, ek word gevind waar ek gesoek word; wanneer gesoek word, word ek nooit gevind nie—Take care, I am found where wanted; when wanted never found—and Mother still drinks of the clean waters of your grandfather, Captain Kok, mother drinks it so slowly today. The great problem of the white people is that their thoughts have come to a standstill, they sit like rabbits on a stone, the young Boers hand over their work to our young people. . . .

I giggled. David gave me his schoolteacher look and continued, Listen to this entry from his diary:

Present-day churches are all military churches. Boys are trained for war; girls are trained for war. Yes the Griqua Choir Girls, there is the new kingdom, for they are preparing for singing when the harlot and the beast is punished in the voice of many waters: Say Hallelujah. . . . No Liquor Brewers, no war material makers, no greedy landgrabbers will be left, no military training, no airforces, no Man-o'-wars will be made by the Girl Kingdom.

Ah, a crackpot visionary and a proto-feminist, I laughed. Does it not prove that the man simply isn't what you want him to be?

He kept silent. The wind howled in its attempt to carry off the roof; the hibiscus tree beat itself against the windowpanes, and, not a little afraid of the vicious wintry night, I was pleased to have David there. Only once, as we sat at the table poring over the type-script, did the electricity falter. The lights flickering on and off added to the bizarrerie of the text, its strange mixture of English and Afrikaans, the outlandish syntax, the madness that dripped from the ill-formed, fallen branches of those sentences.

I'll go back, he said, to my meeting in Guguletu.

What became clear as the lightning flashed across the window was that these texts were no cause for fear and anxiety, that David, having come from the meeting wild-eyed and trembling, was using the Griqua material to displace that of which he could not speak.

Sitting half-propped in his bed, his green eyes ablaze in the weathered brown face, his jaw set with the fury and frustration of years, he hisses at the scribe perched nervously on a three-legged stool, a thin, creaking man who knows that it is not worth his while to interrupt, to ask the old man to go more slowly, to admit that he did not quite catch it. He, the amanuensis, would not dare to ask any questions, would write the words exactly as they fall from the Chief's lips, or improvise where he had not quite heard, not quite understood. The double possessive of the Namaqua *hulle se* surely would be his own, since that is not a construction that occurs in the Chief's variety of Afrikaans.

Justice, he shouts, nothing more than justice is what I demand so don't bring me your English judges no don't bring me your Scottish judges who know nothing of the beauty of the divine scales they may dip or dive this way and that but in the end they must quiver in celestial balance as the truthful mind one that is free of prejudice and greed well the truthful mind settles in divine justice such a mind we have not one among the thieving missionaries look look those scales are ablaze with heavenly light the bush of Moses burns. . . .

As a flash of winter sunlight bounces off the window pane, he struggles against the pillows.

No I won't go to Rhodesia rather again Robben Island or the Breakwater for me I have no fear of prisons but governor of Rhodesia oh no you can't buy me off I am no coloured cur we have fashioned ourselves into a proud people a grand Griqua race no coloured nameless bastards I Paramount Chief of the Griquas the Opperhoof . . .

And then he falls back whimpering, calling for Rachael— Ag, Dorie, Dorie—who is long since dead, so that the thin young man of tired wrists, more adept at tucking him back into bed and soothing his brow with vinegar water, leaps to attention.

Once, in the beginning, he had tried to reason, to assure the old man with his knowledge of history that there was no need to go to Rhodesia, that there had been no question of a governorship, but having roused the Chief's fury, he now desists, and instead, in silence, simply mops the revered brow and strokes his hand, grateful for being a Griqua rather than a currish coloured and, above all, grateful for the break from writing.

But it could not always have been like that. The language is not always that of dictated speech; rather, the typed pages, on long foolscap sheets that ignore the lines, appear to be transcribed from a handwritten text by someone who was neither a good typist nor well versed in English syntax or vocabulary, since he was unable to guess at possible constructions where the writing was illegible.

•

David was skeptical. Surely it is in code, he said, on another late-night visit in that terrible week of relentless wind and rain in which we could barely hear ourselves speak. One surely cannot have such a mixture of good and bad language, such a muddle; besides, it is known that the Chief was fluent in both languages, that he had a way with words.

I explained that it was possible to speak well and not be able to write, that Rachael may have been responsible for the earlier well-written pieces.

He persisted. Why could it not be in code?

Are you able to decode it? I asked.

No, but I could ask people in security who have expertise in that kind of thing.

So, saying what he ought not to have said to an outsider, he revealed the level of his involvement, deliberately, without signalling the act, and I knew that there was more to it, that things were not as they should be, and waited not without fear for what would come next, for it went without saying that such a breach of loyalty could not be without consequence.

I insisted on the influence of an amanuensis. Except, of course, that the Chief's slippage into fantasy also makes his syntax slip accordingly, often introducing a code-switch, by which I simply mean the movement between English and Afrikaans.

I do not overlook the effects of senility. Or the effects of habitual communion with God.

Communion with God brought many miracles, explained Ouma Ragel, fussing about her pots and pans. Unlike Great-ouma Antjie's close, round hut, where little Davie was drugged with wood smoke, the cooking shelter, still round but attached to a new rectangular brick house, was roofless. Here a fire crackled under the three-legged pot, and Ouma's stories of the Chief were flavoured with the rich smell of mealies, beans, and marrowbones that simmered all day long.

The Paramount Chief had written a million letters to Queen

Victoria to show that good woman how her subjects, in the bright light of Africa, had succumbed to the darkness within their hearts. This civilisation thing that Europeans had brought along was on the whole, he had come to believe, like the human heart, a two-sided thing, not altogether bad—even if their hymn-singing was nothing to write home about—but it was the instability, the eggshell fragility of the great idea that made him shake his head in disappointment. Why did it sway so drunkenly between light and dark, unheedful of the cracks revealed for all the world to see? What could be done to preserve the high ideals of civilisation? Le Fleur, bursting with pious energy, had declared himself willing to take on the task. Was it the heat, he asked, that made her subjects arrogant and bad mannered, ungrateful and blatantly uncivil towards their hosts? The good queen had sighed and called for vinegar and brown paper, for truly the problem hurt her head, and thus she had been unable to reply. For King Edward and his role in the prison miracle the Chief had a special regard, and thus high hopes of a solution. He had, after all, approved the presentation of the country's finest diamond, the Cullinan, as a birthday present for the king. But the new monarch, burdened with his inheritance—the multitude of colonies, his crown impossibly heavy with the Cullinan square brilliant, the weight of the Star of Africa in the sceptre such that he could barely lift it—was similarly swathed in the traditional vinegar and brown paper and thus could not muster a reply to the numerous letters.

Lord Milner was furious. What right had the upstart in rough leather breeches to write to royalty? Why did these people not busy themselves with practical things? Would Le Fleur not be better employed seeing to those filthy round huts that no God would risk entering until they have been straightened out into rectangular dwellings? Milner had had enough of Griqua troublemaking. The governor should not have to put up with representations from any Tom, Dick, or Harry; no, he would not condescend to see the man.

But, said Andrew Abraham Stockenstrom le Fleur, this time standing six feet tall in a fine dark suit, he was the Griqua chief, heir to Adam Kok, and in the sharpest of sharp letters he forced that haughty man to receive him. Finding himself at last in Lord Milner's room, into which a young man in a gold-braided jacket had shown him, Le Fleur proudly declined a seat but paced up and down, examining his peculiar surroundings. There he saw, through the contemptuous eye of the liveried attendant, the loftiness of civilisation realised in a high ceiling and elaborate plaster moulding. An intricate ceiling rose carried the weight of a chandelier from which crystal light bounced in the late morning and decorative thistles bristled along the gilt-edged cornices. The pale blue of the walls was covered with portraits of empire builders. In a recess there was a fine engraving of an early Cape scene with slaves going merrily about their business—the only cheer among those austere, ornate pictures—but he averted his eyes from such levity. It was the great men of power, executed in fine dark oils, with their bright white collars, wearing their grandness on their painted sleeves, that held him to attention.

The Chief was thus occupied, leisurely pacing the picture gallery, whilst Lord Milner kicked his heels and drummed his fingers through the minutes he needed to let pass so as to keep the upstart waiting. Under the watchful eye of the young attendant guarding the silver knickknacks, Le Fleur found himself mesmerised by those Argus-eyed walls, drawn into the optical tricks of white collars spinning into the dark paint, until, to steady his palpitating heart, he placed himself among the painted men of power. Instead of thinking of the arguments he had rehearsed all year, he displaced a minor colonial figure to settle himself in the gilt frame where, arranged between two dignitaries, he became yet another image in dark oils with a stark white collar. As the minutes ticked by he saw the advantage of being somewhat to the left where the light fell more kindly, and so boldly supplanted Cecil John Rhodes himself. Now, frowning comfortably in his frame, he saw himself as chief of all coloured people under the banner of Griquas, for why would people choose to carry such an indecent name when they could all be Griquas? And so it came about that Lord Milner found him charming and malleable, meekened with power-pride; the vulgar documents of land claims and petitions remained folded in an inner pocket.

When Le Fleur left, a peacock, waiting on the lawn, raised and spread its jewelled tail in which he saw his own green eyes reflected a hundred times. Then the creature, crying pitifully, steered him down the avenue, so that the man was forced by that Argus-eyed fan to walk backwards, all the way down, along borders of blue-beaked strelitzias, down to the public road where his old Ford waited.

A sellout, David is forced to admit, that's what he became. All those lofty ideals, pshewt, he whistled, lost in their own grand and godly rhetoric. No, I have some sympathy for our comrades who turn the wrong way; it's not easy to resist a meal when you're hungry, not through week after week of not being able to feed your children. But they don't kid themselves that they're doing the right thing; they understand their own treachery, don't turn it into an ideology. Now take our great man: the Chief continued to believe in himself; he had no idea that he was betraying his own ideals, falling into the hands of the policymakers. In fact, he offered them Apartheid, reinterpreted his own words to suit a new belief in separate development. Siss, he said, pulling a face, a separate homeland for a separate Griqua race! He should have been kept in prison; nothing like prison for keeping one's ideas sound, for keeping the politician's hands clean, he echoed.

So you have no sympathy with him?

Of course not. Why do you think I've given my life fighting for a nonracial democracy?

~

DULCIE and the events surrounding her cannot be cast as story. I have come to accept this view of David's, especially since he has been more cooperative of late.

There is no progression in time, no beginning and no end. Only a middle that is infinitely repeated, that remains in an eternal, inescapable present. This is why David wants her simply outlined, wants her traced into his story as a recurring imprint in order to outwit her fixedness in time, in order for her to go on, to proceed, as in the stories he sometimes finds time to tell his children: and then and then and then. . . . Thus, as a result of doing this or that, a jewel is found, a frog turns into a prince, a maiden restored to her true love. But for Dulcie, whose life is swathed in secrets, such resolution is not possible; the thin anecdotes, the sorry clutch of hints and innuendoes, do not lead to anything.

Yes, he confesses, even if a full story were to be figured out by someone, it would be a story that cannot be told, that cannot be translated into words, into language we use for everyday matters.

There is no such thing, I say, as a story that cannot be told.

Then it remains for you to show how it is done, he sneers.

His eyes move along the length of the table, back and forth, lingering over the knots in the wood. Once, thank God, once only—he looks up at me, into me, with irises a ghostly green line of light around pupils black and dilated, like those of a trapped animal, mute, distorted, and it is I who must look away and pray that he will say nothing.

This is an intrusion, a weight that I cannot carry. That no amanuensis should have to carry, I later decide as I ponder the boundaries of my task.

~

Many were given to lying from the mere habit of freely indulging the vagaries of a romantic imagination. They invented stories and enjoyed gossip, they loved the marvellous and exaggerated greatly.

S.J. Halford, *The Griquas of Griqualand*

BEESWATER 1922

When Gert cleared his throat to ask about the function of the quarries, Le Fleur cut him short with a speech about virtue and toil, about fighting idleness and improving their lot. They, men of little faith, were to lift their hearts as they raised their pickaxes, lest the instruments blunder into barren rock and turn blunt.

You will gain nothing by shouting red flag. The only flag that will save you is your pick and shovel. Plant your seed, and whilst others are carrying red flags and shouting destruction and the rights of the worker, your children will be eating the fruits of your labour.

Gert stared in puzzlement. He knew nothing of red flags, had never shouted about any flag; why would anyone shout about such a thing? And as for fruit, the fig and peach they had planted refused to live on brackish water. So that the Chief had to change his tack: only glad souls rejoicing in toil would be rewarded, for even in the most barren patch of earth God had left traces of his bounty. God had not abandoned them, no, he was testing them with the heat and the drought. Without physical toil they would not enjoy good health, and without good health the soul would not grow.

In midspeech he heard the words that old Eduard had borrowed from Sterne—the due contention for mastery betwixt the radical heat and the radical moisture—saw them crack open like stones, revealing themselves loudly, so that he, too, boomed: Here we have the radical heat, right here held in the stones that must be cracked open with pickaxes, even as God demanded in the quarries of Robben Island, but we must balance the heat with a vision of radical moisture. And before his parched eyes rose the image of water, a burn tumbling down a mountain gorge, dashing against the rock its cool white spray, atomised into radical moisture that would be transported to the desert to sprinkle over the entire volk and coax the stubborn trees into fruitfulness.

Take to the water, he thundered. You men of dusty faith must be drenched and baptised into fresh life.

Casting his eyes over the cracked earth and the goats grazing listlessly on ghanna bush, Gert protested, But there is no water, no rain; it will take some powerful medicine men to bring us rain this year.

Well, what kind of talk was that? That was the problem with the fellow, a raw pagan at heart. He felt a pang of shame at his increasing impatience with Gert.

Think, he said patiently, just think of how only a bucketful of winter rain in June or July can turn the veld into a painted sea of Namaqua daisies and the ploughed furrows into bright green lines. It is that idea of rain—except in the memoir he calls it pre-cipitation—that memory of moisture that can cool you down in the heat of the summer sun. Since the rain will not fall of its own accord, well, then, we will send out our intermediaries, our Rain Sisters, who will travel to the Cape peninsula and then to Robberg, and from there bring back the idea of radical moisture that will drench us through the months of drought, so that the wilting pumpkin leaf will lift its head in pride and the orange flower trumpet its praise and this dusty land bellow before God its hidden core of greenness.

Rain Sisters, Gert asked in blunt Namaqua idiom, and what for a thing is that?

There was no need to think through the details. He saw in a flash that the women blessed with the most bountiful behinds, the queens of steatopygia, were the chosen Brides of Christ—that they would be the ones to carry water to the promised land. Not the volksmoeder, Rachael Susanna, who was no longer in good health, but Antjie and four other women who had been shaped by God into perfect vessels for collecting and carrying back radical moisture from the rain-soaked Cape peninsula with which to temper the radical heat of Namaqualand.

Gert muttered that Antjie, unlike the others, was not a virgin, was already middle-aged, but the Chief growled that this was not what Rain Sisters were about and that such vulgar comments were never again to be uttered.

We must revive the old customs Dorie, he said to his wife, those that have fallen into disuse; for he believed the idea, which had been born so smoothly, to be his memory of a lapsed tradition.

I do not recall such a thing, Rachael frowned, measuring an altered brown frock on her youngest, her Deborah, who, having reached an ungainly height, needed an extension to the hem. No, she mumbled, a pin clamped between her lips, I have never heard any-one in the Kok family speak of radical moisture.

You must have forgotten, he said. In the old days I have a clear notion of my own father, Captain Kok's chief secretary—as if she did not know—speaking of the ritual of Rain Sisters carrying water from the peninsula to bring rain to Griqualand West.

As for Rachael, she wondered whether she would have liked to be one of those, to get away from the harshness of the place, the stifling summer, the unrelieved grey of the land, but she had grown too listless to contemplate a journey. Her mouth now stuffed with pins, she could only nod at her husband's insistence that the ritual was a practice of the past. She had certainly never heard of it. In her beloved Kokstad, from where, on still nights, you could hear the distant roar of the Mzintlava, there had not, of course, been any need for water-bearing women of bounteous bottoms.

There are many stories about the Rain Sisters, about how, when they returned from Town after the water gathering trip, their long green Voortrekkerish frocks seemed freshly ironed, their fairy wings of dew-dappled gossamer crisp as the leaves of a new storybook. About how their feet did not quite touch the ground and their veldskoens were transformed into crystal slippers from which water sprayed as they walked. And about how, in the middle of summer, Noah's rainbow curved its colours across a clear blue sky, announcing their arrival. But these are not true, except for the gossamer wings of water, which indeed always trembled in the light above their heads. Otherwise, their Voortrekker frocks of green drill were splattered with filth, their veldskoens grey with dust, their throats and kappies alike caked with the mud of time and travel. For these women who had walked from Clanwilliam, singing their hymns, surviving on water alone, and holding aloft their bulging water bags of canvas, fell at the feet of the elders waiting by the church with a resounding Juig aarden juig. The Chief gave thanks to God, the water was ritually sprinkled over the shoulders of the Rain Sisters, and only thereafter the warm roosterbrood and mugs of steaming coffee brought out for the weary pilgrims.

It was then that Antjie, who fainted on her first return, was caught by the Chief, held in those strong arms, and, in the last second of consciousness, found her eyes drowned in the melting green of his own. But that moment, snared in the hurly-burly of celebrations, did not return as she surfaced from the swoon. Momentous as it was, she remembered little, for all was erased by the sudden darkness at midday when the world went dead still just before warm rain began to fall loudly throughout the Union of South Africa, drenching the earth, swelling the dead tubers so that within weeks the land was ablaze with carpets of Namaqua daisy, with lurid green ghanna bush and with the succulent milkbush that swelled the udders of the cows. In the shade they kept rows of three-legged cast-iron pots in which the excess milk fermented into heavenly curds.

To be a Rain Sister is going to be no ordinary business, no joke, Gert warned in his gentle, irritating manner.

As if Antjie did not know that; as if this burden disguised as an honour did not weigh heavily on her heart. And then there was the business about being thought a virgin, for although she was childless it did not of course mean that they were celibate—not that she would have minded, but Gert being a man of God, was a man all the same. It was altogether an awkward business being in the limelight, being looked at by all. She tried not to think of the intense gaze of the Chief, for that made her blood bubble afresh and then she found herself wanting. Would that she be instructed on her every step, her every thought, but Gert said that that was all foolishness. Miss Rachael said that she had been a fine example of hard work, frugality, and moral uprightness, that honour could not be kept away where honour was due. But she feared that she was just not up to it, quite apart from the physical stamina required to walk all that way without, as the Chief instructed, any frivolous women's talk or gossiping. Since they supposed that all their talk was frivolous women's talk and gossip, they walked in silence in order not to jeopardise the mission. They walked to Clanwilliam, where they caught the post office bus to Malmesbury, from whence they walked again to Cape Town, to the tightly packed lanes and smelly latrines of Welcome Estate, where a Griqua choir revived them with hymns and bathed their feet in mustard. But what if it did not rain for weeks, would they have to stay in those crowded places waiting in the cold wind, so far from home? Miss Rachael said no, it always rained in Cape Town.

If the truth be told, Antjie would have given anything to get out of the vague and heavy responsibilities of a Rain Sister, which she could not quite fathom. Whatever the expectations were of her, she now knew that she could not live up to them. The silence of the journey was oppressive; it brought her face to face with things she could not bear to think about. How often she felt her jumbled prayers spill into the red dust, unfit to soar to heaven, where God could not possibly make sense of the shifts in her distracted pleas or praise. The only constant was a pair of fierce green eyes that rose from the dust to come between her and God, eyes that held her own transfixed and stirred in her breast such turmoil that she had to stop with a hasty amen.

On her return she avoided the others, wandered on her own into the veld for wood or to see to the goats, the better to savour that vision of the eyes, vulnerable as raw yolks on the sand, or to relive the rare moments when that familiar voice midst the sermonising or the barking of instructions grew suddenly gentle, lost its thread in galloping copulas, soft as song, whilst the eyes turned to her, lapping at her own until she heard in their albumen embrace every word translated into a liquid language of love. Or had she imagined it? How delicious to remember and to doubt, for it was a whisper of syllables that she raked together in such reverie, and in truth, she could not have borne to hear it spelt out loud; she would, as she returned with a pile of wood balanced on her head, allow those syllables to scatter once more. Thus she was able to make the fire and cook a wholesome pot of mealies and beans flavoured with kaiings and listen to Gert's rough tales with kindness, lowering her own voice into sweet remembrance.

And so it came about that after the years of barrenness Antjie the Rain Sister conceived a child. Improbable as that was, she had known at once, and marvelled at the miracle of the eyes that had penetrated her body, lapped at every cell, probed every cavity, that had turned into flames licking about her every organ—lungs, liver, kidneys, heart—and made her blood simmer with love. And her womb having been filled in that fire, she felt at last at peace with God, who had taken charge and translated the locked gaze, the whispered syllables, this time into the substance of flesh. Only once did she wonder what it would be like to be with her lover, but, like Mother Mary, knew that it would not do to think of such a thing, was grateful instead, as the child stirred in her belly, for that consummation of the gaze, for the silence of their language. Thus blessed by the radical moisture that in her heart she had carried also for her unborn child, she treasured for as long as was possible her secret of a little boy of strong limbs and stern voice, whose green eyes would blaze as he spoke.

When she finally told Gert, he broke, overjoyed, into the prohibited kabarra dance and declared that they would slaughter a sheep to celebrate. Antjie warned against extravagance, against tempting fate, but no, he said, the old sheepskins would not do for a spanking new child, so he slaughtered the animal and cured the skin himself with utmost care. There were to be no shortcuts as he salted the damp fleece, still warm with the flesh it had carried, and kept a vigilant eye on the drying process, for the softness of the skin depended on manipulating it at just the right moment. A stiff, rough skin would just not do for their baby; it would have to be as malleable after the process as before, and he imagined a new bundle of damp little girl with Antjie's slanted black eyes, wrapped in the fleece that would give her a form, so that she would falter like a newborn lamb in the veld, not quite finding her feet.

There was no need to tell Andrew Abraham Stockenstrom le Fleur of the miracle. He nodded knowingly; he had seen a vision of the child some months before, and said yes, of course, they must give thanks that Antjie had fulfilled her duty as Rain Sister to God and to the volk and had been blessed accordingly. For the first time he took her hand, tenderly, in both his own, but that prudent woman, fearing the language of the eyes and thus for the health of the child in her womb, refused to look up lest her heart burst into flame. The hours went by, and she could not remember when he let go of that hand, which continued to tremble like a captured bird.

She need not have feared; he would never have spoken, never

have acknowledged the feat of telegony, and besides, he was already occupied with the radical transformation of the cult of the Rain Sisters. Since the city had become a den of iniquity, the tradition, like all good traditions, had to be changed. The matron was replaced by a healthy young girl, and the water was now to be collected only a few miles away at Ratelgat. In an elaborate ceremony the radical heat was captured and sealed in a bottle half-filled with hot sand, into which the procured water was poured. God, presiding over the chemical reaction of heat and radical moisture, ensured that the mixture, shaken over the parched earth, raged and frothed so that the rain clouds never failed to appear, bringing a coolness, even if it did not always rain. Never again, however, were they to witness the lusty downpour of Antjie's days as Rain Sister.

The baby was a girl, with bright eyes set like jewels in her brown face and a booming voice that would brook no delay of the breast, so that, in her sling of softest sheepskin, she spent whole days tied to Antjie's chest. It was Gert who declared that she looked like a Le Fleur, and indeed, those telegonous eyes were a brilliant green. Little Ragel, he called her, but not without seeking first the permission of the volksmoeder, Rachael Susannah le Fleur, who was only too happy to have her own Deborah mind the baby, who in the process grew to look so like her minder. The Chief indulged her like a grandchild, called her his own wee Ralie and dandled her on his knee, but was careful to avoid the mother's eyes. Even after the Sunday service, when they all shook hands in a circle outside the church, he barely held hers for fear of another miracle.

And how, I ask, have you arrived at this mumbo jumbo? Was it one of Ouma Ragel's stories?

Not in so many words. Lately I've been trying to put together her many stories and hints, work things out for myself. I'm not convinced that Ouma herself was absolutely sure, but there are so many indications that the Chief cared too much for Antjie—not to mention, of course, the fact that some people think I look remarkably like him, and I must say that in certain photographs I can see a resemblance.

The some people are of course a single old woman literally in her death throes, but I let it pass. I am inclined to believe that there is another, a literary origin for Antjie as Rain Sister, an Afrikaner poem called 'Die Dans van die Reën'—The Dance of the Rain—which I cannot quite remember. These days David, like an old man, is easily transported to his childhood, to the crumbling raw brick of the schoolroom and the daily recitation of poems and prayers. In the afternoon heat that crackled like crossed wires in the reed and clay roof, with dust sifting on to the pages of the book, they chanted in Afrikaans:

> Oh the dance of our Sister!
> First she peeps slily over the mountain top,
> and her eyes are shy;
> and she laughs softly.
> And from far off she beckons with one hand;
> her armbands flash and her beads glitter;
> softly she calls.
>
> She tells the winds of the dance,
> she invites them, for the clearing is wide and it will be
> a great wedding. . . .
>
> she spreads out the grey kaross with both her arms;
> the breath of the wind is lost.
> Oh, the dance of our Sister!

He remembers only these fragments from the beginning and the end, but I also recall the stampede of antelopes as they race to see her footmarks in the sand.

The Griqua Rain Sisters were, of course, without the dance, without the decoration of native beads and copper anklets that Le Fleur would have considered backward and pagan. But we decide that the legendary flower-fairy-cum-princess image is a cultural translation, a severely Calvinised version culled from Eugene Marais's poem, that it is one of the many signs of the Chief's confused adoption of a native voice that was in fact produced by a European.

•

It was at this point that Rachael Susanna's body resisted. Her joints stiffened and refused. The tendons that held things together grew weary, lost their elasticity, and seized up with the glue of despondency, which had leaked into that body since the teens of the century.

Her decline had started with Andrew's first letter to General Louis Botha congratulating that one on becoming South Africa's first prime minister. Since her voice, too, was fading, she could no longer suppress through a hymn those words that came flooding back:

I have done with politics and trust the government entirely to see us justly treated. How necessary it is for our welfare, for the advancement of coloured people, that you should be called to office now. I have given up the quest for restitution. A homeland for the Griquas is all I ask and am sure that we can rely on your benevolence. I have done, he dictated, pacing up and down with his hands behind his back, I have done—do you hear me, Dorie—done with the Griqualand question. Does any man think, after the deception of the kaffirs, we will ever be disposed to trust or even work together with them no matter on what question?

That was when her wrist first twitched with pain, refusing to move across the page, and before her very eyes a gnarled arthritic knob pushed its way up through the not yet wrinkled skin.

But Andrew, she said, all that Sigcau business was a long time ago, and how would we know under what threats the poor man turned informer?

Dorie, you had better think of your duty, woman, was his perspicacious reply.

The thought of duty would have come more readily were it not for the womanly wrist that went limp with pain, rebelling also against him calling her *woman* in that way, for had she not through all his schemes and agitations been a good woman, a loyal wife?

Later that year, at the big meeting in Pretoria, her very ears were to whistle in disbelief. After days of distress, of no eating and much praying, of storming about in bad temper, Andrew was rescued by his God—although she felt sure that it was the devil himself come in disguise, and had he confided in her, that is just what she would have said. Oh yes, never mind about woman's ignorance or foolish heart. She would have said, Andrew, you have now lost all your marbles; how else could you mistake Satan's sour words for those of God?

But no, he made an announcement to the whole wide world, and his solution to the great coloured question—problem, he called it—made her ears suck inward with a whistle of disbelief, so that at the time the words conveniently whizzed past. Now, sitting all day in the large chair that Andrew had himself made for her, those words, surely confused, came to mock her with a horrible clarity:

Coloured, he sneered, coloured! Let us for a moment do without the name given to us by others. Let us think instead of the Eur-Africans, those through whose veins the blood of European settlers visibly flows, and find our own solutions. Let us leave the Union to the Europeans as a white man's country; they, too, must learn to stand on their own feet and do without our labour, make their own arrangements with the kaffirs. Since they cannot look upon their shame, since they must discriminate against their own flesh, we whose very faces are branded with their shame will remove ourselves from their sight. Here good people, is the solution for God's stepchildren: absolute separation. From white and from black. We shall have our own territory, land in which we as a people can live and develop separately. Let us work together as one nation in our own homeland, where, through work and work and more hard work, we can uplift ourselves. With the help of God we will till the ancestral lands of Adam Kok and build a prosperous nation, a separate Griqua nation.

Yes, God's stepchildren. He thought it a fine phrase, and when Mrs. Millin launched her novel of that title only a year after the Rain Sisters set out on their first mission, Andrew was thrilled. He saw no reason to read it; he assumed her story would be an endorsement of his ideas—why else would she borrow his phrase?—and so gave it his fulsome praise.

As for Rachael, not a bar of music came to her rescue, not a line of Juig aarden juig could she summon this time to drown the perfidy. Oh, what chance had she had of persuading him of the evil of his plan when the people drowned his voice in applause. A people bludgeoned into stupidity, who could not see that he was rebelling against God himself.

Too long, he raved, have we been wandering in the desert; we will have our own homeland of sweet grass and precious stones, a virgin soil untouched by Europeans, a soil that cries out for cultivation. For it is in agriculture that our future lies.

Then Rachael had kept silent. Which is not to be mistaken for keeping her peace. She thought bitterly of woman's labour, of the joy of birth that could never be shameful—never a problem, yet there was Andrew, spreading the infection of shame. And if European blood was to flow visibly through the veins of the chosen people, distinguishing them from others, she feared for her own. Had there, in those days, been nylon stockings to stretch over frizzy heads, she may well have done so, for who was to know where lines would be drawn? In this world without song, anything could happen; it was no longer the world of her long-dead uncle, Captain Adam Kok, who spoke a different language—the language of African freedom—as they galloped over the hills to the sound of rushing wind and water.

Even if she then chose not to think of Andrew's strange ideas, to try and carry on as before, her body resisted. She could no longer be his secretary; her wrists seized up in the very presence of a pen, and the smell of ink made her sneeze uncontrollably, scattering the great man's reformed thoughts hither and thither, so that he would rather do without her services.

We shall have to trust to the Boers, he said. I grew up with the Boers in the Free State where they treated us like burghers, sat in the same school benches with Boer children, and will always speak of them with honour and respect.

But the many letters written to President Botha remained unanswered, as that great politician was too busy thinking up good, workable schemes for relieving real black people of the burden of land, so that only after three years in office did he pass the

Natives' Land Act. Then, sitting through a Sunday sermon that failed to lift her spirits, Rachael could not believe her ears as the ignorant Elder Cloete chose to list in his praise prayer the Land Act as one of the Chief's predictions. Oh, she thought wearily, enough is enough, and rose from Andrew's side without thinking, shuffled right out of the church, and settled herself in her chair on the stoep to stare out at the blue of Maskam mountain.

Andrew said not a word, which she took to be a sign of contrition. But in the early hours of the morning he shook her sagging shoulder and in an anxious voice whispered, Dorie, Dorie, is it not so? Was the Land Act not a miracle; was it not my predicted punishment for Sigcau's treachery?

Miracle? she spluttered into her pillow. She struggled to manoeuvre the bounteous behind in which she stored her sadness, so that in those days of silence it had grown quite unmanageable, and, finally sitting upright, still dazed with sleep, said in clear outrage: Miracle, my arse! It's a disgrace, a sin, a bloody disaster; it's the end of all predictions, the very death of us all.

Then there followed profanities and obscenities which cannot be given here. Ugly, unimaginable words that made him press his hands against his ears and stare at her in mute disbelief. Rachael Susanna, her abuse lapsing into gibberish, sank back under the rough sheets and imagined the words safely tucked in her dreams, so that the next morning, as he rose to plump up her cushion and settle her in the chair, there was no need to mention that outburst.

And so it came about that she fell apart, and was held together through the last months only by sitting all day long, in the chair that Andrew had made for her, contemplating Maskam's varying shades of blue.

∼

KOKSTAD 1991

David comes down to breakfast with hair vigorously brushed after a night without sleep, spruce in his mattress-pressed trousers.

The shaven-headed waiter in the far corner of the room is busily organising breakfast. David waits at his table until the man is free to attend to him, to invite him to collect the food of his choice at the central bar as he had done the previous day. Listening intently—for there is something about the man that he can't put his finger on—David allows him to go through the procedure, the entire gamut of food, as if he has not heard it all before. The man has lost his taste for buffoonery; he explains soberly and patiently how one should order bacon, eggs, and sausages from the cook before taking one's orange juice and cereal, so that the breakfast runs smoothly. He is sure that David, being a busy man, has no time to wait, and he turns to the cook to say in his language that their guest must not be kept waiting.

Nkosi kakhulu, David thanks him.

Sir knows our language? the man crows.

A little, David smiles. You know how one comes to know a smattering.

The man is delighted. Yes, in the New South Africa we need to communicate with each other. And then, as if remembering his role, he turns on an American Deep South voice, Yessiree, we sure do.

Ebrahim comes in while he pours his coffee, comes over to see whether his guest is okay, has he slept well. Well, yes, nothing like clean country air to rest the mind and the body.

Listen man, he says, come down to the bar for happy hour this evening at six. This is quite the spot on a Saturday night, everyone gathers here and we can all do with fresh intellectual conversation. You can tell us how the New South Africa is shaping up there in the Cape.

Thank you, yes, perhaps, but I don't know about happy hour—not my kind of thing.

Come on, old chap, and Ebrahim slaps him genially on the backside. You're a coloured teacher, man, and who can keep a coloured teacher from an extra drink, hey?

He laughs uproariously as he walks off.

Through the plateglass David sees Thomas pacing up and down, stamping his feet in the cold, gesticulating, presumably at the Bezuidenhout woman, who is out of vision. That one will give him short shrift. And indeed, it is not long before she totters over to the door to shoo him away.

This is Mandela's country, a free country, I can wait where I like. I'm mos waiting for my friend, Thomas shouts back.

She gives David a glossy red smile as well as a wave, which he returns. Surrounded by people, friends, he smiles to himself; no chance of being lonely in Kokstad.

Which is exactly what Thomas says before he notices the camera that David carries.

Now that's what I call a classy camera, he exclaims.

Not at all, David replies; it's just a regular—

But Thomas interrupts him, Look man, I need to talk some serious business with you. Tell you what, we'll walk out on the Matatiele Road. See, I need a camera and it so happens that I've got just the thing you need.

David smiles, shaking his head.

Say, ou pal, haven't seen you for a while, crocodile. Keeping yourself scarce, hey?

No, no, David laughs. As I said, I'm quite busy. Got a lot of work to do.

But not enough to keep you from djolling at night hey? A married man mos don't always get the chance, so make hay while the sun shines, that's my motto. Look man, you must get around a bit in the daytime also; speak to the right people. These larnie coloureds you been seeing from Twist Valley don't know nothing— how can they if they think their shit don't stink? They tell you a pack of lies tied up with a pink bow and then you go back all mister man with the wrong info.

He holds David's gaze, pausing for the words to sink in. Trouble with you smart guys is you don't see it's your smartness what blinds you to your own needs. Now I can feel your heart is heavy, heavy, my friend; I feel it here—beating his own chest—and what a blessing that the very man to help you is right here, at your service, just when you're getting gatvol of the whole business.

David is firm; he has no time to listen to Thomas's story. He puts a hand on Thomas's shoulder and explains that he really has a full day ahead, a number of appointments to keep, but that they could speak later, in the evening perhaps, at the hotel. So, moving backwards at a half-trot, he says, laughing, See you later, alligator.

The woman at the desk must have given up on her stranger. She does not bother to freshen her lipstick even though she has seen him coming some minutes before, leisurely crossing the square, stopping to buy a newspaper, and this time with a reassuring camera over his shoulder. There is no friendly banter as he enters; only when he stands at the desk does she look up, smile mechanically, hand over the keys, and turn away immediately, swivelling her chair sideways to attend to a document that cannot wait.

Typical, she thinks. He who has always been in a hurry to get away will not leave when there is no encouraging smile.

He picks up a brochure from the counter and, clearing his throat once, twice, says, The Ingeli Forest, hey, must be quite a place, some tourist attraction?

Don't know, she says, without looking up from her columns of figures, Haven't been.

Her left hand fumbles in her bag for a phial of perfume while the right taps at the keyboard. For a moment David is stumped; he has not expected such severe demands on his conversational skills, but at the risk of upsetting her, he stays, leaning intimately against the counter. He resorts to reading aloud from the brochure, about the comfortable hotel, the welcoming crackle of log fires, winding pathways through the pine forests of Ingeli, invigorating walks, solitude, fresh air. Best things in life are free, he adds, then feels the heat of embarrassment rise to his cheeks, but is nevertheless grateful for the cliché. He had not even thought of its suggestiveness.

Concentrating on her work, she makes no reply. He follows the movements of her eyes from the columns of figures on the page to the computer screen. Her painted nails peck independently at the keyboard.

I thought you'd like the countryside. Fresh air and an invigorating walk, he persists, would do you good after a day in this place. Good for the complexion, he laughs.

Uh huh, she grunts, her head moving steadily back and forth.

He says boldly, gallantly, taking a leaf from Thomas's book, taking the risk, We could drive over now, when you knock off; it's a disgrace not to know your own local attractions. Pine smells good in the evening, so how about a twilight walk in the forest, and should you be scared of wolves, here is David Dirkse at your service, ma'am.

It is not the perky, dismissive reply he half expects, or rather hopes for. The fingers of her left hand work deftly at a phial, flicking the plastic top off and taking a dab of its sharp scent to her left earlobe, while she says in a soft, embarrassed voice of excessive regret, keeping her eyes on the ledger, her right hand busy on the keyboard, Sorry, I can't; I'm really very sorry.

Her arsenal of perfume hits the back of his throat, so that he swallows and feels antennae vibrate in the pit of his stomach.

That's alright, not to worry, another time perhaps, David manages to say.

He must not leave in an indecent rush, but the perfume and dyspepsia mingle dangerously, so that he calls, See you then, and turns to go.

She swivels round in her chair. See you. But instead of looking up at him, she strikes at the till, converting her figures into the real thing, he supposes, and he leaves to the jingle of coins and the smell of her perfume lurching about in his stomach.

David has no need of the key. He knows that with certainty as he goes up the stairs. Nevertheless, he stops to listen at his door before turning the handle. Thomas Stewart is in his room, sprawled comfortably in an armchair. He leaps to his feet with a welcoming smile and says, Just in time for tea.

David's eyes whip about the room. At his bedside, Buckland, still open at page fifty-eight, has been moved somewhat to the right. The kettle is indeed about to boil. There is only one chair, so David sits on the bed, but while Thomas makes the tea, he moves the chair to face him directly. They blow at the hot tea and sip loudly, companionably.

Just what the doctor ordered, says David. To tell you the truth, I was feeling rather queasy coming up those stairs, something to do with the receptionist's poisonous perfume, if you ask me.

That's now for you a wakker woman, hey, a sharp woman, drives a mean bargain. That one, yes-like, even her perfume has the kick of a horse. But it seems like it's made you nice and relaxed, ni-ice and re-la-axed, he says soothingly, and that's what we want so we can talk business—

Any messages for me? David interrupts, casting a glance about the room.

No, his guest replies, nothing for you, you've lost your touch, mister, the goosies got you sussed. And he crows with laughter. No, seriously, he says, you're in trouble, man. With all your women. With the world. Let me see now, and picking up David's empty teacup, he studies the uniform trace of tannin left by the no-brand tea bag. He shakes his head gravely.

Things don't look so good for you, ou pal. In fact, it's the end of, shall we say, life as you've known it. Cause why, you been taking on too much, got yourself tangled in politics and now you all wrapped up in barbed wire. He turns the cup round. Here, there, everywhere, no escape, everything's turned against you. So that's where I come in to offer you a new interest, a new line of action, one in which your invaluable skills and experience in the politics business are appreciated and can be put to sensible use.

David paces up and down. The better to hear you, he explains. You're spot on, absolutely right, he says, I am in a bit of a fix and I'm ready to consider any reasonable offer.

Thomas produces a rectangular leather case, not unlike a little cutlery box, which he balances on his knee for a while. He makes as if to open it, then changes his mind, putting it aside.

If you'll excuse me a moment, he says formally, and turns his back on David, who notes the movement of left hand slipping into the breast pocket, clumsily lifting out something that is too light to cause concern.

When he swings round deftly, on his heel, he smiles broadly to display a set of fine white teeth.

Credibility, he explains, that's what teeth give you, but I've not had these long; I'm not so comfortable with them. That's why the credibility is still a bit shaky.

The box is lined with white satin. It has three small depressions in which sit snugly three unremarkable looking stones, one of which is slightly yellower than the rest. As if he has not seen them before, Thomas stares transfixed at the stones while David stares at him.

Beauty, durability, and rarity: such are the three cardinal virtues of a perfect gemstone, says Thomas in a new voice.

David imagines that he has heard these words before, or that he is expected to recognise them. Perhaps they are simply meant to make him unsure.

You wouldn't believe it, Thomas reverently lowers the voice, but these little beauties are diamonds. And they could be all yours. We need to replace a key figure in the business and this is where you come in, a respectable, well-trained person of proven skill who can get in and out of the country unnoticed.

Well, David stalls, it's a great honour, really a great honour, I appreciate your trust in me, but you seem to have got the wrong guy. I'm a teacher you know, in a high school; I do a little work for the UDF, here and there, that I must admit, but I've never left the country; I don't have the skills and experience you speak of. Must have got me mixed up with someone else.

Thomas laughs. Oh, no sir, we've got the right guy alright. We know everything there is to know about you—

In that case, David interrupts, you will know that I'm not inter-ested in diamonds or in making money, certainly not in the IDB business.

But this, Mr. Dirkse, is the time of all-change. A time to be born, a time to die, a time to gather stones together—that's what the Bible says. No, it's time that you start thinking of number one. Have a good look, man, here, touch it. You've given your best years to the struggle and now there's nothing left. Prepare for the future, line your pockets 'cause you deserve it. It's no good just working and working yourself into a ball of barbed wire—for what, for the kaffirs to kick you in the arse when they got no more use for you?

Is that word in the script? They won't find it funny, you know, hearing you calling them kaffirs, David ventures.

He is rewarded by a give away tick followed by a hurried smile.

Look, man, that's—that's cool. Don't you worry yourself about that kind of thing.

No, David says, it's you I'm worrying about. Give me your hand, Thomas. I need to read for myself whether you're the sort of person I could trust.

He studies the brown palm for some time, studies the way the nicotine stains darken towards the fingertips, the crisscross of the dark lines that cut into the paler skin. Then he frowns and pushes the palm away in mock horror.

Ah ha, he says, what a giveaway. Now here it is plainly written, these lines running so closely together, in parallel, and here at the very edge crossing over. What a messy business; I don't wonder you get confused about who I am, about who you're working for. No, man, Thomas, you're too mixed up for me. Sorry, can't do business with a guy who works for Boer and black, who doesn't know friend from foe.

No, wait, says Thomas, this is a delicate matter; we need to keep our heads about this. Tell you what, let's start again, think it through soberly over a drink. Double scotch for me, let's get two double scotches. Go on, ring for service.

While they wait, David takes a stone out of its nest. It is a dull, greasy looking thing, but Thomas, the eager salesman, explains, Don't be fooled by the way it looks. Take it from me, it's the genuine article alright.

Of course, David agrees, most probably from river gravels. And you know the most beautiful thing about a diamond is its internal structure. Turning it this way and that, he lectures: The key thing is the unit cell with its three-dimensional unit of pattern, which determines the structure of the whole stone. A motif that is repeated over and over again in perfect symmetry, absolutely regular, dependable— that's where its beauty lies, inside, beyond what the eye can see.

Nothing to do with the shiny baubles that women, queens, hang around their heads.

Bravo, my friend, bravo. Thomas claps his hands delightedly. See, this stuff is in your blood, man, comes out of our ancestor's soil. It's our heritage; it's your rightful heritage, your Griqua birthright.

He shuts the box and slips it into his pocket when a knock sounds on the door.

It is the headwaiter himself who enters with the drinks. He nods politely at Thomas and fusses over the setting out of pretty coasters with flaming aloes on a background of grey rock. The ice tinkles into the glasses, sparkles in the amber liquor.

Like jewels, David remarks, holding up his glass at the bald man, like picture-story diamonds.

The waiter, keeping a professional distance, smiles politely, asks him to sign for the drinks, but David refers him to Thomas.

Included in the budget, I'm sure, he laughs. Or claim it as expenses. Twice over, and he winks roguishly at Thomas, who obliges by emptying his pockets of silver coins.

As the bald man reaches the door he calls him back. Our friend, Mr. Stewart, is a cheapskate, doesn't think it necessary to give you a tip, hey.

He fishes in his pocket, then tosses an excessively generous ten rand note, roughly wrapped around the lined hit list, into the tray. The man leaves without a word, without looking at the tray.

Do you know what the ancients called the diamond? David smiles at his visitor. Adamas. Hard, unconquerable, ad-a-man-tine, he pronounces. You might as well learn a new word, get something out of our tea party. And now, Thomas Stewart, I would like you to take your stones and go.

Thomas wriggles theatrically in his chair, Listen my friend— But he leaps to his feet when he looks into the gun that David has whipped out of he does not know which pocket.

Move, voetsek, get the fuck out. Go and claim your expenses from all your paymasters, and no more friendly visits.

~

CAPE TOWN 1991

And so it would seem that David has not kept his word. He had promised to ring on Sunday but it is midnight, the children have long been in bed, and still no word from him. Sally walks through the house, from room to room, straightening her skirt, patting her hair in place, before turning on each light. She does not feel the textured fabric under her hands, the resistant silk of relaxed hair, the ribbed plastic of the light switch; her movements are mechanical. She has no notion of having dragged the panty hose off her hair some time ago.

And so, as Sally circles the kitchen table, it is confirmed: Carried away by the woman, he has forgotten entirely about her, about his family. If he were prevented by business, someone would have got a message to her. Thus she must settle down to accept and endure. Like the disciplined cadre that she once trained to be, she knows that there are no further questions to be asked, knows that she must keep still, keep silent, that it is simply a matter of transferring the codes of the Movement to her marriage, for the two can never be separated, certainly not now that they are being so wantonly mixed up in the Crown Hotel in Kokstad. So she does not go to bed, but from time to time prowls through the house, checks the room where the children chatter in their dreams and her mother snores, pats herself once more into presentability before turning on another light, opening another door. Waiting.

It will not be long, she says to herself. By the time the cold morning light creeps up on her, she is able to view herself from a distance, look with pity and contempt at the woman who in the small hours sat hunched in her kitchen with a cup of coffee grown cold and salty with tears. And now she feels pride at the repaired face in the morning mirror, the lipstick she has taken to wearing at all times, her red badge of courage, as she takes the children to school. She will not let herself down, just as she will not telephone.

Ouma Sarie, who has allowed herself an extra few days of

holiday, says that it is a mistake, that lipstick. Makes her look cheap, and there is no need at all to be appearing like that in front of the children's teachers. Pink is not so bad, or even a touch of orange at a pinch, but red, well, that surely is what whores wear; red is no colour for a respectable, married woman. Especially with her husband away. And since her husband is always away there is no need for her to even keep such a thing as a red lipstick. Concentrating on her speech, Ouma stirs the pot of beans and trotter bredie absent-mindedly, not reaching the bottom, which carries on burning as she purses her lips to explain how she has never worn lipstick, never ever, never mind a red one; that Sally's father, Joop, would not allow such a thing in the house, but she supposes the world is changing, although—if you ask her—rather unevenly, too fast in some ways and not fast enough in others. Not that anyone asks an old woman's opinion any more. Look at the electricity pylons within walking distance of her home whizzing their way to the white town, yet making no left turn to her steek-my-weg township behind the ridge, and only then, as Sally sniff-sniffs at the acrid smell of burning, does she see that her wooden spoon has not been reaching the base of the pot. The trotter jelly is quite stuck, just like the stubborn goats they once were, stuck to the bottom of the pot and really, as the smell of burnt food wafts up, she worries that Sally will shout at her, for she has to admit that the dish is ruined and the stain-less steel AMC pot no doubt finished as well. How Sally had fretted for that set of expensive pots. There's no decent coloured house, Mama, without AMC pots, she joked, but the girl's heart was set on it, and she who had not then heard of these new-fangled things, pots that could fry without fat—she'd heard the name as ANC pots, and thought it was just another way of saying the forbidden ANC, ANC, all day long as you went about your business in the kitchen. Sally has shouted at her before for scouring her precious pot with steel wool as if pots weren't meant to be scoured. But there you are, funny how things turn about, that she should fear her daughter's anger—no, that's how it works nowadays in this topsy-turvy world, where children have taken over and there's no respect for old people anymore.

But Sally is not angry; Sally does not shout. Instead, she hugs her dry-eyed, bemused children and comforts them, cooing that everything is alright, that it doesn't matter, that the waste doesn't matter, that the top wouldn't taste too bad. All the time rocking them to her breast. So that Ouma knows that all is not well. That that damned David has brought trouble and heartache as she always knew he would. Which gives her the courage, although she prides herself on not meddling, understands that they are still involved in secret politics business even in these days of change-about and can only hope that Sally will keep her head—but now she just has to ask who it was on the telephone, especially since the child seemed to say nothing at all, just hmm, hmm, hmm, as if anyone needs a telephone for that kind of talk.

David, Sally says. Just a hurried call 'cause things are not going according to plan. He'll be delayed for another day or so, I think.

But I want to speak to Daddy, the boy frets; I have to tell Daddy . . . to tell Daddy . . . and working himself up into a sob, rushes headlong into the curtains where he can wrap up his rage, and where the dust, making him sneeze, brings snot and floods of self-pitying tears.

It was, Sally supposes, one of the comrades who telephoned. Someone she does not know, who said that David has not come to Umtata as planned, that the caller had been expecting him, had been waiting. Had David come home instead? He supposed something important was holding him up in Kokstad. Kokstad, and he chuckled cheerfully, was the sort of place you can't get away from. She was not to worry. No need to telephone; he, the caller, would be in touch shortly.

Sally did not ask his name or why it had taken him so long to get in touch. The unfamiliar voice echoes in her ears, There's no need to worry, no need to telephone. As if she needs such an instruction.

Telephones and faxes and everything these days, it's all change for our people, all these new ideas, Ouma nags, but what the donkey does it bring? Might as well write a letter, if you just want to tell people things and not ask them anything or not want to hear what their story is. If they already know you're okay, know everything about you, so you just have to say hmm, hmm, hmm, then there's no need to use a telephone, hey, no need to speak to you at all. Telephones, she snorts, that wasn't even a conversation; did he not even have time to ask for your news at home?

Sally will not be drawn. She stares at the child, who sobs wildly. Ouma has just the thing in her bag to comfort the child. A rectangular card called Gemstones of Africa, with line drawings of an elephant, a springbok, a lion, and a monkey in each corner. Glued to the card in rows are the even-sized gemstones, ranging from the dark brown of blue tigereye—though why a brown stone should be called blue is beyond her, just the sort of nonsense you get in this country—to pale rose quartz, such a lovely colour. These are stretched across the blue outline of South Africa, which is filled in, if you take your glasses off, with fine pale blue dots. But the shape of the country, its tapering to Cape Point, means that strawberry quartz and jasper, on each side of the last row, have fallen into the sea, which is the white of the card—imagine, white for the sea. Neatly printed, on a white, dot-free strip beneath each stone, is the name of the gem. She had looked at it only last night before going to sleep, read aloud each strange name, beautiful, like words from the Bible: amethyst, carnelian, aventurine, jasper, and sodalite, even if that one does sound like the sinful sodomites. Her favourite is carnelian, a burnt orange that lets in the light, like the jars of preserved orange halves she used to make for the Logan Hotel, with some to display on her own shelves as well. Not like these new-fangled kitchens that look like hospitals, where everything is hidden away behind blind white cupboard doors. She fell asleep with the lovely word on her lips. Carnelian.

And that is where, later on, rummaging behind the bed, she finally finds the card, which must have slipped down the side as she fell asleep. Nice, hey, she holds it out chattering to the child. She saw it in a shop window in town, she isn't sure of the name of the shop, but one of those tourist places full of kaffir things, oops, and there she's done it again....

Don't you have any sense of decency? Sally shouts. You talk rubbish about red lipstick but you don't mind the filth in your own head. If you want to use such words in front of my children then you go home right away and don't come back—Mama, she adds, and just in time, too, for who can stand it being *you*-ed and shoved in such a disrespectful manner.

Now the child, whose crying has stopped for a greedy moment, angrily throws down Ouma's Gemstones of Africa. He has one already, even Chantal does; Daddy brought them each one from his trip to Namaqualand.

Sally picks up the card, stares at its outline, at the lines that carry on beyond the borders of the Republic. Now we are part of Africa, she says, remembering the maps of her school days, when South Africa was an island. She does not remember to admonish the child, whose lips, like Ouma's, are crossly pursed. They are bonded in their sulk.

There is a marked change in David's attitude towards me. He is an affectionate person: I have seen him lifting his children onto his knee while talking politics, nuzzling and petting and holding them close—a man who does not mind being called a moffie. How often he has grabbed my sleeve or even my hand in midconversation. But now, since he has returned from Kokstad, things are not the same.

At first I think that he is simply in an irritable mood. He is cold and distant; his answers are short, terse; he doodles with a pencil on the back of an envelope as he speaks; he waves his hand to silence me as if to save his voice, as if it is too exasperating to speak to me. He has developed a peculiar system of hand signals, and seems irritated when I fail to understand.

I gather that David wants to keep our association strictly businesslike, that he regrets it having slipped into a casual warmth. I recognise a syndrome: He has told me too much, which amounts to betrayal of his comrades, and now, disappointed in himself, transfers the feelings of self-loathing to me. Indifference may in the beginning have moved him to confide in me, but if the battery of speech has revved up our relationship, it has also generated his contempt.

He has little time for those who have not immersed themselves in the struggle—Opportunists, cowards, he raves. Now I watch his lip curl as he skirts about my questions: He has made himself vulnerable, and to a creature who cannot imagine the complexities of political struggle, who cannot understand that a conflictual model of the world is more than a fine phrase, that it is natural for power struggles to erupt in oppositional social units . . .

I switch off when David speaks like a textbook. He is right, I have no stomach for this kind of lecture.

You wouldn't understand the courage and commitment and inviolability of someone like Dulcie, he says, thus placing her on a pedestal, beyond the realm of the human.

No, I say, but neither do I understand why Dulcie, like God, must fend for herself.

Sally thinks that David is withholding the truth from her, that there is a truth, something he refuses to let go of, something over which he cups his hand in order to keep it captive. He does not have such a grasp on the world, that is precisely the problem. The things around him, the old familiar things, this mirror, this chair or mug, these solid things, buckle and sway under his gaze, and in the moments of losing their form, he is taunted by the new, as truth upon conflicting truth wriggles into shape. Yes, this world of swaying and rocking may have been unleashed by Dulcie, but it is not of her making; it is an accident that she has crossed his path, has caused such a disturbance at this very time of liberation.

He will not see Dulcie again. Not after he has seen his own hands tremble and settle on her shoulders. Not after he has held her there, at a distance, and allowed his eyes to mine the depths of her own, to be held by those black eyes, into which were drawn together every scrap of her—skin and bone, her hair, her voice—and only then, as he tried to withdraw his hands and his eyes, for those long seconds, only did the world, the treacherous, helter-skelter world, keep still and hold its peace.

He will not risk it again. It is the swaying world—the smell of blood and the loud report of gunshot—that is for real.

～

DULCIE believes that there comes a time when physical pain presses the body into another place, where all is not forgotten, but where you imagine it relocated in an unfamiliar landscape of, say, bright green grassland cradled in frilly mountains. In such a storybook place the body performs the expected—quivers, writhes, shudders, flails, squirms, stretches—but you observe it from a distance. It is just a matter of being patient. Of enduring. Until the need to relocate once more.

Then you can run through the vocabulary of recipe books, that which is done to food, to flesh—tenderize, baste, sear, seal, sizzle, score, chop—so that the recitation transports you into yet another space. Keeping on the move, like any good guerrilla. Which brings a sense of clarity, as if the mind, too, is being held under a blindingly bright light, and clarity is conferred by the gaze of others. And from that distance, that place, with the promise of further travel, it is possible to endure forever.

They do not speak unnecessarily. For special operations she is blindfolded. They grunt and nod in a shadow play of surgeons, holding out hands for instruments, gesturing at an electrical switch. A woman, who does not always come along, performs the old-fashioned role of nurse—mopping up, dressing wounds. Once, as she left, even lifting the edge of the mattress to tuck in the sheet in a neat hospital fold.

On the very first visit, one of them, the wiry one who seems to be in charge, spoke: Not rape, that will teach her nothing, leave nothing; rape's too good for her kind, waving the electrodes as another took off her nightclothes.

When they speak of her, they do so as people speak of their servants, as if they are not there. Which helps her not to say anything.

She has a feeling that she knows them, or has known some of them perhaps some time ago, in another place. Yes, the figures in their black tracksuits are familiar; the eyes they cannot always keep averted, the black hands, the white hands, these speak of such knowledge. She thinks that she recognises some of the voices, but recognition hovers just beyond consciousness. She hallucinates, turns them into friends, family, comrades. Which brings a moment of pure terror, of looking into the abyss. It is a superhuman effort that brings her back. Never again does she try to identify them. That is where death lies.

Why don't you take off your balaclavas, show yourselves, she said the first time. Won't that teach me something?

Her words lolled obscenely in the pocket of silence, conspicuous, scorned, so that she vowed not to speak again. Besides, what is there to say if you do not know to whom you are speaking? At least whether to friend or foe? For there is an ambiguity about these visitors, something that makes them both friend and foe as they tend to the cracks and wounds carefully inflicted on parts of the body that will be clothed. And so how could she expect answers to her questions? What could they say?

She will not ask for an explanation, will not protest, since they can only offer lies. She has done nothing less than her duty, nothing less than fighting for freedom and justice—even though these words have now become difficult. That too, then, is why she cannot speak. Uttering such tarnished words makes them sound at best foolish, at worst, false.

From the few muted exchanges between them, it is clear that she cannot be killed; that instead they rely upon her being driven to do it herself. They do not understand that for a woman like her— who has turned her muscles into ropes of steel, who will never be driven into subordination, who even as an eager girl in the bush wars resisted the advances of those in power, resisted her own comrades, having worked out that fucking women was a way of preventing them from rising in the Movement, who has resisted all her life, who has known since childhood that tyranny must be overthrown—for a woman like her, there is no submission. She knows that she is tiring them out, that they are exasperated by her. Thus they tiresomely repeat themselves; the knife above her throat hovers listlessly.

What they do understand is that she has supernatural powers. It is as if the rumours about her legendary strength, her agility, her incredible marksmanship, her invincibility that have circulated for some time between friend and foe alike have taken root within her, have grown into the truth.

She has taken her training as a revolutionary seriously—the vows, the beliefs—without, some would say, the necessary pinch of salt. Has her life not been devoted to resisting tyranny? Ah, she knows that she has done it too well for a girl, a woman, but she would, and she clenches her teeth, do it again and again. Resist. No matter how rickety the boat, how choppy the sea, she would remain alive to resist tyranny, to cling with idealism—she knows it to be embarrassing—to that which they wish to break down.

She believes that they know nothing of her secret, her friendship with David.

Marinaded in pain, viewing herself from an unfamiliar place, she would hear a voice repeating the name of Chapman's Peak. Where the familiar road bends sharply to the left—it would take no effort at all, no decision as such, simply a matter of not turning the wheel but rather of carrying straight on, flying off into the unspeakable beauty of the blue below, the bay cradled in mountains. Where she would feel that macerated flesh grow weightless in the water, dissolve in the white spray that beats against the rock. Atomised at Chapman's Peak.

And so each morning as they leave, as a matter of pride and despair, she summons all her strength to get dressed and drive to the sea. Along the coastal road she drives at breakneck speed with the sea roaring below, and slows down only for the baboons who have, through the early hours, come to think of the road as their own. They scurry by with little ones clinging to their backs, the males snarling defiantly by the roadside, and only then would the voice recede, would she wake from the trance, only yards before the beckoning bend in the road, to remember that she will resist, as she has done all her life.

She likes to believe that it is the thought of David that resurrects her at that moment. It seems equally likely that the voice is dispelled by the comic behaviour of the baboons.

Sometimes after minor sessions—there are, after all, limits to what can be done to the human body without destroying it—she gathers her magical strength to chase after her visitors, and on such occasions her legendary marksmanship does not fail.

On such days she knows that the next session will surpass all punishment.

On such days her hands are raw with washing.

~

Ag no, man, says Ouma Sarie, you mustn't say such things about your own husband. Saying is bad luck, and if you're just sucking it all out of your thumb, well then, you should pull yourself together and stop brooding over nonsense. There's nothing that a hymn and a prayer won't put right in the end. Men, she snorts, you can't trust them, but it's just a matter of being firm; press them into doing the right thing and don't put up with any nonsense. Did you find anything in his pocket, lipstick on his collar, something like that, hey? Tell me, why do you say such things?

Oh, I don't know, Sally admits. I did go through his pockets, many times, but there was nothing at all. Except he's behaving strangely, doesn't seem to be himself these days, and then there is that woman.

She had seen him at a meeting looking at the woman, and she knew at once. Caught the woman's eyes several times resting on him, even on her, Sally. And so she knew.

No, he isn't spending more time than usual away, and yes, she has checked up once, twice that he was indeed where he had said he'd be, but she knew all the same.

Is it that he doesn't, does not . . . But Ouma Sarie cannot find the words, so she fishes the bottle of rooi laventel from the folds of her many skirts. Here, she says, have a swallow of this. Nothing like the old Dutch remedies. Next time I'll bring buchu essence, now that's the thing to clean the blood; you must try to find a shop here in town that sells the old medicines. Nowadays you people have it so good, it makes you wasteful, throwing away the crusts of the bread, spreading your bread twice, with margarine under the jam, and then wasting your energies on idle thoughts about ungodly things. No, man, you must pull yourself together, keep yourself busy—you don't need castor oil, do you?—and thank God for each day that passes without troubles.

Ouma Sarie has always felt, as the moon rose and the darkness came with the dipping of swallows, as she gathered together the lamps—never a smudge to be found on her glass funnels, oh no, she cleaned them every morning, polished the glass with newspaper—the weariness peeling off like an apron, the yellow lamplight licking over the wounds of the day. Except, of course, at the time of Sally's disappearances—then she heard the fearful twittering of the swallows and cupped in her hands the paraffin-plump belly of a lamp, dawdled in fear of light, until the darkness would stand no more, before striking the match. Then they ate their bread and drank their buttermilk in silence, under the greedy flicker of the flame. It was then that she stopped polishing the glass, did not want the bright light. The moon and stars will have to do, she said to Joop, who complained about the lamps. Only when Joop finally took it upon himself, with his large, clumsy hands, to rub newspaper inside the glass, which he would surely have cracked did she take it from him and, thank God, pulled herself together. They were, as Joop said, the lucky ones. How many had got through these times without losing their children, their loved ones, seeing them swatted to death like flies, or missing forever, in these years of struggle?

Now Ouma Sarie, hearing again the swoop of swallows, stumbles to the light switch. No, my girl, the trick is to keep faith. . . . You musn't say such things. . . . Saying is bad luck, makes unlikely things come true.

Just the sort of nonsense one expects from old people, Sally thinks. Why on earth can she not keep anything to herself? Why say anything to her mother, of all people, who has no idea of the world? Foolish to bother her, and who knows how the clumsy words will scatter and settle in the various fixed compartments of her stories—among the swallows, the lamps, the red malva, the tiles of the Logan Hotel. Thank God, and she winces at the aftertaste of rooi laventel, thank God her mother hadn't managed to ask about that. Imagine having to explain that, no, there was nothing wrong at all with their private life. In fact, David has never shown such interest in her before, not even in those heady days of not know-ing when they would see each other. Now he comes back late and no sooner presses against her warm, soft behind. . . .

~

DULCIE'S is a story about an obsession with our hero, who cannot, as a man of honour, submit to that which he has produced in her. That is how she views it. That he has lured her into something that has disturbed her equanimity for the worse but upon which he will not act and of which he will not speak. She understands the ques-tion of honour, but what she cannot endure is his silence, the primitive fear that to speak of something will bring it into being, let loose the tokolos. Or the converse: that to not speak of some-thing will divest it of its reality, undo it. Strictly speaking, she is not as obsessed with David as she is with his lack of speech. That makes her storm about with rage. Like a man, she says in moments of bitterness; like a man, he has beckoned her into something which he now pretends does not exist, and worse, he pretends that she does not know he is pretending. Why, then, she would argue triumph-antly, should she care at all for such a windbroek, for such a per-son who is all pretence? That question is not pursued and doubt sets in, for what if she were altogether wrong? Perhaps he is unaware of that which he has produced in her; perhaps she sim-ply has imagined their charged moments of intimacy, in which case it is a matter of folly rather than humiliation on her part. And so Dulcie would swing obsessively between positions. She is enraged that after years of avoiding what is known as love, of not allowing herself to be touched, and after years of resistance, of fighting tyran-ny, of keeping in control and making her measured way to the top, she is left tortured with uncertainty about a phantom lover. David has made her question her own senses, has produced in that strong, fearless body a poisoning doubt that in his absence tinctures everything.

Obsessively she rakes over every exchange between them, checking again in her memory the shift of a facial muscle, the softening of a syllable, the nuanced movements of his articulate hands bound by restraint, only to confirm that which his behaviour the very next day would cast once more in doubt. She knows every word of their conversations by heart, can summon every ambiguity, every inflexion of his voice. She treasures in an ashtray by her bed a stained, gritty sachet from which he had dribbled sugar into her coffee. Every day she promises to throw it away.

When Dulcie reaches the limits of endurance, as she regularly does, she hardens her heart, talks herself into cold indifference, meets him with a brisk politeness. Oh, but then he is distraught, finds an excuse to see her, begs for her return with eloquent eyes until she succumbs. And all without uttering a word, for it is utterance that will translate it into the material and thus for him into infidelity. All is in shadow play, in mime, in a comic strip where speech bubbles taper into think dots that just miss their mouths. She is resigned to the dilation and contraction of her heart, knows that this wordless flurry is the limit, that she can expect nothing more, that perched on a wheel going round and round she is doomed to her obsession.

Dulcie has become an adolescent once more.

There is a fresh crop of pimples on her chin.

She does not know why or how, but notes nevertheless: that this pretence of a relationship coincides with the visits by night; that the coincidence carries a meaning that she has not yet fathomed; that one is a recursion, a variant of the other: the silence, the torture, the ambiguity; and that in such recursions—for if on the edge of a new era, freedom should announce itself as a variant of the old—lies the thought of madness madness madness. . . .

Dulcie longs for the comfort of the quotidian. For warm whole wheat bread with the little square Duens label stuck to the crust. For bacon and boerewors, kidneys and brains, minced liver and lung—but that would have been her preference before the visits. Coloured people prefer to eat something that once had a face: she thinks of the saying with both revulsion and loss.

~

Coloureds had no stomach for blood. They had no traditions and family commitment dating back centuries, or loyalties forged by centuries of war as the black people had. No, the Brigadier thought, the Gentleman was a pure African, and one who dedicated his life to fighting the government.

Thabo Shenge Luthuli, *The Spilling of Blood*

CAPE TOWN 1991

What a toad, I say speculatively, why hire such a creep to try and trip you up?

We are sitting on the slopes of Table Mountain, eating a less than hearty breakfast of muffins and coffee at the café at the Rhodes Memorial, the kind of place that David does not like to be seen in or perhaps genuinely hates. White-middle-class-moffie-wholefood-places, they are known as. But he was so eager to talk with me, adamant that it should not be at my house, that when I suggested Rhodes, he agreed.

No, he says, Thomas is okay, not a creep at all, rather talented, I think, only a bit undisciplined, too theatrical. They don't always find such interesting material, the usual fare is the dull-as-dishwater student of politics or social science, an earnest, bearded young man or a pretty girl, preferably blonde. White students, because we are supposed to be particularly receptive to whites who support the Movement. As if everyone doesn't these days. Try and find anyone who voted for Apartheid and you wonder if you've spent your life chasing phantoms.

There is still no question of explaining the *they;* I am not sure whether David himself knows and it is better not to ask, not to spoil the mood.

David speaks obsessively about his stay at the Crown Hotel. He wants me to be clear about every detail he chooses to disclose. We have met several times since his return. It is inconvenient that he can no longer speak on the telephone now that his tinnitus has returned. There is, he says, a disturbing squeal in the background when he uses the telephone; he fears that his tinnitus will not go away this time. But, using the most transparent excuses, I sometimes call him all the same. The truth is that I cannot help myself, that his contempt binds me to him, that my desire for his story has become rapacious, and it would seem that he, in turn, has been infected by me.

I have become as dependent on seeing David as he is on speaking to me. I abjectly accept his shifts between sullen and less guarded moods, perhaps because I hope that important gaps in the story are going to be filled. Whatever the case, I feel uneasy when he does not keep in touch; I find myself staying in in case he drops by. Today—and I can barely bring myself to confess this—I have taken the morning off in the hope that he would want to meet. Just a hunch, and I thrill with the reward of his terse telephone call.

Perhaps he will speak about the missing day of the trip, the day on which he was supposed to telephone home, unless he assumes that I've not worked out the loss of twenty-four hours.

David proves to be right about this place. He is about to tell me why he has come when the entire black staff assembles at the doorway to sing a hymn, first in English and then the final verse, authentically, in Xhosa. They clap and sway and tilt their heads in unison.

Let's go, I say.

Shall we wait to see what else the proprietors have thought up for the New South Africa? David asks. Perhaps they'll come out to perform the final hallelujah with their workers.

After this display I do not have the stomach for my second muffin, even though the homemade jam is nothing short of memorable. We nevertheless wait respectfully for the ditty about Jesus to come to an end. But we do refuse to put a penny in the hat they bring round to each of the tables, curtseying, for a mission station that would train others to put on shows like this one.

David will not speak of our business in the car. So we wander off to the memorial, beyond the grand Doric columns, down to the bronze horseman called *Physical Energy*.

G. F. Watts, I say, a replica of the one in London's Kensington Gardens, then hope to cover my embarassment by explaining that I have just read that in an old guide book.

But David is indulgent today.

Never mind, he says, as it happens it's a European culture vulture I need to talk to. It's about a painting, about a strange event of a few years ago that I remembered only this morning as I woke up and lay staring, half awake, at the curtains draped over a chair. Sally took them down last night for a wash, left them lying over the chair, and something about the colours or the floral pattern, I don't know about such things, but it brought it all back, even though there's no resemblance, really. . . .

His embarrassment is greater than mine.

David had visited the city of Glasgow in the eighties as a member of a small delegation of teachers handpicked by the Movement. Ostensibly it was a short course on child-centred learning, courtesy of the benevolent city council, but never you mind the real purpose, except, and he chuckles proudly, that it was successfully accomplished in spite of careful National Intelligence surveillance.

Rather incompetent, I would have thought, to lose black people in such a white city.

Never you mind, he says, tapping his nose.

He is hopelessly addicted to this boys' stuff.

Walking the streets of Glasgow in late October proved difficult. He had never, not even in Cape Town, seen such a combination of wind and rain. You have to be properly dressed, he laughs, buttoned up and plastic-coated to survive; then you need to brace your body at the correct angle against the wind, otherwise you find yourself treading water without making any progress.

One of the Scottish councillors lent him a green, gold, and black umbrella produced by the Anti-Apartheid Movement in Britain, and how good it was to sport the prohibited colours and taunt his watcher on an innocent sight-seeing trip. But no sooner had he stepped out than the wind whipped it away and wedged it between the bare branches of a tree. The next day, blown into the railings of a bridge, he clutched at his hat while doing up a throat button, and caught a glimpse of the umbrella sailing down the river Kelvin, and he thought he heard someone snigger.

By then David was getting used to the idea of walking about drenched to the skin, fascinated by a city in which he could enjoy the unfamiliar and yet read the well-known names of streets or road signs. Everywhere the names of places at home: Kelvingrove, Glencoe, Aberdeen, Lyndoch, Sutherland, Fraserburgh, Dundee. There was no danger of feeling lost in Scotland, except that he felt dizzy with the to-ing and fro-ing between rain-sodden place names and the dry, dusty dorps at home. It was as if, along with his watcher, the vast terrain of South Africa had accompanied him as map, now folded and tucked into wee Scotland, and who in such wind and rain would choose to unfold a map?

Then there was Govan, a place to which David's hosts seemed particularly attached. No trouble was spared bussing the delegation into that rundown area of boarded up shipyards and buildings with broken windows, where they held meetings and drank tea with unhealthy-looking citizens who shook their heads and said that Thatcherism and Apartheid were the twin evils of the modern world, that they, oppressed by England, knew exactly what Apartheid was all about. Ye ken, an old man said repeatedly, and that *ken*, soothing for being also the Afrikaans word for *know*, quite made up for everything. Govan Mbeki would be coming there straight from Robben Island, they said, and David wondered about the dampness of the roots the old man would find in such a place.

The grand sandstone buildings, blonde or pink, were indeed old and beautiful as the guidebook said, but the city began to haunt him with its history of elsewhere, so that the majestic structures would, from time to time, before his very eyes, disappear into a fog. Then, on many a corner, there would float into his vision a bank called Clydesdale, the very name of the farm near Kokstad that had driven Le Fleur mad with rage. Out of the fog, too, grew the grand museum called Kelvingrove, the place where as a student David caddied for the wealthy golf players of Cape Town: no blacks, no Jews in Kelvingrove. In this friendly foreign city, his visit had become an exercise in recognizing the unknown, in remembering the familiar that cast its pall over the new.

The cultural tour took him to a huge collection in a park to see the treasures brought from all over the world by a merchant whose name he does not remember. What he wants me to know is that he wandered through it all without looking at a single artefact or painting. There is unmistakeable pride in his voice. Yes, he passed dutifully through ancient Greece and Egypt, through Europe's and Asia's unwieldy treasures, but did not really see anything, could think only of the extraordinary idea of shopping for strange things made by other people for their own particular use and shipping them to a warehouse in Scotland. David had no interest in the artefacts themselves and certainly has nothing to report; he finds the very notion of the man's collection distressing and distasteful; he would gladly be called uncultured. Oh, but the setting was memorable: an airy glass structure in a wooded park—the relief of seeing something modern!—where the trees had turned into a riot of copper and gold and fiery reds as holy as the burning bush of Moses. He had never before seen such a transformation of leaves, just as he had never before looked at paintings, but he knew which he preferred. All this by way of putting off his story of the painting in the People's Palace. I have come to recognize the symptoms: the desire to tell, the stalling, the attempt at withdrawal; thus I keep prodding and provoking.

Yes, of course he looked forward to visiting a museum that celebrates the history of the working people of the city. He remembers entering the People's Palace via its Winter Garden, a huge glass house in the shape of an inverted ship's hull (Nelson's *Victory*, he later learned from a brochure) that housed the familiar Cape flora of palm trees, begonia, poinsettia, hibiscus, and strelitzia, and taking unexpected pleasure in the tender green of the hothouse versions. He listened to the tepid ticktock of moisture dripping from tropical leaves, then heard, through the counterpoint of rain drilling on the glass outside and through the tame roar of an artificial waterfall, the thunderous voice of Le Fleur, roughened by Robben Island, preaching in the Winter Garden in Cape Town's District Six his messages of temperance and of Griqua independence. So that was what a winter garden was. He could not imagine what they would have kept in such a structure at home, unless these plants had only since the knocking down of District Six been driven outdoors to toughen up and propagate.

David took off his wet coat, gloves, scarf, and hat, and sat at a white wrought-iron table to order lunch. His watcher, that day replaced by a bespectacled black man at a table in a far corner, had the same reddish soup with brown bread, which, in that humid ship of glass, protected from the rain, drew them into a fellowship of sorts, so that on a devilish impulse he carried over his tray to join him. Nothing odd about fellow Africans greeting or even speaking to each other in a foreign country. The man was jovial. From Zimbabwe, he said, with a vigorous and heartfelt handshake, and among all those white people it was nice to talk to someone. They chatted genially about the weather and the cosy refuge offered by the Winter Garden. David told him about Cape Town's District Six and Le Fleur's Griqua choirs in their green cotton drill raising the glass roof with song.

And so, says David, I slipped up once again. Just as Sally says, I'm prone to sentimentality, the fake feeling that brings nothing but trouble. And in a foreign city, of all places. There I was, full of bravado and sentiment, a commander of a new cell, doing something as foolish and undisciplined as chatting with the enemy. At the time, of course, I knew nothing about Le Fleur except for snippets of nonsense from my childhood, but I certainly knew who I was talking to. For some reason it didn't occur to me to report our little chat at the time, which means that it can be construed in any way, be used against me.

He holds his head in his hands, which seems to be an exaggerated gesture, surely the very fake feeling of which he has just spoken. Fearing that he might scuttle off into this peculiar and need-less shame, I elbow him in the ribs with a jovial reminder that he has not finished his story about the museum, the People's Palace.

David starts off like a tour guide: The first room celebrates the rise of the city as mercantile centre and focuses on the economic growth of Glasgow in the tobacco trade with the American colonies. There are displays of fine Glaswegian Delft pottery, hand-painted tiles, clay pipes, novelty snuff boxes, a Negro Head tobacco tin with the image of a man in a striped shirt, a slave con-tentedly smoking his pipe. There is an old map of times before the city inched its way westward, towards prosperity. Then, as he turns away from the glass case devoted to tobacco paraphernalia, he sees the painting on the wall.

David describes the painting of John Glassford and his fam-ily, circa 1767, in minute detail. A really glossy picture—is that good or bad? he asks. A sealed, even surface that releases its information with reluctance. He wonders why he is drawn to this portrait of a tobacco lord and his family, of which he can't quite make sense. The white wigged patriarch wears a kindly expression, as does his eld-est daughter, his favourite, standing beside him with a musical instrument that David cannot identify. She is the apple of his eye; her full lower lip droops like his. His other favourite, the fifth, hands him a posy from the flowers she carries in an extravagant green cloth slung from her shoulder. David remembers that there are many more children, all girls except for the an infant of ambiguous gender whose bare shoulders rise above the wrap of the mother's silver-gray frock. He shivers for them all, displaying their bare arms and chests in the cold Scottish air, except for the father, who is buck-led and buttoned up to the chin.

The painting is all hands: clutching, holding, or reaching out for fruit or flowers, as well as the prominent, too-large, limp hand of the mother, whose elbow rests on something beyond the canvas. She leans somewhat towards the edge of the picture, her head inclined, as if she wished to escape from the group.

There is an abundance of flowers: garlands on the heads of flimsily clad girls, flowers in the paisley pattern of the carpet, flowers hidden in the fold of a child's green velvet wrap, posies taken and given to each other, and in the centre, on a tray before the second daughter, a basket of flowers. David is puzzled by how this tray is held up, unless, like a cinema usherette's, it is strapped to her waist. An unnatural bird also perches on the tray.

None of the subjects looks at any other. Neither do they look at the objects, at the instrument held by the eldest or the flowers they give or take. Most marked is the child who hands a posy to the receiving father, a gesture performed with eyes straying elsewhere. The things are there to show their wealth. There is a basket of fruit—grapes, apples, and perhaps peaches—on the oriental carpet. A small child in the foreground, in rich red cloth draped over one shoulder, points to the fruit, again looking away, indifferently, from the object of her desire. Standing on its hind legs with paws on the red velvet of the child's clothing is a little black dog, whose cluttering presence allows for her drapes to merge with that of her mother's red underskirt.

It is then, fixing on the red and the black, the intrusion of black dog between child and withdrawing mother, which at the same time joins their clothing into a single drape of red fabric, that his gaze is drawn obliquely upward, following the gaze of the black dog, along what transpires to be the only sight line in the painting, to the space to the left of the father's head. There, as if being developed in photographic solution, out of the darkness of a wooden panel, the face of a black man takes shape before his very eyes. In three-quarter profile, the distinct face of a bald black man in red livery, repeating the colours of the foreground. David feels himself going cold with fright. The man, who was not there a moment ago, looks directly at him, rather than at the adoring dog. His hands are held together as if in prayer. David steps back somewhat, meeting his steady gaze, and, yes, the man is still there. He does not know how long he stands gazing at that face, but he stays transfixed until the edges of the image start wobbling as if under water, the eyes shift to meet those of the dog, and the colours of that crisp outline dissolve and fade into the high gloss of the paint, leaving just a darkish smudge above Glassford's head.

When he steps forward he reads the plaque underneath. He swears he had not read it before looking at the painting. He remembers the precise text:

John Glassford (1715–1783) tobacco merchant and family at home in the Shawfield mansion. The painting by Archibald McLauchlin, c. 1767, included a black slave on the left hand, which has since been painted over.

Surely, I say, you simply forgot that you'd read the inscription earlier.

But, he insists, there was no mention of slavery in the documentation of the city's economic growth. No mention of the fact that slaves produced the sugar and tobacco in the American plantations, owned and managed by Glasgow merchants like the wealthy Glassford. There was nothing to make him think of a black man, not in the People's Palace, where he did not expect to find the effacement of slavery to be betrayed in representation, as an actual absence, the painting out of a man who had once, alongside fruit and flowers, signified wealth and status and who, with the growth of the humanitarian movement, had become unfashionable as an adornment on canvas. How could he have known about the absent slave without reading the inscription? And that, he swears, he had not done.

David thinks that it is shame that makes the Glassford mother lean out of the picture, away from her family, away from the grasping hands. He wants to know whether I have heard of McLauchlin, whether he is a famous artist, whether the painting is considered to be a good one, what its value might be. I am, of course, unable to answer such questions; I know very little about art, have not heard of the artist. The painting sounds awful, but it is not possible to judge a work that one has not actually seen, that is only reported, I explain.

Look, he says, I've described the painting as accurately as possible.

When I shake my head, he snorts. Now why does that make

me think of Mrs. Thatcher? The South African government has every right to defend itself against terrorists, he intones in that lady's sanctimonious voice. The only judgment one can make of Nelson Mandela is on the basis of his acts of terrorism.

He is not interested in my arguments against this preposterous comparison, and so continues with his story.

I don't understand why it's taken me so long to identify the face of the original. I thought that the man in the hotel reminded me of someone, but I could not for the life of me place him. It wasn't until this morning, when I woke up to the curtains draped over a chair, with their old-fashioned pattern of fruit and flowers crushed in colours similar to those in the painting, that I remembered. Then I knew instantly where I had seen the bald-headed waiter before. He is without any doubt the very man who appeared in the painting. Down to the hands held together deferentially.

Well, well, I mock. Here we have the true descendant of the Griqua chief, the green-eyed visionary who can make a canvas cough up its secret. Although I should point out that the man's hands have changed from the praying position to the deferential.

David says nothing, is lost in thought. Then his face breaks slowly into a smile, Hey, listen to this: strelitzia was discovered by a Scots gardener, that's what the brochure said.

Well, thank God for that, I say, for how would we otherwise have recognised that flower disguised as a golden bird of paradise.

But really I am thinking of how extraordinarily good he looks when he smiles.

Instead of being concerned about the madness of his vision, David is troubled by the idea of false memory.

Fashionable nonsense, I say, but no, he is suspicious of the ways in which the tilt of a hat, the rustle of a palm leaf, or the bunching of curtain fabric will hold its meaning sealed, until one day, for no discernable reason, it will burst forth to speak of another time, an original moment that in turn will prove to be not the original after all, as promiscuous memory, spiralling into the past, mates with new disclosures to produce further moments of terrible surprise. Is one to believe that terror lies dormant in all the shapes and sounds and smells of our everyday encounters, that memories lie cravenly hidden one within another? Surely memory is not to be trusted.

Thus he is reluctant to acknowledge the shaven-headed waiter as the young security department lackey, then sporting a beard and full head of hair. But what else does the memory of the painting ask him to do, if not to return to Angola, to the Quatro camp, where he had arrived just before the mutiny, the envy of rebellious comrades who wished to be working at home. Yes, he had supported their cause, their demands for greater democracy in the army, their stance against the leadership that landed him in solitary confinement, and, yes, all sorts of things that shouldn't have happened had indeed happened, not only to him, his was the least. For the mutineers, unfortunately, things did not go well at all, but what else could have been done, what other ways of dealing with insurrection in the face of a steady infiltration of enemy agents? And who can say even now, with absolute certainty.

Yes, he had argued for the legitimacy of their demands and that earned him days of interrogation and so forth by the big men from security. The young lackey, perhaps in training, had been present once or twice, sitting silently with his head in his hands. Only once, David remembers, was he alone with him, minded by the man whose instruction it was to sit in the corner with his face averted. At one point, perhaps through boredom, he overstepped the mark, and got up to confront his charge.

Imbokodo, he announced pompously, beating on his chest as if he were the entire security department. The grinding stone, he translated.

When David, acknowledging the slight, said he knew that, the man barked for silence.

The boulder that crushes, he added, with the melodramatic turn that David now recognises in his role of waiter-buffoon, and with that returned to his chair.

David is not sure of what he remembers. They were difficult times, times best forgotten. He rubs his face with both hands.

People could not, under those pressures, always afford to be cautious, he explains; it was crucial to act quickly. He does not say why he was at Quatro, but yes, as in any movement beset by treachery there was bound to be paranoia, bound to be some mistakes, and yes, if his treatment had been a mistake it was soon rectified, nothing really serious, perhaps the odd excesses practised by the overwrought. God knows, it was difficult enough. It was war, for God's sake. Every movement produces its crackpots, its power-mongers who cross over into a corrupted version of the freedom they set out to defend. That does not discredit the Movement itself. If things go off course, that course is also determined by the very system we attack. And it's enemy tactics, he repeats, that produce corruption.

I raise an eyebrow.

Oh yes, he explains, by making us insecure about our own members so that we remain suspicious, incriminate the innocent, and do terrible things to our own people. Keeping your hands clean is a luxury that no revolutionary can afford; there's corruption in every institution. It's only you arty types who think of such problems as something special, something freakish that can bring about a climax in a story. Stick to the real world and you'll find the buzz of bluebottles deafening.

Leaning against the bronze horseman, I say nothing; David nevertheless turns on me, his movements stiff with distaste and resentment.

There is no justification for the likes of you to sneer. People who tend their gardens and polish their sensibilities in the morality of art have no idea about the business of survival out there in the bush with no resources. There things do get distorted and ideals do drift out of sight. You who are too fastidious to use the word *comrade,* what would you know about such things? Oh, you can talk about ambiguity or freedom, but you can't face putting the two together, not even from the sunny comfort of your garden chair. That's why you'll never understand about Dulcie; hers is another world altogether.

And when freedom comes, I ask, what are we meant to do with

these different worlds? Which one will survive? Or rather, which one will you choose for me?

My dear girl, he says condescendingly, another bourgeois myth of niceness you've swallowed. There've always been other worlds; there always will be many, all struggling for survival. Then his tone changes. Look, he pleads, I've trusted you with a delicate job. The struggle is sacred; it's been my life. It must not be misrepresented. You know, as all sensible people do, that the fight against oppression is a just one, that it has been managed as justly as is possible in politics.

Together our eyes follow the movement of an ant, stumbling with its burden of an enormous breadcrumb.

Perhaps, I say, as the ant disappears down a crack, it's too difficult. Perhaps we should abandon the whole thing.

Oh no, David says anxiously, no need for that. It's just a matter of being careful, of not distorting things.

I try to think of my walled winter garden where the basil is still green and bushy and the bougainvillea never lets up on its purple rustle. But another image invades, one of worlds as a stack of so many dirty dinner plates that will not come unstuck as each bottom clings to another's grease.

≈

DULCIE's story: Perhaps the whole of it should be translated into the passive voice. Or better still, the middle voice. If only that were not so unfashionably linked with the sixties and with French letters.

David shakes his head in disbelief.

Not only would that be a gross misunderstanding of Dulcie, and as it happens, I do know at least what the passive voice is, but it is also clear that I—and he beats his chest histrionically—have made a terrible mistake in choosing to work with you—pointing rudely at me. I may have overestimated the importance of using someone who is not in the Movement, not of our world; I have certainly underestimated the extent to which your head is filled with middle-class, liberal bullshit.

Naturally we don't speak the same language, I say flippantly, so French letters won't have the same meaning for the two of us.

He has brushed aside my piece on obsession and silence as an absurd exercise in style; it is not surprising that after that he should object to me. Now that our collaboration is on shaky ground—he blows hot and cold in turn—I have nothing to lose and so push ahead with my inventions. Dulcie has, after all, always hovered somewhere between fact and fiction.

If speech is not allowed, she would like to have something written up, or written down. Dulcie once thought that she knew the difference. She would like to think that somewhere there are suitable words with which to say, to ask what she needs to know, to record what she thinks she knows. Then there would be something tangible, something to write, something to read, for even if the words were addressed to David, they would remain hers; there would be no point in presenting him with words.

But she fears for any such writing. Although they come in the early hours she has to be vigilant at all times. Worse than any instrument of torture is the thought of such hard-found words being fingered by them—jabbed, clubbed, defaced into a gibberish that would turn the thing between David and herself into nothing. She had known and accepted that in her position there is no such thing as a private life. Now she insists on keeping a secret. Sometimes, in the clarity of midnight, before they come, she laughs out loud: This is nonsense, kid stuff, what can my private teenage obsession have to do with the weighty matters of a liberation movement? In these times of negotiation, the small, secret world of the guerrilla has grown cracks; her own little secret has come to stand for something else, something to do with a world blown up, enlarged, so that comrades huddle like startled animals in unfamiliar groups.

And so she does not write, neither up nor down; and so she is drawn into silence, becomes his mirror image, silent like him. She winces at the thought of David being special to her because he is like her, or she is like him—of her kind, as our writers also say about race. She is grateful for the ready-made euphemism.

The face of the beloved: she recalls the precise brownness of his skin as her own is being disfigured, the precise colour of his eyes as her own are prised open under piercing light, the precise convolution of his neat girlish ear as silence is blasted at high speed into her own. Is the silence to which we are addicted not inherited from our oppression? Do we not in this resolute silence embrace our oppressors? Put that in your pipe and smoke it, Dulcie would say.

But no, David does not want her voice represented. That is because he wishes to protect her, he says. He has only just explained that I had in fact seen Dulcie once at a party. I can barely summon the image of the large woman of indifferent looks; it is hard to think of such a figure as anything out of the ordinary. But I do remember the voice, hearing her say those very words to someone: Put that in your pipe and smoke it. Sitting with her legs apart, wearing an expensive silk shirt of hideous print, she laughed uproariously. David does not think I am serious when I ask why revolutionaries are so badly dressed.

Once, only once, did David come close enough to place his hands on her shoulders. His fingertips pressed precisely into the wounds under her shirt, plunged intimately into her flesh, caressed every cavity, every organ, her lungs, liver, kidneys, her broken heart, with a lick of fire. She would not have been surprised to see those hands withdraw dripping with blood.

In the silence they have no choice but to be like each other.

You have turned it into a story of women; it's full of old women, for God's sake, David accuses. Who would want to read a story like that? It's not a proper history at all.

What else can I do? If it's not really to be about you, if you won't give me any facts, if you will only give me the mumbo jumbo stuff, my task is to invent a structure, some kind of reed pondok in which your voodoo shadow can thrash about without rhyme or reason, but at least with boundaries, so that we don't lose you altogether. It's impossible, this writing of a story through someone else. The whole thing's impossible. Why, for instance, do you not tell me about the day of your Kokstad trip that's disappeared? Where is it?

Where were you? Why didn't you telephone Sally? You've slipped up, David; you could have got away with it by calling it a day of security meetings. Instead, you choose to pretend that time just skipped from Saturday to Monday without anyone noticing. Or pretend to pretend.

There's surely no need for all the old women. Can't some of the oumas at least be turned into oupas? There's no harm in that, just turning the she's into he's, he suggests.

Harm? I turn the word round in my head. Harm, I suppose, is a category that I ought to take more seriously in relation to this story.

Perhaps Dulcie could be turned into a man, I say. But he will not have that.

No, no, that would not make sense at all. Dulcie is definitely a woman.

I risk another question. Was Dulcie at the Quatro camp in '84?

David looks wistfully at the night sky. At the clouds whizzing across an acid moon, at the stars shrilling in the dark. Or so I presume from the angle of his head. At his insistence, we are outside in my garden, not sitting on the rickety bench but squatting on the grass. He has developed an agoraphobia of sorts since his return from Kokstad and will sit outside even in bad weather. I have a scarf wrapped about my neck against the cold; I sit close up and feel his shoulder against mine. I would like this better if it were not for the peculiar sensation of hearing his tinnitus ring in my ears.

I can't say for sure, he says at last; I don't know if we were there at the same time. But she would have been sent for, I imagine; she might have arrived just after I was cleared and sent back home. You see . . . Dulcie and I kept on missing each other in those days. You see, some of the ringleaders of the mutiny might, I suspect, have been trained by Dulcie. But, of course . . . see, there was always the assumption among some that Dulcie and I were somehow working together, even though chiefs of different cells do not know of each other, never work together. All based, I now believe, on us being from the same Cape community—which, strictly speaking, we are not. (I note the avoidance of the word coloured.) It would appear that we often expressed the same views, the same objections, but as I've told you, we actually met for the first time in Kliprand in quite different capacities, and I now . . . ag, he sighs, then switches to the pompous mode: In guerrilla warfare knowledge of each other's movements is carefully monitored, so they must have known that it wasn't the case. Ag, its all speculation on my part, it's not . . . and he shrugs.

I carry on: And all that stuff, the things that happened in another country, has nothing to do with this story, and besides. . . . We sit in silence; I am conscious of his shoulder tense against mine. Then, when David speaks, his voice drops to a tortured whisper, and I am glad that I cannot see his face in the dark: It's here in close-up, before my very eyes, the screen full-bleed with Dulcie. Who? Is it you put it in my head? The terrible things happening to Dulcie? It's here, in close-up—and he stumbles to his feet with a horrible cry, knocking me over as he charges out.

I scramble fully clothed into my cold bed and pull the covers over my ears.

I no longer know which story I am trying to write. Who could keep going in a straight line with so many stories, like feral siblings, separated and each running wild, chasing each other's tales?

Recently I have become aware of the complexities of walking. It has something to do with the realisation that other people stride purposefully, mark out their paths mentally and do not expect to deviate, so that anyone else, especially a clumsy, steatopygous woman like myself, simply has to get out of the way or risk being knocked down. Looking back to trace my craven zigzag paths, I cannot help but feel a sense of shame. Thus I am practising my walking skills. It is by no means as difficult as I thought it would be. I hope to compensate for the skimpiness of this tale by sharing (as they say these days) the trick with you.

Take a generous space, like St. George's Mall in the centre of Town at about ten o'clock in the morning, before it gets too busy. Mark out your path, lift your chin, and fix your eyes on a landmark well ahead. Now stride purposefully and resolve not to give way to the well-dressed man who comes straight at you. A collision seems unavoidable, but at the very last second and with an expression of disbelief he will swerve to avoid brushing against you. (The same principle, incidentally, holds for developing confidence/competence in driving a car.)

Encouraged by my first success I keep on trying, using expensive middle-aged men in four-piece suits and with attaché cases as practise targets. It works like a dream except that some, who do not get the point at all, tell me sternly to look where I am going.

In spite of practising these manoeuvres again today, I have been knocked rather severely by a youngish man, a windbroek in casual dress—the same one, I swear, for whom I had to leap out of the way in the Claremont Shopping Centre yesterday, the very incident that made me apply myself to the complexities of walking.

Just as I no longer want to have anymore to do with Dulcie's story, as I fear that my inventions on the page might turn into a demon, an uncontrollable tokolos, David does a turnabout. He behaves as if he had said nothing last night and brushes off my attempts to return to that.

All this business with Le Fleur has rubbed off on me. Imagine having visions, he laughs. But it is very important, he now says, that we try to piece together a story for her; now it would seem not to be so impossible after all. There is something manic about his manner. I do not believe that he has changed his position. It may be simply his desire to speak of her; he will be as recalcitrant as ever with real information. He tries to get round me as I resist being drawn into this false cheer.

Howzit with you my friend, he beams, slapping me of all people on the back. At least he no longer tries to call me comrade.

I say, smiling, prevaricating, Fair-to-mild, in imitation of Ouma Sarie's new interjections in English: Yes, because, why, the little ones, her very own Jamie and Chantal with their grand English names, are not sommer-so-platlangs—vulgar farm children—no, they speak their English alright and she, old Saartjie, will have to spruce up her own how-do-you-dos. To this purpose she listens to Radio Good Hope, to the messages of birthday greetings and anniversaries and well-wishings of all kinds, for the sick and the far away and, if the truth be told, messages for people nearby that do not sound so respectable at all. Young people nowadays, sending messages to, as they say, everybody who knows me, no wonder the air crackles with lightning sounds and the weather has gone all topsy-turvy—imagine, proper summer days in the second week of June. No, she will have to set an example, she argues, in order to give herself an all-clear for a message. It's all change nowadays and there is no reason in the world why she, Ouma Sarie, shouldn't cheer Sally up with a radio request and have at the same time the pleasure of hearing her own voice crackle like that of God through a porcelain blue sky.

Ouma Sarie rehearses: A message, please, for my daughter, Sally, whom the Good Lord has seen fit to guide through ups and downs and to bless with two lovely children, Jamie and Chantal, and a very nice house also. Keep it always clean and tidy, tidiness is next to godliness, and keep cheerful, my girl, and the Good Lord will keep his fatherly eye on your efforts.

Ag, no, those words about fatherly eye are from dominee, when he always ends his house visit with a nice little spray of English. No, she'll find her own, but then, thank God, she remembers that you have to speak on the telephone for this radio business, so just as well she hasn't wasted her efforts on that plan. . . .

David interrupts with a clearing of the throat. Okay, he says, that will do for the mother-in-law jokes. How are you getting on with Dulcie?

Let me tell you another story, I say. About Bronwyn the Brown Witch who can do anything at all. Oh, there are tests galore for her, the usual ones of three wishes, three trips into the woods, three impossible tasks. She passes them all. She uses her magical powers to get her friends out of scrapes, to feed the poor, to stave off hurricanes and earthquakes, to drive back the enemy, until one day her friends, the sticks in the forest, come clattering together, lay themselves down on top of each other until they are a mighty woodpile. There is no way out. Bronwyn the Witch must die on the stake.

It's only a wee little story, I say, as I watch his face crumple and his hands foolishly clutch at his person, patting himself, as if looking for a handkerchief or a gun.

You've been to university, you've read all kinds of books, poetry and stuff, he says, you must know about such things, about how things happen, how they twist and turn and become something else, what such terrible things really mean . . . how to write about, how to turn it into a proper story . . .

David's hand shakes. It would seem that he is not dissembling. But how could I possibly know what he's talking about, and who could possibly have such simple faith in formal education?

Just as I think that this man is a windbroek after all, he composes himself and tells me that he has never been able to bear violence of any kind, that to join the resistance movement and overcome cowardice had been the most terrifying decision. That as a child, he dared not confess to his father how his stomach heaved as he had to help with the slaughtering of a sheep, how that brave man, sensing his distaste, had made him hold the severed head from which the warm blood pumped into his hands.

Before his eyes he sees again the black-and-white skin of the sheep hanging in the shed, studded with coarse rock salt. David puts his hands to his ears as his head pounds, presumably with the bleating of a lamb. Or the buzz of bluebottles.

You're wrong, he says, hands still clamped over his ears, eyes shut, haltingly, as if the words are being hauled up from the deep. The sticks won't sacrifice themselves. Yes, she's grown too big for her boots and they've had enough of her. She must give up her power, hand over her uniform, make way for the big men. But that is not enough. She knows too much; knows the very fabrications, the history of every stitch against her. She must—and he stops abruptly.

Why the silence, I ask, why does she not speak out?

Belief. Pride. Pride in belief. The virus of secrecy. Either the very proof of her innocence or the play with secrecy—secrecy turned inside out. Whichever way, they can rely on her; in that world things have different meanings. Just as freedom is not the anaemic thing for us that it is for nice, clean liberals, so violence, too, is not a streaming sheet of blood or gore. That is something you people can't bring yourself to understand.

We sit in silence. Then his hands slide from his ears as he looks up at me. You know, Dulcie will be alright. She'll hang in there by the skin of her teeth and she won't give up a damn thing. Yes, he says slowly, she won't be sacrificed, by God, she's a witch alright.

And he leaves, patting the seat of his trousers repeatedly, as if to check for a handkerchief or a gun, or that shrinking of flesh that turns a man into what his father calls a windbroek.

∿

I ought to explain that there is another page, one without words. One that came just after the Kok family tree that he drew for my benefit. I have had it right from the start.

There are geometrical shapes: squares, rectangles, triangles —isosceles and right-angled—hexagons, polygons, parallelograms, and especially diamonds. The cartoonist's oblique lines that indicate sparkling are arranged about each diamond, but I now see that these have been done with another pen, perhaps added later.

There are the dismembered shapes of a body: an asexual torso, like a dressmaker's dummy; arms bent the wrong way at the elbows; legs; swollen feet; hands like claws.

There is a head, an upside-down smiling head, which admittedly does not resemble her, except for the outline of bushy hair.

I have no doubt that it is Dulcie who lies mutilated on the page.

∿

CAPE TOWN, 1991

There will be an ANC rally on Thursday in the centre of Cape Town.
As if everybody does not know it, there is this peculiar message on my answer-phone. There are no other messages.

As if the 1960s BBC-received pronunciation still used by

SABC newsreaders is not humorous enough, there is something parodic about this newsreader's voice.

There will be an ANC rally on Thursday in the centre of Cape Town. Buses from the townships will arrive by ten A.M. and toyi-toying to the Parade is scheduled to settle down by midday when the crowds will be addressed by Bishop Tutu and Joe Slovo. You are most welcome to attend.

The sixteenth of June—Soweto Day—Youth Day—Bloomsday—Day of the Revolution of the Word—birthday of freedom. I do not usually attend rallies. Except, of course, the historic moment of Mandela's release. But I am impressed with this invitation. Has the Movement managed to infiltrate all the media in the official voice of the newscaster?

It is an invitation I cannot refuse.

Ouma Sarie is miffed that David has been home only for a couple of hours, leaving soon after midnight again for Guguletu. Sally, too, will be going with her own organisation, leaving her to come with the children in the neighbourhood bus. Mrs. January from next door and the Diederikses opposite have been instructed to keep an eye on her, and just as well 'cause Ouma's heart isn't in this business of stampeding and toyi-toying, like those embarrassing people from the Apostolic Church. The neighbours have, since Sally's departure at dawn, been in and out of the house, leaving the door and the gate open, organising their communal picnic, chivvying her along, and Ouma, although not ungrateful for the help, can't but worry about the familiarity of these town people.

No, thank you, she said only yesterday, if you don't mind, Mrs. January, I'll just carry on calling you Mrs. January.

It's just an excuse these younger people have to be disrespectful, so she herself can be you-ed and your-ed and called by her first name. But she must say, even if the woman is now forward, her meat frikkadels are out of this world.

In the bus a young man ties large gold, green, and black rosettes to their jerseys and pretty ribbons around their hats, and although Ouma wishes to nurse her bad temper and her scepticism,

the laughter and babble of the children, the guitar and the jolly singing, and Mrs. January pressing her to eat just a teeny-weeny
frikkadel before they even get on to the highway, soon lift her spirits, so that in no time she is singing along, the children helping her
with the funny black words, so old-fashioned, her little ones,
they know everything about the struggle. How nice and jolly it is
in the bus. Together the big women lift their arms and sway to the
song, happy-y-y like the New Year Coon Carnival she saw on the
TV last year—although that lot with their minstrel faces, she
remembers in time, withdrawing the private comparison, are just
a disgrace. Which for a while makes her compose herself as she concentrates on her dignity. But the mood is too infectious, and by the
time they arrive in Castle Street where the buses park, Ouma
Sarie tumbles toyi-toying out of the bus like everyone else.

It is a perfect winter's day with a jewel of a sun in a bright blue
sky. If she had earlier doubted the wisdom of coming along, she
now knows that God himself is smiling up there, for would he not
have churned up the streets with proper Cape wind and rain if he
had not approved? But this day is a sign that the young people have
been right after all, that what the government these long years have
told them was the straight and narrow path was all the time the ways
of the devil. How could such a fine-looking gentleman like Nelson
Mandela—she just knows that he must have good coloured blood
in him—not be the voice of truth and justice. And so she toyi-toyis
gaily up Buitenkant Street, where a contingent from one of the black
townships joins in so that they all get mixed up together, actually holding onto the bony waist of a sisi—and oh, how good it is,
with everyone out in the warm winter sunshine today.

What a pity her Joop is not there to see how the world has turned
out, how they are all together like Jesus said, singing and dancing,
and when the sisi in front of her—very neat and clean she must
say—falters and faints, she whips out to administer the rooi laventel she had the presence of mind to stuff hastily into her bosom.
With that and a bite of Mrs. January's frikkadel, the old woman is
soon revived, and they all take the opportunity to rest on the shimmering granite wall of the old Standard Bank building, defying the

steward who tries to shoo them along. Ouma Sarie, a country woman who in her youth only dreamt of being a nurse in crisp white uniform, is quite the centre of attention as she ties a scarf tightly around the stomach of a retching little boy and massages the ankle of an old man, with the Zambuk ointment she carries along for the children, until the tendon springs back into place. Her face is aglow with well-being, and emboldened by the events of the day, she tries to take the children into the grand Standard Bank building in search of a toilet. But as she stands at the threshold, a child in each hand, looking at a familiar tiled floor, a geometric pattern of blue, white, and terra-cotta, her heart tilts, and for a moment she is not surprised to find that the heavy doors before her are being firmly shut.

Then Ouma beats at the carved doors and shouts, To hell with the Logan; to hell with the Farquhars. This is now Mandela's tiled floor, Mandela's bank, Mandela's toilets.

The children, trained in chanting, shout after her, Mandela's floor, Mandela's toilet. Another child takes over, Kill the Boer, kill the farmer, kill the bubbi in his pyjama, but he is soundly beaten over the head by a man in an old-fashioned red fez. All of which confuses Ouma, who has to be helped down the marble steps. Memories of 16 June 1976 and of Sharpeville before that buzz like persistent flies around her head, a memory of shooing everyone indoors in case the three black men employed by the Logan Hotel were to go on the rampage. She swats Sharpeville aside decisively, intent on a new vision of peace and justice and harmony, just as Sally explained.

She may not catch all of the speech making, but knows that they are very, very good. Bishop Tutu, say what you like, is a fine, fine speaker, cutting a grand figure in his purple frock, a colour straight from heaven as she has always said, his voice like the engine of a train through a hilly landscape, just gathering steam and beauty as he speaks of those very good things, of rebuilding the country, of food and health and housing for all, of the forthcoming elections and, oh, even her Joop would not have minded his swaying and clapping like an Apostolic, for there comes a season, a time and a place, when even Apostolic behaviour must be overlooked. And what a sensible white man that Mr. Slovo is in his communist socks; she can only hope that he changes them from time to time, even though it's winter, 'cause since he's been back in the country the TV has been speaking nonstop about these red socks. Anyone can see his name in his oupa's own language means *the word*—she read that somewhere—for the words that come tumbling out of his mouth are like the clear mountain stream of the Word which was with God and the Word that was God, a new beginning of light that shines in the darkness and the darkness has not overcome it. Before her very eyes the Word becomes flesh, full of grace and truth, so that the whole city, crammed into the Grand Parade and spilling over into the streets, beholds the glory of justice and freedom finally come, and she blushes for the white people's lies, Boer and English lies fed over the years and foolishly swallowed by her, and then her eyes fill with tears of shame for the poor Mrs. Slovo, a pretty woman, too, blown to bits, they say for standing up against those lies, even if they weren't married—why else would she be called by some other name?—but what does she, old Sarie, care any more about such things in the face of abomination; she will honour the woman with the fine married name she deserves. That the man is a saint and not a communist at all is as clear as this wondrous day that God has given them to celebrate freedom.

As the food is shared around and the children dart about like dassies, Ouma zealously holds her left fist up, stamps her feet, oblivious of the beer being smuggled under her very nose. There is a wonderful smell of herbal smoke in the air, much nicer than cigarettes; there is singing and dancing, and when the bishop sets free clutch after clutch of coloured balloons, lifted by the breeze and kept hovering just out of reach, Ouma, overcome by the beauty of it all, feels, first in her heart, the transformation, turning her inside out, turning her into a princess—yes, nothing short of a princess, waving her fist like a magic wand in this fairyland.

Nkosi sikilele iAfrika / Malu apanyiswe lumu lwayo.

Their voices swoop like summer swallows, weaving up through the balloons to circle the very top of Table Mountain.

The sun is a ball of fire and the sky is streaked with the holiest reds and gold by the time they are finally settled in the bus. Yes, what a business getting themselves together, all these people tired, lost, and jostled, as they must be even in fairyland, where she explains to the whining children, patience also must be practised. But now, as the engine starts up, they fall asleep with heavy bladders, the beauty of the day stamped on their chocolate-smudged faces.

There is no time the next day to shake her head over the newspapers that describe the rally as a day of chaos, pandemonium, of looting and burning by dagga-drunk skollies. David has disappeared. Comrades ring to see whether he has turned up; no one has seen him since early evening, when the crowd dispersed. He was supposed to drive to Comrade K's house for a short meeting, but nothing has been seen or heard of him since that arrangement was made. Sally refuses to take the harmansdruppels mixed with rooi lavantel that her mother puts before her, so that Ouma is forced to slip it into her coffee.

A rally may be no place to practise walking, but I have been too lax. I have fallen down or have been tripped up in the crush, so that, trampled underfoot by toyi-toyiers, my bones are all but broken and my body spectacularly purple with bruises. I try to ring David but his telephone stays engaged. I must confess to feeling a certain fear at this turn of events. When I return from the hospital there is a message on my answer-phone in the same old-fashioned SABC voice.

For broken bones take two teaspoons of harmansdruppels mixed with one spoon of rooi lavantel. Avoid taking with coffee. We repeat . . .

I cannot believe the childishness of this message.

~

The view coming around the bend at Chapman's Peak would have been breathtaking before dawn, at that darkest hour, the bewitched hour when those bewildered by the worlds they have shaped touch the amulets around their necks and grind their teeth. There would have been no baboons, no cars parked in the lay-by, no lone figure firing a camera at the picturesque water and towering rock, no need to slow down at all. There are the tyre marks of a screeching halt, as if he had decided only at the last minute to stop. There is a note on top of the pile of carefully folded clothes on the passenger seat. It is for Sally and the children: there is no explanation, only an apology and an assurance of his love.

In his trouser pocket there is a five rand note, some coins, and a freshly crumpled photograph of himself sitting at a white wrought-iron table, his head bent conspiratorially towards a round-faced, bespectacled man, who listens with a half-smile. They are surrounded by lush tropical vegetation; a palm frond brushes the side of the table, as in an elaborate studio photograph.

The body washed up a few days later is heavy with water; the staring eyes are glassy green bulbs, doll's eyes dropped carelessly into the ashen mahogany of his bloated face.

≈

I am sitting at my desk, looking out onto the lovely walled garden, and hear again the words of the red-faced estate agent: A nice little sun-trap, a very special feature of this place. Actually, he called it a home.

Not many small, two-bedroomed houses have such generous gardens. Not that this is small, he added hurriedly, but it is a very nice, a very private garden. Here, lady, you can sunbathe in your bikini or even in the nude without a worry in the world.

I stared at him coldly so that he said, by way of deleting, Yes, lady, and do a little bit of gardening in these very manageable borders.

These very manageable borders are now bleating with the yellow and orange heads of marigolds in their dark green foliage. The fig tree in the corner, leaning against a back wall that cracks under the burden, carries her proud litter of plump yellow figs. Bees buzz around their dripping ripeness. The whitewashed wall is heavily draped with black-eyed Suzies, their pale yellow or deep orange faces beaming like a million miniature suns. Look into any one of those brilliant black eyes and you will find that you have been fooled. Instead of the apparent protrusion of a fleshy cushion of stamens and stigmas, there is only a dark hole, an absence burnt into that bright face, an empty black cone that tapers towards a dark point of invisibility, of nothingness.

I take a break from writing this impossible story with a turn in my unseasonable garden, slipping a backup disk into my pocket as I always do. Especially since, on my return from the funeral, I found several days' work gone, replaced by a queer message in bold: *this text deletes itself.*

I part the marigold bushes in search of weeds, inhale the crinkled, bunched yellows of their medicinal scent; I nip off shrivelled Suzies, give the fig tree a shake. It is midday. A day without nuances. The sun is a clear yellow disk in a plain sky. Only when I turn to go back to work do I see her sturdy steatopygous form on the central patch of grass, where she has come to sunbathe in private. She is covered with goggas crawling and buzzing all over her syrup sweetness, exploring her orifices, plunging into her wounds; she makes no attempt to wipe the insects away, to shake them off. Instead, she seems grateful for the cover of creatures in the blinding light and under the scorching sun. Blinking, she may or may not, through eyes covered by the hairy filaments of goggas, see a pair of shoes disappearing comically over the wall, a figure lifting itself over into the public street. She yawns and stretches in the warm sun.

Is this no longer my property? I ask myself. I have never thought of Dulcie as a visitor in my garden.

It is midday. A day without nuances. But it is not like that. Sitting at my desk by the window, with my hands and eyes on the keyboard. I shriek as a bullet explodes into the back of the computer. Its memory leaks a silver puddle onto the desk, and the shrapnel of sorry words scuttle out, leaving behind whole syllables that tangle promiscuously with strange stems, strange prefixes, producing impossible hybrids that scramble my story. I look out, across at the full fig tree, where a figure leisurely takes his leave, climbing over the wall and crushing my black-eyed Suzies. Is this no longer my house, bought from the red-faced man with the lacklustre sales talk? Will I never know what's going on? Does no one care what I think? Will I ever be heard above the rude buzz of bluebottles?

My screen is in shards.

The words escape me.

I do not acknowledge this scrambled thing as mine.

I will have nothing more to do with it.

I wash my hands of this story.

∾

Afterword

David's Story is Zoë Wicomb's second book. Writing about her first book, a collection of short stories entitled *You Can't Get Lost in Cape Town* (1987), Toni Morrison said: "Wicomb has mined pure gold from that place—seductive, brilliant, and precious, her talent glitters."[1] The place Morrison refers to is South Africa; more specifically, a small rural settlement in Little Namaqualand in the Western Cape, where Wicomb was born in 1948, and where she lived most of her early life, until leaving for Britain in 1970. Her short stories depict rural life under an increasingly repressive apartheid government, and the growth of organized political resistance in Cape Town.

You Can't Get Lost in Cape Town has often been hailed as the first book of fiction set in South Africa by a woman classified "coloured" under apartheid legislation, but it is pathbreaking in more important ways than this.[2] While Wicomb's writing is given focus by protest against the material and psychological degradations of apartheid, its vitality derives from the daring literary and linguistic play, and from the distinctive positions given her characters in their intricate and subtle rejections of objectification, subordination, and despair. Hindsight helps us see this, of course, but in her short stories history seems to be on her characters' side.

The narrative present of *David's Story* is 1991, after the release from prison of Nelson Mandela, which heralded the beginning of the negotiated settlement that would bring an end to white minority rule in 1994. Now, six years after the country's first ever democratic elections, one hears Wicomb's voice warning about the future. Wicomb lives in Glasgow, but returns often to South Africa, and in one of her essays she writes movingly about returning in 1994 to vote for the first time in her life. Struck by the peacefulness and patience of the long voting queues, she nonetheless adds: "I also fear for our fragile democracy . . . why is this so?"[3] *David's Story* offers something like an answer.

Since the official abandonment of apartheid, South Africa has been engaged in debate about the meaning of nation and national belonging. South Africans have been forging new political, cultural and ethnic identities through the opportunities provided by democracy and a new constitution, and also the Truth and Reconciliation Commission and amnesty hearings, events with which *David's Story* is profoundly, if obliquely, concerned. One subject of debate includes the nature and status of the Khoisan people, and, within them, the Griqua, in whose name are raised questions about ethnic identities felt to have been politically eclipsed in both the old and the new systems.[4] This novel's interest in Griqua history makes it unusual in South African literature. The Griqua, who claim as their original language the Khoi language Xiri (not part of the Bantu linguistic group), have not generally identified themselves with the far more numerous Bantu-speaking indigenous peoples of South Africa,[5] and the concerns of *David's Story* stand somewhat apart from the black-white antagonisms often focused on in South African history. Moreover, the relation between the Griqua and the more general grouping of "coloured" has been variable and complex. Much of the plot centers specifically on Griqua self-definition rather than on this more general grouping, which, again, has been a more standard focus of South African writing.[6]

Simply in these respects, *David's Story* is a novel of its time and place. But it also addresses more general concerns. Self-consciously positioned as a postmodernist text, it does not try to simply "give voice" to those who were marginalised, oppressed, and disinherited by colonial and apartheid powers, or to those who may now feel (like the Griqua) that they are still silenced. Instead, *David's Story* dramatises the literary, political, philosophical, and ethical issues at stake in any attempt at retrieval of history and voice. It also questions notions of ethnic identity. Rather than striving for the illusion of immediacy, the novel uses a first-person frame narrator to fore-ground acts of representation and mediation, and adds other angles of narration (David's, Dulcie's, and a neutral voice) to unsettle any authoritative access to truth.

Zoë Wicomb's novel rises, then, to the challenges of story-telling in our postmodernist and postcolonial times. It uses mate-rial from a dubiously documented South African past, which it has fashioned into a narrative not seamless and entire to itself (as an earlier, realist tradition would have it) but fractured and fissured, and self-critical, even self-mocking, both of its own postmodernist play and of its occasional desire to be other than this. Astonishingly, despite a dominating wryness, the novel nonetheless satisfies readerly demands for a story; one might even want to say that it "brings history alive."

The novel draws to our attention some crucial questions not only about the South African past but also about its present—questions about responsibility, accountability, political integrity, and truth. It also asks us to think about two current issues, and—if we dare—the relation between them: first, about what happened in the African National Congress (ANC) detention camps; and, sec-ond, about the sanctioned treatment of ANC women. It does so with-out any sense of its own political rectitude, or even of its own moral authority. Its skepticism about political truth and its anxiety about responsibility are, in fact, self-reflexive as well: What kind of truth can fiction tell? Can fiction bring about political change? If not, what is its place in the world?

Wicomb is the first South African writer to engage with these post-apartheid issues in so focused a way. The historical, political, and ethical reach of this novel places it as a pioneering text of our time. Its critique of some aspects of the struggle against apartheid is launched from a secure sense of the atrocities of the apartheid past, where for decades a minority government presided over a system of violence in the service of political repression (a violence that was usually quite visible even to that part of the white population which might later pretend not to have seen it). The novel insists on the importance of confronting the past—the history of political subordination and accommodation, the history of women's bodies, the history of slavery—yet also celebrates the stories of courageous resistance that reach back into pre-apartheid days.

David's Story is a quintessentially South African novel, but in its literary and other allusions, it not only proclaims itself part of a South African literary tradition (its more obvious precursors are texts by writers as vastly different as J. M. Coetzee and Bessie Head) but also explicitly sees that tradition as a transaction between European imperialist power and a colonised world. Moreover, the novel positions itself on the world stage, alluding to writers as historically and geographically distinct as Laurence Sterne and Toni Morrison. It also brilliantly deepens its own nature as political fiction through its references to the Gothic novel, on the one hand, and the mystery spy thriller, on the other.

Perhaps the most important, if often also the most subtle, intertextual references made in *David's Story* are to Wicomb's other writing—both her short fiction and essays. Characters seem sometimes to have wandered across texts. For example, Tamieta in "A Clearing in the Bush," in *You Can't Get Lost in Cape Town*, and Deborah in "Another Story"[7] are clear antecedents for the magnificent Ouma Sarie in *David's Story*. Moreover, Wicomb's academic essays restage many of her literary concerns and strategies, whether she is engaged in a sharp critique of the political and aesthetic postures of the time, or whether she is celebrating glimpses of literary and political freedom. No reading could better illuminate *David's Story* than what she herself says about writing and representation.[8]

David's Story might have been called Dulcie's story if it had been possible to give voice to a woman like Dulcie, who is—David says—like a scream through his story (134). For David, Dulcie's is the story that needs to be but cannot be told, just as he finds that *truth* is a word that cannot be written. She is the unrepresentable body in pain, "a disturbance at this very time of liberation" (177). Her body absorbs and gives back the threats and promises of a violently oppressive and violently revolutionary past, a past that has not yet quite passed.

The narrator notes acerbically that there is no point screaming if you cannot imagine a possible rescue (134), but David yearns for an order to which a woman like Dulcie might appeal. So, through its skepticism—and even allowing for the element of play and the arch tones—the novel sometimes counters its pervasively bleak political prognosis with pressing questions about the possibilities of truth, love, and social commitment. These possibilities remain before us, hauntingly real, even if their persistence can be as terrifying to us as the endurance of Dulcie's body—beautiful, grotesque, tortured, and scarred. How do we live, with truth and love, in these violent and hateful times? How has Dulcie survived, and in what form, and at what cost, to herself and to us?

David's Story offers us such questions, and others, yet so elliptically and with such rich ambiguity that any critical response to the novel must find itself hard put to follow standard conventions of exposition and analysis. The novel even mockingly incorporates within itself acts of literary criticism which stand alongside the narrator's (and Sally's) amateur detective work as vain attempts at some certitude or truth. Much that is said in this afterword needs therefore to be seen as provisional; the provisionality of truth stands as one of Wicomb's major themes. Historical account, nevertheless, gives us a firmer place to start, before turning to the novel's relation to literary history, which will complicate the historical contextualization given here.

THE GRIQUA PAST AND PRESENT

The Griqua were descended from one of the largest groups (the Grigriqua or Chaguriqua; *qua* means "people") of the Khoi people, who were among South Africa's earliest aboriginal inhabitants, along with the San. Called, respectively, "Hottentots" and "Bushmen" by early travellers, and by recent historians brought together under the general name Khoisan,[9] these two groups suffered considerable disruption with the advent of the Dutch and the British colonists in the Cape of Good Hope, as well as with the earlier movement southwards of other African groups. In 1774, the Governor of the Cape Colony approved the following resolution: "[I]n the event of the

Hottentots and Bushmen not fleeing from their country, or giving it up on the combined attacks being made, they were to be entirely subdued and destroyed."[10]

In their relations with the colonists, these one-time nomadic pastoralists were left with only two strategies: symbiosis or retreat. Some chose to work for the colonists; others moved into less populated and less inviting parts of the country than those under Dutch occupation. When some travelled north to set up an independent state of their own beyond the Cape Colony, they chose to think of themselves as Griqua, even though they had by that time been joined by runaway—and, later, freed—slaves (brought to South Africa from Madagascar, Mozambique, India, Indonesia, and Malaysia), as well as people of mixed racial origin and a few whites. Moving first through Namaqualand and across the Orange River, they settled in 1804 at Klaarwater, which was renamed Griquastad (Griquatown), recalling an original political independence they were never again able to fully achieve.

In various ways the Griqua and the Dutch colonists came to follow the same lifestyle. They identified themselves in terms of similar myths—notably, the myth of the Promised Land, and the Great Trek or journey it entailed—and spoke a version of Dutch which would, in the late nineteenth and early twentieth centuries, develop into Afrikaans. Both proclaimed themselves Christian. But the Dutch colonists were more and more concerned to identify themselves as white, while the nineteenth-century Griqua embraced a variety of ethnicities. Like the British after them, the Dutch maintained their myth of whiteness largely through the "racial purity" of white women's wombs, turning a blind eye to white mens's sexual activity across racial lines. Racial mixture, in contrast, was an acknowledged part of Griquaness.

David's Story refers to various actual Griqua migrations and settlements of differing magnitude, and many of the characters in the novel's historical sections refer to real-life figures.[11] Adam Kok I led the eighteenth-century trek to Namaqualand, and the early nineteenth-century settlement in Griquatown and what came later to be called Griqualand West took place under the leadership of Andries Waterboer and Adam Kok II. Then, in the 1860s, there was a massive trek over the Drakensberg to what was then called Nomansland, later named Griqualand East, where Kokstad was founded; this involved some three thousand people under the leadership of Adam Kok III. And in 1922, Andrew le Fleur led about eight hundred Griqua (half of those then living in Kokstad, as well as some from other areas) to the southwestern Cape, settling in Beeswater, quite far south of the region first settled by Adam Kok I. (The Afrikaans name Beeswater literally means "cattle water"—that is, a cattle-watering place. In its English pronunciation, "Beeswater" feeds into the novel's Gothic theme, with its play on bees and beehives, cells, hexagons, honey, and water.)

Of particular importance to the novel, too, is the 1917 trek to Touwsrivier in the southwestern Cape, which Le Fleur believed to be rich in mineral deposits. An epidemic of Spanish influenza and a severe drought meant that the settlement (of about six hundred Griqua) largely dispersed during the next four or so years. Le Fleur engaged in various other land-buying schemes. In 1913, for instance, when he was living in Cape Town, he bought a farm from the Logan whose name comes up early in the text in Logan's Hotel (a real hotel, now called the Lord Milner Hotel, located in Matjiesfontein), and in 1916 he bought land on Welcome Estate, Mowbray Flats, in Cape Town. These farms were lost: the Land Bank (the Land and Agricultural Bank, established in 1912) refused to make loans to "coloureds," and the mortgage payments could not be met. Among the various smaller treks of the 1920s, the novel briefly signals the importance of Le Fleur's settlement on Robberg peninsula near Plettenberg Bay in the Cape. In the mid-1930s the group moved inland to Krantzhoek, where Le Fleur died in 1941; Krantzhoek is today known as the "emotional centre" of the Griquas.[12]

The issue of land rights for the Griqua was brought to a head by the move to Griqualand East, which came just before the discovery of diamonds in 1867 in Griqualand West. Griqualand West had by then become part of the Orange Free State, a Boer republic, and in anticipation of this trek, Adam Kok III had authorised an agent to sell his land to the Orange Free State government. There still remained in that territory, under the leadership of Andries Waterboer, other west Griqua communities who also owned land. The Boer farmers of the Orange Free State insisted that Kok had sold them all the land, and both to Waterboer's people and to Kok's people now further east, the rights to this now highly valued land became of immense consequence. When Griqualand West was annexed by the British in 1871 and incorporated into the Cape Colony in 1880, it was the Boers who were compensated for the diamond-bearing land. To add insult to injury, licenses to mine the land, and even to deal in diamonds, were being granted only to whites. The way was now clear for Cecil John Rhodes (a financier and politician who became prime minister of the Cape in 1890) and his De Beers Mining Company to make their fortunes.

In 1879 Griqualand East, too, was annexed by the Cape government, the Griqua once again being persuaded to sell—and in other ways losing their land—to whites. This added to the urgency of the action instituted first by Adam Kok's political heir, Abraham le Fleur, and then by his son, Andries Abraham Stockenstrom le Fleur (later known as Andrew), the paramount chief, or *opperhoof*, who forms the focus of David's research. Andrew le Fleur's fragmentary autobiographical writing—actual historical texts from which Wicomb quotes in the novel—shows how disturbed he was to find the Griqua had "no status as a people,"[13] and his desire to establish national status was based at least partly on the recognition by others of a prior Griqua claim to the land. His fight for compensation, or what came to be called the "forty-years money"[14] in relation to land rights in Griqualand West, and for the retrocession of Griqualand East either to Griqua or direct British rule, meant he was perceived as an agitator, and he was imprisoned several times.

Le Fleur was first detained in 1897 for ten months (without being charged), on suspicion of some unrest involving the African tribes of the Bhaca, Hlangweni and others. On the second occasion, in February 1898, a month or so after Le Fleur and his followers had been engaged in a skirmish with a white farmer outside Kokstad, he was given up to the police by the ruler of the Mpondo people, Sigcau, and was sentenced to fourteen years' hard labour. He had by now become a felt threat to the British. The Cape Parliamentary Papers of 1898 quote his demand, "East Griqualand for the Griquas and the Natives," which, as the historian Christopher Saunders notes, sounded all too like Joseph Booth's "Africa for the Africans."[15] Le Fleur was confined first in the Breakwater prison in Cape Town and then on Robben Island. He served only five years of the sentence through a general amnesty decreed by Britain's new king, Edward VII, and was released in 1903, on condition he not return to Griqualand East. Le Fleur moved to Cape Town, where (from the Winter Garden in District Six)[16] he preached temperance and canvassed support for a Griqua Independent Church, finally founded in Maitland, Cape Town, in 1920. He also edited the weekly newspaper *Griqua and Coloured People's Opinion.*[17]

Then, back in Griqualand East, Le Fleur was arrested in 1920 and charged with theft, forgery, and fraud following complaints by those who had lost land and money through the Touwsrivier scheme. First remanded without bail, and spending four months in prison, he was eventually tried over a period of eleven months, finally being acquitted on the grounds that he was a "muddler or a blunderer" rather than a criminal.[18]

In 1922, a large group of Griqua under Le Fleur had settled in Beeswater in Namaqualand, but, since the land could barely sustain them, they also worked for whites. With Griqua labour, the white economy flourished; they, on the other hand, struggled against low wages and often succumbed to the drunkenness and alcoholism brought about by the "dop system," whereby farm labourers were rewarded for their labor with tots of brandy or wine. Any potential political threat on their part was further diminished by Le Fleur's developing separatism, which echoed a concept proposed by white government officials in the 1920s and 1930s, and, as Wicomb points out, prefigured the later racist policies of the National Party government (78, 150).

The Beeswater community moved to Kliprand in 1983, the "location" (as nonwhite urban settlements are called) bordering a white town. Echoing a moment in *You Can't Get Lost in Cape Town,* Wicomb notes that the modern facilities (clinic, school, running water at the end of each lane) are desirable to most of the community, despite the tall streetlights that attest so crudely to the surveillance that comes with modernity.[19] In real-life, too, the apartheid architecture did not, of course, keep the "terrorists" out: settlements in the same region as Wicomb's Kliprand were immediately visited by members of the newly established United Democratic Front (UDF).[20] As we see from the novel, Dulcie and David's task is to prevail against the Griqua ethnic nationalism Oom Paulse inherited from Andrew le Fleur.

The novel thus starts to make a set of subtly drawn connections between past and present, through which are produced the novel's political themes. Among these are references to ethnicity and political representation, and to diamonds and the land.

David's take on Le Fleur is that he was a sellout to want a separate homeland for a separate Griqua race, thus participating in an ideological line that would cohere with apartheid policy. An essay in Le Fleur's *Griqua and Coloured People's Opinion*, 11 December 1925, claims "dat ons een volk is, dan sal daar drie nasionaliteite in die land wees, nl. die Bantoe, die Grikwas en die Witman" ("that we are one people, then there will be three nationalities in the land, viz. the Bantu, the Griqua and the Whites"). Instead of identifying with Bantu speakers, Le Fleur was hostile towards the ANC, founded in 1912 as the South African Native National Council (SANNC) and generally proclaimed as a nonracial movement.[21] In contrast, the National Party, entrenched in 1948, developed its racial legislation first under the term *apartheid* and then, from the early 1960s, *separate development*. (The latter term was used to justify, often retrospectively, the retribalisation process behind the institution of the Bantu "homelands," the racially differentiated educational system launched from 1952, and the total removal, by 1956, of all remaining nonwhites from the common voters' roll.)

Wicomb shows that under Oom Paulse, too, leader of the Kliprand Council, the Griquas supported what the National Party government started calling in the late 1980s gradual reforms (130). Following Le Fleur's strategies as a Griqua nationalist who struck bargains with the government of the time, Oom Paulse also adopts, as did Le Fleur in his latter days, the fundamentalist talk with which Afrikaner Christian Nationalism, via its Calvinism, was associated. Here, as elsewhere, Wicomb's text makes a set of deft movements between a critique of apartheid government and of current Griqua thinking, which sometimes draws in colonial government policies as well. Wicomb suggests, furthermore, that Le Fleur's paranoid labelling as "Communist" those who disagree with him echoes National Party government attitudes, expressed especially in the way the Suppression of Communism Act of 1950 was used to silence and imprison many non-Communist opponents of apartheid. In addition, his institution of hard labour as a means of control is specifically likened by the text to the quarry digging and futile rock-crushing deployed by the Robben Island prison authorities, which refers back to the representation of his own convict days under the British colonial government, and also to the actual imprisonment on Robben Island of later political prisoners, including Nelson Mandela.

David's politics, on the other hand, lead him to fight for the non-racial democracy promised by the ANC. His interest in Le Fleur breeds suspicion, some of his fellow activists seeing his research as a sign of his own incomplete political allegiance to the liberation movement, perhaps even as treachery, given the Griqua refusal to identify as "black." But they miss the nuances of his interest in mixed ethnicity and the attempted finesse of his political activism: for him, the Griqua separatism which develops under Andrew le Fleur and continues into his own times is indeed problematic, and its betrayal of the black political community is one he works hard to reverse. It is important to stress, then—for an understanding of the novel's contemporary political theme—that the Le Fleur David is striving to recover is the figure uncorrupted by racism. Hence David's enormous pleasure and relief at hearing one of the Kokstad veterans recall Le Fleur's slogan: "East Griqualand for the Griquas and the Natives!" (138). David needs this recuperated, nonethnic Le Fleur as a model to live by, and as a model for present-day Griqua and others, given the (actual) tendency to turn back to the past to find a model for the future.[22]

Thematically, past and present are drawn together through references not only to ethnicity and political representation but also to land rights, closely bound up with national identity (and a still unresolved issue in the politics of reconciliation).[23] When David discusses among his new acquaintances in Kokstad Le Fleur's efforts to retrieve land which the Griqua in Griqualand East had been duped into selling, the text takes the opportunity to hint at the political connection across two temporalities: there is, both then and now, "no beating those white skelms" (138). The novel's major signifier here is diamonds, which are used in the text in more ways than can be noted here. Diamonds may be forever, as the double agent Thomas Stewart says, but they represent a valuable resource stolen, in effect, from the Griqua, and in the story's contemporary account they are used to tempt David into a reactionary illegality. Diamonds also take on symbolic value through David's informing Thomas of the word's etymology: the Greek *a-damas*, that which cannot be conquered or tamed. They stand as an analogue to, and sometimes as a corrupt substitute for, the Griqua national symbol, the kanniedood (literally, "can't die") plant, with its stacked triangular leaves.[24]

For much of his Griqua history, David's major sources (and ours) have been written histories, which turn to the newspapers of the time and also to Le Fleur's own writing. But these accounts are incomplete: to them must be added the stories told to David by his mother, grandmother, and great-grandmother, custodians of an oral tradition. It is through the stories of women (by women and about women) that another set of connections opens up between the past and the present, and looking at the text's reinvention of history through the stories of women will allow us to consider the narrator's suggestion that David may be using his interest in Griqua history to displace a memory of the more recent past, and even of what is happening in the present.

REINVENTION OF HISTORY

In its general details, Wicomb's account is historically faithful.[25] But David and his narrator together construct a startling, fertile, fictional connection between Le Fleur genealogy and the "father of biology," Georges Cuvier (1769-1832), professor of animal anatomy at the National Museum of Natural History in Paris. Although it is in 1688, well before Cuvier's existence, that Madame la Fleur, a Protestant Huguenot, leaves France for the Cape to escape the French Catholic persecutions, David playfully makes her Cuvier's housekeeper, "the good woman being lifted out of her period and grafted onto the wrong century" (35). If we are determined, as good but orthodox critics, to withstand the text's scornful rejoinder to those who "find meaning" in this historical disjuncture (35), we may consider the domestic connection to signal that Madame la Fleur's son Eduard is Cuvier's illegitimate son.

With a century being erased between Eduard's arrival soon after 1688 and Andries's birth in 1867, Andries/Andrew le Fleur is made the grandson of Eduard la Fleur (and thus Cuvier's great-grandson, perhaps). David's own heritage is multiply complicated through this genealogical fiction: Andrew le Fleur's secret union with David's great-grandmother, Antjie, makes David's grandmother, Ouma Ragel, Le Fleur's illegitimate child, so that David himself might be a Cuvier descendent. This will later allow us to ask about what David inherits.

An additional effect of Wicomb's genealogical reinvention is to stress Andries's connection with a French Huguenot line, thus rendering Griqua ethnicity even more complicated than it already is through its local intermixtures. Historically, Abraham le Fleur, Andries's father, was the son of a French missionary and a woman from Madagascar,[26] so through her fiction Wicomb re-establishes the truth of his racially mixed heritage. Using the Dutch name Andries, Wicomb further hybridises the European part of the Griqua heritage, and when, later, Andries Anglicises his name, the text signals the co-implication of Englishness in his developing racial exclusivism. His new name also stands as a neat literary allusion to the fictional figure, Andrew Flood, created by Sarah Gertrude Millin in her notoriously racist 1924 novel, *God's Step-children*, to be the progenitor of the Griqua race.[27]

Wicomb's major reinvention involves the stories of women.

The available written histories give scant information about the role of women in Griqua history, and the real-life figures Lady Kok and Rachel Susanna Kok are but briefly referred to. Wicomb gives the younger of the two (her name is now spelled Rachael) a good deal of fictional space, and also creates for the Beeswater sections the characters Antjie, Ant Mietjie, and Ouma Ragel.[28] Where history is silent, myth often speaks, and Wicomb's reinvention of history needs to deal with a current mythification involving two early South African women, Krotoa/Eva and Saartje Baartman. She confronts through these women the shameful attitudes to body shape that pervade racist South African thinking: as the narrator says, "steatopygia" is the word "that has set the story on its course" (17).

Lady Kok became the wife of Adam Kok III after the death of her husband, his brother, Abraham Kok, in the manner of many African rural patriarchal communities. Tellingly, besides being the object of his discourse on body shape, which Wicomb uses as an epigraph, Lady Kok is described in William Dower's 1902 history *The Early Annals of Kokstad and Griqualand East* as "sociable and talkative" among those with whom she shared "the Griqua tongue" but "shy and taciturn" with others, especially whites.[29] Histories also tell us that Rachel Susanna Kok, daughter of one of Adam's relatives, Adam Muis Kok (*muis* means "mouse"), was appointed as successor to Adam Kok III, with Lady Kok acting for her until she came of age. (Rachel's father was killed in 1878 in the Griqua rebellion against the proposed British annexation of Griqualand East.) It was not standard for women to take such positions. A contemporary historian points out that Britain's Queen Victoria must have provided a model,[30] but Wicomb offers an African model as well, through her reference to M'Ntatisi (38), regent in the 1820s and 1830s of the Batlokwa. (The Tlokwa clan was part of the Sotho; *ba* means "people.")

Rachael Susanna's inclusion in the story gives Wicomb the opportunity to stress both the woman's own authority and her wifely submission: that she passes to Le Fleur the staff of office passed to her by Lady Kok means that his political power is dependent on her. (The staff of office, symbol of political authority, was granted to Adam Kok I by the Dutch East India Company at the Cape.) Wicomb also provides through Rachael Susanna some sharp ironic critique of Le Fleur. Important in the Kokstad and Beeswater sections is her habit of singing in order to cover awkward political moments, but only later—in the narrative of Kliprand—will this kind of strategy open out into a fuller vocalisation of women's own agency and strength: Ant Mietjie's singing allows Dulcie's political intervention to be heard.

Rachael Susanna finds the idea of nation "an unhealthy and accommodating business," and is not silenced (at least not immediately) by the fact that her husband gives her a new name, Dorie, "with which to face this idea" (63). She is particularly repelled by his obsequious letters to General Louis Botha and General Hertzog. Botha, the first prime minister after the Act of Union in 1910, was the man ultimately responsible for the 1913 Natives Land Act, which deprived the indigenous people of most of the land. Hertzog, prime minister from 1924 to 1939, was the man responsible for removing the Cape African franchise. Rachael Susanna's repulsion signals her identification with the larger African community, rather than just Griqua or coloured.

In terms of the events of the novel, rather than the voices drawn in to narrate it, the most sustained inclusion of women is through Le Fleur's invention of the tradition of the Rain Sisters. Le Fleur chooses five Rain Sisters—Antjie and four others—from the most steatopygous women of Beeswater, "shaped by God into perfect vessels for collecting and carrying back radical moisture from the rain-soaked Cape peninsula" (153). Thus the text not only gives the (impossibly difficult) rainmaking position to women, whereas in the San antecedents rainmaking was performed mostly by men, but also accords steatopygia a new meaning in myth and history.

David's memory is haunted by women. In one of his many contradictions, he complains that there are too many women in the story, yet depends on their storytelling, whether for the historical facts and myths they provide or for their critique or for his own emotional stability. He not only chooses a woman as his narrator but also includes as part of his search for truth the restoration of stories about women—and for him, Krotoa and Saartje Baartman are crucial.

Krotoa (renamed Eva by the Dutch) is the first Khoi woman represented in the writing of early Cape Dutch settlers.[31] In or soon after 1652, she was employed in the castle as a servant by Maria de la Quellerie, the wife of Jan van Riebeeck, governor of the Cape. Krotoa later became an emissary between the Dutch and the Khoi. Her marriage in 1664 to a Danish explorer, Pieter van Meerhoff, brought them several children, which—along with her mastery of several languages and her skill as an interpreter—should have put paid to the theories of the eighteenth-century Swedish naturalist Linnaeus that the Khoikhoi were genetically inferior to Europeans.[32]

Saartje Baartman (1789–1815 or 1816) was a young Khoi woman taken to Europe in her early twenties as an ethnological museum exhibit, advertised as the "Hottentot Venus."[33] Displayed in a cage in London's Piccadilly and elsewhere, she suffered an early death, whereupon her brains, genitals, and skeleton were put on display at the Musée de l'Homme, the Museum of Mankind, in Paris, for about 150 years. (They were removed to a back room only about fifteen years ago.) The scientist in charge of the French exhibition was Georges Cuvier.

Despite David's protests, the narrator leaves his story about Krotoa out of the text. She agrees to include his story about Saartje Baartman, but does not. And then she does not—untrustworthy indeed!—honor his request to remove references to his love for Dulcie. What should we make of the distance the narrator sets up between David's and her own story, and what are the connections between Krotoa, Saartje Baartman, and Dulcie, in David's story?

As David's narrator mentions, Saartje Baartman has been the subject of numerous stories and poems in South African writing.[34] Her representation has also been the subject of intense recent debate.[35] Members of the newly established Khoisan Movement in the Cape claim her as an icon, deploying her as a figure through whom they might discard identification as coloured (and as part of the Bantu-speaking indigenous groups). In a similar initiative, the Griqua National Conference asked the French Foreign Ministry in 1995 to return her remains, for a local burial. Likewise, there have been various recent representations of Krotoa, in which she is sometimes positioned as a "founding mother."[36] Although Krotoa and Saartje Baartman are playfully both included and excluded in the text, the narrator's decision to erase David's stories about them flies in the face of these current ethnic identifications. As regards Saartje Baartman, the narrator suggests David is ignorant of the politics of representation, and is naïve to suggest—in his own narrative of nationalism—that she "belongs to all of us"; the narrator makes a sharp retort about the meaning of "us" (135).

There is, too, something David does not come to understand about his relation to women. He is able to interrogate Le Fleur's racism but learns nothing from his attitudes to women. He neither asks himself about his own choice of a woman narrator, nor stops himself from trying to silence her, and he comes to no understanding about his obsession with Dulcie. Moreover, the novel suggests David has inherited a longstanding attitude towards women.

Eduard's eyes are inherited from his mother—emerald green European eyes that are passed down the family line to trouble David Dirkse so.[37] And then Eduard is close enough to Cuvier (whether or not he is Cuvier's biological son) to see his ethnological collection, and either adopts or inherits what Wicomb presents as Cuvier's complex gaze on Khoi women's bodies, a fundamentally fragmenting gaze that manages its desire only through reordering it as contempt. Boldly, then, Wicomb establishes a connection between past attitudes to women and those of the present, whatever the racial affiliation.

Specifically, nineteenth-century attitudes to Saartje Baartman are echoed in the schoolboy behavior towards Dulcie ("they rhymed her blackness with her cunt" [80]). While Dulcie fights back in such instances, she is passive against the men who come to her at night. In another kind of example, Sally's underground political career tells its own nasty story about the "unspoken part of a girl's training" (123). There is a particularly tricky Wicombesque irony here: her trainer says sex with him will relax her, and it does, but just when we are compelled, as readers, to accede to this difficult suggestion, we are shown Sally's body dissolving—relaxation to the point of disappearance, perhaps. As Wicomb puts it elsewhere, Saartje Baartman's story reproduces itself "in puzzling distortions."[38]

Women's bodies are still the objects of an intermingled desire and disdain. David's interest in the past, and his (often ambivalent) belief in the possibilities opened up by women's storytelling, are simultaneous indications of his desire for truth, of his need for models to reconstruct the present, and of his inability to confront aspects of the present—specifically, the ANC treatment of women, and a world where "fucking women was a way of preventing them from rising" (179). Part of what remains untold in his account, then, is his connivance in the processes of idealisation, brutality, and silencing, manifest in his own occasional idealisation and silencing of women, his (possible) actual behavior towards Dulcie, and his refusal to face her fate.

Whereas current debate about Saartje Baartman refers to the need to rebury her body parts on home ground, Dulcie's body refuses burial. Dulcie's is the unwritten, pressing story of our times. Dulcie's story is a story of what has not yet been said about violence and betrayal, political commitment and love, about writing and representation and truth. For David, Dulcie remains at a stage of unrepresentability, not least because certain aspects of her treatment cannot be faced, since facing them would force him to confront his own past not only as victim but also as victimiser. Thus the notion of the unrepresentable, so fashionable a concept in postmodern and postcolonial debate, is deconstructed in Wicomb's text: it is given a historical context and a political force. The narrator's partial exclusion of the stories of Krotoa and Saartje Baartman offers a comment on the difficulties of telling Dulcie's story, and, in turn, Dulcie's story invites us to reinterpret Krotoa's and Saartje Baartman's—to make them less tidy, less readily comprehended.

"An emerging democratic order must acknowledge the fact that even within such an order there are power relations at play," Wicomb wrote in a 1991 essay. "Rather than pursue 'authenticity,' a radical culture would engage with such representations . . . intervene . . . *re*-present in ways that explore and challenge power relations."[39] Along these lines, then, Wicomb's revisionist story of women may be read as a story about women's bodies returning, which will take us, in due course, to the story about Dulcie returning.

THE HISTORY OF THE STRUGGLE

In 1991, when David Dirkse is thirty-five, it is clear to him and to many others that the South African government will soon change hands. When he visits Kokstad, in Griqualand East, the South African flag flying on the courthouse displays its bands of blue, white, and orange. The flag would change after the first democratic elections in 1994, and the birth of what then Bishop Tutu famously and sentimentally called the "rainbow nation."

Born in 1956, David would have been twenty in 1976, the "year of Soweto," and this is why he feels he can speak with authority about "such nonsense" as has entered the general public's understanding of this revolutionary event. He says that schoolchildren did not burst into "spontaneous rebellion over the Afrikaans language" (79), as suggested by the film *Cry Freedom* (a film about Steve Biko's rise as a revolutionary figure). Instead, an underground "military movement orchestrat[ed] the whole thing" (79). Questioning David's reliability here, the narrator's view is different: she calls 16 June the day of the revolution against (in part) the Afrikaans word, "the language of oppressors" (35).[40]

David refers here to Umkhonto we Sizwe (MK; literally, "Spear of the Nation"), established in 1961, the year in which the ANC was banned. This was initially an autonomous guerrilla organisation drawing its members from both the ANC and the South African Communist Party (SACP), but it later developed into the ANC's armed wing. David, like Dulcie, trained as an MK freedom fighter in the Soviet Union, Cuba, and Botswana, and also spent time in Angola, in the camp that later became notorious for its treatment of ANC dissidents, Quatro camp. In 1991, David's official task is to plan MK's role during the period of transition: How should the ANC maintain its army while officially dismantling it? Privately, he is investigating Griqua history in an attempt to retrieve its non-racialism, as a corrective both to the direction being taken by the Griqua community (as evident in Oom Paulse's political stance), and to incipient ethnocentricism in his own political movement, the ANC.

Since the ANC was banned, David and Dulcie's open political activity is conducted in the name of the United Democratic Front, a political movement launched in 1983.[41] The UDF's specific goal was to coordinate opposition to the National Party government's constitutional reforms (reforms which the Kliprand community would have largely supported), whereby coloured and Indian groups were given limited parliamentary representation through the "Tricameral Parliament," made up of three separate chambers which excluded black African voters.

Both the ANC and UDF had proclaimed themselves nonracial. However, there were few formal links between coloured and African areas, and some mutual suspicion based on ethnicity. Similarly, around the time David and Dulcie would have been canvassing in Kliprand, there was intensive debate in the ANC about whether whites, coloureds, and Indians should be allowed to become members of the ANC's National Executive Committee. Open membership was accepted in 1985, but the disagreement was bitter. Even though it tended to refer largely to Indians and whites rather than coloureds,[42] a feared Africanist tendency in the ANC provides a partial context for the suspiciousness among the Kliprand community that David and Dulcie need to overcome.[43]

In addition, UDF canvassers had difficulty making ANC converts in rural communities, given the readiness to believe National Party promises about secure employment and the possibilities of peace, and the rural mistrust of urban-based organisations, as well as a patriarchal conservatism at odds with the leadership roles sometimes being assumed by women. All the more significant, then, is Dulcie's capacity to attract the Kliprand community, although her soothing of Oom Paulse might be seen as something of a feminist betrayal.

David's current task is to go to Umtata, the capital of the Transkei region (one of the so-called Bantu homelands), presumably to consult ANC members there about maintaining an armed force. Here Wicomb interweaves into her political history elements of a mystery spy thriller, much of whose resonance will be lost without an understanding of the reference to the slave in the Glassford painting.

When David visits Glasgow in the mid-1980s, as part of a delegation of black teachers, but also doing underground work as the new commander of an ANC cell, he visits the People's Palace on Glasgow Green, entering it via its Winter Garden. The Winter Garden, a magnificent glass structure in the shape of a ship's hull, was built in 1896, a sign of Glasgow's increasing prosperity through colonial trade. Colonial trade between Europe and the West Indies began in 1707, continuing until the emancipation of slaves and the consequent commercial collapse of the West Indies in the mid-nineteenth century. Glasgow's prosperity was due largely to its position as the port through which West Indian tobacco and sugar were imported. And in Glasgow's Clyde Valley, sugar refining became a key industry—sugar refining having been made conveniently illegal in the British West Indies.[44]

For all its interest in "people's history," the People's Palace bears witness to its own political amnesia regarding the history of slavery and the place of slavery in the economic growth of Scotland.[45] This history mockingly reenters the territory of Griqualand East through the borrowed names of Scottish towns, villages, and banks. Some mission-educated Africans even bear Scottish names: Govan Mbeki, ANC and SACP veteran, for example, named after the Scottish missionary, Dr Govan, also bears the name of a Glasgow shipyard.

Nowhere in this novel is the history of slavery more brilliantly shown as both obscured and revealed than in the evanescent slave-face in the Glassford painting, and its extraordinary reappearance in Kokstad's Crown Hotel. The Glassford painting, which still hangs in the People's Palace, is a portrait of the family of the legendary tobacco lord, John Glassford of Dougalston (1715–83), painted by

Archibald McLaughlin in 1767. Tobias Smollett's novel *Humphrey Clinker* (1771) refers to Glassford's owning twenty-five ships on the high seas, and trading for above half a million sterling a year: he was one of Glasgow's major traders and bankers, and "one of the greatest merchants in Europe."[46] The family's new wealth is represented by, among other things, the red clothing and drapes that recall the red cloaks worn by the Glasgow tobacco lords. The painting also includes the figure of a slave (slaves were conventional signifiers of lucrative colonial connections in the artwork of the time)[47] whose face reemerges as that of the red-and-black liveried waiter at the Crown Hotel. (The song "Smoke Gets in Your Eyes" plays when David first finds the waiter familiar [109].)[48] David's "recognition" returns to him yet another memory, of Angola's Quatro camp, where he first saw the waiter.

David was at Quatro in 1984, an ANC detention camp near Quibaxe in northern Angola, for dissidents from within the ranks. Constructed in 1979, Quatro acquired its name because of its association with the Fort, the Johannesburg prison whose black section was known as Number 4. Because of his support of the mutineers' demands for greater democracy in the army, David was placed in solitary confinement, and (it seems) tortured: hence the deep scars on his feet, and the limp. When he remembers the painting at the People's Palace, he remembers his prison guard thumping his chest: "Imbokodo . . . [t]he boulder that crushes" (195). This was the name given the ANC security department.

Again, Wicomb draws upon historical facts, though barely hinted at.[49] There had been growing tension among guerrillas about the increasing lack of democracy in the ANC. South African guerrillas deployed in Angola wanted to fight in South Africa, against their real enemy, rather than against UNITA, the Angolan rebel army supported by the South African state. But in an atmosphere of paranoia—exacerbated by the unmasking in 1981 of a spy in the ANC high command—even those who simply wished to discuss general camp problems were often detained on suspicion of espionage. Seven ANC mutineers were sentenced to public execution; others were subjected to political reorientation courses in various Angolan detention camps. Of the eleven mutineers taken to Quatro, one man (Zaba Maledza) died in the punishment cell, through either suicide or execution. Although the ANC's Stuart Commission attributed blame for the mutiny partly to the excesses of the ANC security department, security personnel continued to act brutally to detainees. In the early 1990s, after the ANC was unbanned, survivors of the mutiny gave damning interviews in the British press as well as in South Africa. In 1992 Nelson Mandela appointed a Commission of Inquiry to investigate these and other complaints by former ANC detainees. More recently, the Truth and Reconciliation Commission heard evidence against the ANC security department, but many feel that the truth still has not been fully disclosed.[50]

David presents himself as able to come to terms with what he sees as the inevitable violence in revolutionary times. He would have been well aware of cases where guerrillas, captured and squeezed dry of information, would be turned into double agents; or where they would become so-called Askaris, men working undercover for the Special Forces or the police as assassins or saboteurs.[51] During the 1980s and early 1990s especially, immunity from prosecution was being offered to those involved in criminal activity in exchange for information about the ANC,[52] and covert political activity, whether involving security forces aligned to the NP government or to the ANC, was often intertwined with diamond and other smuggling. David's anger at Thomas's offer of engagement in the illicit diamond buying business (called IDB in the text), in exchange for a murder, is to be seen in this context, as is his general suspicion of Thomas and the waiter. His own body bears the marks of the victimised (his tinnitus must partly refer to the practice at Quatro of *ukumpompa*, blows and claps on inflated cheeks which often caused ear damage), but submission to torture, or the refusal to blow the whistle on it, is tied up in David's mind with political commitment. In his engagement with memory and truth, David's story to the narrator both reveals and does not reveal ANC atrocities against dissidents within its own ranks.

Wicomb's text also subtly alerts readers to the tensions surrounding the history of slavery in South Africa. Slavery has been and is still being largely erased in South African reconstructions of the past; to recall slavery is also to recall a mixed ethnic origin.[53] The reference to the changes made to the Glassford painting echoes Le Fleur's visit to Lord Milner (governor of the Cape from 1897 to 1905) in Cape Town. Confronted by Milner's engraving of Cape slaves, Le Fleur averts his eyes, just as he elsewhere denies slave heritage in the Griqua past. And then looking at Milner's portrait of contemporary white leaders, Le Fleur imagines his own figure displacing that of Cecil John Rhodes (149). This moment returns uncannily in the fantasy of his senile years (105, 146), when he believes himself called to be the governor of Rhodesia, which Rhodes had taken from the Matabele in 1890.

In these references to erasure and emergence, the text not only suggests that the mysteries and evasions of present day political and ethnic affiliations may be revealed through a recognition of the historical, colonial past, but also alerts us to the political tensions surrounding acts of memory and ethnic reconstruction. For David, the one-time slave reemerges, as it were, to become known in the present. Whether as an ANC watcher (now) or as an ANC prison guard (earlier), the waiter occupies a position of sinister mastery and control. David's new memory places himself as victim, and, like the waiter, as a witness to torture, and tethers them both to a past characterised by secrecy and their continued entrapment in a discourse of master and slave. The revealed secret may suddenly speak its various "truths," to whoever can hear—but as we shall see, memory screens truth as much as it uncovers it.

THE MEMORY OF WOMEN

David's memory of Quatro releases in him the memory of the terrible things happening to Dulcie "before my very eyes" (201). He does not again refer to what he has recalled. Instead, he is more manic than ever about piecing together Dulcie's story, as if his narrative engagement might allow him to cover over the truth.

In an interview in 1990, Wicomb said, "I don't imagine that I would ever have been able to speak and write if there hadn't been black consciousness, if there hadn't been feminism."[54] These two ethical-political positions continually interrogate each other in her fiction, each position nudging the other closer to the truth, giving rise to an awareness of the ways in which women's bodies are used as signs by political or cultural movements that at the same time refuse to hear what women say.

Wicomb went on to note that the national liberation struggle was suppressing gender issues rather than putting them "on the back-boiler," as contemporary apologists liked to claim.[55] Her concern in this novel with the abuse of women comes at a time when gender issues relating to violence against women still receive insufficient political attention (and virtually no political action). Even in the Truth and Reconciliation Commission hearings, which were meant to unearth a variety of forms of violence, violence against women was rarely a topic. This was first thought to be because the commission hearings were dominated by men, and special women's-only hearings were accordingly convened. Yet even at these segregated hearings, few women, and no active female combatants, came forward to testify. Joyce Seroke, one of the Truth and Reconciliation Commissioners and also chair of the Commission for Gender Equality in South Africa, said of these hearings that "we only began to scratch the surface" of the horror, although there were several "gruesome stories of sexual torture and violence."[56]

This silence excludes two kinds of stories. First, it excludes the stories of torture perpetrated against women by the South African apartheid security police,[57] the implications being that women have been only secondary victims of apartheid (mothers, wives, and sisters of primary victims, who were almost all men), and also that sexual assault against women is less serious than other torture. Wicomb's novel breaks this silence, not least by casting Dulcie as the commander of an ANC cell. Second, this silence excludes the stories of violence against ANC women by ANC men. Such stories are likely to take some years to emerge.[58] Zimbabwe's second Chimurenga, the War of Liberation, has been over for twenty years, but only recently have women guerrillas spoken of the sexual demands, abuses, and violence they were subjected to as part of military life.[59]

Insofar as it is a mystery story, this novel sets up as many mysteries as it solves, and it continually plays games with any attempt on the part of the reader-critic to unravel the novel's "meaning." Hints in the novel lead us to ask: To what extent is David himself responsible for Dulcie's death? Is he one of the men in whose nightly visits Dulcie finds it impossible to retrieve her own will, her own desire and voice? "She would not have been surprised to see those hands withdraw dripping with blood" (199). Is this what passes for love?

Despite her refusal to have sex with military colleagues, Dulcie's body may now be in sexual service to the struggle. She is of course agent as well as object, for we see her washing the blood off her hands. (Handwashings and other cleansings form an important trope through the text.) But does this dual existence mean that some of the questions we pose about David's political commitment and silence apply to her, too? Are her lover-torturers from the ANC's security branch or the apartheid state's? If the text implies that the signs of her torture are like a slave's branding (19), how would Dulcie's scars turn into something as miraculous as the living tree that Sethe in Toni Morrison's *Beloved* has on her back?[60]

It is the point of the novel not that such questions might be answered, but that they are posed; hence the novel's epigraph from Frantz Fanon: "Oh my body, make of me a man who questions."[61] Fanon has been an important influence in black South African thinking, and the focus Wicomb gives him here is telling,[62] for it reminds readers that a revolutionary stance should include self-questioning. Of course, this epigraph is ironic, too, not least since one sometimes finds in Fanon an idealisation of women similar to David's.[63]

If the plea reflects on David as the "man," it refers sardonically to his displacement onto his body, and from there onto Dulcie's body (and onto his woman narrator) a critical response to current political orthodoxies and erasures that he himself cannot directly face. If the plea is the narrator's, or the author's, the epigraph registers their own imperative to question through the body, which also takes us to Dulcie's body: if her body is in sexual service to the struggle, is it in sexual service to writing as well? Does the focus on her body mean the loss of her voice?

As the shrewd Ant Mietjie notes at one point, David's disturbance has to do not just with political commitment and political doubt but with love, with the place of love in the political struggle, and with the place of politics in love. (Sally's life with David offers a quotidian, less elevated staging of this issue.)

In her critical work, Wicomb has turned to issues raised in Bessie Head's writing. In Wicomb's fiction, too, Head stands alongside Toni Morrison as an important literary precursor. Head wrote in her novel *Maru* about relations between the Tswana and the enslaved and degraded Masarwa (one of the peoples of the San), using the perspective of a marginalised Masarwa woman to interrogate Tswana nationalism, and resurgent nationalism in general.[64] Wicomb's attention has been caught particularly by Head's interest in the inseparability of the struggle against racial and gender oppression, and by Head's concern to move beyond "a question of power"[65] in conceptualising relations between subject and nation and between women and men. In *Maru* a woman, and specifically her art, transforms, and then also fails to transform, an inherited patriarchal, racist world.[66]

Borrowing metaphors from Head, Wicomb draws attention to Dulcie's potentially transformative powers. Dulcie has a vision of her own heart rising over the city of Cape Town, hovering on the horizon and then bursting "to bathe the world in soft yellow light," and she hopes David might "see that heart in the eastern sky and feel his own drawn into its embrace of light" (115). In *Maru*, Margaret sees Moleka's love as "half suns glowing on the horizons of her heart"; the half suns represent her beloved's glance "like the early morning sunrise" into her heart.[67] As she stares "deep into her own peaceful heart," she imagines a new kind of male-female relation: "Maybe it was not even love as people usually think of it. Maybe it was everything else; necessity, recognition, courage, friendship and strength."[68] These connections emphasize Wicomb's interest in what can only be called a shared being between women and men, a love which has nothing to do with subordination or humiliation, and which involves a cooperation between women and men far from the asymmetrical relationship that in reality exists.[69]

Of course, David is too "preoccupied" to accept what Dulcie offers (115). Wicomb's ironic sword comes down once again.

WRITING BACK

Wicomb refers in her epigraphs and in the narrative itself to a large and wide ranging set of texts: colonial and South African texts by William Dower, Andrew le Fleur, Eugène Marais, Sarah Gertrude Millin, Nadine Gordimer, Bessie Head, J. M. Coetzee, Breyten Breytenbach, Thabo Shenge Luthuli, among others, as well as a more geographically and historically dispersed set of writers, such as Miguel de Cervantes, Hart Crane, Laurence Sterne, Joseph Conrad, James Joyce, Frantz Fanon, and Toni Morrison. Some of these writers are named in the novel; others remain unnamed. While the narrative allusions have a diverse function, the epigraphs, usually ironic, indicate the resistance offered by Wicomb's own text to a (mostly South African) literary tradition. For instance, early South African texts (Millin's, Dower's) act as a reminder of the English liberal tradition that preceded apartheid and is often indistinguishable from it, and later ones (Breytenbach's, Luthuli's) are placed to suggest a continuing racial bias.

There is a particular postcolonial satisfaction in seeing so much racist thinking from the past so smartly dispensed with. Within the presented world, too, we are given comforting representations of spirited rejoinders. Thus, for instance, soon after its publication in 1902, Le Fleur writes to the press objecting to the lies, omissions and slurs in Dower's *The Early Annals of Kokstad and East Griqualand*. Many of the intertextual references function, then, as part of the novel's strategy of "writing back,"[70] which occurs on three levels: that of the author, or the novel itself; that of the two major storytellers, the narrator, and David; and that of Le Fleur and other characters as well, if we include verbal retorts.

The postcolonial interest in "writing back" often involves not just the native writer's response but also the writer's representation of the native's existence prior to the coloniser, and hence his or her prior authority. Thus the term *back* may function in two ways: to mark the assertive retort, and to mark a temporal shift back to pre-colonial days. Yet Wicomb's intertextual references are usually more complex than this, weaving richly through the novel in an exploration of authority, memory, and truth. As we know, for example, from David's two different memories of meeting the old man to whom he gives, or does not give, his precious stone (23-24, 142), the novel is deeply engaged with questioning memory, and thus with the authority to which personal experience lays claim. Furthermore, when the text asserts that boerewors is not the sausage of the Boers at all, but was invented by "the Kok ancestors, those slave cooks who would go nowhere without their spices" (132),[71] it is not the precoloniality of Griqua identity being asserted.

The intertextual use Wicomb makes of a poem by the Afrikaans writer, Eugène Marais (1872-1936), suggests one kind of complexity and play. As the narrator and David tell us, Le Fleur derives his rain-making tradition from the poem "Die Lied van die Reën" (The Song of the Rain), which Marais first entitled "Die Dans van die Reën" (The Dance of the Rain).[72] In the narrative leading up to the poem, apparently based on a tale told Marais by a "Bushman" informant, Krom Joggom Konterdans (krom means "crooked") plucks at his four-string violin, making songs that sound like the rain. Around his neck is a copper necklace from Heitsi-eibib, the Khoi God, given him by the old woman Nasi-Tgam. (Antjie's and, later, Ant Mietjie's and Ouma Rhodes's expletive "Heitse" comes from this name.) At the end of the story he sings a song which Marais later published as a separate poem under the new title, changing the name Joggom to Jan. The song evokes the rain as a young girl whose bracelets and beads sparkle as she moves; she wears a copper ring round her neck and on her forehead a bright feather; her light footprints are the drops of the rain. The wild animals of the region race across the plains, and bend to see the footprints; the little folk under the earth hear her feet, too.

The novel's allusion to Marais's use of indigenous narrative incorporates Le Fleur's borrowing, David's borrowing, and its own borrowing from Marais and elsewhere, and is actually a smart joke about hybridity, authenticity, and the impossibility of true origins (to say nothing of its sly invitation to the critic to pursue these trivial issues of scholarship). David's rendition of the first two stanzas and final lines of the poem is faithful to Marais's poem. But when the narrator refers to an additional line—the "stampede of antelopes as they race to see her footmarks in the sand" (159)— it is remembered through its reference not to "big game" (*grootwild*), which is the term Marais uses, but through "antelopes," which gives more detailed substance to the image used by Marais, and also seems to assert the prior reality of the indigenous, remembered world. But this prior reality is itself marked as fictional, not least since the word "antelopes" derives not from Antjie but from the English translation of Marais's poem by Jack Cope and Uys Krige, found in *The Penguin Book of South African Verse* (1968). In another instance, too, the text both asserts a prior vision and destabilises it. In typical Wicomb irony, Antjie has simply been hearing goats (97), neither antelopes nor even part of Marais's (or Konterdans's) "big game," so that Le Fleur's invented tradition is additionally undercut. In all this, as part of its thematising of memory and true origin, the text offers a dizzying relation between "fiction" and "reality" which is, after all, no more than a relation between texts. It is simply the novel's "illusion of reality" which points to the indigenous past as a source for Marais's poem in a clever destabilisation of the notion of origin.

Another kind of "writing back" exists in the intertextual relations between *David's Story* and *God's Step-children*. Eduard la Fleur being placed in the progenitive Griqua position, instead of Andrew Flood,[73] Wicomb's (imagined) historical fact precedes Millin's and thus topples the authority of Millin's account—quite sensibly, since this kind of racial mixing in South Africa dates properly from the seventeenth century rather than 1821, which is when Millin placed Flood's arrival.

In *God's Step-children*, Millin generally approves the Griqua choice of a separate homeland from which to build an "uplifted," obedient Griqua nation. Following Dower on the Griqua, she also offers some patronising praise to the political order developed by the Kokstad community—"it was crude, but it worked"—yet sneers at the spectacle of idleness and of grasping entrepreneurship she manages simultaneously to create.[74] Heading a section set in Kokstad in 1991, Wicomb includes as epigraph a quotation from *God's Stepchildren* that ends: "but here, round about Griqualand West, they were nothing but an untidiness on God's earth—a mixture of degenerate brown peoples, rotten with sickness, an affront against Nature" (63).[75] The same passage from Millin is used in Wicomb's 1991 short piece, "Another Story," where the main character, Deborah, like Ouma Sarie, does all she can, as a good coloured woman, to be tidy and godly and not like Millin's type.[76] Yet Deborah's and Ouma Sarie's refusal to fit the stereotype is obedience, as well, as they subject themselves to the fundamental thinking from which racism springs, believing as they do (in the European Calvinist tradition) that "tidiness is next to godliness" (202).

Therefore, Wicomb's use of Millin is more complex than mere rebuttal, for it addresses notions of "implicatedness," even of contamination. Le Fleur in his later days is also in some ways a figure who has strayed from Millin's text. Following European definitions of "savagery," his vision of Griquaness repudiates, for example, the drawing of patterns on dung floors: "[W]e are no cousins to Xhosas; we are a pure Griqua people with our own traditions of cleanliness and plainness and hard work" (94). Le Fleur's social pronouncements direct the Griqua to behave oppositely, especially as regards idleness, a stereotype so frequently launched against indigenous South Africans.[77] Yet this reactive behavior does not free him from the racist symbolic order at root.

Wicomb sees the stereotype as part of a historical discursive tradition inherited by all South Africans. This insight is, of course, not new, and can be said to be a dominating interest in postcolonial writing. But Wicomb's focus is on the way this discursive order causes characters to behave in a certain way. Their reactions against racist slurs and predictions—by nature of being reactions—cannot suggest liberation from the symbolic order which gave rise to them. Wicomb then examines possible ways out of the characters' merely oppositional stance in an effort to produce alternative forms of identification. This constitutes an important intervention on her part, and, as we shall see, directly impacts on the reconstruction of memory to withstand damaging stereotypes.[78]

Wicomb's treatment of "shame" is a case in point. The notion of shame, its repression on the one hand, and its exorcism on the other, informs the novel in more ways than can be dealt with here. Most economically, however, we can refer back to Millin. Shameful, according to Millin, are the sexual unions that give rise to racial mixing, and in *God's Step-children* she developed a powerful and insidious "poetics of blood," relentlessly tracking down the "degenerate seed" from one family to the next.[79] Le Fleur anticipates Millin's notion of shame—"we whose very faces are branded with their shame will remove ourselves from their sight" (161)—in a gesture which enacts the racial separatism which white colonisers and settlers imposed on blacks. In contrast, for Rachael Susanna, birth can never be shame: it is not the "degenerate seed" that threatens to be spread, but instead "the infection of shame" (162). Thus Wicomb neatly transfers back to Millin obsessive notions about taint and flaw. Shame, instead, on those who spread such words!

And then, following through on this gradual liberation from oppressive discursive formations, Wicomb has David remember lying in his Ouma Antjie's lap, in so "ancient" a sleep that he can retrieve a different kind of thinking than that offered by white racism. Enmeshed with David's recall of his grandmother's lap is a memory of a visit to Cape Town's Natural History Museum, where he saw a diorama representing a wrinkled Khoi woman squatting by a fire (100). Wicomb depicts the same museum scene in "Another Story," but her character Deborah cannot speak of it, so shameful does it seem, even though she recognizes its absurdity: what Khoi woman would sit at an unlit fire?[80] In *David's Story* the diorama combines with a living scene, where Antjie is busy at the fire. David reclaims the stereotype from its stasis or timelessness, and at the same time exorcises shame, banishing it without denying its presence or power.

Laurence Sterne's novel *Tristram Shandy* (1759–67) is another important intertext for *David's Story*. Sterne parodies through Walter Shandy the Elizabethan belief in the four humours—the bodily fluids supposed to determine temperament and health—by referring to "the due contention for mastery betwixt the radical heat and the radical moisture."[81] In *David's Story*, these words are recited (152) and are said to come from Sterne's fictional manservant, who is indeed named in Sterne's *A Sentimental Journey* (1768) as La Fleur. Eduard, whose ill health keeps him in "darkest Africa," practices his uncle La Fleur's medical advice, and passes his sage words on to Andries (88). But in the process, the Irish writer's parodic voice has been lost, divested of its ironic signifying tones. So when Andries le Fleur encounters Walter Shandy's words—"O blessed health! . . . health depending upon the due contention for mastery betwixt the radical heat and the radical moisture"—and the word *radical* rushes like wine through the young boy's mind (88), it is a confusion of decontextualised words and discredited science about the humours that guides Le Fleur to his mad and community-disrupting vision—a vision of water springing from rock (152). And it is this discredited science, too, which urges Le Fleur to combat the radical heat of the newly settled land by deploying women's bodies as bearers of radical moisture (153). Secular texts have by now, we are told, largely replaced hymns (88). Wicomb's intertextual reference signifies thinking from Europe that knows nothing of the South African climate, and should be of no use to the Griqua. It is Dorie, and not Rachael, whom we hear repeat, "[A]ll will be well when we find the radical moisture" (96). Her voice is not her own.

Tristram Shandy is more extensively used in *David's Story* than can be addressed here. When Dulcie's steatopygous fat oozes from her body like the "oily and balsamous substance" Walter Shandy describes as the body's "radical moisture,"[82] Dulcie's body is asserting its own physicality, an assertion made against the kind of masculinist vision promoted by Walter Shandy in which "the lively heat and spirit of the body" is understood to be semen.[83] Le Fleur's associating this moisture with women's bodies may be radical in this context, yet he uses women's bodies as cultural signs rather than letting women speak for themselves. The representation of Dulcie's body, which is sometimes associated with beehives, bees, and insects attracted by honey, not only addresses Millin's references to Hottentots "swarming", and to their huts as being like "hives", but also echoes the language used in Walter Shandy's digression on methods of characterisation, in which he posits a dioptrical beehive as a device for truly observing the human soul with "all her maggots from their first engendering to their crawling forth," a soul seen clearly through its "dark covering of uncrystalized flesh and blood."[84] Dulcie's uncannily oozing body partly stands as a mockery of this kind of truth; partly, too, it suggests the disturbing psychic return of the betrayed body—betrayed by male comrades who stole her honey, and by David's representation, as she becomes a "glittering mummy of his making" (128).

There are other kinds of equally rich intertextualities which, again, often direct themselves into questions about authority, representation, writing, and truth. Conrad's *Heart of Darkness* (1902) is used to remind us that the truth about empire is its unspeakable horror.[85] It also indicates David's refusal to hear—or inability to bear—the truth about the political world he inhabits, and, further, emphasises his incrimination in the political horrors he attempts to disclose: "Has he, the intended, been directed into acting, into becoming the agent for others?" (117). In *Heart of Darkness*, the woman Kurtz intends to marry is placed as the feminine ideal, so unsullied by the business of empire that she may not be told the truth about the colonial exploitation of Africa. At the same time she is the purpose to which Kurtz's endeavor is (or pretends to be) directed: the proxy of Empire.[86] Wicomb's surprising gender-switch—Conrad's "Intended" become male—is underlined by the fact that the hit list is written in a "girlish hand" (113). Readers may even feel invited to turn the reference back to a question about Dulcie, that other "intended" in *David's Story*, and from there to move into a metafictional question about the use the text makes of Dulcie as the signifier of an unrepresentable excess, sometimes figured as "the feminine" in deconstructionist criticism.[87] And from there we may voice some anxious questions that tremble beneath the text itself: Is the narrator (and behind her, the woman writer) herself producing a preordained script, writing through Dulcie yet another version of the idealisation of the feminine? Or is this idealisation negated by the blood on Dulcie's hands? These are not the critic's questions, but the text's. Erasing Dulcie's name inscribes her into the plot, just as in the cases of Krotoa and Saartje Baartman. In an attempt to deny his responsibility for Dulcie's "erasure," David writes her name on a fresh piece of paper, claims, "It is they who obliterate her name" (119), and hands the hit-list (back) to the waiter (171).

"Writing back," for Wicomb, relates crucially to the rewriting of stereotypes, which undergo reversals, shape changes, and historical reorientations in her hand. The pernicious stereotype of the idleness of indigenous people, for instance, is instead made applicable to the "ladies in the Logan Hotel" (117) in a sharp joke about who works in this place. Wicomb celebrates the sounds of words: *carnelian*, for instance (175) and *steatopygia* (17). But, as David points out, the term *steatopygia* has become tarnished by white people's pathological interest in Khoi women's bodies. Wicomb's text renews the term, so that what is signified—"the natural fat padding of the buttocks" (17)—is often lovingly regarded instead. Steatopygia is linked by colonialists to concupiscence, and the narrator lightly suggests that indeed it is (96), and elsewhere ensures its erotic appeal (46), while at the same time questioning the colonialist linkage through the opposing term *windbroek* (34, 204 et passim), which also designates concupiscence, and an altogether more cowardly response to social realities that have to be faced. There are many other textual engagements with the word, which Wicomb restores as rich, complex, nuanced: changing shape, as it were, as it changes context.

The corruption of words, and their recuperation, is a focus of *You Can't Get Lost in Cape Town*, too. The last story, "A Trip to the Gifberge," divests the protea bush of the symbolism given it by the colonizer: "a bush is a bush; it doesn't become what people think they inject into it."[88] Cleansing language of its history, or cleansing history of its language, is not an easy task, nor can it be an unproblematic desideratum of writing. In "Another Story" Wicomb presents a nervous reminder of some of the difficulties attendant on cleansing language of its past; as she suggests in her character's

treatment of the apartheid label "coloured" and the reactive qual-
ifier "so-called," political correctness does not necessarily offer a model.[89]
Certainly, however, the horror of the stereotype depends on who
is doing the talking. In what we may take as a reference to Homi
Bhabha's essay on Morrison's *Beloved* and Gordimer's *My Son's Story*,
to which Wicomb has made a sharp retort,[90] Sally complains that
"there is always something to read about the tragedy of being
coloured and therefore, it would appear, in limbo," and about
black women's "great sturdy hams," yet she herself refers to her "very
own good heavy hams" (117).[91] Similarly, Wicomb is happy to use
the term "woolly" for hair (64). Context is all. Moreover, meaning
depends on the angle one adopts: Rachael Susanna Kok's tying of
her bonnet strings reads to her husband like obedience, but to her
it is the reverse (48).

WRITING AND THE POLITICS OF REPRESENTATION

David's Story is not only about revolutionary struggle; it is also about
a revolution in language. Hence the reference to Soweto Day,
when the schoolchildren of Soweto, and many other schoolchildren thereafter, rebelled against the language imposed on them by the
Bantu Education Act; 16 June is also James Joyce's Bloomsday, the
"day of the revolution of the word" (35).[92] (It is on this day that David
and Dulcie meet, and on the day after this, in another year, that David
disappears.) In 1993 Wicomb wrote of the need for "a radical ped-
agogy, a level of literacy that will allow our children to read works
of literature that will politicise them into an awareness not only of
power, but of the equivocal, the ambiguous, and the ironic which
is always embedded in power . . . that will sensitise those whose priv-
ilege has blinded them to the ironies of power."[93] Unlike the political slogan, or the propositional statement, or the either-or choices
upon which, for instance, the judicial system is based, writing
offers ambiguity, ambivalence, and nuance. One of the tasks of
the writer is to be both comprehensible and innovative, to represent
reality (or the illusion of reality) as it is commonly believed to be
experienced, as ordered and sequential, and at the same time to show

its actual ambiguities and confusions, the richness of its unknown and unconscious processes, the underside that is not commonly seen. "The oppositionality of writing," Wicomb has said in her essay "Why I Write," resides in the unexpected, the hitherto unsaid—"the known which . . . turns out to be what we had not known."[94]

In one of the most tantalising and elliptical of her statements about her own writing, Wicomb has referred to her need to write in a realist mode and at the same time not to impose order on reality: "[P]recisely because there isn't order, there's conflict and that's not only in the South African situation . . . I think it's important to have chaos on the page." She explains "chaos" as "an alternative to the camouflage of coherence that socio-political structures are about,"[95] and we may think of it also as that which has not yet entered language as proposition, or as cliché, or as meaning, or truth. This "chaos" is to be both feared and welcomed in reality as well as in writing; Wicomb cites the socio-political disorder in South Africa during the 1970s and 1980s, with the increase of violence by the state but also by the revolutionary forces that freed South Africa from white minority rule. For the narrator of *David's Story*, the physical "chaos" that Dulcie's body represents, lying peacefully in the writer's garden, and oozing its honey, may seem to be one thing; the "chaos" caused by the bullet in her computer may seem to be another, as words leak out and lose the kind of relation to one another that produces meaning (212). Yet both dramatise David's and the narrator's own fearful relation to writing: the celebration of truth and beauty may look all too like an act of mutilation.

The text makes an acerbic comment about the incapacity of the ANC to handle the truth (140), yet notes its own difficulty. David muses about metaphors such as the truth "in black and white" and "colouring the truth" (136) in a way that leads us to ask: What kind of world do we live in where truth cannot coexist with nuance? How can we be post-apartheid (in the metaphysical sense) if truth is still "black and white"? Moreover, what kind of world do we live in where love constitutes political betrayal? David says of his love for Dulcie, "To indulge in such passion is to betray the cause, and there is far too much of that already" (137). In the world he inhabits, rape and torture seem acceptable, as if the (understandable) paranoia of the political struggle makes them valid forms of behavior. Similarly, nuance may seem to be a betrayal. Wicomb offers a compelling contextualisation of women's silences here: in the face of Le Fleur's political accommodations and ethnic divisions, Rachael Susanna's voice starts fading, her body falls apart, and her buttocks grow vast with despair. This is a foreshadowing of Dulcie's transfiguration.

Dulcie represents a kind of flux and flexibility that both represents the chaotic act of writing and charts the contradictions and difficulties of her representation.[96] Of course, Dulcie is very much herself, too—a woman in political command, and under political subjection—but she nonetheless stands in this novel as an elusive force, the "bewitching phantom" Sterne speaks of in *Tristram Shandy* when he refers to the endless search for truth.[97] Indeed, if her representation fluctuates between the mythic and the real, so too does her name alert us to these two possibilities. For the mythic, a partial prototype is Dulcinea, the imaginary, idealised mistress in Miguel de Cervantes's *Don Quixote de la Mancha* (1605–1615), in whose name Don Quixote undertakes his various enterprises. For the real-life, a partial prototype is Dulcie September (1935–1988), ANC activist, whose murder in Paris still remains officially unresolved. When David and his narrator ponder a way to write about Dulcie, they allude to the possibilities offered by this story. "Perhaps," says David's narrator, "the whole of it should be translated into the passive voice. Or better still, the middle voice. If only that were not so unfashionably linked with the sixties and with French letters" (197).[98]

The novel offers opposing images of writing as truth—the rustle of the bougainvillea, for instance, and "a stack of so many dirty dinner plates that will not come unstuck as each bottom clings to another's grease" (197). When the narrator asks why Dulcie does not speak, David's answer, in effect, is that she has not developed the right tongue: "Just as freedom is not the anaemic thing for us as it is for nice, clean liberals, so violence too is not a streaming sheet of blood or gore" (204). All in all, it is a different and a more difficult truth that is being striven for than the one which depends on existing political discourse—and as in all great writing, questions are posed, rather than answers given. Dulcie remains to haunt us with questions about representation, history, revolution, and truth: her protean shape (35) is, as Wicomb has said of language, a "slippery system of signs" which "prevents it from being wholly appropriated by a dominant group as an instrument of repression."[99] She holds onto idealism, however embarrassing it seems; she has been serious as a revolutionary; she has done it too well for a woman; she would do it all again. (180)

Wicomb makes no claims for the material effectiveness of the literary. In a 1992 essay, she asks about the function of writing in a world where "beggars [are] beating at our doors for food."[100] And in "Why I Write" she says, "It seems dishonest to claim that you write in order to bring about political change. There are other shorter and more effective routes to that end."[101] Still, her interventions are profoundly political, like those offered by philosophical deconstruction, in that they work at the discursive formations which order the world. The literary and historical reinscription offered by *David's Story* strives for a truth beyond ideological construction yet nonetheless recognizes itself as text.

So all the while Wicomb's crisply ironic voice infuses the novel, at its sharpest around political orthodoxies or the claiming of authoritative positions: Antjie is "a good Griqua" (97); underground political activity is "boys' stuff" (187); and when Ouma Ragel insists the Griqua are not a drunken people, we see her "[s]truggling drunkenly to her feet" (95). And through Ouma Sarie's voice, comes the most distressing irony of all, for within it is embedded a question not only about South Africa's political future and its entrapment by the past, but also about the capacity of language to manage—and yet not manage, after all—to give harmony and peace and pleasure to the world. Ouma Sarie says, "And now, how everything's turning out alright, De Klerk letting Mandela out to help him fix up the country nicely and her Sally all settled down decently, herself a mother" (122). The writing does make it sound all right in the beautiful passage that follows, about "the pleasure of all that shimmering water in which her children play like fish knowing their way through the waves" (122). But soon enough Ouma has to "surfac[e] out of the cool blues and greens of sleep," and a little girl is sobbing (123). As Dulcie would say, "Put that in your pipe and smoke it" (199).

Dorothy Driver
University of Cape Town
October 2000

NOTES

My thanks are due to the University of Cape Town Research Administration for providing research funds to help in the preparation of this essay, and to Meg Samuelson for sterling assistance. My thanks also to Christopher Saunders and Tony Morphet.

1. Wicomb, *You Can't Get Lost in Cape Town* (1987; New York: Feminist Press, 2000). Morrison's comments appear on the cover of the first U.S. edition (New York: Pantheon, 1987).

2. See Carol Sicherman's afterword to the Feminist Press reprint of *You Can't Get Lost in Cape Town.* Sicherman lists useful critical responses, to which should be added the following: Judith Raiskin, "'Miskien of Gold Gemake': Zoë Wicomb," in *Snow on the Cane Fields: Women's Writing and Creole Subjectivity* (Minneapolis: U of Minnesota P, 1996) 205–233.

3. Wicomb, "Comment on Return to South Africa," *Kunapipi* 16.1 (1994) 576.

4. For an important indication of contemporary debate, see Andrew Bank, ed. *The Proceedings of the Khoisan Identities and Cultural Heritage Conference* (Cape Town: Institute for Historical Research, U of the Western Cape, in conjunction with Infosource CC, 1998). The Griqua have recently been accorded First Nation status by the United Nations, a status also granted to the San and Khoi people (and in other countries, the Australian Aborigines, the natives of Greenland, and several indigenous American peoples).

The development of Griqua ethnicity may be seen as a reaction to two major indications of official government attitude, one under a white minority government, and the other under a black majority government. Under apartheid, Griqua was a sub-category of Coloured. Following a practice established in the 1904 census, where Coloured and African were differentiated for the first time, the Population Registration Act of 1950 broadly distinguished between White, Coloured, and Native (i.e. African), and allowed for further subdivision according to the ethnicity of the two latter groups. In 1959 the coloured category was divided into Cape Coloured, Cape Malay, Griqua, Indian, Chinese, "other Asiatic," and "other Coloured." Despite the legal rigidity, confusing practices of racial classification continued to characterise the apartheid era. Classification was based on appearance, on general acceptance and repute, as well as on the idiosyncracies of government officials. Griqua were sometimes classified as African (in which case they would then be educated through the medium of one of the Bantu languages, under the Bantu Education Act of 1954). For this and further information, see Muriel Horrell, comp. *Laws Affecting Race Relations in South Africa (to the end of 1976)*(Johannesburg: South African Institute of Race Relations, 1978) especially 16–17.

The development of Griqua ethnicity may also be seen in the context of a recent speech made by Thabo Mbeki, then deputy president of the country, that the "Bushman" and "Hottentot" had perished as a people. The claim was made in a speech called "I Am An African," delivered at the opening of Parliament (8 May 1996) on the eve of the Constitutional Assembly accepting the new Constitution for South Africa. Speaking at the Khoisan Identities Conference, advocate Mansell Upham, Khoisan representative, said: "This incident perhaps illustrates best the extent of what I would turn [sic; i.e., term] 'Our national shame' . . . Unfortunately, the negotiated settlement that saw the official demise of apartheid purposely ignored the aboriginal peoples of the land" (Bank 42). A recent newspaper article by wellknown columnist John Matshikiza shows how politically charged Griqua identity remains, for it involves competing claims to the paramountcy, competing definitions of Griqua identity, and increasingly intense canvassing on the part of South Africa's major political parties for Griqua support. See John Matshikiza, "In Search of the Griqua and their real leader," *Weekly Mail & Guardian* (Johannesburg) 21 May 1999. In a recent conference paper (publication forthcoming in conference proceedings), Linda Waldman discusses the various different Griqua political groupings in current politics, and their strategic alliances. "No Rainbow Bus for Us: Building Nationalism in South Africa," paper presented at the conference entitled "Africa's Indigenous Peoples: 'First Peoples' or 'Marginalised Minorities,'" Centre of African Studies, U of Edinburgh, 24–25 May 2000.

5. See Joseph H. Greenberg, "The Click Languages," in *Studies in African Linguistic Classification* (New Haven: Compass, 1955) 80–94.

6. In the context of a rising tide of racial segregation, early proposals that the name Griqua simply replace that of Coloured depended on drawing coloureds into rural communities and establishing their economic independence in self-segregating homelands. In contrast, the African Political (later, People's) Organization (APO) attracted urban coloured support on the basis of integration into the wider society. (The APO was established in 1903 and flourished under the leadership of

Dr Abdullah Abdurahman from 1905 to 1940.) For relevant histories of coloured South Africans, see Ian Goldin, *Making Race: The Politics and Economics of Coloured Identity in South Africa* (London & New York: Longman, 1987); Gavin Lewis, *Between the Wire and the Wall: A History of South African 'Coloured' Politics* (New York: St Martins Press; Cape Town: David Philip, 1987); Mary Simons, "Organised Coloured Political Movements," in Hendrick W. van der Merwe and C. J. Groenewald, eds. *Occupational and Social Change among Coloured People in South Africa* (Cape Town: Juta, 1976) 202–237; and R. van der Ross, *Myths and Attitudes: An Inside Look at the Coloured People* (Cape Town: Tafelberg, 1979).

Recent Griqua nationalism distinguishes itself from the more general coloured grouping by being more ethnically understood. At the Khoisan Identities conference, Alan G. Morris felt the need to stress that Griqua identity should depend on "its special history as identifiable political and social communities . . . and diverse biological origins" rather than the "almost unwavering focus of the GNC [Griqua National Conference] on the Khoikhoi cultural origins of the group" (Bank 371). He also pointed out that the 1980 census figures of nearly 100,000 Griqua was so much higher than the 1860 figures that "a significant in-migration" is suggested, rather than natural demographic increase, due to the prior receptivity of the Griqua to outsiders (Bank 370–71). See also Alan G. Morris, "The Griqua and the Khoikhoi: Biology, Ethnicity and the Construction of Identity," *Kronos: Journal of Cape History* 24 (1997) 106–118. In relation specifically to the Nama people, another grouping within the Khoisan, Emile Boonzaier observes that, while they objected in the early 1980s to the label Nama and preferred coloured, by the late 1980s they asserted Nama identity. See "People, Parks and Politics: Resolving Conflicting Priorities in the Richtersveld," in M. Ramphele and C. McDowell, eds. *Restoring the Land: Environment and Change in Post-Apartheid South Africa* (London: Panos, 1991) 155–162. For a study of coloured literature, see Grant Farred, *Midfielder's Moment: Coloured Literature and Culture in Contemporary South Africa* (Boulder: Westview Press, 2000).

7. Wicomb, "Another Story," in Sarah Lefanu and Stephen Hayward, eds. *Colors of a New Day: Writing for South Africa* (1990; New York: Pantheon, 1991) 1–15.

8. Especially important is Wicomb's essay "Shame and Identity: The Case of the Coloured in South Africa," in Derek Attridge and Rosemary Jolly, eds. *Writing South Africa: Literature, Apartheid, and*

Democracy, 1970–1995 (Cambridge: Cambridge UP, 1998) 91–107. Here Wicomb addresses the white pathologising of black female sexuality and coloured complicity, the ethnocentric mythologising which excludes other cultural and political groups, the replacement of "the narrative of assimilation" (provided through the political activism of the 1970s and 1980s) by the "ambiguous coloured exclusion and self-exclusion from national liberation politics" (98), and the erasure of slavery and the loss of "all knowledge of our Xhosa, Indonesian, East African, or Khoi origins" (100). As her title indicates, she is interested in the operations of shame and silence in ethnic representations and self-representations: "We do not speak about miscegenation; it is after all the very nature of shame to stifle its own discourse" (92). Her essay proposes that instead of denying history and fabricating a totalizing colouredness, "multiple belongings" be accepted (105).

9. See Isaac Schapera, *The Khoisan Peoples of South Africa: Bushmen and Hottentots* (London: Routledge & Kegan Paul, 1960).

10. Qtd. in Samuel James Halford, *The Griquas of Griqualand* (Cape Town: Juta, [1949]) 13.

11. See the family tree on pages vi and vii. The genealogy of the Kok family is taken from William Dower, *The Early Annals of Kokstad and Griqualand East* ed. Christopher Saunders (1902; Pietermaritzburg & Durban: U of Natal P, Killie Campbell Africana Library, 1978) 169. Besides Halford and Saunders's edition of Dower, I am generally indebted to the following for historical information: Robert Edgar and Christopher Saunders, "A. A. S. Le Fleur and the Griqua Trek of 1917: Segregation, Self-Help, and Ethnic Identity," *The International Journal of African Historical Studies* 15.2 (1982) 201–20; Richard Elphick, *Khoikhoi and the Founding of White South Africa* (Johannesburg: Ravan, 1985); Robert Ross, *Adam Kok's Griquas: A Study in the Development of Stratification in South Africa* (Cambridge: Cambridge UP, 1976); Christopher Saunders and Nicholas Southey, *Historical Dictionary of South Africa*, 2nd ed. (Lanham, Md. & London: Scarecrow Press, 2000); Alf Wannenberg, *Forgotten Frontiersmen* (Cape Town: Howard Timmins, 1980).

12. Edgar and Saunders 220.

13. Le Fleur qtd. in Edgar and Saunders 203. Le Fleur's manuscripts are to be found in the Natal Archives and in the Cape Archives.

14. The term derived from the belief that forty years after an agreement made in 1848 between the Griqua and the British Cape

government, the Griqua would either recover possession of three million acres of land ceded to the British or be compensated for their loss (Dower 119–120).

15. Saunders's editorial notes in Dower 166.

16. The Winter Garden was the name of a building in District Six, whose ground floor was used as a hall for church meetings and dances. District Six, once a mixed-race community close to Cape Town city center and the docks, was declared a white group area in 1966, and subsequently demolished. Restitution is now underway. The District Six Museum is an important research resource whose website can be found at www.districtsix.co.za. In "Shame and Identity," Wicomb addresses the mythologising of District Six (94–96).

17. *Griqua and Coloured People's Opinion*, edited by Le Fleur, includes carefully detailed agricultural budgets that project a dream not only for Griqua prosperity but also "a happy future for all" (27 Feb. 1925). It runs notices of Le Fleur's countrywide tours, and exhortations about controlling the youth, especially through organisational structures for girls, and about the importance of "handcraft" (manual work) rather than book-learning for "our race [to become] industrious and self-supporting" (7 Feb. 1925). It is also worth noting that in its frequent reprinting of correspondence between Le Fleur and officialdom, some letters pass through P. Wicomb, secretary for the Griqua office in Cape Town.

18. *Cape Times* 30 Sept. 1921; qtd. in Edgar and Saunders 214.

19. In "When the Train Comes" in *You Can't Get Lost in Cape Town*, Frieda Shenton says: "We packed our things humming. I did not really understand what he [her father] was fussing about. The Coloured location did not seem so terrible. Electric lights meant no more oil lamps to clean and there was water from a tap at the end of each street" (30).

20. A recent history of the UDF notes that several trips were made to the West Coast and Namaqualand in the early 1980s by Cheryl Carolus and two male colleagues. Carolus was secretary of the Regional Executive Committee, and a leading figure in the United Women's Organisation. See Jeremy Seekings, *The UDF: A History of the United Democratic Front in South Africa, 1983–1991* (Cape Town: David Philip; Oxford: James Currey; Athens: Ohio UP, 2000) 82.

21. Some early African leaders addressed the possibility of equitable land segregation. While they knew that a fair division was unlikely under European hands, and were suspicious of the way land segregation was

deployed to abolish direct political representation, it is noteworthy that even their entertainment of this idea was later used to discredit them within the ANC. See Peter Walshe, *The Rise of African Nationalism in South Africa: The African National Congress, 1912–1952* (London: Hurst; Berkeley & Los Angeles, U of California P, 1970) 54.

22. For example, the GNC currently sees itself as retrieving the basic values of past Griqua communities, offering the following statement: *"[I]n die bruinman se soëke na sy siel moët daar weer gekyk word na dit wat ons voorouers vir ons nagelaat het, om daarna voort te bou op die pad wat ons in die nuwe bedeling van ons land moët loop."* This translates literally as follows: "[I]n the brown man's search for his soul we must re-examine what our ancestors left behind for us, and then build upon it on the road we have to take in the country's new dispensation." Tellingly, its somewhat free translation by one of the Griqua conference delegates uses the word *identity* for *soul*, and takes pains to stress the notion of a model from the past: "[I]n the brown man's search for identity it is critical that we go back to the lessons of our fathers and grasp at the values which were such an endemic part of the Griqua community" (Bank 6–7).

23. In 1995 the GNC sent a memorandum to then president Nelson Mandela asking for the return of all Griqua land. Their claim is complicated by the fact that the Land Rights Act of 1994 refers primarily to the restitution of land removed from South Africans by the 1913 Land Act, whereby 87% of the land was reserved for whites. For additional information, see Steven Robins, "Transgressing the Borderlands of Tradition and Modernity: Identity, Cultural Hybridity and Land Struggles in Namaqualand (1980–1994)," *Journal of Contemporary African Studies* 15.1 (1997) 23–43. The webpage for the Commission on Restitution of Land Rights can be found at www.restitution.pwv.gpv.za.

24. The kanniedood plant (tech. Gusteriah) is a small genus of the lily family closely related to the aloe, and grows only in the western and southern Cape regions. Known as "Khoisan rice," its flowers are edible, and its swollen roots provide water. It is represented on the Griqua flag as a national emblem. Richard Lee, at the Khoisan Identities Conference, noted: "This is a true survival plant like the people that it commemorates . . . It shelters under thorny Karoo bushes and camouflage to avoid grazers, small pieces of the leaves will take root and produce new plants and that is what I see coming out of this gathering. We are taking root and producing new plants" (Bank 47).

25. The historical texts cited in these notes provide information not fitted into this afterword. Wannenberg records, for example: "[Le Fleur's] mission in life is said to have been revealed to him on May 9, 1889 when, while searching for his father's donkeys in the veld, a voice told him to reunite the 'dead bones of Adam Kok' as a people" (186).

26. Edgar and Saunders 201.

27. Sarah Gertrude Millin, *God's Stepchildren* (1924; Johannesburg: Donker, 1986). The original title uses a hyphen: *God's Step-children.*

28. The continuing importance to the Griqua of oral tradition recounted by women, and of women as figureheads, is attested to by the following comment: "The Grand Lady of Griqua oral history is 'Volksmoeder' [Mother of the Nation] Dollie Jones of Krantzhoek, only remaining child of Die Kneg [God's servant, the name for Andrew le Fleur]. Nearly in her eighties, she has a vivid memory of, and can relate incidents in the lives of her 'oupa,' Adam Muis Kok, and other great men in the finest detail" (R. K. Belcher, "From Literature to Oral Tradition and Back Again," in Richard Whitaker and E. R. Sienaert, eds. *Oral Tradition and Literacy: Changing Visions of the World* [Durban: Natal U Oral Documentation and Research Centre, 1986] 269). Rachel Susanna le Fleur was president of the Griqua Women's Christian Association, established in 1920. See supplement to *Griqua and Coloured People's Opinion*, 10 July 1925, which refers to her simply as Mrs. R. S. Le Fleur. An unpublished essay by Sophie van Wyk, referring to Ragel Susanna le Fleur, notes her status as the Crown Mother of the Griqua (cited Bank 245, 252), as does Belcher (267). Other women in Wicomb's novel may be based on historical figures. Antjie is possibly derived from Annie Jood, in real-life the wife of Abraham le Fleur, and Andrew le Fleur's mother. The Rain Sisters are possibly based on the famous Griqua choirs established by Andrew le Fleur in 1919 (Wannenburg 187, Belcher 268). Lady Kok is also referred to as Margaret in historical accounts, as in the genealogy on page vi.

29. Dower 57.

30. Halford 128.

31. See G. M. Thom, *The Journal of Jan van Riebeeck* 3 vols. (Cape Town & Amsterdam: Balkema, 1952–1958). For further information about Krotoa, see Elphick 106–10 et passim; Christina Landman, "The Religious Krotoa (c. 1652–1674)," *Kronos: Journal of Cape History* 23 (1996) 22–35; V. C. Malherbe, *Krotoa, Called 'Eva': A Woman Between* (Cape Town: Centre for African Studies, U of Cape Town, 1990); Julia

Wells, "Eva's Men: Gender and Power in the Establishment of the Cape of Good Hope, 1652–74," *Journal of African History* 30 (1998) 417–437.

32. One of the Dutch officials of the East India Company, Johan Nieuhof, decides on this basis to call her "white": "It has been found by experience that a girl who was reared from her birth among our folk in the Castle, and grew up there, was as white as an European woman." (R. Raven-Hart, ed. *Cape of Good Hope 1652–1702: The First Fifty Years of Dutch Colonisation as Seen by Callers* [Cape Town: Balkema, 1971] 19.) But after her husband's death, she was said to prove through a life "irregular . . . adulterous and debauched" that "nature . . . again rushes back to its inborn qualities" (obituary; qtd. in I. Schapera, ed. *The Early Cape Hottentots* [Cape Town: Van Riebeeck Society, 1933] 125).

33. See the film directed by Zola Maseko, *Life and Times of Sara Baartman—The Hottentot Venus*, Film Resource Unit (fru@wn.apc.org), 1998. See also Sander Gilman, "Black Bodies, White Bodies: Toward an Iconography of Female Sexuality in Late Nineteenth-Century Art, Medicine, and Literature," *Critical Inquiry* 12.1 (1985) 204–242.

34. For some of these, see Stephen Gray's chapter in *Southern African Literature: An Introduction* (Cape Town: David Philip; London: Rex Collings, 1979) 38–71. Entitled "The Hottentot Eve," Gray's chapter refers to both figures, Krotoa/Eva and Saartje Baartman.

35. See Yvette Abrahams, "The Great Long National Insult: 'Science', Sexuality and the Khoisan in the 18th and early 19th Century," *Agenda* 32 (1997) 34–48; and "'Ambiguity' is My Middle Name: Research Diary about Sarah Baartman, Myself and Some Other Brown Women," unpublished paper delivered at the African Gender Institute, U of Cape Town, 6 August 1996; also at Gender Equity Unit, U of Western Cape, 26 September 1996. Abrahams argues that white critics like Gilman re-enact in their interest in Baartman's representation the strategies of white colonial eugenics. She also claims Baartman as Khoisan, and, through her, establishes her own Khoisan rather than coloured identity. For a different view, see Zimitri Erasmus, "Same Kind of White, Some Kind of Black: Living the Moments of Entanglement in South Africa and its Academy," in Barnor Hesse, ed. *Un/Settled Multiculturalism(s): Diasporas, Entanglements, Transruptions* London: Zed Press, 2000) 187–207. Erasmus argues that Abrahams uses Saartje Baartman to turn away from a part-white heritage that needs to be claimed and dealt with (187–189). For Wicomb's discussion, see "Shame and Identity" 91–93.

36. For recent representations of Krotoa, see Karen Press, *Bird Heart Stoning the Sea, Krotoa's Story, Lines of Force* (Cape Town: Buchu Books, 1990); and Trudie Bloem, *Krotoa-Eva: The Woman* from *Robben Island* (Cape Town: Kwela, 1999). For discussion of other representations, see Carli Coetzee, "Krotoa Remembered: A Mother of Unity, A Mother of Sorrows?", in Sarah Nuttall and Carli Coetzee, eds. *Negotiating the Past: The Making of Memory in South Africa* (Cape Town: Oxford UP, 1998) 112–119. Coetzee argues that contemporary Afrikaner writers have started to claim Krotoa as their foremother in order to gain "what seems like legitimate access to the new rainbow family," despite the general denial of nonwhite ancestry among the Afrikaners (114–15). She turns to Abrahams' representation as preferable. Yvette Abrahams: "Was Eva Raped?: An Exercise in Speculative History," *Kronos: A Journal of Cape History* 23 (1996) 3–21. Wells, however, has argued that Krotoa should not be seen as unambiguously a victim.

37. At the Khoisan Identities conference, Chief Joseph Little, self-styled leader of the Hancumqua grouping of the Griqua, drew attention to his own green eyes: "[In England and Ireland] some of the people said that I would have a tough time proving that I'm a Khoi *met die groën oë and die haakneus* [with the green eyes and the hook nose]. But it's something that is in the blood, it's in my line, *ek kan ook oor die lyn gespring het and Whitie gespeel het* [I too could have jumped over the line and played Whitey].... I thank God that it didn't happen because we have eventually found each other" (Bank 7).

38. Wicomb, "Shame and Identity" 92. Saartje Baartman's reemergence is suggested partly through the repetition of names: Sally, Sarie, and Saartje or Saartjie are all diminutive forms of Sarah. Wicomb goes on to say: "I adopt her as icon [in this essay] precisely because of the nasty, unspoken question of concupiscence that haunts coloured identity, the issue of nation-building implicit in the matter of her return, her contested ethnicity (Black, Khoi or 'coloured'?) and the vexed question of representation" (93).

39. Wicomb, "Tracing the Path from National to Official Culture," in Philomena Mariani, ed. *Critical Fictions: The Politics of Imaginative Writing* (Seattle: Bay Press, 1991) 248, 250.

40. See Stephen Ellis and Tsepo Sechaba, *Comrades Against Apartheid: The ANC and the South African Communist Party in Exile* (London: James Currey; Bloomington & Indianapolis: Indiana UP, 1992), whose analysis combines the views of David and the narrator, but tends

more to the latter: "It is generally agreed that the 1976 rising was spontaneous and that it was sparked off in the first instance by the language issue. . . . It is also true that individual ANC or Communist Party members still living inside South Africa had contacts in Soweto and may have been in touch with small groups of participants. . . . But such contacts were only of minor importance in accounting for the turn of events. Few of those who took to the streets of Soweto seem to have had more than the most rudimentary awareness of organisations such as the ANC, the PAC [Pan African Congress] and the Communist Party. . . . [T]he nationalist organisations had been eclipsed since they were forced into exile sixteen years earlier" (83). David claims ANC authority over the children.

41. Part of the UDF's success was that it was a movement rather than an organisation, loosely affiliated to a large number and variety of organisations including trade union organisations, on whose behalf it offered a sense of unified and widespread resistance. It had massive popular support. Banned in February 1988, it continued under the guise of the Mass Democratic Movement, and then, at the end of 1989, courageously and unilaterally declared itself unbanned. It was partly in response to the increasing strength of public opposition, in the UDF/MDM as well as the Congress of South African Trade Unions (COSATU), that the government unbanned the ANC early in 1990, released Nelson Mandela and other political prisoners, and entered the process of the "negotiated settlement" that led to democracy in 1994.

42. Ellis and Sechaba 148.

43. African UDF activists were sometimes critical of the disproportionate influence wielded by Indians and coloureds in Western Cape branches, with Western Cape UDF activists sometimes expressing anxiety about African nationalist tendencies. See Seekings 20, 78–80.

44. Eric Williams, *Capitalism and Slavery* (1944; London: Andre Deutsch, 1964) 75–76. For information about nineteenth-century Glasgow, see Sir James Bell and James Paton, *Glasgow: Its Municipal Organisation and Administration* (Glasgow: James MacLehose & Sons, 1896).

45. C. Duncan Rice argues that the critique of slavery developed by the Scots in the 1760s sat uneasily with their commitment to economic growth, and that Scottish humanitarians were interested less in the plight of enslaved Africans than in the theoretical issue of how to balance economic growth with political liberty. "Archibald Dalzel,

the Scottish Intelligentsia, and the Problem of Slavery," *Scottish Historical Review* 62.2 (1983) 122, 134.

46. Tobias Smollett, *Humphrey Clinker* (1771; London and Glasgow: Collins, 1954) 249.

47. David Dabydeen, *Hogarth's Blacks: Images of Blacks in Eighteenth-Century English Art* (Manchester: Manchester UP, 1987) 85.

48. The song's title is used in the headnote to a recent essay on the Glasgow tobacco lords, whose full text reads: "Smoke gets in your eyes—but it also made the fortunes of the Clydeside merchants who shipped in the golden leaf from the New World and transformed Glasgow into an international commercial centre." See Tom Devine, "The Tobacco Lords of Glasgow," *History Today* 40 (May 1990) 17. Pipe puffing, often represented in eighteenth- and nineteenth-century art, was used in Hogarth's paintings as a satirical reference to colonial exploitation (Dabydeen 86). There is no real-life Crown Hotel in Kokstad; there was, until recently, a Royal Hotel, which was built and opened in about 1880 by a man known as "Yankee Wood," according to Dower an African American who had been mixed up in illicit diamond deals in Kimberley (117–118). The name "Crown" recalls the British crown, with its (stolen) Griqua diamonds.

49. For information about Quatro, see Ellis and Sechaba, especially 132–136; 192. See also "Inside Quadro [sic]," *Searchlight South Africa* 2.1 (1990) 30–68. This article contains a long report by ANC guerrillas on camp conditions: Bandile Ketelo et al., "A Miscarriage of Democracy: The ANC Security Department in the 1984 Mutiny in Umkhonto We Sizwe," 35–65. The writers refer to prisoners being instructed to sing in order to drown the noise of screams. They also say that released prisoners had to sign documents committing them to silence. In the interest of exemplifying David's position vis-à-vis the ANC, and also of stressing the political courage of *David's Story* itself, it is worth noting that one of the authors of *Comrades Against Apartheid* uses a pseudonym; the book's introduction tells us that although "Tsepo Sechaba" is critical of some of its practices, he remains faithful to the ideals of the ANC, something like David, perhaps.

50. The Truth and Reconciliation Report was presented to Nelson Mandela, then President of South Africa, on 29 October 1998. It can be found at www.truth.org.za. Just before the presentation, Thabo Mbeki, then deputy president, made application to the Cape High Court to prevent publication, on the grounds that the report contained inaccuracies

about the ANC. Subsequently, the ANC was quoted as saying that the attempt of the TRC to establish "a new jurisprudence governing the conduct of warfare" was "comical, irrational and absurd" (*Weekly Mail & Guardian*, 29 October 1998). Nelson Mandela, however, backed the findings, saying that nobody could deny the deaths in ANC detention camps, although he reiterated that the war against apartheid had been just.

51. Ellis and Sechaba 112.

52. Ellis and Sechaba 167.

53. Some recent movements harness a slave heritage to their construction either of a unified coloured identity (which threatens to alienate black Africans) or of a specifically Cape Malay past (which exaggerates the number of slaves brought in from Malaya, focuses on a Muslim heritage, and again has an exclusionary bent). See Kerry Ward and Nigel Worden, "Commemorating, Suppressing, and Invoking Cape Slavery," in Nuttall and Coetzee 201–217.

54. Wicomb, "Zoë Wicomb, interviewed by Eva Hunter, Cape Town, 5 June 1990," in Eva Hunter and Craig MacKenzie, eds. *Between the Lines II: Interviews with Nadine Gordimer, Menan du Plessis, Zoë Wicomb, Lauretta Ngcobo* (Grahamstown: National English Literary Museum, 1993) 88.

55. Wicomb, interviewed by Hunter 90. In 1990 Wicomb wrote: "In South Africa the orthodox position whilst celebrating the political activism of women, is that the gender issue ought to be subsumed by the national liberation struggle. . . . I can think of no reason why black patriarchy should not be challenged alongside the fight against Apartheid." "To Hear the Variety of Discourses," *Current Writing* 2 (1990) 37.

56. Seroke was speaking at a conference called "The Aftermath: Women in Post-War Reconstruction," 20–22 July 1999, University of the Witwatersrand, Johannesburg; qtd. in Vanessa Farr, "How do we know we are at peace? Reflections on the Aftermath Conference," *Agenda* 43 (2000) 28.

57. The Federation of Transvaal Women (FEDTRAW) has compiled a list of sexual assaults on women perpetrated under apartheid during the latter part of the 1980s. See their *A Woman's Place is in the Struggle, Not Behind Bars!* (Johannesburg: Fedtraw, [1988]).

58. Thenjiwe Mtintso, an MK commander in Uganda during the

1980s, and now Deputy Secretary General of the ANC, has spoken of the expectation in ANC camps that female comrades would provide sex for male comrades. See Beth Goldblatt and Sheila Meintjes, "Gender and the Truth and Reconciliation Commission," May 1996, www.truth.org.za/submit/gender.htm. Thandi Modise, also a former MK commander and now deputy president of the ANC Women's League (and chair of the Parliamentary Portfolio Committee on Defence), has referred to women learning karate specifically to protect themselves against men in the ANC training camps. Yet she dwells on sexual insults and leering rather than coercion and rape. Robyn Curnow, "Thandi Modise: A Woman in War," *Agenda* 43 (2000) 37–40. It is noteworthy, too, that even in Vanessa Farr's report, cited in the previous note, there is no specific reference to sexual abuse or torture of ANC women in ANC camps.

59. Chiedza Musengezi and Irene McCartney, eds. *Women of Resistance: The Voices of Women Ex-Combatants* (Harare: Zimbabwe Women Writers, 2000).

60. Toni Morrison, *Beloved* (1987; New York: Penguin, 1988) 79; also 16–18.

61. Fanon's quotation comes from *Black Skin, White Masks* (1952) trans. Charles Lam Markmann (London: Pluto Press, 1986) 232.

62. Although Fanon's works were banned in South Africa, he had considerable influence on black South African thinking. See Steve Biko, *I Write What I Like: A Selection of His Writings* ed. Aelred Stubbs (New York: Harper & Row, [1978]) especially the chapters entitled "We Blacks" (27–32) and "White Racism and Black Consciousness" (61–72).

63. Fanon's chapter "Algeria Unveiled," in *A Dying Colonialism* trans. Haakon Chevalier (New York: Grove Press, 1965), bears interestingly on *David's Story* regarding, for example, the ways women transported arms during the revolutionary struggle (Fanon 61, *David's Story* 19). For discussion of Fanon's self-interrogation, see Homi Bhabha, "Foreword: Remembering Fanon: Self, Psyche and the Colonial Condition," in Fanon, *Black Skin, White Masks* (1986; New York: Grove Weidenfeld, 1991) vii–xxv.

64. Bessie Head, *Maru* (1971, London & Portsmouth: Heinemann Educational Books, 1987).

65. Head, *A Question of Power* (1973; New York: Pantheon, 1974).

66. For Wicomb's discussion of Head's *Maru*, see "To Hear the Variety of Discourses," *Current Writing* 2 (1990) 43–44; and "Nation, Race and Ethnicity: Beyond the Legacy of Victims," *Current Writing* 4 (1992) 17–18.

67. Head, *Maru* 93.

68. Head, *Maru* 99.

69. There are other productive connections. For instance, in *Maru* the two major male characters, each of whom is driven by a startling combination of ruthlessness and tender compassion, are transformed through their contact with Margaret and her paintings. Moreover, *Maru* addresses rather than erases the topics of slavery and "miscegenation", and deploys as a narrative strategy an easy movement between the mythic and the real reminiscent of Wicomb's strategy regarding Dulcie.

70. See Bill Ashcroft, Gareth Griffiths and Helen Tiffin, *The Empire Writes Back: Theory and Practice in Post-Colonial Literatures* (London & New York: Routledge, 1989). Wicomb refers briefly to "writing back" in her 1990 interview with Hunter. Speaking of her admiration for Nadine Gordimer, J. M. Coetzee and Njabulo Ndebele, she says: "[Y]ou can't separate yourself from the products of your culture even if you do write in reaction against certain things" (82).

71. See Belcher (261) who cites two Griqua legends about the origins of the name Kok in the noun *cook*.

72. The four stories that later made up Marais's series of so-called dwaalstories (perhaps to be translated as "dream stories"; to *dwaal* is to daydream or to ramble, as in a kind of walking) were first published in four issues of *Die Boerevrou*, from May to August 1921; anthologised with other stories in 1927, under the title *Dwaalstories en ander vertellings*; and saw their first, separate publication as *Dwaalstories* (Cape Town: Human and Rousseau, 1959). Marais's separate publication of the poem can be found in his collected works, *Versamelde Werke* ed. Leon Rousseau (Pretoria: Van Schaik, 1984), vol. 2, 1018–19.

73. Millin's use of an Englishman entrenches her attack on English liberalism as inappropriate to a South African context. See Michael Wade, "Myth, Truth and the South African Reality in the Fiction of Sarah Gertrude Millin," *Journal of Southern African Studies* 1 (1974) 100–112. Millin's figure is partly based on the Dutch missionary, Dr. J. T. van der Kemp, who came out with the London Missionary Society in 1797, married a Khoi woman, and had four children with her.

74. Millin 107–108.

75. Millin 313.

76. Wicomb, "Another Story" 11.

77. See J. M. Coetzee, "Idleness in South Africa," in *White Writing: On the Culture of Letters in South Africa* (New Haven & London: Yale UP, 1988) 12–35. Dutch and, later, British settlers used the apparent idleness of the indigenous people in order to justify their take-over of the land, which was said to belong to those "who make best use of it" (16). Hence Le Fleur's eagerness to work the land as part of nation-building.

78. In her 1990 interview with Hunter, Wicomb refers usefully to Morrison's treatment of stereotypes: "I suppose what I'm trying to do [in *You Can't Get Lost in Cape Town*], rather unsuccessfully, is what Toni Morrison now has done in *Beloved*, where ... she's not concerned about 'covering up', but concerned with exposing, actually uncovering the economic and historical bases of such stereotypes" (87–88).

79. See J. M. Coetzee, "Blood, Taint, Flaw, Degeneration: The Novels of Sarah Gertrude Millin," in *White Writing* 136–162.

80. Wicomb, "Another Story" 15.

81. Laurence Sterne, *The Life and Opinions of Tristram Shandy, Gentleman* (1759–67; New York: Odyssey, 1940) 394.

82. Sterne, *Tristram Shandy* 397.

83. "What evils since!—produced into being, in the decline of thy father's days—when his powers of imagination and of his body were waxing feeble—when radical heat and radical moisture, the elements which should have temper'd thine, were drying up; and nothing left to found thy stamina in, but negations" (296); "Now the radical moisture is not the tallow or fat of animals, but an oily and balsamous substance; for the fat and tallow, as also the phlegm or watery parts are cold; whereas the oily and balsamous parts are of a lively heat and spirit, which accounts for the observation of Aristotle, "*Quod omne animal post coitum est triste*" (397). See also Walter Shandy's warnings about the need to prevent the boy child from running into either fire or water, "as either of 'em threaten his destruction" (398); that is, the destruction of his semen, that vital fluid.

84. Millin 7, 14; Sterne 74–75.

85. "It was as though a veil had been rent. . . . He [Kurtz] cried in

a whisper at some image, at some vision—he cried out twice, a cry that was no more than a breath—'The horror! The horror!'" Conrad, *Heart of Darkness* (1902; New York: Penguin, 1999) 111.

86. For Marlowe's lie, see Conrad 121. For pertinent discussion of *Heart of Darkness*, see Padmini Mongia, "Empire, Narrative and the Feminine in *Lord Jim* and *Heart of Darkness*," in Gail Fincham and Myrtle Hooper, eds. *Joseph Conrad After Empire* (Cape Town: U of Cape Town P, 1996) 120–132; also in Keith Carabine et al. eds. *Contexts for Conrad* (Boulder: East European Monographs, 1993) 135–150; and André Brink, "Woman and Language in Darkest Africa: The Quest for Articulation in Two Postcolonial Novels," *Literator* 13.1 (1992) 1–14.

87. See Luce Irigaray, "The Power of Discourse and the Subordination of the Feminine," in *This Sex Which Is Not One*, trans. Catherine Porter (Ithaca: Cornell UP, 1985) 68–85; Jacques Derrida, "Choreographies: An Interview with Jacques Derrida," ed. & trans. Christie V. McDonald, *Diacritics* 12.2 (1982) 66–76.

88. Wicomb, "A Visit to the Gifberge," in *You Can't Get Lost in Cape Town* 181.

89. "It grieved [Sarah] that she so often had to haul up the 'so-called' from some distant recess where it slunk around with foul terms like half-caste and half-breed. . . .Lexical vigilance was a matter of mental hygiene." Wicomb, "Another Story" 7.

90. Responding to Bhabha's introduction to *The Location of Culture* (London & New York: Routledge, 1994) 1–18, Wicomb suggests that Bhabha's theoretical placement of coloured South Africans on "the rim of an 'in-between' reality" (Bhabha 13) ignores their actual political positionings ("Shame and Identity" 101–102). This disagreement should not obscure the, arguably, many similarities between Bhabha's and Wicomb's thinking on language, literature, and politics.

91. In her essay "Shame and Identity," Wicomb says: "Gordimer has never missed a chance to comment on the good, strong legs or large buttocks of black female characters" (103).

92. James Joyce's *Ulysses* (1922) is the story of Stephen Dedalus, Leopold Bloom, and Molly Bloom on 16 June 1904, since then known as Bloomsday.

93. Wicomb, "Culture Beyond Color? A South African Dilemma," *Transition* 60 (1993) 32.

94. Wicomb, "Why I Write," *Kunapipi* 16.1 (1994) 574.

95. Wicomb, interview with Hunter 92.

96. For pertinent discussion, see Derek Attridge, *Joyce Effects: On Language, Theory, and History* (Cambridge: Cambridge UP, 2000) especially 78–85; Dennis Porter, "*Orientalism* and its Problems," Francis Barker et al eds. *The Politics of Theory: Proceedings of the Essex Conference on the Sociology of Literature* (Colchester: University of Essex, 1983) 179–93; and *Haunted Journeys* (Princeton: Princeton UP, 1991). In the first of the two cited texts, Porter refers to the "self-interrogating density of verbal texture" and the "textual dissonances" by means of which literary texts measure their distance from the "hegemonic unity" of ideologically less complex and nuanced works. In the second, he notes in some useful ways his indebtedness to Roland Barthes and Homi Bhabha (5–7).

97. Sterne, *Tristram Shandy* 90. Compare David's preference for the palindrome *trurt* (135) with Antjie Krog's comment in her book on the Truth and Reconciliation Commission: "I hesitate at the word; I am not used to using it. Even when I type it, it ends up as either *turth* or *trth*. . . . I prefer the word 'lie.' The moment the lie raises its head, I smell blood. Because it is there . . . where the truth is closest." *Country of My Skull: Guilt, Sorrow, and the Limits of Forgiveness in the New South Africa* (1998; New York: Three Rivers Press, 2000) 50 (second ellipsis in the original).

98. Dulcie September's political activities cast back to the early 1960s: as a member of the National Liberation Front, in Cape Town, she was imprisoned for five years and then banned on her release. After she left South Africa for Britain in 1974, she joined the ANC, and in 1984 she was appointed chief ANC representative in France, Switzerland and Luxembourg. Dulcie's name may also refer to the wellknown line, "*Dulce et decorum est pro patria mori*" (It is sweet and fitting to die for one's country) in Horace's Ode III.2, which is generally celebratory of manly courage and loyalty.

99. Wicomb, "Classics" [review of *Mittee* by Daphne Rooke, and *At the Still Point* by Mary Benson] *Southern African Review of Books* (Summer 1988) 16.

100. Wicomb, "Nation, Race and Ethnicity: Beyond the Legacy of Victims," *Current Writing* 4 (1992) 19.

101. "Why I Write" 573.

GLOSSARY

Aapstert. Literally, monkey tail. Type of whip.

Ag. Exclamation expressing dissatisfaction, frustration, or resignation.

Ant; Anties. Aunt. Also used as an honorific, not necessarily indicating a blood relationship.

Atjar. Vegetable pickle.

Baas. Honorific for white man, used primarily in rural areas.

Bedoeked. Wearing headcloths.

Boboties. Traditional dish of curried mincemeat and dried fruit.

Boerewors. Sausage.

Braaivleis. Barbecue.

Bredie. Stew

Bra. Informal term for brother, not reserved for family relations. Used primarily as a form of address.

Broekies. Panties.

Bubbi. Muslim shopkeeper.

Buchu. Herb.

Coons. Coloured carnival celebrating the new year.

Dagga. Marijuana.

Dassie. Hyrax.

Djolling. Having a good time; partying.

Doek. Head scarf.

Dominee. Minister of religion.

Dorinkie. Little thorn.

Dorp. Very small town.

Frikkadel. Meatball.

Gatvol. Literally, arseful. To be sick and tired of something.

Goggas. Insects.

Goose; Goosie. Mildly derogatory term for a woman.

Harmansdruppels. Old Dutch patent medicine.

Heitse. Exclamation of surprise, delight, or admonishment. One of few words from the Khoi language that still survives in rural areas.

Hotnos. Shortened version of Hottentots. Derogatory name used by many whites for the Khoikhoi people.

Ja-nee. Literally, yes-no. Used, however, to signify a doubly strong affirmative, an emphatic yes.

Kabarra. Khoi dance.

Kaffir. Derogatory term for a black person.

Kak. Shit.

Kaiings. Crisp twists of meat fat.

Kappie. Bonnet.

Karossie. Animal skin worn over shoulders.

Karoo. Semidesert terrain.

Khoikhoi. Collective name for a major group of indigenous peoples of the Cape of Good Hope.

Knobkierie. Stick used as a club; a traditional weapon.

Konfyt. Candy made of melon; a South African delicacy.

Kraal. Animal pen or fold.

Kroeskop. Frizzyhead.

Larnies. Posh people; wealthy whites.

Lekker. Nice. Common modifier.

Lofgedig. Song of praise.

Magou. Fermented mealie-meal drink.

Malva. Geraniumlike plant.

Mamma-se-boklam. Literally, mother's kid (baby goat). Term of endearment.

Mealies; Mealie-meal. Maize (corn); maize-meal.

Moffie. Derogatory term for an effeminate homosexual man.

Mos. Indeed; at least. Used as an intensifier.

Mtombo. Homemade sorghum beer, brewed in rural areas.

Muis. Mouse.

Nkosi kakhulu. Nguni term equivalent to *thank you.*

Oom. Uncle. Also used as an honorific, not necessarily indicating a blood relationship, especially in rural communities.

Opperhoof. Paramount chief.

Ou. Old. Often used to indicate familiarity or affection rather than age. Also used as a noun, the equivalent of *guy.*

Oubaas. Older white man.

Oulik. Cute.

Ouma. Grandmother. Also used as an honorific for any elderly woman.

Oupa. Grandfather. Also used as an honorific for any elderly man.

Pap. Porridge made of mealie-meal, similar to polenta.

Pensenpootjies. Literally, stomach and trotters. Sitting with feet folded under the body.

Plaasjapie. Country bumpkin.

Pokkenkô. Stiff, crumbly version of pap.

Poeskop. Cunthead.

Pondok. Shack; hut.

Poort. Pass, as in a mountain pass.

Potjiekos. Traditional slow-cooking meal made in a single pot.

Ramkie. Homemade musical instrument, usually similar to a guitar.

Roesbolling. Rough; vulgar.

Rooi. Red.

Rooibos. Redbush; a plant used for tea.

Rooi laventel. Old Dutch patent medicine.

Roosterbrood. Griddle bread.

Sago. Pudding made from the pith of the sago palm plant.

Siss. Expression of disgust.

Sisi. Older black woman.

Skinderbekke. Gossipmonger.

Skokiaan. Home-brewed liquor.

Skollie. Hooligan.

Sommer-so-platlangs. Vulgar; lowdown.

Steek-my-weg. Literally, hide me or tuck me away. A term used ironically to describe a township built at a far distance from any white towns.

Strelitzia. Blue-and-orange flower, commonly known as bird of paradise.

Tokolos. Mythical evil creature of popular superstition.

Toorgoed. Fetishes; magic objects.

Toyi-toying. Engaging in a well-known defiant dance-march developed by black youth during the years of resistance.

Trekgedagte. Yearning or itch for trekking.

Veldskoen. Shoes made of rawhide.

Voetsek. Get away. Imperative exclamation used toward animals.

Volk. The people; the nation.

Volksmoeder. Mother of the nation.

Voorloper. Leader of a team of oxen.

Voortrekker. Boer pioneer who took part in the Great Trek from the Cape Colony in 1835.

Wakker. Literally, awake. Lively or sharp.

Windbroek. Literally, wind trousers; lacking full buttocks. Man without courage or nerve.

Yirrer. Blasphemous expression.

ACRONYMS

ANC. African National Congress.

IDB. Illicit Diamond Buying.

MK. Umkhonto we sizwe—in Nguni, literally, spear of the nation. Secret military wing of the ANC.

Iscor. Iron and Steel Corporation.

PAC. Pan African Congress. Rival resistance movement to the ANC.

UDF. United Democratic Front. Popular resistance movement of the 1980s.